PRAISE FOR ~~THE PLYMBURY WITCH~~

The Plymbury Witch offers a little something for everyone: a little magic, a little intrigue, a little romance—and Ravenna, a modern-day witch to root for. Ravenna's struggle for self-acceptance and love in the small New England seaside town of Plymbury, peopled with judgmental locals and a handful of kindly souls, speaks to the resonant theme of coming into one's own and refusing to be marginalized. Author Kendra Vaughan writes with jewel-like precision and clarity, bringing her characters and their lives into view and etching them onto the reader's heart forever.

—**Jan Elizabeth Watson, author of** *Asta in the Wings* **and** *What Has Become of You*

In *The Plymbury Witch*, Kendra has crafted a story about the dangers of generational trauma, the friction between two spiritual paths that willfully choose to misunderstand one another, and the woman whose choices heal all involved, most importantly herself. Themes such as the magic of compassion, growing past what one has been taught, reaching out to support others, and taking risks in order to challenge what we have been told is true will resonate with readers. *The Plymbury Witch* teaches us that grief and loss are balanced by love and hope throughout all our lives, and sometimes embracing the magic inside us is the only way to move forward.

—**Arin Murphy-Hiscock, author of** *The Green Witch*

THE
PLYMBURY
WITCH

THE
PLYMBURY WITCH

KENDRA VAUGHAN

CRANBERRY HOUSE PUBLISHING

THE PLYMBURY WITCH

Published by Cranberry House Publishing, Plymouth
www.CranberryHousePublishing.com

Library of Congress Control Number:
2024916624
ISBN: 978-1-961103-00-9 (hardcover)
ISBN: 978-1-961103-01-6 (paperback)
ISBN: 978-1-961103-02-3 (ebook)

Cover art and design by Holly Dunn Design

First Printed Edition: 2024

To Alec and Alana,
May all your wishes come true....

SPRING

1

RAVENNA GAZED OUT THE window, listening to the people waiting outside her shop. Locals and tourists alike carried on about having their wish granted by the witch with one green and one brown eye. The line stretched down the cobblestone walkway from the Sea Glass Apothecary, curving east across the footbridge and stretching to the beach where the festivities had already begun. She watched the sun in its climb over the maypole, its ribbons flapping in the breeze, and took a deep breath, anticipating the most demanding weekend of the year.

Moon jumped on the windowsill and rubbed her body into Ravenna's shoulder. *We've done this every year for the past twenty-three years. Why the hesitation today?* The cat's voice was clear in Ravenna's mind.

Ravenna petted her silky fur. *Oh, Moon. You know me too well. When I came in this morning, I found a noose hanging on the doorknob with a note. It said, 'Just like in Salem.'*

Skye burst into the shop, closing the door quickly so the crowd gathered on the breezeway couldn't squeeze inside. "Do you hear everyone, Mom? And look at the beach! The maypole is already up, and so is the Ferris wheel. Do you think I could sneak away later for a little while?"

"I was hoping we could all go tonight for the bonfire and fireworks," Ravenna said.

Moon jumped to the floor with a meow, and vanished into the opening of the cat-sized passageway between the Sea Glass Apothecary and the family home in the other half of the building.

Maeve and Klay fought their way in next, closing the door against the crowd as Skye had.

"If I wasn't with your grandmother, I could have come in unnoticed, but she's hard to miss in that getup," Klay said.

Maeve's long, colorful skirt swirled and her headscarf with gold coins jangled as she waved a hand, her golden bracelets clinking. "Well, I never had this many people in line during the Annual Wish Festival when I was the Plymbury witch. But I wasn't famous like you are, either."

"Maybe it's the new sign the Plymbury Town Hall put up," Klay said.

Maeve pointed out the window. "That one by all those protesters? When did they put that up? What does it say?"

"It says 'Home of the Plymbury Witch' on the side facing left. The right side says 'Sea Glass Apothecary: Where All Your Wishes Come True.' They put it up last week," Skye said, "and there have been protestors ever since."

Maeve peered out the window to get a better look.

"You're not Romani, Maeve. You're a witch. Why are you wearing that outfit? It calls attention to us." As Ravenna walked toward Maeve, she again caught sight of the protestors' signs that had sickened her earlier in the week.

SWIM THE WITCH

HANG THE WITCH

THOU SHALL NOT SUFFER A WITCH TO LIVE

Maeve wrinkled her face into a sourpuss, then busied herself organizing shelves of sea glass jewelry. "Is that why you're dressed so plain? You don't want to attract attention?"

"I'm not wearing anything special either, Great Maeve," Skye said.

"But your sweatshirt has a pentacle on it. See that, a pentacle," Maeve said, pointing at Skye's shirt. "She's proud to be a witch."

"Please, Maeve. I have enough to worry about," Ravenna said.

"Ravenna's proud to be a witch, Maeve, but she's never been one to flaunt it. I learned that about her years ago." Klay laughed and pulled Ravenna in for a hug, then whispered to Maeve so Ravenna could hear him. "She doesn't flaunt that she's bad at math either, so it's a good thing I run this place."

Ravenna poked Klay. "Very funny."

Klay pretended the jab hurt and released her. "It's seven forty-five. Only fifteen minutes until opening," he said. "Is everyone ready? The next two days will take a lot out of us. Ravenna, why don't you head into the wish room and take a few minutes alone."

2

RAVENNA STUDIED THE SILVER star affixed to the oak door behind the sales counter. She ran her fingers across her name etched in the center, and pushed the door open. Inside, the wish wall, painted midnight blue, served as a backdrop for thousands of twinkling stars fading in and out and painted ocean waves rolling and crashing loudly with excitement. The full moon painted on the upper left corner shone her rays down on the round table below, covered with a black crushed velvet cloth. Ravenna lit a white candle next to the bowl filled with white sea glass stars resting on the cloth, and waited for Moon to return and jump onto the table to take her place.

Are you ready, beautiful? Ravenna petted Moon, sinking her fingers into her chocolate-colored fur.

Moon's sapphire-blue eyes gazed into Ravenna's. *I'm ready.*

There was a faint knock on the door.

It sounds like they're scared, Moon said.

Ravenna opened the door. The noise from the now-crowded apothecary floated into the wish room, along with the smell of burning sage. A petite woman with shoulder-length brown ringlets of hair, wearing white capris and an untucked salmon blouse, holding a Louis Vuitton bag, stood at the door. Onlookers stretched their necks to see inside the room, and reporters raised their cameras to snap photos from above the crowd. Ravenna welcomed the woman in and closed the door, shutting out the press of people and attention.

She showed the woman to a chair, then sat at the table across from her. "Your name?"

Moon pushed her head under the woman's shaking hands and purred to help calm her.

"I'm Jill," she said.

Jills often have psychic powers, even if they don't know it, Moon said.

Ravenna smiled at Jill. *Look how nervous she is. She's shaking.* Aloud, Ravenna said, "Please pick a star." She handed Jill the bowl, and she took a sea glass star from it. "I'll need to go over the rules for wishing with you, so please listen carefully:

"A person can have only one wish in their lifetime. The wish cannot provide financial gain. The wisher cannot travel in time. The wisher cannot bring someone back from the dead. And the wish can harm none. Got it?"

"Harm none? How can I possibly know if my wish harms none?"

Ravenna leaned forward and gazed at Jill. Jill's eyes shifted back and forth between Ravenna's green and brown eyes, unable to settle on either.

"We can't know, Jill. Not for sure, anyway. However, if you ask with sincere and loving intentions, I will know your heart. It's a gift of mine to know whether people are sincere when they speak. Then I'll decide whether to grant it."

I think you mean it's a gift of mine, Moon said.

Ravenna glanced at Moon and petted under her chin. *That depends on how you interpret it. After all, Maeve gave you to me as a gift.*

"What happens if I am sincere and loving, and you decide to grant it, but then it harms someone?" Jill said.

One of the few with a conscience. I told you she was psychic—one of us, Moon said.

"I can't say. Any decision we make in life comes with risks, and only you can decide if it's worth it," Ravenna said. She waited for Jill's decision in silence.

"My husband and I have tried to have a baby for seven years with no luck. I'd like to have a baby." Tears fell from Jill's wet eyes, and Ravenna handed her a tissue.

"Do you want a biological child, or would you like to adopt?"

"Oh! I'd like to experience pregnancy."

"Well, there's no better time than the holiday of Beltane for babies. Shall we begin?"

The stars on the wall twinkled faster, and the waves roared with purpose. Jill's eyes darted around the room, and she let out a cry. Ravenna reached her hands across the table and cupped Jill's. "It's okay. Just relax. Open your hands when you're ready."

Are you ready, Moon?

Ready.

Jill's hands crept open. Her fingers twitched as if debating whether to close them again, and her breaths became rapid and shallow. Ravenna's right eye turned from grass green to a bright, iridescent emerald hue that illuminated the star in Jill's hand when she gazed at it.

Steady, Ravenna. Focus, Moon said.

Ravenna recited the wish chant:

"Light that once hung in the sky, you turned to glass and fell from high, into the ocean and tumbled free. Now grant this wish. So mote it be!"

Jill's eyes widened, and she gasped when a white light inside the sea glass appeared and flickered, dislodging itself from the star, then floating up in the air and attaching to the wall. The other stars surrounded the new one, dancing with glee, and the ocean below rumbled with joy. Every time Ravenna witnessed the power of desire in action in this room it struck her how believing in wishes opened people to a world of possibilities previously unseen.

"Are all those stars granted wishes?" Jill said.

"Yes, but the only one that matters is yours. Let me know when the test comes back positive."

Jill looked at her stomach and then up at Ravenna. "Really? Oh, wow. How can I ever thank you?" Jill dropped a one-hundred-dollar tip on the table and hugged Ravenna on her way out, still clutching the sea glass star in her hand.

Ravenna smiled. *Shall I let the next one in, Moon?*

By lunchtime, Ravenna had granted thirteen wishes.

"I'd like to eat whatever I want and not gain weight."

"I'd like to speak a foreign language fluently."

"I'd like to stop self-limiting thoughts."

"I'd like to have work and life balance."

She had also denied ten wishes.

"Can you make an exception just this once? I'd like to win the lottery."

"I'd like to meet with my deceased mother one more time." Ravenna wanted to say yes to that one, but after battling with her conscience and Moon's refusal to help, she decided against it.

"I'd like my ex to have an accident that kills him." When Ravenna refused, the client changed it to, "I'd like my ex to pay the child support he owes me."

Through all twenty-three wishes, Ravenna was thinking of her own secret wish. *I'd like relief from social judgment.* But Moon had told her that a witch couldn't grant her own wish, and Maeve had refused to do it for her, telling her that when others judged Ravenna negatively, it built up her character while tearing theirs down.

The crowd in the apothecary cheered when they saw Ravenna emerge from the wish room. She met them with an obligatory grin. Not that she didn't appreciate the people or want to help them, but with fans came haters, and she didn't want to be disliked by anyone.

After signing her name on admirers' souvenir postcards and memorabilia, she excused herself from the reporters snapping photos and drilling her with questions about the wishes she'd granted.

Ravenna scanned the mass of people and spotted Skye helping a customer. She wove her way through the crowd toward her. "I'm going to take a walk on the beach to bury my feet in the sand and ground myself," Ravenna said.

"Okay, Mom." Skye hugged her, directing her energy into Ravenna.

"You're going to need that energy, sweetie. It will be like this until late tonight."

Skye giggled. "I'm fine, Mom."

Every year, as the Annual Wish Festival approached, Skye's excitement overtook the very air Ravenna breathed. Skye loved this crowd, of course, because she was just like her father. Tristan had been revitalized by the energy created by crowds of people. She thought that if he could see Skye now, he'd be so proud of the outgoing young woman she had become.

"Next year, Mom. Then I'll be eighteen and can help you grant wishes," Skye said. Ravenna squeezed her shoulder, and left without saying anything else.

ON THE BEACH, RAVENNA passed carnival rides, pop-up shops, and food huts. Live music floated in the air as boys and girls wove the ribbons of the maypole beside a fifteen-foot pile of oak logs intended for the bonfire later. Ravenna passed the firecrackers lining the shore to reach Ashley's food hut, and jumped up and down behind the crowd there, waving her arm in the air to get her attention.

Ashley waved back and zigzagged through the crowd to hand Ravenna a slice of pizza. "I'm one more hour here, and then back to the café. I'll catch up to you at some point," Ashley said and disappeared back into the crowd.

A man materialized from the swarm of people. "Well, how lucky am I? I didn't expect to see you today, Lady Ravenna. Isn't that what they call you? It's quite an event the town hosts in your honor. Of course, this is my first time at the festival. And how rude of me. My name is Reverend Chase Wilkinson. I'll be taking over the ministry at Living Waters here in Plymbury. I believe the church is only five doors down from your Sea Glass Apothecary. Am I right?"

"Yes, that's right." Ravenna took in his soft blue eyes, the gray streaks in his dark blonde hair, and his fair skin surrounding a cleft chin. "I'd love to stay and chat, but I have to get back."

"Yes, of course. I'll visit you soon," Chase said.

Ravenna's stomach tightened. "Visit?"

"Well, we are neighbors, aren't we?"

"No. I mean, yes. But I'm sure you're too busy." Ravenna folded her arms across her body, still holding the plate of pizza.

"I'm sure you'd prefer it that way, Lady Ravenna. However, I'm committed to love thy neighbor, even if she is a witch," Chase said. He melted back into the crowd.

Ravenna shuddered, pulled off her sandals, and sank her feet into the wet sand. She was watching the children circle the maypole and taking a bite of her much-needed food when an anonymous hand reached out and knocked the plate to the ground.

"Burn in hell!"

Shocked, Ravenna scanned the faces around her, but couldn't determine where the voice had come from. She wondered if it had been someone from Living Waters.

3

"I don't think you'll be able to grant wishes for all the people in line today. What should I do?" Klay said when Ravenna returned to the crowded apothecary.

"Just ask fifty people if they wouldn't mind being first in line tomorrow, and offer them something for the inconvenience."

"Like what?"

"I don't know. Ask Maeve. I'm sure the two of you can come up with something." Ravenna ran to the wish room, waving her hand for the next woman in line to join her. "And remind me later to tell you what happened on the beach."

After granting the woman's wish and saying goodbye, Ravenna felt an unexpected wave of heat course through her body. She grabbed her chair to prevent herself from falling and took a sip of water.

Are you lightheaded from a lack of food? Moon said.

I'm not sure, but it's passed. I'm fine now.

Ravenna scooped Moon into her arms, nuzzled her face into Moon's belly, and kissed her all over. *I couldn't imagine my life without you, Moon. You care so much about me.*

Moon giggled. *I've loved you since the day you were born.*

The noise on the other side of the door grew louder, and Maeve knocked. "Ravenna. Ravenna. There are angry people out here, and we need your help."

As much as I love the belly rubs, you'd better go see what's wrong, Moon said.

12

Maeve's knocking almost punched Ravenna when she opened the door. "Hey. Hey, be careful. What's the matter? I told Klay to give fifty people something for their trouble."

"Fifty shmifty. Never mind that. A group of people are outside the shop, and they've gone mad. They're yelling about you tricking them and taking advantage of them, and something about stomping on pizza."

Before Ravenna could answer, Ashley had forced her way through the crowd.

"I need to talk to you. Right now, and it can't wait," Ashley said.

Ravenna pulled Ashley into the wish room. "Do something about the people outside, Maeve. Call the police if you have to."

Ravenna shut the door, blocking out the chaos on the other side. "What are you doing here? I'm sure your café is just as crazy, Ash. Wait, you don't look well. Is your MS flaring up?"

"No, I'm fine. I came to help you."

"You have enough to worry about this weekend. I can handle this."

"Ravenna, listen to me." Ashley grabbed Ravenna's shoulders and stared into her brown eye. "You know that Reverend Todd from Living Waters left a couple of weeks ago, right?"

"Yes," Ravenna said.

"Well, they've replaced him."

"I know. I met Reverend . . . Wilkinson, I think it was, earlier on the beach."

"What? You met him?"

"Yes. Right after you gave me the pizza."

"Ravenna, those angry people outside. The ones who want to hang you. He sent them. He's telling the whole town that he's come to strip you of magic and run you out of Plymbury."

"Are you sure? I knew he wasn't sincere when I met him, but that seems extreme. Maybe you misunderstood."

"I didn't. I'm sure!"

Ravenna shook her head in disbelief and paced the room, recalling her conversation with Wilkinson and her uncomfortable feeling when talking with him.

The crowd in the apothecary grew louder.

Ravenna flung the door open. "What's going on out here?"

"No, Ravenna. Wait!" Ashley said.

The crowd had pushed toward Ravenna. There was nowhere for her to go; she and Ashley were trapped in the wish room. The walls of the apothecary spun around her, and heat filled Ravenna's body again, but this time it didn't pass.

The protestors were closing in, their shouts merging into a terrifying roar. The air thickened with a sense of danger as the crush of bodies grew tighter. Ravenna's pulse quickened, and she suddenly wondered where Skye was in the crowd. A storm brewed at Ravenna's core, her vision narrowed, and her breaths became short and ragged. Her hands tingled from energy surging up her arms, searing hot and wild.

Then a burst of fire shot from her fingertips.

Ravenna's eyes widened, and her mouth opened into a silent scream. She watched the uncontrollable blaze scorch the wish room ceiling and threshold. It surged outward ten, then twenty feet into the apothecary. The glass display cases and windows shattered instantly. The ceiling, walls, and pine floor caught fire, and the flames spread out of control.

"Oh, my God. Fire! Get out of the building!" Klay yelled. "Someone call nine-one-one!"

People screamed, and a bottleneck formed at the front door. Some customers threw open the enormous bay windows and jumped out. Ravenna ran past Ashley back into the wish room and plunged her burning fingers in her glass of water. A sizzle came before the burning smell of sulfur filled her nose.

She turned back, but the apothecary beyond the wish room door was obscured by smoke. The crackle of flame made her heart leap into her throat. What was happening?

14

"How can we get out?" Ashley said, panicking.

"Come with me." Ravenna grabbed Ashley by the wrist and pulled her to the back corner of the wish room. She opened a trap door set in the floor, revealing a stairway. They climbed down, ran through a dank cement passageway lit with dim electric sconces on the walls, and came out on the other side of the building, climbing out another trap door into the cool, dim, soil-scented air of Ravenna's garden shed. Sirens were blaring in front of the house.

"Hurry, I need to find Skye," Ravenna said. She threw open the shed door and bolted through the flower and herb gardens, inhaling the delicate odor of daffodils and crocuses wrapped in thick, bitter smoke.

She ran around the side of the house with Ashley trailing behind, where a firefighter waited in front of the building, watching the crowd carefully. "Where's my daughter? Where's Skye? Is she safe? Skye! Skye!" Ravenna stretched her neck, hoping to spot her across the street.

"Everyone's safe, Lady Ravenna," the firefighter said.

Ravenna let out the breath she'd been holding. "Thank the Goddess." Then:

"Wait, Moon! Where's Moon? Did you see my Siamese cat?"

"Yes. She's safe with your daughter." The firefighter led them across the street, where police held back the crowd.

Ashley whispered in Ravenna's ear, "I don't know what happened in there or how we ended up in your garden shed—we need to talk."

"I don't know, either. Nothing like that's ever happened to me before," Ravenna said, her voice trembling. She glanced down at her hands, still feeling the lingering warmth from the flames that shot from her fingertips and shook them, trying to rid herself of the realization that she possessed a power she neither understood nor could control. A bead of sweat trickled down her temple.

Ashley tugged Ravenna's arm, and they ran to meet up with Skye, Moon, Maeve, and Klay. Ravenna scooped Moon from Skye's arms, and hugged her.

"Mom, what happened?"

"I'd like to know that, too," Klay said.

"Yes, I just asked the same thing," Ashley said.

Maeve is quiet. I wonder if she knows something she's not telling you, Moon said.

A firefighter stepped out of the apothecary and crossed the street to where they gathered. "We extinguished the fire as quickly as we could. Your home in the other half of the building is fine, but the apothecary will need repairs before you can safely use it again. I turned the gas off, tagged it unusable, and put a note on the door that it's closed until further notice."

"No, you can't. Please. Just let me get through the weekend, and I promise to have all the repairs done right away," Ravenna said.

"I'm sorry about the festival, Lady Ravenna, but I can't do that."

The police began to direct people away from the area, and yelling came from deep within the crowd.

"The witch should have burned to death!"

"Burn in hell!"

"She's a fraud!"

"She shot fire from her fingers!"

"That witch is dangerous!"

Maeve tapped Ravenna on the arm. "Let's go. We need to get you somewhere safe. Ravenna?"

"Maeve's right," Klay said. We need to hurry and get out of here. The police can't hold that crowd back forever, and they're angry. Let's go. Now!"

But Ravenna stood frozen in the middle of the street, staring at her blackened fingers, while reporters snapped photos of her.

4

RAVENNA REMOVED THE SIZZLING bacon from the oven. She placed it on the burner next to the hash browns cooking with fresh thyme and oregano from the herb garden—leftovers from what she'd wrapped around her fingers overnight to heal the burns. She cracked two eggs into a pan and stared out the eastern window toward the ocean, her eyes gazing past the carnival rides that swirled with screaming people. She scooped Moon up from the floor and petted her silky fur. Moon settled with her head nuzzled into Ravenna's neck.

What would I have done if anything happened to you, Moon?

I was here at home with Skye. She took me to join her for a late lunch.

I'm so grateful you were both here together and safe, but—

But what?

Ravenna strolled to the worn pine kitchen table and ran her fingers across the beaten surface, admiring it for standing strong after being battered for over four hundred years.

Do you remember my fifth birthday, Moon? When I sat right here with you, waiting for my birthday cake?

Yes, I remember. I remember every minute we've ever spent together.

That was the birthday that Maeve told me she'd given you to me when I was born and that you'd live with me forever. Forever, that is . . . unless you got killed. Oh, Moon. I could have killed you yesterday. I could have killed all the people I love, and innocent people, too.

"Mom! Mom!" Skye's yells forced Ravenna and Moon out of their conversation. Ravenna turned around to find smoke billowing, filling the kitchen with a rotten stench, and the ceiling fan spinning at full speed above them.

Skye lunged past, pulled the egg pan from the stove, and shut off the heat. "That's all we need is the fire department coming here again. Hey, Mom, are you okay?"

Ravenna lowered Moon to the floor and examined her hands, which showed no sign of soot. "Yes, honey, I'm fine. I was just talking to Moon and not paying attention. Let me cook you some new eggs."

"It's okay, Mom. I'm meeting some friends on the beach, and I'll pick something up from a food hut." Skye looked up at the blades whirling and buzzing overhead. "You can tell the ceiling fan to shut itself off now."

Klay entered the kitchen, yawning. He rubbed his caramel-brown eyes and stretched his arms over his head, exposing tight abs between his shorts and t-shirt. "You're letting her go with that sweatshirt on?"

"What's wrong with my sweatshirt?"

"Does every shirt that kid owns have a pentacle on it?" Klay said to Ravenna.

"So what if it does? Are you seriously going to give me a hard time for a pentacle, Mr. Witch-wanna-be?" Skye said.

"That's enough, Skye. Klay stayed here on the couch last night because he thought someone might try to hurt us."

Skye rolled her eyes and headed up the living room stairs. "Klay makes a better fill-in for a father than a security guard. I came down twice for water last night, and he didn't even move. Just sayin'."

Klay eyed the fan. "Can you all calm down? I'm freezing."

Maeve barreled in the kitchen door, startling them. Maeve's unkempt red hair and the dark bags underneath her eyes told Ravenna she hadn't slept all night. At least she'd changed out of the Romani outfit she'd worn yesterday.

"Next time, you could knock," Klay said.

"Knock shmock. I have something important to show you." Maeve waved her iPad and put it on the table next to Ravenna. She headed to grab a cup of coffee, now cold from the fan's gusts.

Ravenna wanted to ask Maeve how she had shot fire from her fingers, why Maeve hadn't seem surprised, or why she had never warned Ravenna it could happen. Moon had said that Maeve knew something, and Ravenna wanted to know why Maeve would keep this from her. It didn't make any sense. Maeve was the woman who had raised her. Maeve was the one who had taught her everything she knew about the Goddess, life, and magic. She loved Maeve like a mother, and just couldn't believe Maeve would ever keep anything important from her.

Skye returned to the kitchen. "All changed. Are you happy now?"

"Very. Thank you." Klay hugged her.

"See you all later." Skye kissed Ravenna and Maeve on their cheeks and left.

Ravenna cleaned the egg pan and was cracking two more eggs when there was a knock at the door.

"What did she forget? She probably needs money," Klay said.

"Wait. Who is it? Don't open it. I have to show you something first." Maeve choked on her coffee and pointed multiple times to the iPad on the table.

"How do I know who it is unless I open it?" Klay said.

Maeve closed the kitchen window. "Shh! Don't let them know we're home."

"That's ridiculous, Maeve. Just open the door, Klay."

Maeve dashed across the kitchen and tried to pull Klay's arm away from the knob, but he ignored her and opened the door. Ashley brushed past him on her way inside.

"What is this? Grand Central?" Klay said.

"More like South Station," Ashley said. "Did something happen last night that I should know about? There's a strange vibe in here."

"Maeve was paranoid and wouldn't let me open the door."

"Why didn't you want him to open it, Maeve? What's the big deal?" Ravenna said.

"Well, you're the big deal. You're famous, remember? Those reporters are as bad as the paparazzi. It's right here on the home page of *The Boston Globe*." She picked up the iPad and turned it so everyone could see the headline: "The Plymbury Witch Shoots Fire, Burns Shop During Annual Wish Festival," with a photo of Ravenna in the street, holding Moon, staring at her blackened fingers. A picture below showed flames bursting from the shop windows with firefighters working to extinguish them.

"Oh!" Ashley grabbed hold of the table and sank into a chair.

"I'm worried, honey. That mob was serious yesterday, and someone might try to hurt you or Skye," Maeve said.

"I agree. That's why I stayed here last night," Klay said.

Ravenna examined the screen and hung her head low. She hadn't asked for any of this. She had been born into this magical family and had no choice, but she certainly never imagined anything like what happened yesterday would ever happen. So far she'd managed to ignore the sneers and snickers from some people around town, but recently, things had gotten worse, making them more difficult to ignore. And after what happened yesterday, it all seemed unbearable to her.

Moon jumped on the counter and rubbed her head into Ravenna to comfort her.

"It was an accident. We'll figure out how it happened, and it won't happen again." Klay rubbed Ravenna's back and brushed away the strands of her hair that the ceiling fan was blowing in his face. "But right now, we need to do some damage control."

"Yes, Klay's right," Ashley said. "You need to come up with a good reason for how the fire started, and why your fingers were black. Then we need to circulate that story. We also need to figure out what Reverend Wilkinson is up to, because I don't trust him. He may have something to do with this. I was clearing an outdoor table at my café and saw him talking with you in the driveway, Maeve. What did he want?"

Ravenna gave Maeve a pointed look. "Wait. You know Reverend Wilkinson? Why didn't you tell me?" Ravenna pushed her hair out of her face. The ceiling fan blew it back.

"I only met him earlier yesterday. He wanted to be sure nobody got hurt. I told him everyone was fine, and you weren't up for visitors."

"He asked to see me? What if I wanted to talk to him? You didn't even ask me." Ravenna dropped breakfast plates and silverware on the table, and glared at the ceiling fan. "Shut off already. You're making this whole situation worse!"

"Why would you want to see him? You said he gave you the creeps when you saw him at the beach yesterday," Ashley said.

"I think we need to find out what's up his sleeve," Klay said. "He did a good job intimidating you. I saw your face before the flames flew out of your fingers. You were terrified of the crowd closing in on you, Ravenna."

"You saw him yesterday at the beach? What did he say? Why didn't you tell me?" Maeve said.

"Like grandmother, like granddaughter. You don't like it much either, do you?" Ravenna said. "And I was kind of in shock yesterday. I think I still am. I don't know how flames shot from my fingers. Do you?"

"I've been wondering about that too," Ashley said, handing Klay the sugar he was reaching for.

"Let's not worry about that now. I came to show you something," Maeve said.

Ashley glanced at her buzzing cell phone. "I have to go. I need to get back to my restaurant because the place is chaotic, but I wanted to check in on you." Ashley leaned down to hug Ravenna from behind her chair, and hobbled to the door.

Ravenna turned her chair around, scraping it on the timeworn pine floor. "I'm so sorry, Ash. I've been dwelling on all of this and haven't asked how you feel. Is the sea glass anklet I gave you helping you cope with your symptoms?"

Ashley lifted her pant leg to show Ravenna she was wearing it. "I'd hate to think about how much worse I'd be without it, but I've been getting sicker. I'm going to see my doctor about switching to an intravenous treatment."

"Please, Ashley. I know you think I'm too busy or crazy or something, but please let me know how it goes."

"I promise." Ashley blew kisses on her way out.

Klay took a break from shoveling food in his mouth. "I think you should contact the reporter and explain what happened. Tell him you were in the wish room when the fire broke out. The cloth on the table was on fire, so you grabbed it and tried to douse the flames, burning your fingers. That's when you realized how bad the fire was, and ran."

"Great idea, except how do I explain why my fingers look perfectly normal now?" Ravenna raised her hands, turning them for Klay and Maeve to see.

"We'll wrap your fingers and hands in bandages, honey. You'll have to keep them like that for at least a week or two, pretending it hurts to touch things," Maeve said.

"Oh, great. Well, at least it will give me time to look for a temporary shop to sell my jewelry," Ravenna said. "I can't just close up shop till the repairs are done. I have bills to pay."

"When we find a place tomorrow, I'll put up a sign here letting people know where you are until the renovations are done," Klay said.

Ravenna pushed cold potatoes and eggs around her plate. A tear slipped from the corner of her green eye. When it landed on the food, it went brown, rotting immediately. *All this,* she thought, *just because I'm a witch.*

5

RAVENNA PLOPPED ONTO THE car seat and tucked her hands under her legs. She looked out the windshield without even so much as glancing at Klay.

"Are you cold?" Klay said.

"It is fifty-five degrees out, you know."

"I know. But you always say that long hair of yours keeps you plenty warm. And I do have the heat on."

Ravenna stared out the window, watching crows gather on a nearby fence, surrounding a raven. The raven peered past the other birds, making eye contact with her.

"How did you expect to keep it from me?" Klay said.

"Keep what from you?"

Klay laughed. "Okay, I'll play along. Could you hand me a tissue in the glove box, please?"

"Fine. I'm not wearing the stupid bandages." Ravenna pulled her bare hands out from under her legs and folded her arms across her chest. "Don't you know me better than that? I won't lie."

"I didn't think you'd go along with our plan, but you've surprised me before. Did you at least call the reporter and tell him the story we all agreed to?"

"No. What kind of mother teaches their daughter it's okay to lie? You know how I feel about it. Living with one lie is enough. Besides, inner peace only happens when your inside matches your outside."

"Do you really think you're going to have inner peace if the whole town thinks you're some sort of freak who can shoot fire from your fingers?"

In her mind's eye Ravenna saw the six-year-old boy she'd met on the school playground, who had a way of making her laugh when she thought her entire world was crashing in. She didn't know then that his world was crashing, too, or that they'd spend the next thirty-five years riding the waves together, keeping each other afloat. She needed Klay now more than ever and was so grateful for his friendship, even if he thought she was making a mistake. "Do you think I'm a freak?" she said.

"Never. Just a little . . . stubborn. Hey, maybe no one even read the article, or believed it if they did."

Klay pulled out of the driveway, heading west down Seacrest Street, and turned right onto Ocean Drive. The quaint gift shop was a few hundred feet down on the right. Klay parked the car and grabbed the bag with samples of Ravenna's sea glass jewelry he had packed the day before. They entered the store together, the bell jingling, and walked past counters displaying high-end jewelry sparkling with diamonds, shelves of handcrafted Plymbury Beach sand art, and others displaying Waterford crystal animals and figurines. Wall-sized photographs of Plymbury, taken by a sought-after local photographer, hung on the walls with tiny price tags dangling from the corners. Klay read one and gasped. "Five thousand dollars for a photograph?" Ravenna elbowed his ribs and glared at him without saying a word. "What?"

A lanky woman appeared, wearing a pink mod-style dress with a high ruffled collar and beige sandals. She eyed Ravenna up and down. "Hello, Lady Ravenna. Right away, let me say that we don't allow anyone in the store to wear jeans or flip-flops, even if they have cute pieces of sea glass on the straps. And that belt buckle." She pointed to Ravenna's waist. "If my customers saw that pentacle, especially after that newspaper article, you'd scare them all the way to Provincetown. Of course, I'm a bit more open-minded than them, but business is business. So I'm afraid I will have to ask you to leave."

"Wait. I'm Klay Mitchell. I called you on the phone. Your ad said you had a space for a local artisan to rent. Ravenna's here to rent the space." Klay nudged Ravenna forward and opened the bag to show the woman some samples. "Her high-quality, custom crafted pieces will—"

"I'm afraid I've already rented the space."

"Between now and an hour ago?"

Ravenna turned to Klay. "I think we should go."

"I'm sure she'll change her mind once she sees this." Klay pulled out a platinum necklace with a seafoam green piece of sea glass nestled atop an ocean wave. He held it in front of the woman. "Isn't it spectacular?"

Ravenna recognized the piece. Her heart skipped a beat.

"Klay, no! Put it away," Ravenna said through tightened lips.

The woman stared at the necklace and was reaching out to touch it when the bells on the front entrance jangled. She snapped her hand back. "I'm going to have to ask you to leave now. Through the back door." She pointed to a door on the far wall and moved briskly to the front of the store to welcome the customer.

RAVENNA WATCHED THE PINES whiz by as they drove down Ocean Drive. She was furious. "Are you serious? You showed her the persuasion necklace. That piece isn't a toy, Klay. I designed it for Ashley to get custody of her kids, and she gave it back to me once they settled the case. It's too powerful. I hid it. How did you even find it? And how dare you bring it without asking me!"

"I care about you, Ravenna, and love Skye like a daughter. It's not like you can move into my place with my dad and all the dogs. I need to be sure you can support yourself and Skye until your shop's fixed. I'm willing to do whatever it takes."

"Even lie?"

"Yes, if I have to. A little white lie won't hurt anyone."

"You didn't tell these people it was me who wanted to rent their space, did you?"

"No, but someone will rent to you. I just know it. After they touch that persuasion piece, it'll be all over for them."

"No. We're not using the necklace. I do this on my own, or I don't do it at all. Got it?"

"Sure. Whatever you say."

6

THE FOLLOWING SIX SHOPS went the same way, except Ravenna refused to let Klay show the persuasion necklace to anyone else. But it didn't matter. No one cared how exquisite her sea glass pieces were. They only cared about getting Ravenna off their premises, for fear she might burn the place down.

A bald man in a business suit owned the seventh shop, a vintage A-frame cottage with cathedral ceilings converted into a jewelry store. He welcomed Ravenna and Klay, peering at them through a monocle, shaking Ravenna's hand with short, chunky fingers that matched his squat body. He clung to her hand as he spoke. "Well, well, Lady Ravenna, I'm Jim Dalton. It's a pleasure to meet you—someone so famous, living right here in Plymbury. I can't believe you're standing here in front of me. I'm quite fond of your grandmother, Maeve. She and I have known each other for years. Did she tell you to come and see me?"

"She didn't. I had no idea." Ravenna glanced at Klay.

"Maeve and I go way back, but that's not important right now. You need a temporary place to sell your jewelry, no?" He patted Ravenna's forearm with a disfigured hand and released his grip.

"Yes. Yes, I do."

"Please follow me, and I'll show you where you can display your pieces."

Klay flashed a smile at Ravenna and walked behind her, whispering. "See, I told you."

"Here we are," the man said. "This display case has—"

"Excuse me, Mr. Dalton," a woman said, walking toward them. "There's someone here to see you, and they insist that they speak with you immediately. I couldn't convince them otherwise."

"I see. If you'll excuse me for a moment. I'll be right back." The woman followed him through a door on the far wall.

"Wow! I can't believe it. Tell me you didn't pull out that persuasion piece when I wasn't looking," Ravenna said. They both laughed.

Klay peeked inside a glass display case across the aisle. "I guess we lucked out that he knows Maeve. Hey, did you notice that in all these shops, there's not a single diamond smaller than that?" Klay pointed to a solitaire engagement ring glimmering atop a black velvet platform. "I'll need a raise if you want one that—"

"Shh!" Ravenna pointed to the man coming back toward them.

"I'm sorry for the interruption," the man said. "Where was I? Ah, yes. I'm afraid there's been a misunderstanding, and I don't have a space to rent after all. I'm sorry, but I'll let you know if things change. I'm sure you can see yourselves out. Please give my regards to Maeve."

"But, sir, the case is empty. Surely you could benefit from carrying healing sea glass jewelry in your shop?" Ravenna said.

"Here, I'll just take a few pieces out to show you how crazy talented Ravenna is," Klay said.

The man pointed a shaking hand in the direction they had entered. "The door is that way."

Ravenna marched straight for the exit and crossed the street. She sat on a bench in Beach Plum Park, lowering her face into her hands. Klay sat next to her without saying a word.

"What am I going to do? I need a shop, and I need one fast. I have bills to pay." She glanced at Klay. Only it wasn't Klay sitting next to her; it was Reverend Chase Wilkinson.

"I'm sorry to hear about your troubles, Lady Ravenna, but I can help," Chase said.

Ravenna shot up. "What are you doing here? And where's Klay?" Her eyes scanned across the street.

"I'd heard what happened and came by your house yesterday. You know, the visit I promised, but you weren't up for company. Funny, it appeared there were people visiting."

Ravenna stretched her neck, hoping to spot Klay. "Look, I don't know what you want from me, but why don't you just leave me alone, and I'll leave you alone? Sound like a plan?"

"That's not very neighborly. I'll tell you what. I want to be a good neighbor, and I'll make you an offer." Chase stood to meet Ravenna's eyes. "There's a room behind the church sanctuary with easy access to a driveway. The perfect place for you to sell your trinkets. You're welcome to use it until your shop's fixed if you'd like."

"I don't sell trinkets."

"My mistake."

"I sell sea glass jewelry and designs. They're healing."

"You grant wishes, too, no?"

"Yes."

"Then grant yourself a wish and find a better offer."

"I can't grant my own wish, but my answer is still no." Ravenna caught sight of Klay exiting the shop, heading across the street.

"It might be wise to reconsider, Lady Ravenna. If you change your mind, you know where to find me." Chase waved to Klay in the distance and sauntered up the paved pathway.

"Who was that?" Klay said.

"That was Reverend Chase Wilkinson. I'm not sorry you didn't meet him. What took you so long?"

"You ran off, but I wanted to talk to the guy in the shop. He insisted he rented the space, but then I ran into the woman who interrupted us. I asked her if someone had shown up to rent it. She told me someone showed up, but only to make sure it didn't get rented. I pressed her for more information, but she wouldn't tell me anything else. What did Wilkinson want?"

"To offer me a space in his church to sell my jewelry. I refused, but I'm not very hopeful we'll find another solution. And who says I have to trust him? Even if the guy's shady, what can he do to me with his entire congregation there? It's not like I'll be alone, and it's close to home. What other choice do I have?" Ravenna said. She was trying to convince herself more than Klay.

"You're a witch, Ravenna. Tell me you're not seriously thinking about this."

Ravenna's legs felt weak, and she fell back on the bench. The Cleveland pear trees lining the park had long lost their blooms, and the days were growing warmer as summer approached. Klay took off his sweatshirt and tossed it on the bench. He sat next to Ravenna and ran his hand through his hay-colored hair.

Ravenna felt comforted with him there, but noticed he was clenching his jaw. "Klay, what do you love so much about being a witch?" she asked to distract him.

"Spending time with you." His cheeks changed to a warm red, bringing out the gold in his caramel eyes.

"You could spend time with me if you weren't a witch. Ashley does. What do you really love?"

"I love calling nature home. When I'm fishing, I become one with the sea. It's like I'm floating on a different plane of existence, and the Klay I show the world is gone, and I'm left with the Klay I really am—a free spirit."

"Do you think you could feel that way if you weren't a witch?"

"I suppose, but why would I want to find out?"

"So you've never thought you might not want to be a witch?"

"Not since that day thirty years ago when we prepared my Wiccaning ritual, and I declared it three times under the stars and the full moon: 'I'm a witch. I'm a witch. I'm a witch.' I'll never forget it, or how much I hoped I'd be given the magical powers you have. I was such a foolish kid."

"I wish we were still kids. Back then, I thought my magic was cool, too."

"What are you saying, Ravenna?"

Ravenna studied a bed of pink and purple tulips swaying carefree in the warm breeze, with no concern that in a few more months, they would perish. She didn't reply.

7

No one took hurricane warnings seriously in Massachusetts, especially not late in May. Hurricane season didn't start until June, if at all, and almost every nor'easter predicted over the winter was nothing more than a few inches of snow. The winds had already picked up to a gusty thirty miles per hour, and marbled gray puffs hovered low in the morning sky. Ravenna had cut all the herbs she could, tied them into bundles, and hung them on the drying rack over the kitchen's butcher block island to use later in tea. Now she and Skye headed out to pick up Ashley and her kids for the Unitarian Universalist church's Sunday service.

"Do you think we'll get this one? There's a lot of hype about it in the news," Ashley said when they pulled into the church parking lot.

"I doubt it. When was the last time we had a hurricane? Four, maybe five years ago," Ravenna said and grabbed her raincoat from Skye's lap in case she needed it.

"Look over there. Isn't that Chase Wilkinson coming out the side door of the church? Why would he be in the UU church?" Ashley said.

"He's the president of the Interfaith Council now, so maybe he had some business to discuss with Reverend Logan," Ravenna said.

"I don't trust him. Ever since he showed up in town, everything's gone rotten."

"Yeah, even the weather," Skye said. She twisted and tucked her straight black hair into the hood of her black sweatshirt. "Why did I even bother straightening my hair today? And my eyeliner's going to run all down my face."

Gina, Ashley's eleven-year-old, mocked Skye from the back seat, rubbing her hands over her face and tossing her blond hair. "Oh, my face. It's all black, and my hair is a frizzy mess." The younger kids giggled and made the same gestures. Skye groaned, rolling her eyes. She opened the door and ran across the parking lot, followed by Ravenna, Ashley, and her kids.

About half as many people as usual stood in the church's entryway, and only two greeted Ravenna on their way to join the congregation. Ashley's kids joined others running downstairs for their Our Whole Lives sexual education class, and Skye met up with her friend Kerry.

Ravenna and Ashley found a simple pew a few rows away from the altar in a large room that looked more like a high school cafeteria than a sanctuary. "Did Skye take OWL with Kerry?" Ashley said.

"She did, with five other girls who have all become excellent friends. They're from different towns, so the church is a chance for them to spend time together." Ravenna noted Ashley's ghostly appearance and her hollowed eyes with dark circles around them. "Are you feeling okay, Ash? What happened at the doctor's appointment?"

"She's putting me on the intravenous treatment. It should slow the progression of the disease."

The organ prelude rang through the room as Reverend Jennifer Logan sat at the altar. Ravenna closed her eyes and let the music soften her tense muscles, thinking it wasn't only Skye who loved the church, because she loved it just as much. Reverend Logan had been a loving and supportive addition to the church, especially to the Pagan community, ever since she'd arrived ten years ago. Ravenna loved the church so much that she'd thought about becoming a UU, but most Christians in the community didn't accept UUs either, so why bother?

Jennifer stood at the entrance to the meeting room after the service to hug and chat with parishioners.

"Hey, I'd rather not wait in that long line. I don't feel well, and my legs would never hold me up that long," Ashley said.

"Why don't we go around and enter from the other side of the meeting room?"

Ashley held onto Ravenna for balance as they walked. "No luck with any rental spaces you and Klay visited?"

"No, but I want to catch up with Jennifer to ask her about selling my sea glass jewelry here. I don't know what I was so worried about. There's an empty classroom downstairs. I know she'll let me use it."

"That's a fabulous idea. She's always willing to help her congregation."

Ravenna took two cheese pastries off the fellowship table, and jumped when thunder crackled outside. She handed a pastry to Ashley as lightning flashed through the windows, highlighting the worry lines etched on Ashley's face. They stared at each other when rain began slamming against the roof.

"It doesn't sound good out there. We should grab the kids and go," Ashley said.

Ravenna spotted Jennifer walking across the room toward her. "Can I just have five minutes to chat with Jennifer, and grab a key?"

"There you are, Ravenna. I need to talk to you. Please join me in my office?" Jennifer said.

Ravenna smiled and whispered to Ashley, "She must have had the idea before I did."

Ashley held her hand out for Ravenna's car keys, then yelled back as she shambled across the room, holding the chair rail, "I'll take the kids home and swing back to pick you up."

"HAVE A SEAT, AND I'll be right back," Jennifer said. She closed the door on her way out.

The office decor was more ornate than the rest of the church. A large mahogany desk stood in front of Ravenna with matching bookcases along the back wall, filled with titles like *The History of the Unitarian Universalist Church* and *There is No Religion, Only God*. The walls were painted dark olive green and held photos of people gathered at church events, holding awards earned over the years. Ravenna spotted Skye and herself in several of them as she sank into the plush chair and released weeks of tension that had built up in her body. The church was her haven, and the next best thing to her private meditation room at home. She took three deep breaths, closed her eyes, and waited for Jennifer to return ten minutes later.

"I'm sorry. I had a small fire to put out. Oh, terrible choice of words," Jennifer said. She closed the door and leaned against the front of her desk, facing Ravenna.

"Since you brought up the fire, there was something I wanted to ask you." Ravenna's cheeks flushed red hot with embarrassment. "My apothecary is unusable, and I hoped I could use a classroom downstairs to sell my sea glass jewelry until it's fixed. Maybe a couple of months?"

Jennifer folded her hands and spoke in a condescending tone. "I don't think that would be possible."

Ravenna watched Jennifer's eyes twitch, making her thick mascara look more like spiders stuck to her face, weaving intricate webs that spread to the corners of her eyes. Thunder crackled outside, and Ravenna's stomach turned sour.

"There isn't a place for you and Skye in this church anymore," Jennifer said.

"What are you saying?"

"Let's just say . . . the church isn't getting involved in all the controversy. I assume nothing here belongs to you?"

"No. But—"

"I'm asking you nicely to leave the building. And if you don't leave immediately, I'll have no choice but to call the police and have you removed."

"What about Skye? You can't just—"

"Yes, I can." Jennifer tugged Ravenna's arm, pulling her out of the chair, and pushed her into the hallway, closing the door behind her.

Ravenna couldn't hold back the sting that had built up behind her eyes, and the tears poured as hard as the rain outside, burning holes in the linoleum floor. She looked back at the closed door, hoping for it to open and for all of this to have been a mistake. The only other time she'd experienced a shock like this had been seventeen years earlier when Tristan had died, leaving her with a six-month-old baby. Except then, the church had been there to help her pick up the pieces.

8

KLAY PREPARED A HOT cup of tea with mint from the herbs gathered earlier that morning, and placed it on the table in front of Ravenna. "You didn't talk the entire ride home, just stared out the window. Did you even notice it was me who picked you up and not Ashley?"

Ravenna listened to the wind whistle as the rain ran down the window, making patterns like tree branches meeting at the trunk. The howling gusts seemed to blow through her, swirling around her insides, each pulling them tighter until she couldn't breathe. She wrapped her hands around the mug and soaked in the heat, then lifted it to her nose, inhaling the cool, minty aroma, letting it fill her lungs. Her chest shook as she exhaled. "Yes, I knew it was you. I just can't believe it," she said.

"You can't believe what? Ashley said you met with Jennifer. What happened?"

Ravenna dropped the cup on the saucer's rim, causing it to topple. Tea cascaded like a waterfall over the table's edge, setting her words free. "She told me we can't go back to the church again."

Klay grabbed a kitchen towel to clean up the mess. "Wait a minute. I don't get it. Why would she say that? Maybe you misunderstood. Jennifer would never say that. She's too nice."

"You think I'm lying to you, and that I want to tell my kid she can't spend Sundays with her closest friends anymore?"

"Of course not. I mean, maybe you misunderstood her."

"I didn't. She stood right in front of me and said it to my face. What part of 'You and Skye are no longer welcome in this church' could I have misunderstood?"

"Is this because of the fire? That makes no sense. It's not like she doesn't know you're a witch, and Skye had nothing to do with it."

Ravenna recalled one Sunday, when Skye was only seven years old, Klay had called in sick, and she had to take his place to work in the apothecary. After Ravenna had explained that they couldn't go to church, Skye cried and ran outside, screaming that she hated Ravenna. She was so loud that nine-month-pregnant Ashley had waddled into the apothecary, introduced herself, and said if Skye didn't stop screaming, all the customers would leave her café. It wasn't how Ravenna had wanted to meet her new neighbor. But after some coffee and conversation, Ashley had offered to take Skye to church with her that day. Skye hadn't missed a Sunday since.

"How am I going to tell Skye? She loves that church," Ravenna said.

Klay's face drained of color. "Maybe you don't have to tell Skye. Let's talk to Jennifer. I'll call and make an appointment, because I'm sure there was some miscommunication here."

Ravenna grabbed Klay's cell phone before he could get it. "No, don't call. Please? I know she meant it, and I don't want her calling the police because she thinks I'm harassing her."

"Someone needs to talk to her."

"Someone already did. When we pulled into the parking lot, Ashley saw Chase coming out of the building."

"He keeps showing up in places where things go all wrong for you, doesn't he?" Klay massaged the back of his neck.

A gust of wind and a loud crack of thunder made Ravenna shake. She gazed out the window at the intensifying storm, thinking about what Klay had just said, knowing he was right. Each wind gust blew harder against the window, whipping Ravenna's fear and anger until it finally reached an uncontrollable frenzy. High in the sky, a jagged bolt of raw power tore through the clouds. It hit a large oak, and the tree split in two, burning and sizzling in the rain.

Klay sank into the chair next to her, still rubbing the back of his neck. "Take a deep breath and relax. Everything's going to be fine."

Moon jumped onto Ravenna's lap.

What's happening to me, Moon?

Just like the winds of a hurricane, thoughts can spiral out of control and leave destruction in their wake.

Ravenna's gaze shifted out the window, her eyes tracing the tendrils of smoke that twisted up from the broken tree.

9

Ravenna knew Plymbury Beach would be empty after the nor'easter left seaweed littered along the shore and the accompanying stench of rotten eggs hovering in the air. She didn't care. More than anything, Ravenna needed to think about how to find a shop so her business would get back on track. Maybe if she and Chase could come to some mutual understanding about each other, he'd stop trying to sabotage her by turning the whole town against her.

Ravenna eyed two seagulls playing in the sky, swooping and swirling in unison, taking turns chasing one another. They looked happy and carefree. It reminded her of how much the burden of the Greene family lineage had weighed on her, now more than ever. She couldn't help but think that if she'd died when her pregnant mother had fallen down the flight of stairs, the legend would have died with her. Or if she had been born into some other family, her life would be different, and she wouldn't have to think about what accepting Chase's offer might mean for her.

Two hours later, her feet and shins were soaking wet and red from the cold, chilling her to the core. Black yoga pants that reached below her knees and an oversized hooded sweatshirt hadn't been enough to keep her warm from the storm's trailing winds that forced saltwater droplets into her mouth and left an unpleasant taste. But it wasn't a wasted morning. Not at all. She held three small buckets filled with hundreds of pieces of multicolored sea glass, all glowing in that pulsating way that only she knew how to use for healing.

After climbing onto the footbridge, Ravenna turned to gaze at the coast before leaving. She removed her hood, letting her hair whirl around her body, and lifted her face to the sky. The sun's rays warmed her eyelids, and a surge of gratitude flooded her heart. "Thank you."

"You're welcome."

Ravenna whipped around to see Klay standing behind her. "What are you doing here?"

"Just thought you'd be here, and maybe you'd want to walk home together. Looks like you found a lot of sea glass to keep you busy until we reopen the apothecary. Any idea when?" Klay reached out and took the buckets from her.

"A few months, anyway. The insurance company said that outside of all the cosmetic damage, the fire shorted out the whole electrical system. In a house that old, it could take longer to fix than we originally thought."

"Whoa, a few months? I didn't realize the fire caused that much damage. We really need to find a temporary place."

"I know. Should I think more about Chase's offer?" Ravenna held her breath, waiting for Klay's answer. Her words hung between them like the thick ocean air, heavy and oppressive. Klay gazed down at the ground, ignoring her.

"Did you hear me?"

"I'm putting together a bunch of places where we can inquire. Some are outside of town, but not too far." Klay placed the buckets on Ravenna's lawn next to the driveway and climbed into his car. "I'll swing by when I finish the list in a few days, and we can figure out a plan. Okay?"

"Okay." Ravenna was grateful for Klay, and how his steadfast loyalty shone in his thoughtful gaze. It was a lifelong friendship that could never break, no matter what the future held. She picked up the buckets and went inside.

10

ASHLEY SAT ON A granite bench under an oak tree overlooking Plymbury Bay. Ravenna handed her one of the iced coffees she had bought at Dunkin' across the street.

"So you're not coming to church anymore? Jennifer said you couldn't sell your jewelry there, so you just up and quit?" Ashley said.

"Quit? Someone told you that? Is Jennifer lying and telling everyone I wanted to leave?"

"Lying? I heard you talked with her and said you and Skye were leaving because you needed time to sort things out. It makes sense, but why didn't you tell me sooner? I would have understood."

Ravenna's head spun. She sat beside Ashley and thought about the past three weeks since getting kicked out of the UU church—a blur beyond recognition. "I didn't want to leave. We were kicked out," Ravenna said, jealous of the ocean's tranquil demeanor, the seagulls gliding in the sky gleefully singing their songs.

"Who would kick you out? Just talk to Jennifer. She'll tell whoever it was to back off," Ashley said. "I hope you wouldn't let some idiot scare you away, because you have plenty of support there. I don't think anyone even cares about the fire anymore."

"Trust me, people still care, and it was Jennifer who kicked us out."

"What? Hold on. She can't do that, because the congregation runs the church. She doesn't run the congregation."

"I wondered if she had the authority, and wanted to ask you since you're the chair of the Committee on Ministry. So, how do we get back in? Oh, and I don't want any of this discussed with Skye yet, okay?"

"I could have sworn I saw Skye at church this morning."

"You did. I haven't had the heart to tell her, and I feel sick about it. But she won't get away with showing up there forever. We need to get back in fast."

Ashley freed windblown strands of her hair stuck to the plastic cup. "Maybe you could ask Jennifer about Skye. How could a well-behaved seventeen-year-old kid be a problem?"

"She made it clear that neither of us was welcome anymore. What can I do to come back?"

"I know you'll have to meet with the Committee on Ministry. It's a hearing where you'll tell your side, and Jennifer will tell hers. Then the committee will vote on it."

"That's going to go well. Hi, committee. I was at church one Sunday, and Jennifer asked to talk with me, and then she kicked me and my daughter out. Oh, why? I don't know. Maybe it's because of some stupid gossip about me starting a fire in my apothecary. Why don't you ask her yourself since she's sitting right there?"

"I don't think sarcasm is going to help you. I'll see what I can do."

Ravenna got up from the bench and wandered to the grass's edge that lined a ten-foot drop down to the beach area. A narrow stretch of sandy shore extended beyond an incline of rugged boulders, and to the left was a long breakwater with a smooth gravel walkway. Ravenna called back to Ashley, "Hey, do you want to walk the Plymbury Jetty with me?"

Ashley shook her head. "I'd love to, but I don't trust myself walking on that narrow path. You go on. I don't mind waiting."

Ravenna followed the grass to the jetty's entrance and strolled along the gravel pathway that led nowhere but as far out into the ocean as it could reach. The waves crashed into the rocks flanking the walkway, and saltwater droplets sprayed Ravenna's feet and legs. The bitter cold water forced her to run in a zigzag pattern to avoid the mist raised by the waves. She looked up at the sun and summoned its rays to penetrate her body with a comforting warmth. She wanted to cling to the present moment, but she reluctantly pivoted on her heel to return to Ashley. At the other end of the jetty, she spotted her daughter on the beach. Skye's long black hair whipped in the wind, and she'd planted herself with her hands on her hips, tapping her foot. Like her father, Tristan, she had never shied away from a conflict, and Ravenna thought she was a strong, determined young woman because of it. Ravenna wasn't going to be able to avoid whatever bothered Skye unless she dove into the ocean.

"Like, seriously? You didn't expect anyone at church to say anything to me? You made me look so stupid," Skye said as Ravenna drew near. "Why would you do that to me? Why didn't you tell me we were taking time off? I don't want to leave the church!"

"I was hop—"

"Jennifer told me I couldn't go back until you said I could. So why can't I go? I want to be with my friends."

"I never said we wanted time off. Jennifer's lying to you. She kicked us out."

"Kicked us out? *You're* lying. Why can't I go?"

Ashley came up from behind Skye. "Your mom's telling the truth. She didn't want to upset you."

"Why? It makes no sense. Why would we get kicked out? Is this because you don't know how to control your magic? You're ruining my life!" Skye made fists, her arms stiff at her sides, and stomped off, snapping, "Thanks a lot, Fire Queen."

"With her in that mood, I'm glad she doesn't have a car," Ashley said.

"I should have told her. How soon can you set up the meeting?"

"I'll talk to the committee next Sunday. Hopefully, we can set something up in a month."

"I have to wait over a month? Maybe Skye's right. Maybe I am ruining her life. Now that she's not helping me after school, she's off doing who knows what and where. She needs something to do to make her feel good about herself. Could you use some afternoon help in your café until my shop's fixed?"

"You know, things are more difficult for me lately. I'm getting tired much earlier, and my motor skills are getting worse. Yesterday, I spilled a full tray of food on a customer. She wasn't happy about it and made a huge scene, but thankfully, most people are regulars and understand. Sure, I could use the help. I'll ask her."

"Thanks, Ash. What can I do for you?"

"Keep your fingers crossed that this medication works, and I don't need to ask you to finally do my wish magic," Ashley said. "You know I'm saving it."

The burn of bile filled Ravenna's throat, and she swallowed the sting, thinking about how focused she'd been on her own problems. She admired Ashley for dealing with a disease that limited so much of her life, and on the heels of a brutal divorce. *And somehow, Ashley wakes up every day with joy, willing to give so much of herself to others.* Ravenna wrapped her arms around her. "You'll be okay, Ash. You're my hero."

11

Ravenna and Klay huddled together, their heads bent over papers full of names and phone numbers of potential places to rent.

Klay pointed to one of the sheets. "These look like our best options."

"I'm not sure my local clients would drive two towns away. Plus, I prefer to be close to Skye. Maybe we can set up a pop-up shop in the garden." Ravenna bit her lip.

Klay laughed. "Do you really think jerkface would let you off that easy? As soon as you put it up, he'd summon Jesus, and that tent would be windblown and destroyed in less than an hour. Come on, Ravenna. It's not like I'm suggesting we go all the way to Boston. Maybe these Marshfield people won't know about the fire."

Before Ravenna could answer, the hammers pounding next door echoed through the air. Their unrelenting beat rang like a call to action, and she needed to decide fast. "I think we should—"

"What? I can't hear you."

The noise stopped. Moon leaped onto the table and rolled across the papers, crumpling sheets under her body. Others scattered, falling to the floor.

Hey! We need those, Ravenna said.

And I need a belly rub.

Klay grabbed Moon from the table.

Wait. I just want a belly rub. Please? Just for a minute?

"Let me have her." Ravenna scooped Moon from Klay's arms, turned her on her back, and rubbed her belly.

"You're rewarding her for destroying everything? How do you expect her to know she can't do that?" Klay sighed and picked up the fallen papers.

Please don't do that again. If you want a belly rub, all you have to do is ask.

I'm bored, and I miss doing wishes together. Can you find a place soon so we can do more?

Ravenna scratched Moon's head and kissed her face. *Okay, I will. Today.*

"Wow. I've never heard her purr that loud. What did you say?" Klay placed the papers back on the table, then reached over to pet Moon. "Don't touch them again, you little monster."

Moon giggled, but only Ravenna could hear it. She hugged Moon and placed her on the floor, then she and Klay returned to talking about the apothecary. But it wasn't long before the kitchen filled with the clamor of clanging, drilling, and banging from across the breezeway again, causing ear-splitting, mind-numbing discomfort. The pounding of hammers echoed, and the high-pitched whine of a circular saw sliced through the middle of their conversation.

"Do you want me to call and set up appointments at some of these places? They won't be available for long." Klay said.

"I can't hear you, and I can't think with all this noise, either." Ravenna held her hands up to her ears.

"Maybe we should go someplace more quiet." Klay gathered the papers strewn across the table, and they headed toward the door.

Ravenna spotted Moon slinking through her private tunnel toward the Sea Glass Apothecary. "I don't want her in there with all that construction."

"Then tell her to get her kitty butt in the house until the repairs are done."

"She's going to listen to that, all right." Ravenna rolled her eyes. "Let's go get her, and I'll bring her back."

Ravenna took the lead across the breezeway until she faltered, and Klay bumped into her. Her body tensed as she gazed at the apothecary's doorknob, remembering the threatening noose that had hung there the morning of the Annual Wish Festival. She stared at the handle, like a movie stuck on a frame that couldn't move forward.

"Are you okay?" Klay said.

"I forgot to tell you. A noose. On the doorknob. The morning the shop burned."

"What? I can't hear you."

The door flew open, jarring Ravenna. A painter waved his brush in a fury, splatting paint everywhere. "I'm sorry. Hurry! The front door was open. Your beautiful cat. She ran. Chased a chipmunk. Out in the street!"

Ravenna gasped and ran down the walkway. She turned right and sprinted down Seacrest Street after Moon. White picket fences and towering oaks flashed by, her sandals pounding on their long shadows stretched across the pavement. Her heart thundered against the ragged rhythm of her quick, shallow breaths.

The shrill cry of screeching tires filled the air, and she covered her ears against it as the smell of burnt rubber filled her nose.

"Oh, Moon." She bolted toward the noise while clutching her stomach, fighting back nausea. And there, on the side of the street, at the corner of Seacrest Street and Ocean Drive, Moon lay still.

"Moon. Moon. Oh, Goddess, no!" Ravenna gasped for air and dropped to the ground, pulling Moon's motionless body onto her lap. *Moon, you can't leave me. I need you. Now more than ever.* Ravenna's pouring tears soaked Moon's fur.

I'm sorry. I have to go now. I love you.

Oh, no, Moon. No. Stay. Please stay. Ravenna sobbed like a child and choked. *I love you too, Moon. Forever.*

Moon gurgled aloud and took her last breath. Her body lay limp, leaving a vacant space in Ravenna's mind and a searing agony in her heart.

Klay bent down and placed his hand on Ravenna's, deep in Moon's wet fur. "I'm so sorry, Ravenna. I know she was your best friend."

"You're my best friend, Klay. Moon's been a part of me since I was born. How can I live without her?"

Ravenna's sobs grew deeper and louder. Through a blurry haze of tears, she looked up at a crowd gathered across the street, their eyes fixed on her. The sounds of their joyful cheers and celebrations pierced the air, threatening to suffocate her. "How could they?"

"Come on. Let's bring Moon home to the catnip garden. It was her favorite place," Klay said.

Ravenna stood with Klay's help and steadied herself. She clung onto Moon, hugging her lifeless body. "I want to know who killed her, and I won't rest until I find out," she said and stared at the people across the street.

Klay wrapped his arms around her and led her away from the mob.

12

Ravenna knew she had to find a new familiar, but shopping for a cat only three weeks after Moon died seemed overwhelming and excruciating. She had asked why she even needed one, and Maeve said, "Because it's what we Greenes do. Familiars aid us in our magic, and you can't be without one." But it seemed to Ravenna that a lifetime of magic and memories couldn't simply vanish. Death didn't threaten to unravel the inseparable loving bond she and Moon had spent a lifetime building. Foolish tradition did. But she didn't say that to Maeve. Instead, she did what Maeve instructed, just like always.

Ravenna and Klay drove over five hours to a cat shelter on the Union River in Ellsworth, Maine, hoping to get far enough away so no one would recognize her. When they approached the desk, a woman in her early twenties with sandy blond hair and a deep golden tan greeted them.

"My friend lost her cat recently in a hit and run, and she'd like a new fam . . . ahem, pet," Klay said.

"I'm so sorry for your loss. No wonder you're wearing your sunglasses indoors. When my cat died, my eyes were red and swollen for weeks," the woman said. "So now, I work here. We're a no-kill shelter, and I get to cuddle cats all day until they find a home, and that makes me happy, not sad. You know what I mean?"

Ravenna forced a smile with the same insincerity that the people in Plymbury now did when seeing her. "My cat was a chocolate point Siamese. You don't have any Siamese for adoption, do you?"

"We have one hundred and thirty-two cats and kittens available for adoption, but only one Siamese. She's a lilac point, not a chocolate. They sent her to us after a fire in California destroyed her home, and we think she's about a year old. Would you like to see her?"

"Yes, we'd love to see her," Klay said.

Ravenna wiped tears from her cheek and was planning to turn around and leave when Klay placed his hand on the small of her back, nudging her forward instead. They followed the woman through a metal door leading to a long corridor of floor-to-ceiling cages that spanned the entire length.

Ravenna gasped. "I can't. It's so sad."

"Let's just focus on the cat you came to see, okay?" Klay said.

Ravenna continued walking, trying not to hear all the cats mewing in their cages, begging for attention. She shuffled past them with a heavy heart and eyes lowered until it was too much to bear, and then she ran to the closest cage, sticking her fingers inside. An orange tabby pressed his head against her fingers, causing the cat in the next cell to cry louder. She zigzagged down the hallway, going from cage to cage, shoving her fingers as far in as she could, giving each one as much love and attention as she could in a brief time. "I want to take every one of them home with us. Look how desperate they are for love."

"The Siamese is two cages down on the right. Why don't I take her out so you can hold her," the woman said.

"What's her name?" Ravenna said.

"Lilly." The woman placed the cat in Ravenna's arms.

Ravenna felt Lilly's ribs protruding through her fur and a gentle rolling purr in her neck. She gazed into Lilly's deep blue eyes, and her grateful mews riled up the other cats.

"Can I hold her somewhere else? Somewhere quiet where I can see if we bond," Ravenna said.

The woman pointed to a door at the end of the hallway. "There's a small room in there where you can go. Just place her back in her cage and come find me at the desk when you're done."

Ravenna opened the door, and Klay followed her inside. Flooded with light from the south-side windows, the room had dozens of scratching posts and cat trees. She placed Lilly on the floor, happy to give her the freedom to stretch and feel the sun's warm rays penetrate her body. But Lilly just wove around Ravenna's legs, rubbing her head into Ravenna's feet and calves, mewing louder than any cat she had ever heard.

"Siamese are notorious talkers," Klay said. "I think the only reason Moon didn't meow as much was because she could talk to you in other ways."

Ravenna lifted Lilly and placed her in a round, carpeted circle at the top of a cat tree so she could look into her eyes. *Lilly, can you hear me? I want to talk to you.*

The cat cocked her head and sat frozen like a statue.

"Does she hear you?" Klay said.

"I don't know. She stopped moving when I spoke to her. It's like she's trying to listen."

"Try again."

Do you know your name is Lilly? I'm Ravenna.

The cat jumped down from the cat tree and turned in circles, curling herself into a ball on the floor where a stream of light could soak her fur.

"I don't imagine they see much sunlight. Poor thing. She just wants to sleep there," Ravenna said.

"Did she tell you that?"

"She didn't have to. Look at her."

"Sorry, I'm a dog guy. Did she tell you anything?"

"Yeah. She told me to get Maeve off my ass."

"Come on."

"I'm not looking for another familiar. These shelters are depressing, and now I want to take Lilly home, even if she can't talk to me. This was a mistake."

Klay bent down to pet Lilly. She lifted her head and pushed into Klay's hand. "I have an idea. Why don't we take her home? You can tell Maeve that you found another familiar and just stop the search. She may not be Moon, but I'm sure she'll be great company."

Ravenna scooped Lilly into her arms. "Do you want to come home with me?"

Lilly clawed up to Ravenna's shoulder and nuzzled her head into her neck.

"I'm going to take her and find her a home," Ravenna said. "But I won't lie to Maeve again. It's too hard keeping the truth from her."

13

A WEEK AFTER ADOPTING Lilly, Ravenna still couldn't help but wonder if she could have done something different to prevent what happened to Moon. She wished she'd listened to Klay and not let Moon go into the apothecary that day. Instead, she had been too focused on her own troubles, and let Moon fend for herself. Now, the gray morning clouds made her world seem even more lonely and filled with regret. And while she knew she couldn't change what had happened, the guilt tortured her mind.

Ravenna trudged up the familiar footbridge from the beach toward her home, her buckets heavy with sea glass she'd collected over the past few hours. She neared her house but didn't want to go inside. The dreary day mirrored the emptiness that had taken hold of her, leaving her heart with nothing but a barren void. She'd spent sleepless nights with her mind racing through the memory of the faces and cars passing the intersection the day Moon died. Her need for closure had overtaken her.

She was happy to see Klay standing in the driveway, waiting for her. He'd been so loving and supportive in the weeks following Moon's death, and she was grateful for his help in her search for peace, promptly reporting any leads he'd discovered.

Klay pried the buckets from Ravenna's icy grip. "You can let go, and I'll put them wherever you'd like."

Ravenna pointed next to the porch stairs, climbed two steps, and sat down. She slipped off her wet sweatshirt and replaced it with a dry one waiting on the railing.

Klay sat beside her and placed his arm around her shoulders. "You're shivering. Why don't you go inside?"

"Nothing can make me feel better, at least not until I find out who killed Moon. Have you found out anything new?"

"No."

"Nothing at all?"

Klay sighed. "I know how hard this is for you, Ravenna. But you have to move on."

Ravenna winced as though a physical blow had struck her. "Really? You're acting like I should just get over it. Is that what you want me to do? Just turn my feelings off?"

Klay stood to face her. "That's not what I said. Feeling sad and mourning is okay, but seeking revenge isn't healthy. And honestly, you're consumed with it, and it's taking over your whole life."

Ravenna wondered how Klay could even think that, never mind say it. But she felt a twinge of self-doubt, wondering if he was right. "I don't want revenge. I thought you knew me better than that. I need closure."

"You can't have closure unless you know who killed her? Seriously? How's knowing going to change your world?"

"I just want to know what happened. Did the driver not see her, or see her and not care? Did they intentionally want to kill her because she was my familiar? I need to know."

Klay looked at Ravenna, his eyes filled with a gentle warmth. "No, you don't need to know. It's just like you always say about granting wishes. People choose what they want to believe. You need to make sense of this in a way that feels right for you. I believe it was a genuine accident, that someone made a mistake and didn't want to show their face because they feel so bad about it."

"What if it was Chase or someone in his church? I saw people across the street high-fiving and jumping up and down. They probably couldn't wait to bring him the news."

"I suppose anything's possible, but we'll hear about it in time if that's true." Klay sighed. "Look, I've been thinking, and I feel like we should stop searching for whoever killed Moon."

"What? What do you mean, stop searching? I won't rest until I find out who killed her. She was my everything. How could you say that?" Ravenna stared at him.

"I don't know. I just think we won't get an answer."

"Then we need to look harder."

"What are you planning to do if you find out who killed her?" Klay sank onto the lower step and began pulling weeds growing between the walkway cobblestones.

"Well, I . . . I don't know, but I want to know who it was."

"So then, what's the point? I'm letting this one go, and you'll have to search on your own."

Ravenna shot to her feet and looked down at Klay. "You're serious, aren't you? Klay Mitchell, I thought you were my best friend and would do anything for me. How could you? You know how important Moon was to me."

"I do, but I think it's time to move on. This search isn't making things any easier for you."

"I think you mean it isn't making things easier for you. What's this sudden change all about? Are you hiding something from me?"

Klay plucked a blade of grass and played with it between his fingers. "I just think it's time to let Moon rest in peace."

"She is resting in peace. I'm the one who's not. I'm the one who tosses and turns all night because I can't sleep. I'm the one who struggles to perform magic alone." Tears leaked from her eyes, falling on the walkway, killing the grass they landed on.

"I'm sorry, Ravenna. I'm not changing my mind."

"Fine. I'll keep searching alone. Thanks for nothing." Ravenna grabbed her wet sweatshirt and stomped inside.

14

SOMETIMES, WHEN RAVENNA NEGLECTED her meditation practice for long periods, she felt remorse for ignoring her special room at the top of the stairs leading to the attic. Tristan had built it for her, spending all the time he wasn't flying an emergency shipment of medical supplies across the country up there, building it to exact specifications. He cut and installed a dormer window twice the size of the existing one so that Ravenna would have a better ocean view. "No amount of meditation or yoga can relax a woman more than an ocean view," he'd always said. He hung sheetrock, designed built-in shelves for her magical books, and painted the walls her favorite color, lilac. He laid wide pine hardwood floors that matched the rest of the house and hung shelves from the slanted ceilings to store mason jars full of dried herbs and sea glass. He added a custom-built altar and meditation bench that fit squarely under that eastern-facing window, crafted from cedarwood that he loaded on his cargo plane in California and flew home just for her. Ravenna knew he'd been building something upstairs, but she'd assumed it was a man cave because he was so secretive about it. That was, until her twenty-fifth birthday when he said he had a gift for her.

At nine months pregnant, she could barely climb the extra flight of stairs to see the surprise, but Tristan insisted, holding his mouth closed so he wouldn't blurt it out before she reached the top. He gave Ravenna a moment to catch her breath, then handed her a key that fit smoothly into the doorknob of a solid three-panel door framed with Shaker-style trim. Not sure what to expect,

Ravenna opened it. The morning sun rising on the horizon shone through the oversized window, blinding her. Tristan ran across the room to pull the shade down just enough to stop the glare. "Happy birthday, my love!" He smiled, beaming with pride, and spun in circles with his arms wide open, showing her all that was hers.

Ravenna gasped, covered her mouth, and scanned the room in disbelief. She breathed deeply through her nose and smelled white sage from a recent smudging, mixed with the earthy scents of cedar and pine. The room pulsed with pure love, bringing Ravenna to tears.

"So, you like it, then?" Tristan said.

"It's incredible," Ravenna said, wiping her eyes. "You made this for me? It's the kindest thing anyone's ever done for me. How can I thank you?"

"By using it." Tristan took her hand and walked her to the window. He slid it open and lit a white candle on the altar.

Ravenna turned from the dreamy ocean view and hugged him, then gazed into his gentle eyes, grateful to love a man so deeply, knowing he felt the same about her. "Thank you, Tristan. I love it."

Tristan wiped tears from her cheeks and leaned in to lick the salty taste that had reached her lips. Ravenna reached behind his head, grabbed his thick, wavy hair, and pulled him in for a kiss. There, in front of the altar, they became one with the rhythm of the rolling ocean waves.

Today, the sun rose over the horizon, blinding Ravenna just as it had that day. Tristan had gifted her this room, wrapping her with love and nostalgic memories that never faded. Mornings like today made Ravenna grateful it looked exactly the same as it did when he presented it to her. That was, until the Sea Glass Apothecary burned, and the wish room's wall of shimmering stars and crashing ocean waves had vanished, only to resurface here.

It wasn't like she had a choice. The wall had just appeared in the meditation room the next day. Ravenna didn't mind sharing the space with the stars and waves, at least not until the shop got fixed. But to use it, it meant she had to share her private meditation room with clients who wanted their wishes granted, who had to walk through her private home to reach the room at the top of the house. The thought had made her feel ill, all the more so as her troubles had compounded over the months since the Annual Wish Festival. Between avoiding her meditation room, not granting wishes, and losing Moon, her magic was suffering.

RAVENNA HEARD A KNOCK on the door and let in her first client.

"Whoa. I didn't even know this room existed in this house. Hi, I'm Orla." She stood holding the doorframe, wearing a straw hat almost as wide as the entrance, holding her breath. Her eyes moved over the room.

Ravenna smiled. She motioned Orla in and asked her to sit across from her at the table she had brought in when she had decided to try granting wishes in the meditation room. Ravenna lit a white candle next to the glass bowl filled with white sea glass stars.

"What can I do for you today?" Ravenna said.

"I'm not entirely sure I want my wish today. If I use it, it's the only one I'll get in my lifetime, right?"

"That's right. Let me go over the rules for wishing with you. Please listen carefully." Ravenna recited the rules:

"A person can have only one wish in their lifetime. The wish cannot provide financial gain. The wisher cannot travel in time. The wisher cannot bring someone back from the dead. And the wish can harm none."

"My wish won't break any of the rules, but . . ." Orla studied Ravenna.

Lilly jumped on the table.

"I'm sorry. She's mine temporarily," Ravenna said.

"Temporarily?"

"Yes, until I find her a home."

Lilly stood on her hind legs and placed her front paws on the bouncing rim of Orla's hat, extending her claws to play. Orla grabbed the top of her hat with one hand and unhooked Lilly's claws with the other. "I'm sorry. I love cats, and yours is sweet and precious, but I didn't want her to ruin my hat." Orla petted Lilly.

"Lilly, now is not the time to play. Leave Orla's hat alone. Would you like me to take it for you and place it on the altar until you're ready to go? I wouldn't want Lilly to decide she wants to play again and ruin it." Ravenna reached for the hat.

"Oh, no. That's not necessary, but . . . while you're standing, could you turn around for me so I can see how long your hair is?"

"That's an odd request."

"I understand, but would you mind?"

Ravenna pulled her hair out from around her neck and turned slowly around, but only so far as she could still see Orla.

"That's it," Orla said. "I want my hair like yours, minus about six inches, and medium brown with soft blond highlights, not black. Yours is too long for me and too dark. Yeah, the middle of my back would be perfect."

Ravenna's eyes widened, and she sat back in her chair. "Oh, wow. Um . . . no one's ever asked me that before, and I don't know how I feel about it. Why do you want to use your wish on your hair?"

Orla removed her hat and put it on the table beyond Lilly's reach. Bright orange, unkempt, tight curls fell to her shoulders.

"My parents are both Irish immigrants. I'm an only child, and it's a good thing because I would hate to think I had siblings who had to endure the torment I've had with this hair. It's way too curly, out of control, and . . . well . . . orange. I've learned to wear hats to hide it."

"Why don't you just color it? You could have any color you want, and your curls are so full of life." Ravenna reached out and sprang the closest curl she could reach.

"That's why. Because everyone tries to touch it. Some people don't think it's real, some think I'm a freak, and others say they wish they had hair like mine. I want to fade away by running into the orange setting sun, if you know what I mean. No amount of color will change how curly it is, and even hair straightening treatments curl at the roots after only a few weeks. I hate the curls, I hate the color, and I don't want to deal with my hair. I'd be in the salon every three weeks for hours. Honestly, I want to start all over again and be someone entirely different."

Orla's last words grabbed Ravenna's heart and transported her somewhere else, the way a plane humming across the sky might transport her to some faraway destination. Ravenna found herself daydreaming about something she had never thought of before—changing her green eye to brown to match the other, so she'd look more mainstream and normal. Ravenna remembered Moon warning her that a witch couldn't perform magic for themselves, but wondered if something that simple could actually change a life for the better. So how could she deny someone else the chance to find out? "Okay, Orla. Pick a star."

The stars on the wall blinked, and the waves roared. Ravenna reached across the table and cupped Orla's hands that held the star. Orla's face lit with excitement. Ravenna's right eye turned from grass green to a bright, iridescent emerald hue that illuminated the star in her hand.

She recited the wish chant:

"Light that once hung in the sky, you turned to glass and fell from high, into the ocean and tumbled free. Now grant this wish. So mote it be!"

Orla opened her hand wider. The sea glass turned white, flickered, then faded away. The ocean waves and stars on the wall remained still.

"Oh, no!" Ravenna ran to grab a hand mirror off the altar for Orla to see.

"What's wrong?" Orla grabbed the mirror and eyed the reflection staring back at her. She stroked her locks, then looked up at Ravenna. "What happened? It didn't work."

"I don't know," Ravenna said. But she did know what had happened. Moon had died. And her magic hadn't been the same since.

"Hmm. Okay, well, maybe it's harder to change than I thought," Orla said. Ravenna grabbed Orla's hat. "Here. Just put this back on. I'm so sorry."

Orla reached into her bag and pulled out a cash roll with a one-hundred-dollar bill on top. She dropped it on the table.

"No. No. I didn't give you what you wanted." Ravenna picked up the money and tried to hand it back.

"Keep the money. But I have one more request."

"What is it?"

"Lilly. Could I possibly adopt her? She said she'd love to come home with me."

"What do you mean she said that?"

"I would have thought you of all people would know that cats can talk to us. All we have to do is listen. And she said she wants to come home with me."

Ravenna looked into Lilly's wide blue eyes, trying to decipher if she truly wanted to go with her. "Is it true? Do you want to go home with Orla?"

Lilly jumped off the table and traced figure eights around Orla's legs, rubbing her face and body into them. Orla giggled and lifted her. Ravenna felt the intense love blooming between them, reminding her of the way she and Moon used to look at each other. Her eyes prickled with tears.

"I didn't expect to find what I was truly searching for when I came here today," Orla said, her voice tinged with introspection. "But I did, because Lilly loves me just the way I am."

SUMMER

15

RAVENNA SPOTTED CHASE WILKINSON walking toward her on the beach. "What brings you here tonight? On a witch hunt, Reverend?" she said. She laughed at how foolish it sounded when spoken aloud. He was close enough now that she could see defined muscles bulging beneath his blue t-shirt, and inhale his musky cologne mixed with summer's salty air.

Chase stepped back, keeping more than an arm's length of distance between them. "You gave sea glass to one of my parishioners, and she's boasting all over town that it was a miracle—that it's how she got pregnant."

With a gentle tug, Ravenna freed her feet from the grip of the sand and turned to face the full moon. She gazed out over the glistening sea, listening to the hypnotic rhythm of the shimmering waves. Knowing that the moonlight would be illuminating her silver belt buckle, Ravenna looked down at it, confident Chase would look, too, at the star nestled inside a circle, a piece of green sea glass set in the center, glowing with magic and mystery. "I'm glad I could help," she said.

"Help? Are you joking? You gave her false hope. Only God can give life."

"There's nothing false about hope. It's the purest form of magic. And I think you mean Goddess."

Chase stared at her, shifting his focus from her green to her brown eye. She was used to people staring at them, but the way Chase scrutinized her, she would have sworn he was searching for her soul.

"Have you reconsidered my offer to sell your sea glass in my church until your shop is repaired?" Chase said.

"I gave you my answer. There's nothing more for me to think about."

"I'm sure there is, Lady Ravenna. After all, I may be the only one in town willing to take you in after your fire episode."

"Why is that, Reverend Wilkinson? First, you're pissed off at me for helping someone in your church, and now you're still offering me a space. Why? Why aren't you afraid I'll burn your place down, like everyone else?"

"Because fear is for the weak-minded."

"The weak-minded?"

"Those who don't trust God."

"You mean the Goddess?"

Chase snickered. "I'm sure you've never read the Bible."

"Why would I read the Bible? I have no use for it." She eyed him with a steady gaze. "Nature is my teacher. I learn from observing wild animals and changing seasons. It's more than any book could ever offer me. Haven't you ever felt so minuscule in the vastness of, say, the ocean," Ravenna said, opening her arms to show all that surrounded them, "that you can't catch your breath because you're in the presence of something so powerful? That's when I know I'm one with the divine." Ravenna saw the confused look on Chase's face, and thought again how curious she was about him.

"You don't need to be a witch to appreciate nature," Chase said.

"Right, because there is no difference between Christians and Wiccans. We're all the same, and if you disagree, Reverend, tell me why?"

Chase shifted his weight from one foot to the other. "To begin with, Christians believe in one God, and Wiccans believe in many."

"Are you sure about that? There are more Wiccan beliefs than Wiccans, but we almost all agree on a belief in the divine feminine, the cycles of nature, and the power of intention, which isn't so different from your idea of faith and prayer, is it?"

Chase spoke with unwavering confidence. "Nature is more about survival of the fittest." His eyes narrowed. "Speaking of which, reconsider my offer, Lady Ravenna. I think you'll find it's the only one you'll have."

Ravenna watched him walk away, like receding ocean waves that left an emptiness in their wake. She'd reached out, had engaged in conversation about belief, hoping for some mutual connection, but now all she had was sand sinking beneath her feet.

16

RAVENNA WALKED ACROSS THE street to Watson's Café. Ashley's restaurant was a popular spot for locals and tourists at the entrance of the footbridge to Plymbury Beach. White wrought-iron tables and chairs filled the restaurant's outside courtyard, enclosed by white stanchions and chains. It was a quiet afternoon, and Ravenna approached Skye, sitting at a table in the far corner of the courtyard, talking with another waitress.

"Are you on break?" Ravenna said to Skye.

"Uh huh."

"Can I join you?"

"Do I have a choice?"

Ravenna sat across from her, and the waitress took Ravenna's order—a large extra cheese pizza with half pepperoni and two bottled waters.

"I'm hoping you have time to have a bite with me."

Skye stood, rearranging her apron and receipt holders neatly in the pockets. "I need to work now."

"I'm sure Ashley wouldn't mind if you spent a few minutes with me. Please, Skye? I want to talk to you, and you're never around anymore. I ordered your favorite." Ravenna smiled.

"Right. I'm never around because I'm serving tables and not in the apothecary, where I belong. It's not my fault you don't have any time with me. I'm busy."

"Do you like working here? I know you're a huge help for Ashley."

"You mean, do I like people asking me why we left the UU church? No, I don't like it. I especially don't like being lied to and not knowing what the truth is."

"I want to talk to you about this, so can you sit down with me?"

"I have to get back to work."

"Tonight, when you get home?"

"I'll be too tired."

Ashley carried a pizza to the table. "Hey Ravenna, I made it myself, and Amy will bring out your waters. Skye, relax and sit with your mom for a while. I'll pay you for the time." She stepped past Skye, set the pizza and two plates on the table, and smiled at Ravenna.

Skye sat, and grabbed a slice of pizza and a plate. "Then, what's the truth, Mom?" she said, and took a bite.

Ravenna loved Ashley's pizza more than any other, and remembered how hungry she had been at the Wish Festival when the slice she held got slapped out of her hand. "Something strange has been going on, and—"

"Mom, I'm not a child. Just tell me the truth already. Why did you want to leave the UU church? Oh, that's right, Jennifer kicked us out. Give me a break." Skye let out a heavy sigh and rolled her eyes. Her fingers tapped against the tabletop as she stared into the distance at a group of skateboarders whizzing past.

"I told you the truth, Skye, but it sounds like she wants everyone to believe we left."

"I don't believe it. I don't believe any of it! Why would she kick us out for no reason?" Skye's eyebrows squeezed together, and she looked down at her plate.

"Politics, honey. Money has a powerful voice."

"But I thought ministers were poor."

Amy placed the waters on the table and asked if they needed anything else before leaving.

"Honey, the church still needs money to survive, and it gives ministers a free place to live."

"Now you sound cynical, like Great Maeve. And we gave the church money, so I don't get it."

"So do other people." Ravenna pointed to the mansions across the street next to her house. "The influence comes from people with the most money because it gives them that power." She wondered if a witch couldn't grant their own wish because it would give them too much power.

"But we help people, so why hurt us? Why is that okay?"

Ravenna noticed Skye eyeing the courtyard tables around them, filling for early bird specials.

"It isn't okay. That's why we're going to—"

"It's getting busy, Mom. I have to get back to work." Skye stood, retied the strings to her apron, and walked away.

"You're welcome!" Ravenna said, but Skye didn't look back, and she hadn't finished her pizza, either. And now Ravenna had lost her appetite. She stared at Skye's half-eaten slice and felt Ashley's hand on her shoulder.

"It's okay. She'll come around. Just give her some time," Ashley said, and sat in Skye's seat.

"Thanks for helping, Ash. She wouldn't have stayed with me if you hadn't said something. She's been doing a great job of keeping busy and avoiding me. I'm at a loss. We were so close, but since the fire, everything's changed."

"I don't think it's the fire that changed everything. I think it's him." Ashley pointed at Chase, standing by the café's door.

Ravenna spotted him and snapped her head back around to Ashley. "Oh, no. I need to leave fast. I'll slip in the side door to the café, and once he's seated, I'll go. Face him away from the front door."

"I don't think you can hide. He's heading over here now."

"Shit."

"Good afternoon, Lady Ravenna." Chase looked Ravenna in the eye and nodded. "I'm not sure I ever noticed how green your eye is in the sunlight. Piercing." He faced Ashley. "And you must be Ashley Watson, owner of the café. One of my parishioners pointed you out at lunch the other day."

"That's right," Ashley said. "Is everything all right?"

"Perfect. I'm picking up takeout, but I also wanted to see you. I'm Ch—"

"No introductions are necessary. I know who you are."

"News travels around here, doesn't it?" Chase said and glanced at Ravenna.

"Can I help you with something?" Ashley said.

"I was hoping we could chat for a minute if you have the time. Otherwise, I'd be happy to schedule a time more convenient for you."

Ravenna knew Ashley would want to get away from Chase, but she'd never leave her alone with him. She thought, *Ashley's the kind of friend who sacrifices herself for the happiness of others.* "Ash, I'm sorry I asked you to sit and talk about Skye's schedule with me. You're busy, and I have to go, too. We can talk another time. It's getting crowded." Ravenna stood.

"Leaving already?" Chase looked at the table. "You haven't even finished your meal."

"I'll have to get back to you, Reverend Wilkinson. The day has already escaped me." Ashley stood and smoothed down her skirt. "Ravenna, why don't you come in with me, and I'll wrap your leftover pizza so you can take it with you." She hooked her arm around Ravenna's, grabbed the pizza tray, and began walking. Ravenna felt Ashley leaning on her for balance.

"Sure. Sure. Call the church to schedule a time," Chase said.

"Will do," Ashley called over her shoulder.

"That was a close one. I can't believe he didn't want to talk to me for once. What do you think he wants to talk to you about?" Ravenna said.

"I'm sure he only wants to talk about you. He seems obsessed."

Ravenna helped Ashley into the only free chair in the café's corner and grabbed a bottle of water from the bar. "Here, drink this. Can you take the rest of the day off and rest?"

"I had my first treatment yesterday. It's okay. The doctor told me I'd feel this way and be more myself in a day or two. Grab an empty box on the bar and go before Chase thinks we planned the exit."

Ravenna laughed. "Yeah. Because we're so smart, he'd never suspect a thing."

On her way out, Ravenna waved to Skye, pouring a cup of coffee at the outdoor coffee station. "See you later."

Skye looked up, then turned away.

17

WHEN A PET DIES, you lose a family member, but when a familiar dies, you lose yourself, Ravenna thought, lying in bed, watching the ceiling fan whirl in circles above her. By now, Moon would have insisted she open the window shades and let the sun inside. She'd yell for Ravenna to get up, even though Klay opened the shop on Saturdays. Moon loved Saturday mornings, jumping to the cat perch in front of the window, chirping and chattering at the birds in the catnip garden, and observing the raven. Until, in typical cat fashion, she couldn't hold her eyes open any longer, and curled up in a ball with the sun's rays shining down on her, keeping her warm. Ravenna gazed at the closed window shade and the empty perch in front of it. Her heart gushed with anxiety when she remembered that Moon wasn't coming back. She hated that feeling. Losing Moon was hard enough, but those random sharp pangs of twisting agony reminded her how much it hurt, as if a switch flipped, shut her body down, and left her numb. Memories blurred Ravenna's eyes, causing shadows from the spinning fan to play tricks on her. She spotted Moon jumping on the perch and peering at her, disappointed the shade was still down.

I think I'm going crazy. I know you're not here, Moon, but I'll put the shade up for you, just in case. Ravenna wiped her tears with the back of her hands and opened the shade. The blazing sun stung her wet eyes. She raised her hand to block the rays and noticed Maeve in the catnip garden. Ravenna laughed through the sorrow. *Now you know what it feels like, Moon. She's not letting you rest this morning, is she?*

Ravenna threw on jeans and a shirt, brushed her hair, and headed out to meet Maeve in the yard. "Why don't you trim the herbs and leave Moon to rest? You're keeping the raven away, too, and it's Moon's favorite entertainment."

"Raven shmaven. It'll come back when I'm finished. You look terrible, honey. Are you sleeping?" Maeve hugged Ravenna.

"No. I toss and turn all night."

"Why don't I finish here and grab some takeout at Ashley's? She makes the best New England breakfast. Those pancakes are fluffy and comforting, with just the right touch of maple syrup to lift your spirits, and when it mixes with the egg yolks . . . ah, I can taste it now." Maeve lifted her hands to her mouth.

"I'm not hungry, but you go get some. I'll make coffee and meet you inside."

Maeve returned with two takeout containers and transferred the food to plates.

"I told you I didn't want any," Ravenna said.

"Well, let it sit in front of you, then. You need to eat, and once you smell those eggs and maple syrup and see me digging in, you'll eat it." She put the plates on the kitchen table by the coffee mugs Ravenna had filled, and sat across from her.

Ravenna knew Maeve ate when she was sad or upset, but also knew she simply loved food, and her waistline proved it. Ravenna had watched Maeve mix everything up on her plate her whole life. That's how she ate, and that's how she lived. Everything jumbled into one messy ball. And yet, somehow, it all turned out perfect for her. But Ravenna knew what she was about to say might make things a little too messy, even for Maeve.

"Go on. Take a bite. It's scrumptious, and if you don't start eating soon, you'll waste away to nothing. Moon loved you too much to want to see that happen."

Ravenna took a small piece of pancake and held the shaking fork up to her mouth. "Grandma, have you ever thought about what life would be like if we weren't a family of witches?"

"What are you saying, Ravenna? Our family has been at the heart of Plymbury's folktale for centuries. We're the family of witches that the local legend talks about, who found the stars that turned to glass and fell into the ocean, the ones who use that tumbled sea glass to grant wishes." Maeve pointed two fingers toward her eyes. "We have one green and one brown eye, just like the legend says. Look at me, Ravenna. I have one green and one brown eye, and your mother did, too." She pointed at Ravenna's eyes. "You do. So does Skye. And make no mistake, it didn't start with me. All Greene women have had them—every one of us. And for crying out loud, Ravenna, you've made us famous. Now our name will go down in history with the legend. Look at the legacy you're handing to Skye and her daughters."

"Come on, Maeve. You know as well as I do that fame brings out the worst in people."

"Only if you let it. So don't let it."

"Did you forget I burned my shop down? I don't even know how, or whether it could happen again, and I got kicked out of the UU church because of it. My daughter hates me now, and I lost my familiar. I lost Moon!" Ravenna put her elbows on the table, cradled her face in her hands, and wept.

"I hope you're not blaming yourself for Moon's accident. It had nothing to do with you."

"Maybe not, but don't tell me you think it's coincidental that all these things are happening at once. I'm listening to what my intuition is telling me."

"That's not intuition. That's self-sabotage."

"I'm sorry, Maeve. I need some fresh air and time with Moon right now." Ravenna walked out, leaving the kitchen door swaying open on its hinges.

THE CROWS SCATTERED WHEN Ravenna collapsed in the catnip garden.

I can't live without you, Moon. Ravenna ran her shaking hand over Moon's memorial stone. *Everything's changed, and I'm changing, too. Is it supposed to be this way? Did losing you mean I was supposed to lose myself at the same time?*

Maeve ambled across the lawn and placed her hand on Ravenna's shoulder. "I know how hard this is for you, but you are who you are, and you'll get through it."

"I just don't know if this is what I'm supposed to be doing with my life anymore, Grandma."

Ravenna spotted the raven watching her from the branch of a nearby pine tree, but her curiosity dissipated when Maeve grabbed her arm, pulling her to her feet.

"Of course it is, Ravenna. You're just mourning right now. Don't you remember? You've always loved sea glass, and it's your whole life now. Well, that and Skye. You've given this life to Skye, and she loves it as much as you do."

"Don't you get it? I never had a choice, and neither has she. While the shop is being fixed, she's working for Ashley across the street." Ravenna pointed toward Watson's Café. "What if she decides she loves working there more than fulfilling people's wishes? What if she wants to go to college? I want her to explore and decide what's right for her. I can't ask her to do something that her whole heart may not want, just because of this town's folktale."

"Maybe you missed the memo, but Skye has never had more joy on her face than when she's in that shop. She's asked for a pentacle tattoo, and can't wait to grant wishes next year."

"Stop. You're pushing my daughter where you want her. You did that to me, and I won't let you do it to her, too!"

"Maybe it's not me. Did you ever think maybe it's you who's pushing Skye to have the life you want for her, and have you bothered to notice she doesn't want it?"

"She's too young to know what she wants. I want her to know there are more options, that she's not being forced to do anything she doesn't want to."

"Ravenna, the sea glass has given you purpose and helped you learn to accept who you are. Even your different colored eyes, which you used to say were the worst curse on any human. Do you remember when you came to me in high school and insisted on attending the Massachusetts College of Art and Design for your BFA in Jewelry and Metalsmithing? You wanted to learn how to make jewelry from the pieces of sea glass you couldn't use for wishes. You knew all the glass had healing properties and wanted to use them to help people. But that wasn't all. You wanted people to feel beautiful and special while they healed, and what better way than by wearing jewelry? I didn't deny you what you wanted. I didn't choose that for you. You were the one who found more uses for the sea glass. You were the one who became the Plymbury witch. It's a blessing—an opportunity to help others. So what's changed? You're still the same person."

"I burned my shop down."

"Burned shmurned. No one in town even cares about it anymore." Maeve waved her hand as if to dismiss the problem into thin air.

"Maeve, I've lost everything, and you taught me when things don't feel right in my gut, then something has to change."

"Yes, but when you lose someone, and it causes unbearable pain, it's best to wait until you can think clearly before making any major decisions in your life. I'm sorry about Moon, but give it a year. If you still feel this way, then I'll talk seriously about it. Okay?"

Ravenna kneeled in the catnip. Her heart bled, and her stomach twisted from the hole left inside of her. She wanted to think with clarity and work this out in her mind, but Moon's were the only conversations she'd ever had in her head. Now, she didn't even know what to say to herself or, worse, how to answer. She had relied on Moon for every major decision in her life, and the bond between them was stronger than any silver cord binding two souls. Moon guided her through the darkest of nights with the voice of a wise sage. She was a friend and mentor who had woven her way into the very substance of Ravenna's being. Moon had been her partner for life and the mystery behind her magic.

Ravenna's sobs grew guttural, and the herbs beneath her began to wilt and die from her fallen tears. The catnip was all she had left of Moon, and now that was dying, too. Ravenna kissed her hand and brushed it on Moon's gravestone. She rose and walked out of the garden to a stone bench surrounded by mulch, where she could let her tears run freely.

Maeve sat next to her.

"I can't think. My head is so empty," Ravenna said.

"Remember the first time you let Moon run through the catnip garden? She rolled all over the place for an hour, then stumbled into the house like a drunkard. She didn't have a responsibility in the world, and you said your head felt empty then, too. You said it felt empty every time she rolled around in the catnip, but you also said you loved seeing her so free and happy. Do you remember that?"

"Yes, I remember. Why?"

Maeve embraced Ravenna. "Because she's probably rolling around in an endless sea of catnip now, free and happy."

"I know. I just wish I wasn't so sad."

18

RAVENNA ASCENDED THE STEPS of Living Waters Church. After each one, she stopped and inhaled deeply, trying to muster her courage. At the top, she touched the doorknob, hot from the summer heat, let go, and walked back down the stairs. She paced back and forth in the parking lot, then ran up again and turned the knob, hoping for a locked door. But it clicked. She let go, allowing it to snap back into place, and turned to descend the steps.

"Lady Ravenna, such a pleasure to see you here. Was the knob stuck from the heat? I'll be sure that gets fixed."

Ravenna spun around to see Chase holding the door open, gazing at her with sharp focus.

"Please, come inside. At least there's no rain." He looked up at the sun-filled sky. "Wouldn't it have been terrible if you melted? To think, a real live witch, visiting my church."

Ravenna's cheeks burned fiery hot, knowing that Chase had seen how much she struggled to come inside. His words made her feel like he was making fun of her, to see her squirm.

"I imagine this visit must be something important. Should I invite you in? After all, you've never invited me into your place."

"I . . . I didn't even think to offer." Ravenna said evasively, knowing she had no intention of ever inviting him into her home.

"Never mind that now. Come in." Chase moved aside to let her into the entrance, where people who'd just attended the Sunday service stood and gawked at her. She spotted Jill and watched her walk past with a huge smile, pointing to her stomach. She mouthed, "Thank you," and caught up with others passing in the hallway.

"Let's talk in my office," Chase said.

Ravenna followed him past the church office and down the hall to a door on the left. His study was simple, Puritan style, and Ravenna wasn't sure why she would have expected anything different. A computer and scattered papers sat on a Shaker-style pine desk with a matching swivel chair. A pair of chairs sat across from it. On the far side of the room was a pine table with framed photographs set on top, and matching bookcases standing like bookends, flanking a picture window overlooking the marsh. Ravenna stepped toward it to take in the view.

"If you look to your right, you can almost see the beautiful flowers and herbs you grow in your gardens," Chase said. "Sure, it's a ways away, but I can see when you tend to them. I used to watch my mother tend to hers, too, and when I was old enough, she taught me to garden. It's one of my favorite things to do. From what I've seen, I think it's just as enjoyable for you. No?"

Ravenna turned around to face Chase. "Yes. You watch me?"

"I just see you sometimes when I'm walking the grounds."

"But you said you see me from this window."

"I said that? Well, I imagine I could. I mean, if I can see you from outside it."

Ravenna stared at Chase while she moved forward to sit in front of his desk. He walked backward and swayed his body around the side, his eyes fixed on hers, sitting in the chair behind it.

"Should I close the door?" Ravenna said.

"It's better if it stays open." Chase placed an elbow on the desk, leaned toward her, and wrapped an index finger around his cleft chin. "What can I do for you, Lady Ravenna?"

"I've been thinking about your generous offer to let me sell my sea glass jewelry here in your church. I assume the offer still stands?"

"Yes, of course. I offered the room behind the sanctuary." His blank face gave way to a raised eyebrow.

"Could I use a space near where I entered by the side of the church? I assume that's the popular entrance."

Chase's muscles tensed visibly beneath his tight shirt. He leaned back in his chair and crossed his arms over his chest. It seemed he wasn't used to a woman speaking her mind, much less asking for what she wanted.

Ravenna tried to soften the blow to his ego. "I just thought it would be better for everyone. You know, more visible exposure, so people coming in and out of the church can find me. My business partner, Klay, plans to put up a sign at the Sea Glass Apothecary to let people know we're here, which could give your church more exposure down by the beach." Ravenna knew Klay had planned to make a sign, but if the apothecary was temporarily at Living Waters Church, that might be reason enough for Klay to forget he'd made that promise.

"Let's go see the room I had picked for you," Chase said.

"Why are you doing this for me? You don't even know me, and after the newspaper article and your church members staring at me in the entrance earlier, it just seems odd." Ravenna pulled her straight black hair over her shoulder, twisting it into a thick rope that reached her thigh. It was an old habit that brought her comfort.

Chase stared at Ravenna coiling her hair, then shifted his gaze to a pen on his desk. "Just being neighborly."

He seemed self-conscious, and she couldn't help but feel a twinge of sympathy for him when he shot up from his desk and smoothed the wrinkles in his shirt.

"Shall we?" he said, motioning to the door.

Chase escorted Ravenna past the side church entrance, the main office on the hallway's right, and a long craftsman bench beside a closed door on the left. The ancient building creaked from the winds billowing outside as they approached the sanctuary doors in front of them. Chase heaved open the solid, twenty-foot oak doors and waited for Ravenna to enter. She ran her fingers across the wood's grain on her way inside. Images of a brig and the names Weston and King Caesar appeared in her mind. The expansive cylinder glass windows along the walls spanned from waist height to just below the fifty-foot cathedral ceiling. A massive antique brass chandelier hung over the congregation area, with simple wooden pews with red velvet cushions, flanking the sixty-foot aisle leading to the sanctuary. Three steps up, behind the altar, wood-carved Ten Commandments hung prominently enough for people in the street to see them. Ravenna turned in circles, taking in the sight of all the handiwork, breathing in the smell of aging wood. "It's incredible. Spectacular," she said, and groped as if blind, feeling for a pew to sit and catch her breath.

"It is. Overwhelmed me the first time I saw it, too. Wealthy shipbuilders built it in Greek revival style in the mid-nineteenth century."

Ravenna stared at the imposing Ten Commandments hanging ominously ahead. She thought about the only Christian Bible quote Maeve had ever taught her, and the picket sign outside the apothecary the day of the Annual Wish Festival. *Thou shalt not suffer a witch to live.* Her breath became shallow and quick, and she began to feel warm. She scanned the sanctuary for its exits.

"The room is over there." Chase pointed to a doorway beside the altar. "Come, let's have a look."

"Wait! Maybe this was a mistake. I'm sure I can find another place to sell my jewelry. I should probably go."

"If I didn't know better, I'd say something scared you. Has the Good Lord spoken to you, or is it me you're afraid of? Is it worth it, Lady Ravenna?"

"Is what worth it?"

"Witchcraft. Is it worth it?"

"What do you mean?" Ravenna thought about the noose hanging on the apothecary door the morning of the Annual Wish Festival, and the angry protesters who closed in on her before the fire burst out. "Are you threatening me?"

"Why would I threaten you? Didn't I offer to help you?"

Ravenna took a deep breath and grounded herself, releasing her fear and anger into the wooden floor. "Yes. That's why I'm here."

"Come then. It's behind the sanctuary."

They stepped through a curious door off the side of the dais area housing the altar and lectern. Dull light seeped through hazy windows, casting eerie shadows on the walls. The absence of furniture and decor gave the room a desolate, forgotten feel. Across the room, Ravenna spotted another door leading to a small private parking lot.

"With a little cleaning, I think this spot would be perfect for you. It's plenty private, with your own entrance, and no one ever uses this room or that parking lot. You can't see inside from any part of the church or its grounds, even when the windows are clean, but you'll get plenty of sunlight."

For a minute, Chase fooled Ravenna. She thought he genuinely wanted her to occupy the perfect place to grant people's wishes and sell her jewelry, but then it struck her like a bucket of icy water being poured over her head. He intended to keep her hidden and vulnerable. A deep chill set into her bones, replacing the initial shock and numbness. "Would it be possible to see the room I asked about across from the church's side entrance? It's busier over there, with much more foot traffic."

"I don't think so. The church uses that room to collect items donated for the annual spring fair," Chase said.

As a child, Ravenna had attended the church fair with Maeve. She had played in the children's section while Maeve supported the church by purchasing gently used children's toys and books for her to take home, along with some antique dishes and silverware for herself. One year, Maeve bought a handcrafted wooden rocking chair for the front porch of the apothecary. She'd brought it with her to the house she purchased on Mayflower Lane when Ravenna took over. Maeve believed Christians would leave the Greene family alone if she showed their church hospitality. Still, she had always warned Ravenna not to trust them, but never provided a valid reason why. Standing here with Chase now, Ravenna thought there might be some truth to the warnings Maeve had spewed all these years. He was up to something, and it smelled like today's catch down on the docks.

"I won't be here long, a few months, tops. I can't imagine any later than . . . the fall." Ravenna swallowed hard. "Klay and I would happily move everything and return it when we leave."

Chase stiffened, but led her back to the door in the hallway.

Ravenna crossed the threshold to be greeted by an overwhelming display of colors. Trinkets filled every space, and books stacked as high as the ceiling filled the thick air with the musty aroma of yellowed pages. Ravenna's eyes widened, and she felt like she'd stumbled upon a hidden treasure, a portal to an ancient world.

"If you choose this room, you'll need to move all this to the space behind the sanctuary and back again when you leave. And outside of moving all of this twice, there is one more caveat."

"What is it?"

"You can't perform any sea glass wishes here. I don't want anyone in the church exposed to that kind of sorcery. I'm sure you understand."

"No. I'm afraid I don't. Are you saying I can grant wishes in the other room? I've been seeing clients in my meditation room at home, but I'd prefer not to have people in my house. So I'll reconsider the other room. Could I see it one more time?"

"Let me make this perfectly clear for you, Lady Ravenna. There will be none of that witchery nonsense anywhere in my church!" Chase's nostrils flared, and his voice lowered to a growl. "If I find out you're granting wishes anywhere, even in your home, I'll kick you out. Do you understand me?"

"But that's what I—"

"Do we have a deal or not?"

"I need to think—"

"Yes or no, Lady Ravenna? I won't offer it again. Now or never."

"Yes. We have a deal."

Ravenna understood that not keeping her word meant more than being kicked out of Chase's church. It would mean she couldn't support Skye, and the thought of failing her was unbearable. Besides, Ravenna was all too familiar with the burden of living with a lie and refused to live with another.

After all, she thought, *this was only temporary.*

19

RAVENNA SPOTTED KLAY FISHING on the shore as her yoga class wrapped up, and knew she'd have to face him eventually. She bowed before her yoga instructor and headed toward the water, already feeling a knot forming in her stomach and discomfort in her neck. Klay stood at the beach's edge as the last few rays of sun swallowed the sand dunes behind him. His lean muscles and sun-soaked skin contrasted with a faded blue t-shirt and khaki shorts. Ravenna watched him open a small Styrofoam box full of pogies and grab one, fresh and glistening. He held the fishing rod between his legs, grabbed the hook, and pierced the fish.

Ravenna winced. "That poor, innocent fish. How can you do that?"

"If I don't hook him, I'll eat him and all his friends, too. I'm hoping for something bigger and tastier tonight," Klay said. "If you don't want to watch, turn around. Go on. Don't look."

Ravenna faced the dunes, watching the sky turn from pink to dark orange. The waves crashing on the shore behind her filled the air, growing louder, and her uneasiness rose with the incoming tide.

"Don't hurt the fish. Please?" she said.

"We both collect treasures from the sea, and mine just happen to swim."

"Yours only swim until you kill them. Mine pulse with life for eternity. Did you catch anything tonight?"

"If I caught something, I'd be home grilling it for dinner. So what's on your mind? I know you didn't come here to watch me fish. Let me see if I can remember what you said about this. Oh, I know. You said, 'Can't you just eat vegetables?', and 'If you need some quiet spiritual time, why not just meditate?'"

"At least I know you listened to me," Ravenna said, unsure she wanted him to pay attention this time. Klay already believed she wasn't thinking clearly, so she contemplated working at Chase's church alone. But deep down, she needed Klay. He'd lay his life down for her, and she relied on his loyalty.

Ravenna eyed Rich, Klay's father, as he approached, walking one of his Dobermans.

"Hey, Dad," Klay said.

"Did you catch dinner yet?" Rich waved to Ravenna.

"I'm kind of distracted. Can I meet you up at Ashley's?"

"A distraction like that's hard to leave. Take your time," Rich said and smiled at Ravenna.

Ravenna managed a return smile and thought that after all these years, Rich might have gotten the hint that she and Klay were just friends and business partners, but nothing more. Ravenna waited for Rich to be out of earshot. "How many places have we tried, Klay? No one will rent to us."

"I don't know, but I have six more places lined up. Some farther than Marsh-field, but that doesn't mean it isn't a good idea. Maybe it will give the people in Plymbury a chance to miss you."

"I found us a place."

Klay spiked his rod into the sand. "That's incredible! I told you the hype would settle down, and people would decide the truth for themselves. Where is it?"

Ravenna picked up a rock and skipped it across the waves.

"Stop it! You're scaring the fish away."

"I'd offer to pay for dinner, but since you won't help me find Moon's killer, you're lucky you still have a job."

Klay watched his father cross the footbridge to Ashley's. "I told you how I feel about it."

"Yes, and I don't agree."

"We don't always agree on business stuff either, but we compromise and make it work."

"I must have missed it. Was there a compromise about finding Moon's killer?"

"No, there wasn't. I'm sorry, but I don't have one."

"You're not sorry. I have something to tell you, and I won't compromise either, so you're going to have to deal with it."

"Are you trying to get back at me, here?"

"I accepted Chase's offer."

Klay rolled his eyes. "Goddess. Please tell me you didn't?"

"I did. It's not like I had a choice. The man's ruining my life, and it was my only option."

"So if the frying pan burned the bacon, you'd stop it by jumping into the pan? Because you and I both know he will burn you, and it won't be in a frying pan. It'll be right here on Plymbury Beach when it's crazy busy. Hmm. Yes, maybe on the Fourth of July. He'll bind you with ropes to a post built on a platform so everyone can see." Klay opened his arms to indicate the expanse of the beach. "Then he'll pile logs around you and spread straw from the horse farms on top of it. His sinister laugh will reverberate across the beach as he turns the spark wheel of his lighter and lowers it to the hay. Poof! In an instant, you're engulfed in flames." Klay snapped his hands toward Ravenna with open fingers. "And then, in celebration, fireworks."

"And what will you be doing? Standing there, watching me burn?"

Klay picked up his fishing rod and started packing his gear. "What else would I do? It's not like you tried to run away or anything."

"Come on. You won't let me do it alone, will you?"

"I'm seriously thinking about it."

"What happened to the guy who would do anything for me? Fine, I'll go alone. Maybe I can get some of Skye's guy friends to help me move everything in." Ravenna walked away, but Klay went after her. He grabbed her arm and turned her to face him.

"You didn't give me a chance to answer. I didn't say I wouldn't go."

"You will when I tell you I agreed not to do any wish magic."

"Man, Ravenna. What's wrong with you?"

"I need a space."

"I guess I'm not shocked he won't allow magic in his church, but you'll take clients at night in your meditation room, right?"

"I promised not to do magic anywhere in town while I'm selling in the church, and I may have agreed to outside of town, too, but I don't know how he'd even know if I did. Anyway, it doesn't matter. I can't." Ravenna gazed down at the sand.

Klay laughed. "The man's a fool. He obviously doesn't know your entire being is magical. This might actually be fun."

"It's not a game, Klay. I need to provide for Skye. Otherwise, I never would have accepted."

"Okay. Okay. I need the money, too. We have a new litter of pups that the mom won't feed, so Dad and I have been taking shifts around the clock, hand-feeding them. It's expensive."

"Funny, I thought you'd want to sleep more than you'd want money."

"Looks like you've got me figured out, all right."

"Will you go with me?"

Klay looked into Ravenna's eyes. "I really wish you hadn't accepted his offer, because I know he's up to something. But I won't let you go alone."

20

RAVENNA WONDERED IF CHASE cherished garden time with his mother as much as she did with Maeve. Ever since she was a young girl, they would spend days in the garden together, sometimes talking more than gardening, watching Moon roll around in the catnip or chase the raven. Today was different, and it wasn't because Moon was gone. Maeve was unusually quiet, spending the entire morning in the flower bed that mysteriously bloomed all year long on the far side of the yard, while Ravenna tended to the bleeding hearts closer to the house. Twice, Ravenna brought Maeve a water bottle and asked if she needed help.

"I'm fine," was all Maeve had said.

Ravenna knew she wasn't okay, but didn't press her because she could only remember one other time Maeve had been quiet like this. It had been when Ravenna was a teenager, and had lied to her about the senior prom.

"WERE YOU ASKED TO the senior prom?" Maeve had asked Ravenna.

"Yeah, but I don't know if I'm going."

"Why not? Everyone goes to their prom, and there are some nice Pagan boys in Plymbury." Maeve winked her green eye. "Which one asked you?"

"It doesn't matter, because I'm not planning to go."

You're not going to tell her the truth, are you? Moon said, curled up in Ravenna's lap.

No. I'll tell her I'm going out with my friends, bring my clothes to Meghan's, and get ready there.

What if there are pictures in the newspaper?

There won't be because I'll avoid the cameras. Don't worry so much, Moon. Ravenna rubbed Moon's belly.

Moon nuzzled into Ravenna's neck. *I think you should tell her.*

"I hope you'll change your mind. I'd love to see you all dressed up, and I know you'd have a wonderful time," Maeve said.

"I'm not going."

Ravenna never told Maeve she went to the prom, but the next day, Ravenna spotted the newspaper sitting on the living room coffee table, opened to a picture of her and her date walking down the school's red carpet. She'd asked the cameraman not to photograph her, and he didn't, but that didn't stop Meghan's mother from submitting the photos she'd taken to the local paper.

So Ravenna searched the house and found Maeve outside in the garden. "I'm sorry. I should have told you, but I knew—"

Maeve held her palm up to Ravenna.

"You won't talk to me?" Ravenna said.

Maeve didn't speak to her for five days.

The fifth night at the dinner table, Maeve said, "If I ever catch you with that boy again, or any other Christian boy, you can forget college." Her nostrils flared. "So long as you live in this house, I make the rules."

MAEVE MADE THE RULES all right. She'd made them Ravenna's whole life, and now, as an adult, Maeve was still trying to control her.

Ravenna marched to the other side of the yard where Maeve was splitting hostas. "If there's a problem, I'd like to know about it."

"Oh, there's a problem. I thought I raised you better than that."

"Better than what?"

"How many times have I told you that you can't trust Christians?"

Ravenna stomped back to her garden, thinking Klay must have told Maeve she was moving the apothecary to Chase's church.

Maeve trailed behind her. "Keep walking, because we're going over there right now and telling Wilkinson you changed your mind."

Ravenna stopped and faced Maeve. "No, we're not."

Maeve lifted her hand with the trowel and pointed it at Ravenna. "Yes, we are."

"Maeve, I have no choice. I need to provide for Skye. It's my only option, and get that thing out of my face!"

"Face shmase. If you want me to put it down, you have two choices. You can come with me to tell him you made a mistake, or you can tend your gardens alone. I don't trust him, Ravenna, and I'm not letting you go there." Maeve threw the trowel at the ground, just missing Ravenna's foot.

Ravenna's eyes widened, and her body tensed. "You could have hurt me with that thing."

Before Maeve said anything, Ravenna heard the kitchen door open and saw Skye stepping out of the house.

"Whoa, what's all the yelling about?" Skye said.

"Get back in the house," Ravenna said.

"Why don't you come here, Skye, so I can tell you how foolish your mother is?"

"Don't put her in the middle. Go ahead inside, Skye."

Skye didn't listen. She followed the flagstone pathway to where Maeve and Ravenna stood.

"Your mother wants to move the apothecary to the Christian church down the street," Maeve said.

"Mom, why would you do that?"

"Because it's my only option."

"Because your mother wants to let them finish the job they started the day the shop burned."

"Finish the job?" Skye said.

"They were trying to kill her, you, and me."

"Great Maeve, that's extreme. Don't you think? They weren't the ones who lit the fire. Mom was."

Maeve stared at her. "Make no mistake, Skye. They wanted your mother to start that fire."

"That's ridiculous. I've never lit anything on fire before," Ravenna said.

Maeve watched the raven fly in circles above them. "I'm going there myself to end this foolishness."

"I'm not in high school anymore, Maeve, and don't you dare ruin my only chance of supporting my family."

"You'll regret this, Ravenna, and not just because of the wedge you're driving between us." Maeve stormed off, and Skye followed her.

Ravenna shuffled to Moon's grave and knelt in the catnip. *I think I'm losing everyone I love. You would have understood, Moon. Wouldn't you?*

21

THE BATTERY-OPERATED DRILL TOOK longer than one with an electrical cord, but Ravenna never understood why some sea glass artists drilled in water with electricity. She knew how they drilled holes for jump rings was a preference, but getting electrocuted wasn't on her list of things to experience in her lifetime. Ravenna placed a wood block into a plastic container filled with water, put the sea glass on top, and set the drill at a low speed, enjoying the meditative pace, watching the water swirl in wide circles as the bit sank in.

The door to her meditation room flew open, jarring Ravenna out of her contemplation. Her hand slipped as she jumped, jamming the drill into the water. She whirled around to see what had startled her, then turned back. "And there, my friend, is why I don't use an electric drill. Thanks for that." Ravenna pulled the wet drill out of the water and placed it on a dry towel.

"Oh, sorry," Klay said. "I was looking for the boxes to bring to jerkface's church and thought they might be up here."

"Did it ever occur to you to knock? And please stop calling Chase jerkface. We both know he's a jerk, but being nice might help make this easier."

Klay grunted, then spotted the wish wall. "Oh, wow! I didn't know it had moved in here. Do you think it'll follow you to jer . . . um, Chase's church?"

Ravenna hadn't considered that the wall might follow her there. "Shit. I hope not. I don't think they'd be so happy about my wish wall in their Christian church."

Ravenna wrapped the sea glass jewelry she'd made over the past few days in bubble wrap and placed them into boxes labeled with their metaphysical properties. Klay took them to the car.

"Here's the last box," Ravenna said when Klay returned from his fifth trip outside.

Klay grabbed the bubble wrap and swathed the bowl of sea glass stars.

"No, Klay. I won't need those. They can stay here."

"Look, I know things are harder for you without Moon, but you're the Plymbury witch, and everyone comes to you for wishes. You can't just stop doing them."

Ravenna felt heat rising to her face. "How about you don't tell me what to do? Should I tell you what to do? Okay, I will. Get out of here and go look for Moon's killer." Ravenna pointed to the door. "How about you do that?"

Klay grabbed the box of jewelry and slid out the door.

Ravenna followed him. "You drive. I'm walking."

"What did you say?"

"I said I'll meet you there." Ravenna hopped onto the sidewalk and followed it, trailing her hand across the next-door neighbor's white vinyl fence, letting it fall limp between the wide slats. She gazed at the massive front lawn flanked by Cleveland pear trees that led up to a mansion, surrounded by tall rhododendrons at each corner of the house and blooming pink and purple hydrangeas filling the spaces between. Ravenna stood in bitter silence, wishing the chipmunk Moon chased had run into this enormous yard instead of down the street to the intersection. *I miss you so much, Moon.*

Klay yelled out the car's window as he rolled slowly past Ravenna. "Hey, you'd better get a move on. I'm going to get there before you, and no telling what I might say to jer . . . I mean, Chase."

"Shh! People can hear you."

"Well, if you don't want me saying embarrassing things down the street, then get in." Klay stopped, leaned across the passenger seat, and opened the door.

"Fine." Ravenna jumped in and slammed the door.

"I know you're mad at me. And I know you want to keep searching for Moon, but I think—"

"If you don't say that you're going to help me find her killer, then you'd better stop talking, or I'll jump right out of this car."

"Okay. Have it your way."

Ravenna was thankful that Chase's church was only down the street, so she didn't have to endure Klay's heavy silence in the car for long. When they arrived, she dug her hand deep into her pocket and pulled out a key while Klay tried to balance too many boxes.

"He gave you a key? That seems a bit personal to me. If you know what I mean." Klay winked his eye a few times.

"Don't be ridiculous. This is where my shop is for now, and I'll need access when no one is here."

"That's what they all say," Klay said and laughed, almost dropping a box.

"Can you please be careful? I don't need you ruining the pieces I just finished making, and it's bad luck to break them."

"Yeah, we don't need any more bad luck these days. Walking in this place is bad luck enough."

"Come on, Klay." Ravenna held the door open for him.

"It's kind of eerily empty for six on a Sunday evening. Don't you think?" Klay said.

They followed the dimly lit hallway, and Ravenna flipped on the light inside the room she and Chase had agreed she'd use. She glanced up at the suspended ceiling tiles. "Ugh. Fluorescent lights. I really hate fluorescent lights. They make everything look puke green and dark at the same time."

"Let's just hope we're not here long," Klay said.

"At least the sanctuary's beautiful. Do you want to see it?"

"No. Not at all. There are only three places where you'll see me in this hellhole. The entrance when I come in and out, this room, and the bathroom. That's it. And the sooner we can move out, the better."

It didn't take long to unwrap the jewelry and set up display cases. After working with Klay for over twenty years, Ravenna knew he preferred an organized system sorted by color and metaphysical properties, so when a customer needed something in a specific color or healing specialty, it was easy to find. However, Ravenna felt no need for the organization. She knew the pieces and why she made them, but if it made Klay's life easier, she'd do it since he was always the one in front of the shop serving customers while she granted wishes in the back.

"You'll notice I labeled the boxes for you," Ravenna said. "Can you put the lighter colors by the window? I know sunset light instead of sunrise seems strange, but those pieces will still look best when sunrays shine through them. Also, it doesn't look like there will be enough moonlight to clear them, so we'll have to smudge every morning."

"I'm a step ahead of you," Klay said. From a nearby box he pulled out a white sage smudge stick with matches sitting in a quahog shell. "Figured you'd want to smudge the place, anyway. I know I do. Heck, we should smudge the whole freaking building while no one's here."

When they finished arranging the jewelry, Ravenna lit the smudge stick and wafted the smoke around the room to neutralize the energy. She and Klay were relaxed in two folding chairs, planning the store opening the next morning, when Ravenna heard the church door swing open, followed by footsteps.

Chase entered the room. "Well, good evening, Lady Ravenna, and . . . ?"

Ravenna and Klay jumped to their feet, and Klay extended his hand. "I'm Ravenna's business partner, Klay. Klay with a K. Mitchell. I guess we were bound to meet."

Chase shook his hand. "Yes, I've heard about you, and I see you've both made yourselves comfortable. Perhaps a little too comfortable." Chase stared at the incense burning in the shell.

"It's been a long day, so we thought it'd be okay to discuss business here before we left," Ravenna said.

Chase sauntered past the display cases and picked up a sea glass bracelet. He brought it close to his eyes, inspected it from every angle, and placed it back down.

"Would you be interested in that piece, perhaps for the missus? Light green sea glass is always a favorite, and promises to soothe the wearer by removing irritation and stress," Klay said. He picked the bracelet up, holding it out to Chase.

Chase walked away, ignoring him, but turned back when he reached the doorway. "There is no missus, and there'll be no incense burning in my church, either. Put it out, and don't let me see it or smell it again. Understood?" He didn't wait for an answer, but marched across the hallway and out of the building, letting the door slam behind him.

Klay stuck his chest out and yelled across the empty hallway. "Ya, guess again, jerkface. I'll light incense wherever and whenever I want."

"Now listen to me. You will not light incense here, and you will not call him jerkface anymore. I've had enough." Ravenna grabbed the shell and rubbed the smudge stick in it, crushing it flat. "You're going to play nice and by his rules. Don't forget, I have a kid to feed. Tomorrow, we'll bring the circles of selenite with us to clear the jewelry."

"They aren't big enough. And how am I supposed to get this Christian slime off of me?" Klay wiped his hand on his jeans three times.

"Take a shower."

"I couldn't take one long enough."

22

RAVENNA SAT IN A folding metal chair, bouncing her foot up and down, holding a cell phone in front of her mouth. "Yes, I can design that with the intention—" Ravenna heard a click, then silence, and looked down at the blank screen. "Damn it! How am I supposed to work when my phone keeps disconnecting? It's been two days since we moved in, and they still haven't given me the Wi-Fi password."

"I'm sure they know we have poor reception and will come by to give it to you," Klay mumbled, laying on the floor with his lips tightly gripping a screw, holding a drill in one hand and a pencil in the other.

"Why don't you finish fixing the bottom of that display case? I'll see if I can find the church's admin to get the password. If I can connect to their Wi-Fi, I don't think I'll drop any more calls."

Klay waved from half inside the display case.

RAVENNA ENTERED THE CHURCH office, and the scent of freshly brewed coffee and blueberry muffins filled her nose. A printer hummed a series of clicks and whirs, depositing freshly printed sheets onto a tray. A cockeyed corkboard hung on the wall behind it, threatening to fall, littered with announcements, upcoming events, and religious tracts. Off to the left, a woman stood behind a schoolhouse metal desk, and everything about her, including her age, looked sixties. A broad white headband held her brown flipped-up bob in place, and her black and white brocade print skirt with black lace trim looked like she should wrap it around a lamp rather than her waist. Blue eye shadow, bright red lipstick, and long fingernails starkly contrasted her white button-down blouse with puffed sleeves. Ravenna wanted to look under the desk at the pilgrim-buckle pumps she had to be wearing on her feet, but fought the inclination, fearing she might not hide her distaste.

"You must be Lady Ravenna. Who else would wear jeans and flip-flops in a house of worship? And look at your crazy long hair. So disrespectful to our Lord." She eyed Ravenna up and down. "I'm surprised the pastor didn't insist you wear something more appropriate."

Ravenna cocked her head, and her eyes widened, surprised that anyone would be so forthright in their disdain, even if they shared the same sentiment toward one another.

"Wow, and those eyes! The pastor told me not to fear them. He said some people have different-colored eyes, and you happen to be one of them. He muttered something about heterochromia, so I looked it up here online." She pointed to the computer at the corner of her desk. "He was right. He's always right, and such a great catch for my daughter," she said, and crossed her hands over her heart.

"I didn't know he was engaged."

"Oh, they're not, but they will be soon if I have anything to say about it."

"Do your daughter or Chas . . . er, Reverend Wilkinson, have any say?"

"Was there something I can help you with? Maybe you'd like one of those pamphlets?" She walked out from behind the desk, and Ravenna couldn't help but see them: yellow pilgrim-buckle pumps.

The woman grabbed a tract from the corkboard and pointed to a blueberry muffin beside the coffeemaker. "Would you like a muffin?"

"Thank you, but I didn't mean to bother you. I need the Wi-Fi password. Would you mind giving it to me?"

The woman handed her the tract. At a quick glance, Ravenna saw the words *God* and *Hell* in large print on the front. Her fingers began to heat, so she tucked it in her back pocket.

"Hmm . . . I'm not allowed to give the password to just anyone. You never know who might try to breach our security, so you'll have to talk to the pastor about that." She eyed Ravenna up and down with a plastic smile on her face.

Ravenna knew there was no way the woman was checking her out, but that would have made her feel much more comfortable than knowing she didn't trust her.

The woman ran to answer the ringing phone. "Living Waters Church. This is Barbara. How can I help you?"

Ravenna waved and headed down the hallway, dropping the tract in the trash can outside Chase's office before knocking on the door.

"Come in."

Ravenna stuck her head just inside the door. "I don't mean to bother you, but I wonder—"

"No bother at all. Come in and open the door wide, will you?"

"Open the door?"

"Yes, you can use the stop at the bottom to hold it in place."

"I won't keep you. I was hoping you could give me the Wi-Fi password, because all of my calls have been dropping, and when I asked the admin for it, she said to ask you."

He pointed to a chair in front of his desk. "Have a seat. I see you've met Barbara?"

"Yes. Is there a problem with how I'm dressed? Because if there is, you said nothing about it to me. How was I supposed to know? You could have just said something. And what about my hair?" Ravenna pulled her hair all in front of her shoulder and sat. "Honestly, if I had known it would be a problem, I would never have accepted your offer. The Goddess doesn't care what I wear or even if I wear nothing at all." Chase stared at her. "Umm . . . you know what I mean, right?"

"You must know there are people here who are afraid of you, Lady Ravenna, and it doesn't help that you're a little . . . shall I say, unruly."

"Unruly? What the fu—what is that supposed to mean?"

"Point and case."

Ravenna leaned over the desk and spoke with a raised voice. "Are you going to give me the password or not? It's kind of hard to run a business without a phone."

"It's kind of hard to keep a congregation calm when there's a witch among us, too, but I'm managing, and so will you."

"What? You asked me to come here. You're seriously not going to give me the password? Do you think I would try to harm you or the church? What do you think I am, some kind of crazy person?"

Chase sat stoic, without expression, save a slight twitch in his jaw.

"You'd give it to me if I dressed like I lived in the sixties and wore my hair in a headband, wouldn't you? Or if I read that foolish tract that I threw in the trash outside your door."

"Lady Ravenna, we don't judge others. God loves all his children."

"Right, and I'm not his child. Is that it?"

"He loves you too."

"You're damn right she does, so can you please ask your staff to stop handing me religious tracts and to mind their business about what I'm wearing?"

Ravenna heard a voice come from the hallway.

"I wasn't eavesdropping, I'm just going to the ladies' room. But I offered her a muffin, too."

Chase smiled, and Ravenna realized she'd never seen him smile before. Somehow, it made him look less sinister, human even, and approachable. "Maybe next time we should shut the door when we talk," Ravenna said, waiting for Chase to agree.

Again, she heard Barbara in the hallway. "Gentlemen don't lock themselves in rooms with women, and especially not wi—"

"I'll take it from here, Barbara," Chase said to the hallway.

"Can you just give me the password so I can go back to work? I'll look out your window while I wait." Ravenna strolled across the room to view the gardens, now blooming with a kaleidoscope of color mixed with multicolored greenery. She eyed rows of red, pink, and yellow flowers leading to her yard acres away, and could have sworn she spotted Moon running across the lawn, chasing a raven that flew out from the giant cherry tree in the magical garden that boasted clusters of delicate pink blossoms. The bird turned midair and flew at record speed toward the window where she stood. It came to a halting stop when it reached her, hovered a moment, cawed, and then flew away. Ravenna wondered what the bird was trying to tell her, but pushed the thought away. She turned around to find Chase staring at her from behind his desk, his eyebrows pinched together.

"Is there a problem? I thought you were getting the password for me?"

"I don't recall saying I'd get anything."

"You're not making this easy for me, are you? Could I please have the password?"

"From the sound of it, you really need it, and I just might relinquish it if you say you'll attend the service this Sunday. So you attend on Sunday, and I'll give you the password."

"The only other church I've ever attended is the UU church here in town, but you already knew that, didn't you."

Ravenna thought about what Chase had offered and why it was so important to him for her to attend. "Can I think for a minute?"

Chase nodded, and Ravenna's eye was caught by the table full of old photographs. Her gaze drifted from one picture to another until it rested on one of a young boy, a woman, and a man wearing a suit. She leaned in for a closer look and noticed the man's face riddled with scars. She reached for the photo to bring it closer to her eyes, but gasped at the jolt of Chase's firm grip pulling her hand away.

"You said you wanted time to think, not to inspect my office, Lady Ravenna. So what will it be?"

She wanted to ask about the man in the photograph, the woman, the child but knew Chase didn't trust her enough to tell her anything about it. She realized that if she was going to achieve any level of mutual respect with this man, she had to attend. "Would it be all right if I attended the service just like I am?" Ravenna looked down at her clothes and touched her belt buckle in both hands. She wanted Chase to see it and know she'd wear a pentacle in his church among the congregants. She would go, but as a witch.

Chase looked down at her belt buckle and quickly lifted his head, his eyes settling on hers. "Come as you are," he said.

RAVENNA BOUNCED WITH EXCITEMENT back to the apothecary room.

"I'll get the Wi-Fi password on Sunday, but I had to give a little to get a little, and I'm not sure how I feel about it."

"Don't tell me jerkface asked you on a date?" Klay said and laughed. "Could you imagine? I don't know what would be worse: a witch dating a Christian minister, or a Christian minister dating a witch. Or how about a witch selling her magical sea glass in a Christian minister's church? Yeah, that's bad enough."

"He didn't ask me on a date. Don't be ridiculous."

Ravenna hadn't thought about dating since Tristan passed. She had Skye to take care of and the apothecary to manage. It was enough. The thought of dating anyone was as distant and complex an idea as the moon in the sky, and even though the moon was mesmerizing and stirred something deep within her, she couldn't understand its unpredictable moods or why sometimes it only revealed slivers of light through the darkness. She'd spent a lifetime studying the moon's ways, and didn't have time to learn a man that deeply. Like the moon, she was happy to admire it from a distance and savor its mystery without ever attempting to grasp it.

"Then what did you have to give him?" Klay said.

"My time at Sunday's service."

"You agreed to it? That's a joke, right?"

"No. It's not. I need that password."

Klay rolled his eyes. "Don't even ask, Ravenna, because I'm not going with you. You'll have to figure a way out of this mess alone."

23

Ravenna thought it best to enter the service from the church's front door at the back of the congregation to avoid attracting attention. That way, everyone would be looking toward Chase at the lectern, but only he'd see her when she sat in the last row of pews. Yes, she'd agreed to attend, but she didn't agree to make a spectacle of herself.

Having never been to a Christian service and not knowing what to expect, she wasn't prepared for a few hundred people to turn in their seats and stare at her when she entered anyway.

"Welcome, Lady Ravenna. I'm glad you could join us today. Would you like to share something with us?" Chase's voice boomed through the speakers hanging at the room's corners. "Someone hand her the microphone, please."

Ravenna's heart sped up, and she felt her face and neck flush red, highlighting the beads of sweat snaking toward her chest. She'd worn a black hemp cord necklace with a chunk of polished hematite for grounding, and clenched the stone in her left hand, waving the man with the microphone away with her other. She closed her eyes for a moment and recited a silent prayer. *Oh, Goddess. I can do this. With you, I am strong.*

The man shoved the microphone in her hand. "We pass the microphone to give anyone who would like to share a chance to lift up the Lord," he said.

"You worship the Lord? What about the Lady?" Ravenna didn't realize the microphone was already on, amplifying her words so everyone could hear them.

The congregation gasped and laughed, leaving Ravenna a deeper shade of red. "Did I say something wrong?"

"There's only one Lord, the ruler of all. His reign is supreme. We don't know the lord and lady you're referring to, but Christ Jesus is the one and only Lord of all," the man said.

The congregation broke out in "Praise Jesus!" and "Amen!"

Ravenna scanned the congregation and spotted a group of women huddled in the corner, looking in her direction.

Chase eyed her, waiting for her to speak. "Why don't you share something with us, Lady Ravenna?"

She wanted to say no and give the microphone to the woman sitting alone in the pew beside her, but she needed that Wi-Fi password. "I just want to thank everyone for welcoming me today, and sharing your love of the divine with me."

Chase smiled. Ravenna observed people scowling at her, whispering.

"Did she just say divine?"

"I don't want that witch here."

"It's bad enough she's selling her jewelry here, but now she's in our sanctuary?"

"She's evil."

"Going to burn in hell."

"If she doesn't burn us down first."

Ravenna wished Klay was with her, but he had made his intention to not attend very clear. He'd never even gone to the UU church with her and Skye. The only exceptions were church events open to the public, or plays that Skye performed in as a child. Klay was anti-organized religion. Period. The day he'd embraced Wicca was the day he made nature his one and only sanctuary.

It had been Tristan's idea to join the UU church, thinking that a UU community would give them a sense of belonging and a connection to open-minded people, spiritual people representing all faiths. He wanted Ravenna and Skye to have support when he couldn't be home with them. He'd said, "There aren't many Wiccans for you to have a circle with in Plymbury, but even if there were, your fame would draw too much media attention. Most witches don't want public scrutiny." She didn't want scrutiny either, and it was getting much worse since Chase came to town. Being born with one green and one brown eye was reason enough to cause people to move away from her and walk on the other side of the street or to whisper behind her back, but recently, it seemed like the whole town was prejudiced against her.

"Pastor, can I share a story?" said the woman in the pew beside Ravenna's.

Chase motioned for her to rise. "Go on and stand up, Grace."

"I'd like to say I saw a woman on the public bus. She was scrounging through her purse for the fare. I asked if she knew our Lord. She smiled and said, 'Oh, yes. Praise Jesus.' She was a Christian! So I took out a five-dollar bill and handed it to her to pay the driver."

A thunderous proclamation of "Glory be to Christ Jesus" erupted in the sanctuary, sending vibrations reverberating off the walls, cascading upward toward the cathedral ceiling, echoing and swirling, rising higher and higher, until it filled every inch of space, then faded away. The room became still and quiet.

Ravenna leaned toward the woman. "You wouldn't have given her the money if she wasn't a Christian?"

"We help our own," the woman said and nodded as if it were the only logical answer.

"Why wouldn't you help anyone else in need? Why would it matter if they're a Christian or not?"

Grace tilted her head to the side like a curious dog. "Well, she was. You know?"

Ravenna didn't know, but knew enough to stop asking questions when she spotted the vein bulging on Chase's temple and his tight lips forming a straight line.

A woman turned around and snarled at Ravenna. "Shh! The pastor's starting the service."

Everyone opened the Bible they'd brought with them or took one from the rack behind the pews in front of them. Ravenna grabbed a Bible but didn't know what page to open it to. She cracked it open, and her fingers trembled with fear. She wondered if it was offensive to the Goddess to hold it. It felt heavy, but her hands weren't as weighted down as her wavering heart. She ran her fingers over the pages, noticing how thin they were and how easily they could tear. The words on the page seemed incomprehensible, as though written in a foreign language she didn't understand. She scanned the fine print, so intricate and tightly spaced that it appeared to weave a spell. The words seemed to conjure an enchantment so mesmerizing that they looked like an incantation, each letter resembling a magical sigil. She tried to navigate this unfamiliar book, but felt lost and overwhelmed. With no idea where to begin, the ancient text seemed more daunting than the first time she'd opened her family's Book of Shadows.

"Don't spend your time with unbelievers. For what good can come from a mix of good and evil? Or what light can come out of the wicked darkness?" Chase said.

Ravenna felt a sudden tightening in her chest. The words felt like an athame cutting into her soul. She knew everyone there saw her as an unbeliever, as someone wicked, and felt exposed, given a sharp rebuke, a damning judgment. She thought about fleeing the church, but remembered what Maeve had taught her. *Deny anyone the right to belittle you and embrace your self-worth. When you are on the minds and lips of others, they've given their power away to you. Take that power, use it wisely, and let the radiance within you shine.*

Deep in thought, Ravenna missed all but the last sentence of Chase's entire sermon.

"And do not trust a wolf in sheep's clothing."

Everyone shouted, "Amen!"

Soon, a hush fell over the congregation, and the worship team took their place, guitars and microphones in hand. The first chords of the song echoed through the church, and melodic voices filled the air. The music sounded contemporary, and the entire room swayed, clapped, and sang along. She didn't stand; she wasn't worshipping Jesus. Besides, she didn't know the words and didn't want to sing. She didn't even want to be there. Shifting in her seat, she listened to the lyrics that told stories of redemption and forgiveness, and watched hands rise in surrender. As the last notes of worship music faded away, chatter filled the room. Ravenna observed as two people made their way to the altar, tears streaming down their faces. They knelt before Chase and said something she couldn't hear.

Chase spoke into the microphone. "Jesus, feel the weight of their sins lifted, for they have accepted you into their hearts. Praise be to Christ Jesus. Amen!"

The congregation burst out in another "Amen!" and some ran to the altar, embracing the women with open arms. Over the passed microphone, people welcomed them into the community of believers.

The service was over. Ravenna spotted others standing in groups, their heads bowed, and heard one on the left side of her pew ask God for protection against the evil in the room. She was about to quietly leave through the back door when a woman approached her, holding the porcelain vase that had been sitting on the altar. She couldn't help but admire the delicate sprigs of lavender and smell their strong fragrance wafting to her nose. The velvety petals of bright pink peonies burst with color, and the tiny star-shaped creeping phlox clung to the vase's edge. The woman extended her arms, holding the flowers toward Ravenna. "I'm Ava. Here, take them and bring them to your shop. It's gloomy in that room, and maybe the flowers will brighten it up and help your sales. I arranged them myself."

"They're spectacular. Are you a florist?"

"No, no. Nothing like that, but I love flowers, and this is my hobby. I arrange the flowers for all the church services and events. I wanted to tell you that I have an intimate connection with the natural world. I thought you might appreciate that about me. So here, please take them," she said with a genuine smile.

Long, curly brown hair framed her face, accentuating blue eyes that radiated a sense of calmness. Her sundress's intricate pattern communicated a sense of style Ravenna couldn't help but appreciate. Ava embodied a Pagan aesthetic, and Ravenna felt drawn to her warm, kind energy. "I wasn't expecting anything like this today. Thank you."

"The congregation agreed to volunteer to help paint the Plymbury Community Center. Will you join us when we confirm the date?"

"Oh, um . . ." Ravenna's mind raced, trying to think of a way to say no, then thought it might be better to say yes, but then wasn't sure what to say.

"Think about it. I'll drop by your shop in a few weeks, and we can talk more," Ava said.

"Okay, but will Cha . . . I mean, Reverend Wilkinson be there?"

"Yes, he will."

Across the room, someone called Ava's name.

"I've got to go. See you soon," she said and went to meet her friends.

Ravenna was halfway out the door when she heard Chase's voice behind her. "Leaving so soon?"

"I kept my end of the bargain. Can I have the Wi-Fi password now?"

"I'll bring it to you later today, but why sneak out? It's much easier to get to your shop by going through the church."

"I didn't want to bother anyone any more than my presence here today already has. And I can't help but wonder if you catered the service directly to me, Reverend Wilkinson. Is that what you think of me, that I'm wicked, a wolf? I suppose all of you are sweet, innocent Little Red Riding Hood's grandmother just waiting to be chewed up and swallowed? Is that what you want, for everyone to be afraid of me, to hate me?"

Chase eyed the blotchy red hives Ravenna felt sprawling across her face and neck in response to her stress. Then his eyes settled on the vase of flowers she held. "By the looks of it, it didn't work," he said, and winked at her.

Ravenna didn't know what the wink meant, but as she walked outside into the bright sun, she felt herself softening after seeing it.

"I'm surprised you took them. They reek of Christianity," Klay said.

Ravenna inspected the flowers Ava gave her, now sitting on the counter of their makeshift apothecary, and wondered how they could have a religious scent. She inhaled deeply, noticing only a single familiar, ancient smell. She stepped back and heard the flowers singing in unison, and watched the brightly colored petals stretch upward as if they were worshipping, nature itself celebrating creation. "Funny, I think they smell Pagan."

Before Klay could answer, Ravenna heard the church's side door open. Bold footsteps made by high heels echoed through the hallway, a sound that demanded attention as if the person wearing them was announcing her arrival. Ravenna peeked through the apothecary's entrance. Barbara was running from the church office to greet a slender woman in her thirties with loose blond curls cascading below her shoulders. "Wow!" Ravenna said.

Klay stood behind her. "Who's that?"

Ravenna elbowed Klay in the ribs. "Shh!"

The woman was stunning, standing tall and upright, her chin held high with an aura of confidence. She wore a black pencil skirt that hugged her body, elongating her already long legs. Her matching blazer had a tailored fit, and the white blouse underneath exposed a plunging neckline, hinting at the curves beneath, seeming risqué for a Christian church. *There was a woman who knew what she wanted and wasn't afraid to go after it*, Ravenna thought.

"Faith, it's unfortunate you couldn't make the service," Barbara said and hugged the woman.

"Sorry, Mom, I couldn't get out of work. I can't believe I missed today, of all days."

"I'll tell you all about it, but why don't you visit Chase first? I'm sure he'd love to see you."

Barbara returned to the church office, and Faith followed the hallway to Chase's. She knocked, and Chase welcomed her in.

"Do you think he's dating her?" Ravenna said.

"Christians date? I thought they courted with a chaperone."

"This is the twenty-first century, Klay."

"You obviously haven't noticed that these people removed the twenty. It's like time travel gone wrong, because instead of going back in time, they brought the past here and think it's the future."

"She didn't look so first-century to me."

"Christians are supposed to keep it in their pants until they're married, but who knows, maybe he'll think it's worth giving it all up for just one night. He can always repent after."

Ravenna laughed. "You talk a good story, Klay Mitchell, but you wouldn't. It's not like you're Mister Playboy."

"A guy can fantasize."

Ravenna wondered if Faith was the type of woman that attracted Chase, if all he wanted was sex and not a relationship. Then she wondered why she even wondered that, and why she even cared who Chase dated.

Klay interrupted her thoughts. "When's he bringing the Wi-Fi password? I bet he lied to you, and you attended that awful service for nothing."

"You didn't like the service?" a woman's voice said. Faith walked into the shop.

Klay rushed toward her. "Can I help you?"

"No. I'm here to talk with her." Faith pointed a long, manicured fingernail at Ravenna, gray with a diamond-shaped French tip, making her look even more elegant. But what came out of her mouth was far from that, because it was harsh and offensive.

"It's no surprise you didn't enjoy it. Witches don't belong in houses of worship. They belong in the Lake of Fire."

"The Lake of Fire?" Klay said.

Faith let out a sinister laugh. "Hell. You'll both burn in hell."

"Oh, trust me. We're already here," Klay said.

Ravenna turned to Klay behind her and gave him the shut-up stare.

"The pastor asked me to give you this paper on my way back to visit my mom." She waved the folded paper in front of Ravenna's face. "But I've decided not to give it to you. And how unfortunate, Reverend Wilkinson has left for the day."

Klay barreled past Ravenna and attempted to grab it from Faith's hand, but she quickly tucked it into her shirt.

"I don't imagine you want to go fishing for it. I know. How can you resist? Come on, go for it." She stood with her arms down and her chest pushed forward, tempting him.

Klay stared down at her and spoke in a deep voice. "You couldn't pay me enough to catch a fish with that rancid bait."

"I guess I'll just offer it to the pastor, then. I'm sure he'd be happy to feel his way around for it," she said with a sly grin, making eye contact with Ravenna.

It surprised Ravenna to feel a twinge of jealousy. Her mind raced with thoughts of Chase touching Faith. Her chest constricted with a tightness she couldn't explain, and her palms grew clammy as she tried to shake the feeling.

"This is going to be so fun. The pastor loves a good challenge, and I'm just the person to give it to him. I always give it to him," Faith said.

"I'm sure he's smart enough to kick you out on your ass, but maybe that's giving him too much undeserved credit," Klay said. "We have nothing more to discuss." He grabbed her by the arm and pushed her into the hallway.

Faith looked back at Ravenna, scrutinizing her. "You can fantasize all you want, but he'd never go for someone like you." Her face scrunched in disgust.

"Me interested in Chase? That's a joke, right? Trust me, he's all yours."

Ravenna listened to Faith stomp down the hall into the church office, and shut the door. "Damn it! I needed that Wi-Fi password. Why do people assume that just because you're Pagan, you'd jump into bed with anyone?"

Klay wrapped his arms around her. "They only think that about beautiful Pagans, and it seems little Miss Christian Temptress is jealous of you."

24

THE FOLLOWING SUNDAY, RAVENNA sat across from Skye at the kitchen table, trying to find something to discuss during dinner. Skye answered with nothing but grunts and groans.

"The apothecary should be fixed in a few months. Are you looking forward to getting back in there as much as I am?" Ravenna said.

Skye lifted her head from her dinner and shrugged her shoulders.

Ravenna pushed the salad on her plate, thinking about the fire. Moving her business to Chase's church had had a major impact on Skye, and she didn't know how to snap Skye out of this funk. She wanted to apologize, to say it was difficult for her too, but no words passed the lump in her throat. Ravenna remembered life was hard enough as a teenager carrying the burden of being born a witch, but it made her body ache to know she was adding to her daughter's pain. Lately, even being in the same room with Skye was difficult, so Ravenna tried to avoid her and the constant reminder of their strained relationship. Looking down at the white and pink sea glass bracelet on her wrist, she closed her right hand around it, pressing the glass into her skin. She focused on absorbing its energy, but knew her powerful jewelry alone wasn't enough to mend their broken relationship. Ravenna yearned for the closeness they once shared, but that bond had burned with the apothecary. She thought that maybe when the shop reopened, she'd get her daughter back. "When the shop is ready and we work together again, you can still help Ashley if you want to."

Skye stood and slammed her fork on the table. "Is that what you want, to keep pawning me off on someone else?"

"No. I was considering your feelings. I just assumed you'd want to, but you're free to make that choice for yourself."

"Really? Really? You didn't give me a choice when you moved to the stupid church down the street. You made me go to Ashley's." Skye grabbed her dishes and tossed them in the sink. The ceiling fan started to whirl, dispersing the crashing sound through the kitchen.

"Is that what you think, that I didn't want you with me? That place is awful, Skye. I was trying to spare you."

Skye's eyes widened. "I think the fire did something to you, Mom. Since then, you've forgotten how to tell the truth."

Ravenna's lips parted, but no words escaped. She was stuck in disbelief, shaking her head as Skye marched out of the room.

"I CAN'T SAY I blame her, because moving to that church was foolish. How many times have I told you to stay away from Christians? But no, you don't listen. I thought I taught you better than that," Maeve said to Ravenna over the phone.

"I didn't call to talk about this. I was hoping you could spend some time with Skye. Maybe you can get through to her, because I certainly can't. No matter how hard I try, I make things worse."

"Should I come over?"

"No. Give her time to cool off."

"I'm not sure why she thinks you're lying to her. Lie shmy. Have you ever told a lie since your senior prom?" Maeve said and laughed. "Wish I could say I've never told one."

Ravenna remembered Maeve once telling her that when you lie, it becomes easier to tell more lies until they get all jumbled up, and you can't keep them all straight, or worse, you believe they're true. She wondered what Maeve lied about, but didn't ask.

"Look, Ravenna, maybe I should come and talk—"

"Hang on, someone's knocking," Ravenna said. "I'll call you back." She ended the call and opened the door. She felt her face flush. Just when she thought the day couldn't get any worse. "Chase. What are you doing here?"

"I don't recall saying that to you when you showed up unannounced on my church's steps."

"That's because my name's Ravenna," she said and stepped out into the breezeway, forcing him to step back.

Chase chuckled. "And you're still not going to invite me in, are you?"

Ravenna glanced down the street to see if Chase had come alone.

"Were you expecting to see someone else?"

"Why exactly are you here?"

"Because, Lady Ravenna, when I say I'm going to do something, I do it." Chase's voice was laced with condescension, as if talking to a child.

"Yeah, Faith wasn't a good enough servant for you, I guess. At least not when delivering messages, but I'm sure she's plenty good at other things."

Chase's eyebrows shot up. "Contrary to what you may believe, Lady Ravenna, witches don't know everything." He pulled a piece of paper from his pocket and handed it to her.

She turned it in her hand, studied it, and raised her green eye to him. "And why is it a different paper than the one Faith waved in my face earlier? Did that one get destroyed somehow?"

"I don't know. Maybe it's because I never gave her one. Have a good evening." Chase turned his back to Ravenna and strode down the cobblestone walkway.

Ravenna stood speechless, almost wanting to call him back and invite him inside, thinking maybe she was wrong about him. Her eyes traced his steady gait in front of her house. Then she spotted the raven swooping down from an old oak across the street, heading toward him, its wings flapping gracefully, gliding through the air. He didn't notice it, but Ravenna watched the bird land on a tall pine in her yard. It eyed Chase until he was out of sight.

25

Drop whatever buckets of sea glass you have off at your house and get here fast, Klay texted Ravenna.

It was six o'clock in the morning, and Ravenna had arrived at the beach only fifteen minutes earlier. *This had better be good*, she thought. Never had she given up an early low tide in August searching for sea glass, and missing out on it could cost her hundreds of dollars. She ran home, took a quick shower, and arrived at the church thirty minutes later. She followed a quiet rumble leading to the door of her shop, where Klay met her and she took in the jarring sight of the wish wall on the left side of the room. The sound of the waves grew louder and more insistent as they climbed higher and higher, swallowing the stars as they rose and crashed with an explosive roar, as if impatient, coaxing her to perform magic. Ravenna stared at the wall in disbelief that it would leave her meditation room and show up here. She tried to calm her racing thoughts. "Shit! What are we going to do?"

"Pack up our stuff and call it a day?"

"I'm screwed." Ravenna looked at her phone. "Chase will be here in an hour."

"Let's put our heads together. I'm sure we can figure something out," Klay said.

"I can't get kicked out, Klay. Things would get much worse for me."

"Hey, maybe we don't need to stay here much longer. Or let's just leave anyway."

"Even if that were true, the wall might not leave with us, so we need to hide it. And what would we tell Chase if we left before the shop was ready?"

"I'm sure we'd think of something to tell jerkface."

Ravenna felt her anger rise. "I'm going to stay here and try to get the waves to settle. You run over to the hardware store and get some pipes we can put together to drape a cloth over. Make sure it will cover the entire wall, and then grab some heavy material at the fabric store to hang over it."

Klay took the wall's measurements.

"Hurry, we have less than an hour."

In thirty minutes, Klay returned with pipes and fabric and began constructing the screen to cover the wall. "There's one thing we didn't think about, though."

"What?"

"The noise. This screen may quiet those waves, but you can still hear them." Klay tightened the last pipes together, and Ravenna helped drape a dark blue cloth over the frame.

"Oh, no! We only have two minutes," Ravenna said, looking at her phone. "Think quick."

"Good morning, Lady Ravenna. Klay with a K. Is there something I can help you think about? Why is it so noisy in here?" Chase stood in the doorway, eyeing them.

Klay grabbed Ravenna's phone from her hand. "Yeah, so we were listening to white noise while setting up this display to hang earrings, and we can't get it to stop. Have you ever noticed that sometimes your phone plays random music, and you don't know where it's coming from, and you can't shut it off? Hopefully, we'll figure it out at some point."

Ravenna glanced sideways at Klay, holding her breath, waiting for Chase's fury, but he only looked into the hallway when the church door slammed.

"Hello, Reverend Wilkinson," Ava said. "Do you have a minute?"

"Let's go to my office," he said.

"Don't go away, Ravenna. I want to talk to you, too, and I'll be back in ten minutes," Ava said. "Oh, and I like the sound of the waves. They're soothing, and it feels like our church is closer to the beach."

Ravenna watched them turn into Chase's office, and whispered to Klay, "How did you think of that so fast?"

"Divine intervention?"

"You know it wasn't divine. Why did you lie?"

Klay hung earrings in pairs on the new cloth screen. "You'd rather get kicked out because of something you have no control over? Do you want your life better, Ravenna, or would you rather keep sabotaging yourself?"

"I can't lie, so we need to figure out how to get this wall out of here."

"Good luck with that," Klay said.

Ravenna called Maeve and left a message: "I have a problem, and I need your help. Call me as soon as you get this message, or drop by the church." Then she punched in Ashley's number, but hung up before it rang when Ava walked into the shop. "What can I help you with, Ava?"

"I wanted to talk with you about volunteering to help us paint next week at the Plymbury Community Center. I'm sorry I didn't come sooner, but I've been busy volunteering at the homeless shelter, the animal shelter, and the soup kitchen."

"It sounds like you do a lot of volunteering."

"I'm selfish, to be honest. It makes you feel so good and sets off all kinds of endorphins. It's addictive, like drugs. You know what I mean. It looks like you're addicted to sea glass, and I can't believe you made all these." Ava moved from one display case to the next, studying the pieces. "But how does sea glass heal?" Her finger pointed to a notecard that read *If you need healing for something specific, please ask Lady Ravenna for help.*

"It's nature's magic. The ocean takes discarded broken shards of glass and turns them into something new, but the glass holds all the information that transformed it. So when you wear it, you absorb their mysteries, and your own brokenness changes and heals, too," Ravenna said.

"I get it. That's why I love Jesus so much. He does that for the sea glass and me, and he gave you the gift of making these beautiful jewelry pieces out of someone else's trash. It's incredible."

Ravenna felt like Ava was saying Jesus was nature, and that was fine with her. The divine was the divine, no matter what anyone called her, and Ava, with her earthy-crunchy Pagan vibe, would have loved the Goddess if she wasn't a Christian.

"I'd love a piece, but I don't know which one to choose. They're all so beautiful," Ava said.

Klay finished hanging the earrings and approached to help her. "Is there something you want to change in your life? Something you're struggling with?"

"I don't know. I usually pray and leave it in God's hands." Ava said.

"It's okay, Klay. I can help her," Ravenna said.

"All right, then I'm off to get some coffee."

Ravenna held her hand out, encouraging Ava to grab hold of it. "If you give me your hand, I can tell you which piece is best for you."

Ava hesitated.

"If you don't want my help, you can pick one that speaks to you. Sometimes our intuition knows best."

"You're saying you can tell me which one I should wear? How do you know?"

"It's just a feeling I get from your energy."

"Could you be wrong?"

"Anything's possible, but no one ever said I was."

"I'll give you my hand, but only if you agree to help the church paint the community center next week," she said.

"What is it with Christians and bribes?" Klay said as he returned.

"I'm not trying to bribe her," she said to Klay. "I want Ravenna to come because I feel we have a lot in common, and we're meant to be friends."

Ravenna scooped up Ava's hand. "Maybe we should just plan coffee together sometime."

"Please? Will you join us?"

"Sure. And you need blue sea glass for the strength to say something that's hard for you."

Ava's jaw dropped. "How do you know that?"

"Have you ever felt like God speaks to you, and you know what you're supposed to do?"

"All the time."

"Then you know I don't know anything, because I'm just the messenger."

"It seems to me there's light inside of you, Lady Ravenna, so don't let anyone tell you otherwise. Sometimes, Christians are afraid of the dark, but your shop proves that gems emerge even from the shadows below the ocean's surface. You just have to look close enough to see it." Ava hugged Ravenna.

"Come on. I'll show you the blue pieces," Klay said and led Ava to a display case in the room's far corner.

Ravenna held a piece of loose sea glass in her palm, examining what was once a discarded piece of useless glass whose edges had softened, turning it into a treasure. She ran her thumb across its smooth surface, wondering why people couldn't see each other the same way.

26

THE WAVES BEHIND THE curtain let out a low rumble that could have come from an iPhone, but Ravenna wasn't sure Chase believed it, and she didn't want to find out.

"Lady Ravenna, correct me if I'm wrong. I thought we had an agreement," Chase said. He moved from one display case to another, tapping on the glass and peeking inside with a curious eye.

"Is there something wrong?"

"Where's that ocean wave sound coming from?" He looked at the cloth screen. "Somehow, I think if I walked closer to those earrings, it would get louder, wouldn't it?"

"Of course it would." Klay pointed to Ravenna's phone on the table beside the wall. "Her iPhone is right there. It doesn't take a genius to figure that out."

"Maybe I should look at her phone, then, because even a non-genius like me could figure out how to shut it off."

"Is it disturbing anyone? If it is, they could tell us. We prefer people who are direct and to the point."

Ravenna observed Klay stood two inches taller than Chase but wasn't as muscular. Then she wondered why she'd noticed.

"If you don't mind, I'd like to speak with Lady Ravenna alone. Maybe you could keep Barbara company in the office," Chase said.

"I don't think so. Anything you have to say to—"

"Klay, I'd love a cup of coffee. Would you mind?" Ravenna said.

"Yes, I would mind." Klay stared at Chase. "I have no intention of leaving you alone with jer . . . him."

Chase raised an eyebrow.

"We only need ten minutes," Ravenna said.

Klay stomped out and slammed the door.

"Tell me you made him from sea glass, brought him to life, and you can reverse the magic," Chase said, and laughed while opening the door again.

Ravenna knew Chase wanted to be alone with her because Klay was usually the one who answered all his questions, and he wanted answers about the waves directly from her. She thought giving them to Chase might show she wasn't hiding anything and hoped he'd trust her. "When I perform magic, there's a star wall that reacts to it. I have no control over it. When my shop burned down, it moved from there to the meditation room of my house, and now it's here, but we covered it so nobody will see it. It just wants to be with me. This sounds weird. How about I show it to you?" Ravenna grabbed the cloth to pull it aside.

"Nice try." Chase winked. "Why don't you figure out how to turn the music down?"

There was that wink again, Ravenna thought, not knowing if he believed her. "I'll see what I can do, but I'm curious. Why do you keep opening the door when we talk?"

"I wouldn't want anyone to get the wrong idea, Lady Ravenna. Christians believe the devil tempts them in all kinds of ways, and witches have tempted Christians for centuries. That's why they built historic houses in New England with slanted windows on the second floor, to prevent witches from flying in and tempting men in their sleep."

"Are you calling me the devil? Do you think I'm trying to tempt you? And what about Christian men? Maybe misogyny has something to do with that fable."

"Believe me when I tell you, some hatred toward witches is with good reason."

"And the rest?"

"I only care about you."

"It doesn't sound like care is the right word here. Do you care, or is it something else entirely? Why are you trying to ruin my life, Chase?"

"Lady Ravenna, how about I spew some metaphysical words you love so much right back at you? The only person who can ruin your life is you . . . or maybe your family's karma. Wouldn't you agree?"

Ravenna tilted her head. She struggled to decipher his words, and nothing seemed to make sense. What had started as a warm conversation shifted, leaving her with an uncomfortable chill.

"You gave Ava sea glass and told her it would help her heal. I thought we discussed this before. You're performing magic on my parishioners again, and here in my church," Chase said.

"No. I didn't. I haven't broken our agreement."

"Then why don't you tell me how the sea glass works without magic?" He folded his arms across his chest as if guarding himself against the unsettling truth that threatened to change his mind.

Ravenna grabbed a piece of pink sea glass. "Why don't I show you? Are you a righty or a lefty?"

"I'm right-handed. Why?"

Ravenna reached out to uncross his arms and grab his left hand, but as soon as she touched him, he pulled away, backing up to the door.

"I'm not tempting you. I touch everyone. Please hold your hand out, and I won't touch you."

He raised his cupped palm, and when she dropped the sea glass into it, a surge of energy passed between them. Their eyes met, and she couldn't help but think how much stronger it would be if she'd touched his hand. He quickly looked away, trying to dismiss what she knew he'd felt, too.

"Now close your eyes," she said.

Chase didn't close his eyes. "If it's not magic, then how did . . ." He inspected the glass. "I saw white, brown, green, blue, and even yellow glass cases in this room. Why did you give me pink?"

Ravenna told him the truth. "Because I know you came here mad, and it's supposed to soften your heart. Pink is supposed to fill you with compassion. You know, universal love. Let me clarify that I have nothing to do with it. It's just a piece of glass from the ocean. No magic, unless you believe nature is magic."

"But you perform magic with sea glass, don't you?"

"Not anymore." Ravenna's voice cracked, and she felt queasy. "Maybe try closing your eyes and focusing on how it feels in your hand."

"I'll give it a whirl, but I don't expect to feel anything."

"It's better without expectations."

Chase closed his eyes, and Ravenna studied the wrinkles in his forehead and his tense shoulders lifting close to his ears. "You'll need to relax."

Chase opened his eyes. "I am relaxed, and nothing." He extended his hand to give the glass back to her.

Ravenna gazed into Chase's soft blue eyes, hoping he would see her sincerity. "You keep it, and hold it any time you need more compassion. I'm sorry I didn't let you in my house when you came by the other day. Next time. I mean, if there is a next time." Ravenna felt her cheeks flush and the unwelcome hives begin to spread across her chest.

"I'm not sure I'd have a reason to come by again. I only came to deliver the Wi-Fi password I'd promised you."

"Maybe you'll want to exchange that piece of glass for another one. I keep my best pieces at home."

"I'll have to remember that."

130

27

RAVENNA HEARD THE CHURCH'S side door slamming and a familiar voice urgently echoing in the hallway. "Ravenna, what's wrong? Where are you?"

Before she could answer, Barbara flew out of the church office to confront Maeve. "We don't raise our voices in a house of worship."

"Voices shmoices. What are you, a librarian? Get out of my way, where's my granddaughter?" Maeve said, brushing past Barbara and catching sight of Ravenna. "I got here as fast as I could."

"I didn't say it was an emergency."

"I know when you're panicked. What is it?"

Ravenna took comfort in Maeve's unwavering support, even if she was melodramatic, but didn't know if having her come to the church was a wise idea. Maeve wasn't happy Ravenna was there and wouldn't make getting on their good side any easier, especially since Maeve didn't filter what she thought before saying it. Christians found Maeve abrupt and aggressive, but Maeve didn't care what anyone thought about her. Ravenna cared, though, and was trying desperately to be liked and accepted.

Barbara eyed Maeve up and down. "If you're not here for church business, I will have to ask you to leave."

"Ah, a shapeshifter. What are you, a watchdog now?" Maeve said. "Speaking of watchdogs . . . we haven't spoken in weeks, and I have something to tell you, Ravenna."

"Can we deal with my problem, Maeve?"

"Yes, because the sooner I leave, the better. You know I'm vehemently opposed to you being here. It's a foolish decision. Why couldn't we talk about this at your house?"

"Come here," Ravenna said. She grabbed Maeve by the arm and pulled her into the makeshift apothecary. Barbara followed close behind.

"Excuse me. I don't recall asking you to join us," Maeve said to Barbara.

Before Barbara could enter the room, Klay greeted Maeve and attempted to whisk Barbara away. "I could use a fresh cup of coffee. Would you mind helping me make a pot?"

Barbara stretched her neck, trying to see what Ravenna and Maeve were looking at.

Klay walked toward the church office. "It's okay, never mind. I can make it myself."

"No. No. I'll make it for you. You know I don't like anyone touching the office gadgets. No one has any respect for other people's things arou . . ." Barbara's voice trailed away into the office with Klay.

Ravenna didn't tell Maeve what hid behind the curtain, but the faint rumbling gave it away.

Maeve gasped. "Oh, no! How could this happen? The wall always stayed in the apothecary's wish room."

"Not exactly, because it moved to my meditation room when the shop burned. Until now."

"It moved? Why would it come here? It knows Christians and witches don't get along, especially not in Plymbury since your m—I mean, because we're the witches that fulfilled the prophecy."

"I don't know, but it needs to go. Chase has heard it twice now, and he's suspicious."

Klay returned with two coffees and handed one to Maeve. "Yup, he's not buying that the sound is coming from Ravenna's cell phone. He's actually smarter than I thought, but honestly, not by much."

Maeve plopped into a chair. "I think I need something stronger than coffee."

"Don't tell me we can't move it, because there has to be some family magic for this."

"There is," Maeve said.

Ravenna lit up with hope. "What is it? What do we need to do?"

"It's not we. It's you."

"Tell me, and I'll do it right now."

"You need to get the hell out of here. I will not allow this for one more minute. They're out to get us, and you can't hide this wall. Let's go!" Maeve grabbed a box and started haphazardly packing Ravenna's jewelry.

Klay laughed so hard that he spit out coffee, then scrambled to find a paper towel to clean it.

"There's nothing funny about this. And where do you suggest I go?" Ravenna grabbed the box from Maeve. "There's nowhere to set up shop, and I need to take care of my daughter. You would have done the same for me, so don't tell me you wouldn't have."

"I don't mean to get in the middle, but I agree with Maeve. Let's cut our losses and get out of this hellhole," Klay said.

"If I wanted your opinion, I would have asked for it weeks ago."

"Being here isn't helping you. They're trying to destroy you and our family. If you want to protect Skye, then move away from this place and trust the Goddess will provide until the shop is repaired. You can't trust Christians," Maeve said.

"Why? You've never told me why. I want a reason."

"Not now, Ravenna. Let's pack up and go."

"If we left, would the wall go, too?" Ravenna said.

"I don't know, but it seems to follow you wherever you are, so there's a good chance."

Ravenna sank into a metal chair. "This isn't helping!"

"I think it's mad because you're not doing any wish magic. It's like it wants you to," Klay said. "If we leave, you can start doing magic again."

"What do you mean, you're not doing wish magic?" Maeve said.

"It's only temporary because I can't while I'm here. It's part of the agreement."

"You've gone mad, Ravenna!"

The rumble behind the screen grew louder, piercing Ravenna's ears. She jumped up and ripped back the sheet, yelling at the wall to go back home. Her eyes widened, and her heart beat faster, witnessing the thundering waves respond by crashing with fury, growing so loud she had to cover her ears. Now reaching the ceiling, the waves unleashed a violent symphony of thunder as turbulent winds lashed out, howling with untamed fury. The air thickened with the stench of seaweed, and a salty taste pierced Ravenna's tongue. She pulled the cloth back in place. "Grandma, please help me! I don't know what to do!"

"There's nothing I can do. Only you can. Wear who you are with pride, Ravenna, or others will strip your magic away."

"What if I'm someone else? What happens then?"

No one heard Ravenna over the wave's noise. Her voice drowned in surrender, and everything went quiet, as if nothing had happened. But Ravenna knew better. Deep down, she could feel the wall watching her, waiting for her to do magic.

28

RAVENNA ARRIVED AT THE Plymbury Community Center when the night dissolved into day, and the sky boasted elongated streaks of pink, orange, and yellow hues. Ravenna approached the paint-chipped building, a modest, wooden structure in the center of town with large windows facing the ocean, and spotted familiar church members already painting the exterior.

"Hey, Ravenna!" Ava waved from the side of the building, wearing painter's pants covered in a blend of bright colors that matched her outgoing personality. She pointed to a table with muffins, doughnuts, and a Box O' Joe from Dunkin'. "Help yourself. Then come over here so I can show you what needs painting."

Ravenna pressed the spigot, filling a paper cup with coffee. She eyed Chase on a ladder, wearing jeans and an old t-shirt with rolled sleeves that showed off his chiseled muscles. Flecks of blue paint highlighted his hair. Ravenna thought he looked relaxed and approachable, so she made her way toward him, but Faith jumped in front of her.

"Where are you going? Ava's that way," Faith said with a twisted, sour face and pointed in the opposite direction. "I'm not surprised she invited you, because she may as well be one of you."

"Should she be more like you?"

"Like me? Well, of course not. Only one of us can be the pastor's wife," she said, then looked over her shoulder, smiling at Chase, who was out of earshot. He smiled back.

Ravenna thought that Faith's shorts seemed shorter than a Christian would wear, with a white shirt so tight you could almost see through the thin material. "Well, for now, he's my landlord, so if you'll excuse me, I'd like to say hello."

Faith huffed as Ravenna walked past, brushing against her shoulder.

Chase descended from the ladder. "Lady Ravenna, I'm glad to see you here today."

"I'm glad to be—"

"I'm surprised, frankly," Barbara said from about twenty feet away, loud enough so everyone could hear. "I didn't think witches volunteered their time for the benefit of others. They say witches are hedonistic, after all. Don't they, pastor? Watch out for that one." She pointed at Ravenna.

"Where did you hear that?" Ravenna said.

"Barbara, I've got this. Why don't you focus on painting?" Chase said and lowered his voice so only Ravenna could hear him. "She's very protective."

Ravenna thought, *Not protective, predatory.* But Barbara was right, because Ravenna didn't want to help paint the community center. It wasn't because she was unwilling to volunteer her time or talent, but because she wanted to preserve herself. Every time she spent time with groups of Christians, whether in the Sunday services she now frequently attended or when they visited her shop, Ravenna felt the need to protect herself, even if Chase had softened over the months she'd been in his church. Still, she couldn't read him. He ran hot and cold, teetering on the edge of both wanting to know more about her and fearing her. But despite his occasional coldness, Ravenna sensed something genuine about him.

"Oh, I almost forgot. I was on the beach earlier, and found something I thought you might like." Chase reached into his pocket, pulled out a dime-sized piece of yellow sea glass, and handed it to Ravenna. "I don't remember seeing a lot of yellow pieces in your shop, and figured it was a rare color."

"It is. That was kind of you to think of me."

Chase winked. "Let me help you get set up."

"Thanks, but Ava said she would." Ravenna looked past Chase. "She's on her way over to get me."

"There you are, Ravenna. Come on, I have a spot ready for you where I'm painting," Ava said.

"Looks like you're in excellent hands. I'll come over later to see how things are going," Chase said.

Ravenna watched him climb back up the ladder.

Ava led Ravenna to the other side of the building. "I'm saving you from Barbara. Of course, everyone thinks Chase is hot, but who will admit it in a Christian church? Well, I will." Ava laughed. "But that Barbara, she thinks Faith has a chance with him. Give me a break. The girl shows up half-dressed, and he doesn't even look at her."

"Why not? She's beautiful."

"Yeah, if you're talking about the outside, but we all know there's something sinister inside. Besides, Chase says that the church is his bride. It's kind of odd. He's not a Catholic priest, so there's no problem if he married. I asked him about it once."

"You did?"

"Yeah, he said he wouldn't consider marrying until he made peace with the past."

"Did you ask what that meant?"

"No. What, are you crazy? When someone gives you a cryptic answer, they don't want to tell you. So it's best to leave it alone."

"I could never do that," Ravenna said.

"That's because you're not a Christian, and it's one reason I like you so much."

After grabbing some supplies, Ravenna started painting the other half of Ava's wall, but that didn't stop the stares and sneers from others in the congregation.

"Are you okay with me here? If you want me to move somewhere else, I'd understand," Ravenna said.

"I'm only here because I knew you were coming. Otherwise, I would have spent the day volunteering at the soup kitchen. Just ignore them. Not everyone here's against you. Some see your effort and believe Jesus is working in you."

Ravenna didn't know how that comment made her feel. She understood they were Christians and everything was about Jesus, but not everyone believed in him, and she felt that proselytization violated personal freedom. As each Sunday passed, she had a greater understanding of their faith, but the magic she held was older than any religion and more powerful than any prayer. She was one with the universe, and stood as a living testament to the strength of her spirit and the depth of her power. She was a witch, and magic had always been her truth. And yet, without it, she was being accepted, and things were stirring inside her that she hadn't felt since Tristan died.

Ravenna painted in silence, coating the wall a deep shade of blue, lost in soaking up the warm sun and breathing the salty air. Peace washed over her as she focused on the brush strokes, each motion a small spell transforming the mundane into something transcendent. She felt a deep sense of satisfaction, knowing she was bringing some happiness into the world, until she heard crying. She searched to find where it was coming from and observed Chase consoling a woman with his hand resting on her shoulder, nodding in understanding. He reached into his pocket for a cloth and wiped her tears. She smiled, and they embraced. This was the side of Chase Ravenna witnessed in church services, too. He had a way of putting people at ease, of making them feel seen and heard. Ravenna admired his magic, his ability to uplift others with a few kind words or a comforting touch, and wrapped her hand around the piece of glass he'd given her earlier.

"Find a logical place to pause, and let's grab some lunch," Ava said.

Ravenna relinquished her thoughts of Chase, acknowledging a hunger pang, and realized she'd been painting for hours. "Wow, I can't believe how late it is."

"You were so deep in thought that I didn't want to disturb you. I imagine things can't be easy for you these days."

Ravenna took the paintbrushes and squatted before a nearby water spigot to rinse them while Ava pounded the paint cans closed.

Chase stood behind Ravenna, holding out his paintbrush. "Would you mind rinsing mine, too?"

She twisted to take it and lost her balance. Chase grabbed her wrist so she wouldn't fall and reached under her arm, lifting her to stand. Her eyes met his, and they froze. Her heart sped up.

"I didn't mean to grab you, but you were falling," Chase said.

She heard a softness in his voice, the one he used when consoling people in his congregation. Ravenna relaxed in his tender grip for what seemed like a year and a day as he stared into her eyes. It was different from that day on the beach. He wasn't searching to see if she had a soul this time. He was searching to connect with it. And when he did, a heat between them crackled through the air. Ravenna felt his gentle touch linger on her wrist as paint from the brush dripped, an intoxicating brew twisting around their hands, leaving her breathless. Her skin tingled, and she couldn't help but wonder how it would feel to have his lips on hers, a dangerous thought that could lead to all kinds of complications. But she didn't care. Chase must have felt it, too, because he looked away, breaking the spell between them.

"Thanks for taking care of the paintbrush," he said, and walked away, leaving Ravenna wondering what had just happened. She scanned the church faces, hoping no one else saw whatever it was.

Ava appeared beside her, moved her eyes to the right, and nodded her head. "Wow! Look over there."

Ravenna focused past her to see Faith wiping the paint off Chase's hand. He was uncomfortable and trying to pull away, but Barbara grabbed a cup of water and poured it over Chase's hands.

"Look, the poor guy's surveying the terrain and trying to get away. He's one of the few men who call themselves a Christian and mean it," Ava said.

Ravenna's insides ached. She knew how it felt to be held hostage by someone else's desire, but watching them together stirred an undercurrent of something entirely different.

29

"Wow, Skye, it's a big deal that Ashley's leaving you to run the café while we have dinner on the beach." Ravenna knew she was interrupting Skye from waiting on the outdoor tables, but it was important for her to hear it.

"Give me a break. You'll be twenty feet away on the beach and there for what, an hour?"

Ravenna clasped Skye's arm and turned her around. "There are at least four other servers here tonight and a bartender. Did she ask any of them?"

"No, but—"

"She's counting on you, Skye. It's a big deal."

"At least someone appreciates me." Skye looked over Ravenna's shoulder at Ashley, shuffling toward them.

"That's not—"

"Hey, Ravenna. I packed the cooler, and it's inside at the bar. Would you mind grabbing it?"

Ravenna picked up their meals, and she and Ashley followed the footbridge toward the beach. On the short walk, Ravenna couldn't help but notice Ashley's gait was slow and unsteady. Every few feet, she'd hold her hand out and latch onto Ravenna's arm for balance. She would have held Ashley's arm the entire way, but she knew her too well. The walking had to be on Ashley's terms, and if she needed help, she'd reach out.

At the end of the footbridge sat two folding chairs and a table Ravenna had secured in the sand earlier. Ashley made herself comfortable and closed her eyes. The colors in the sky reflected off her face, casting a warm glow over her blond hair and pale skin. This was the first time in months Ravenna had seen Ashley let her worries melt away. The waves rolled onto the shore, the sound blending with children's playful cries.

"Do you hear the kids?" Ashley said. "Something about that sound and being here on the beach instantly relaxes me. I wish I could come more often."

Ravenna knew Ashley's health was getting worse, and that she couldn't walk the crossover or the sandy beach alone anymore. She pulled a piece of jewelry out of her pocket. "I made you a necklace."

Ashley opened her eyes and gasped when she caught sight of the pendant hanging from the end of a silver chain. Five individually cut triangle-shaped pieces of green sea glass surrounded a clear quartz crystal. "It's spectacular, but how is it different from this incredible piece you already gave me?" Ashley lifted her sundress to expose her anklet.

"The pentacle is a symbol of wholeness and perfection. This is what we want for your body, right? Green sea glass is best for healing physical ailments. And I added the quartz crystal because it amplifies the glass's healing energy."

"Oh, thank you. I love it, and if I could get up right now, I'd give you the biggest hug. Will you help me put it on?"

Ravenna clasped the necklace around Ashley's neck, then unpacked salads with arugula and kale, topped with cherry tomatoes, diced mango, and creamy avocado slices. Ashley's culinary skill shone through with an unexpected blend of sweet and sour dressing, reminding Ravenna of the past several weeks around Chase and how he teetered between hot and cold. She'd run over every encounter with him in her head repeatedly, and still couldn't figure out why he was softening.

"Don't forget about your hearing at the UU church next week," Ashley said. She smiled with a look of accomplishment.

Ravenna had indeed forgotten that the hearing was approaching. She wasn't pining to return to the UU church anymore, and hadn't thought about it in months. "Maybe I should reschedule the hearing and stay at Chase's church until my shop's repairs are finished. Chase and his congregation have been more tolerant of me lately."

"That's not tolerance. They're pretending to be nice because they're afraid of you. Besides, this is probably just a case of showing up for the hearing, and then all will return to normal after that."

Ravenna knew some who attended Living Waters were afraid of her, but not everyone anymore, especially not her new friend Ava. She was learning more about Christianity, too, which made it easier to explain why they didn't need to be afraid of her. Even Chase was warming up. Ravenna realized that she wanted to stay until her apothecary was fixed. "Ash, I think I'd like to postpone the hearing until after I'm back in the shop. Maybe when things get back to normal there, the transition will feel better because I can get back in my shop and the UU church at the same time."

"Do you have any idea how hard it was for me to get you this hearing? I'm sorry it took so long, but I don't think postponing is a good idea. If you wait, they may change their minds."

"I'll take the risk. It's been good at Chase's church, and business is picking up again."

"What about Skye?"

Ravenna ran her fingers over the rough, sandy surface of the table, feeling the grains move and shift. The windblown sand below her feet flowed like waves, calling out, and the grains leaped from under her hand to join them. Ravenna observed how the sand moved in unison as one, more powerful together than any single grain alone, and knew she needed a friend to help her sort through her feelings.

"Ash, it's selfish of me to burden you, but I need some help. You're the only person I can talk to about this, and oddly enough, it's because you're a UU."

"Are you okay?" Ashley said.

"Not really. I mean, yes, but no. Every time I'm near him, this crazy energy passes between us. He winks at me, I don't know why, and smiles a lot now, and gave me sea glass and I almost fell, and he made me want to kiss him, but I didn't, I couldn't, maybe he didn't want to, but I know he did. I can't even look at him without feeling it, the energy, but maybe it's just me, but it isn't. Oh, and those muscles and the way he looks at me. You know what I mean?"

Ashley's head bobbed and tilted the entire time Ravenna spoke, and came to a stop when she did. "You can't be . . . talking about Klay this way, right?"

"No. Not Klay," Ravenna said and chuckled. "I've never even thought about him that way. He's like a brother."

"I'm confused. Do I know this person?"

"Yes, but don't judge, okay? Please be open-minded."

"Sure. I think of myself as an accepting person."

Ravenna took a deep breath. "It's Chase."

Ashley's mouth dropped, and her salad spilled in her lap. She scrambled to pick up the pieces to put them back in the to-go container, and Ravenna jumped up to help.

"What happens when your whole life falls apart because of that asshole? It won't be as easy as picking up a spilled salad when it happens," Ashley said. "You can't just pick up the pieces and move on. Trust me, Ravenna, I know what it's like to fall for a guy that treats you like crap. Don't do it. He doesn't care about you. He's trying to destroy you, and you're falling for it."

"But it's not like that anymore, Ash."

"I thought Jason was decent too, and don't think I'm not petrified about what might happen now that my health is worse."

Ravenna took the container and handed Ashely a stack of napkins. "I'm sorry, Ash. I shouldn't have burdened you with this. What you're dealing with is much more important. Is there anything I can do to help?"

"I don't know. I've been thinking that I may need to ask for my one wish."

Ravenna sat back in her chair and watched a group of kids playing frisbee, running, giggling, and shouting. She'd always longed for her life to be carefree, unburdened by the responsibility of other people's happiness. But Ashley was her closest friend. She'd always thought she'd do anything for her, but now she wasn't sure. She didn't know what to say, and swallowed hard to keep the salad she'd eaten from spilling out of her mouth.

"Should I let you know when I'm ready for my wish?" Ashley said.

"Try to hang on until I get back into my shop, okay?"

"I know the stairs up to your attic would be hard for me, but at least I wouldn't have to worry about coming back down. It'll be a breeze once you've performed the magic. I think about that, and other things that would be so much easier for me all the time," Ashley said. She winked, reminding Ravenna of Chase again.

"How about we talk about the wish magic another time?" Ravenna said.

"Are you still stuck on Chase? Come on, Ravenna. Get over him, and fast. He's bad news, and I don't want to see anything like what happened at the apothecary happen to you again, or something worse."

"Nothing like that would happen again."

"Please tell me you're not serious about him, that it's just a physical attraction you'll get over in a week or two? Like the guy in my café who I had the hots for, and he turned out to be running from the police. Guys like him and Chase will make you think they care about you when they want to swindle you out of something. For me, it was my café, and he wanted my money. For you, it's your magic. Don't give it to him."

"Never," Ravenna said, and couldn't help but wonder if she already had.

AUTUMN

30

THE AIR WAS GETTING chilly, and the leaves on the trees would soon turn color. The thought of being back in her own shop before winter was exciting, but dulled by the idea of leaving Chase's church when things were getting better with him and his congregation. Ravenna couldn't help but fear that the warmth he'd shown her might not continue if she left.

Ravenna was running late to work after scouring the beach for sea glass and checking her attic to see if the wish wall had moved back. But it hadn't. Klay had said the wall was quiet when she wasn't near, but as soon as she showed up, it rumbled a low growl, reminding her it was impatiently waiting for her to do magic. She thought up ways to try to move it out of the church, but nothing worked. So all she could do was hope Chase forgot about it and that it would return to her wish room when the shop was ready in a few weeks.

An hour later, Ravenna entered the church. Barbara was in her usual place in the office, glancing up from her computer to see who'd walked in—no wave or smile from that one, at least not for Ravenna.

Inside the shop, Klay was rearranging display cases. "Have you seen the progress on the new apothecary yet? I bet it's more beautiful than it was before."

"Oh, Klay, it's spectacular. I can't wait to move back, and I hope Skye's excited, too."

"But what about Ashley? I'm sure she'll still need help in the café."

"I've been trying to avoid that conversation with Skye, but I was hoping we could work something out where she could spend half of her time with me in the apothecary and half of her time at the café."

Ravenna hadn't seen or spoken to Skye much since the apothecary burned. They still avoided each other as much as possible, and it pained Ravenna to her core. She didn't know what had happened to the girl who wanted to spend every waking moment with her. Ravenna couldn't comprehend how a child could go from loving their mother so deeply one day to feeling complete disdain toward her the next. The thought made her choke, unable to breathe, and she couldn't help but feel a twinge of anger toward her own mother for dying and leaving her alone. Ravenna knew she needed to confront Skye if she wanted their relationship to mend, but she couldn't bear the idea of facing her emotions, let alone Skye's.

"I can't believe Skye started her senior year. She'll want to train to do wish magic and help you when she turns eighteen. You will do wishes when you return to the shop, right?" Klay said.

"Yes, of course. The agreement to stop was while I'm here in Chase's church."

"I hope so. I wouldn't put it past jerkface to make up some new rule to keep you from doing them."

"No, he won't."

"I need a coffee. Do you want me to get you one?" Klay stopped before stepping out into the hallway. "Wait. Shh! Come here and keep your voice down. What's Maeve doing in the church office?" he said.

"I don't know. Let me go see."

Klay held his hand out to prevent Ravenna from leaving the room. "Hold on. Who's with her? Isn't that the Dalton guy from the store downtown?"

"Jim Dalton? Why would she be here with him?" Ravenna said.

"Back up. They're coming out of the office."

Ravenna and Klay made themselves look busy, waiting for Maeve and Jim to enter. Only they didn't, and the church side door didn't open either. Klay poked his head out. "Look. They're headed into jerkface's office."

Ravenna watched them go in and close the door. "What? He closed the door. He never closes the door. Why did he—"

"Who cares? What the hell are they doing in his office?" Klay said.

"Go see if you can hear anything."

"What if I get caught?"

"I don't know, but you're quick on your feet and can figure it out. Better yet, don't get caught."

"Oh, okay, sure. I'll just throw on my invisibility cloak. Now that I think about it, I don't need one. I'm already invisible."

"Hurry, Klay, I want to know why they're in there."

Ravenna peeked around the doorjamb, watching Klay sneak down the hall. She glanced back and forth between Klay lingering near Chase's door and Barbara typing away at her computer in the office. If Barbara got up, she'd see Klay and cause a scene. Klay looked at Ravenna with wide eyes and an open mouth. He put his ear closer to the door and listened. Ravenna jumped when she heard the church's side door open, and saw Faith entering the church. Barbara looked up from her desk and stood to greet her. Ravenna ran into the hallway to block their view of Chase's office door.

"What is it with you, Faith? Can't you keep your claws off that man?" Ravenna regretted saying it as soon as it came out of her mouth.

"How dare you? Since when do you think you can control Chase's love life? You don't have a chance with him, Miss Bitch-Witch, so go fly on your broomstick with the devil and let this prim and proper Christian woman have at him." Faith stared into Ravenna's brown eye. "In fact, why don't you go back into your little stupid glass shop, and I'll tend to real business."

"Don't waste your breath on her, honey. Chase is busy in his office right now, so come spend a few minutes with me until he's free," Barbara said.

"No. I'm not done talking to you," Ravenna said.

Faith looked Ravenna up and down with the same sour face she'd had the morning they painted the community center. "I have nothing else to say to you." Faith flicked her wrist as though Ravenna were an inconvenient fly buzzing around her head. "It's fine, Mom. Chase won't mind if I disturb him for a minute to flash him a smile."

"Didn't you hear her? Chase is busy and doesn't want to be disturbed."

Klay must have used Ravenna's distraction to slip into the men's room. Faith stomped down the empty hallway, with Barbara running after her. Ravenna ducked back into the apothecary, waiting for Klay to return, and heard Faith banging on Chase's door.

"Oh, I didn't know you had . . . I was going to say company, but that's not . . ." Faith's voice trailed off when she stepped inside and closed the door.

Klay ran back to the apothecary.

"What's going on?" Ravenna said.

Klay lifted his index finger for Ravenna to wait a minute. Maeve and Jim Dalton walked past the apothecary and left the building.

"Why would Maeve talk to Chase and not even visit me? Why was she with Jim, and did she think I wouldn't see her?"

"Didn't you have plans with Skye to spend the day at Faneuil Hall and see Katy Perry tonight at TD Garden, before she changed her mind and refused to go with you? Maeve must think you're not here."

Ravenna picked up her phone and looked at the date. "Skye must have told Maeve we were going, but never told her we weren't. But wouldn't she know you'd be here?"

"I don't know, but she obviously didn't say hi. And from what little I could hear, I swear I heard Jim say that he wished he rented his space to you despite Chase."

"So Chase did convince him not to rent to me! But what did Jim mean? And why is Maeve with him?"

"I tried, Ravenna, but I couldn't hear anything else. Thanks for the warning that the bait trap was on her way down the hall."

Images flashed into Ravenna's mind, thinking about Faith in Chase's office with the door closed, but then her insides burned with fury because it didn't matter anymore. Ashley was right. She couldn't trust Chase, and now she couldn't trust Maeve, either.

31

RAVENNA TENDED TO HER magical garden, surrounded by the fresh scent of flowers that bloomed year-long and a gentle wood-smoked breeze from a nearby fireplace. Crisp autumn leaves rustled as if sharing secrets, stirring the mystical energy of Ravenna's ancestors who could be felt there. The garden was a peaceful sanctuary, an escape from the world's demands, and a place where a witch's soul could rest and heal. Ravenna often wondered if that was why Maeve preferred to look after this garden more than any other in her yard. If Maeve was trying to heal from something, Ravenna didn't know what it was. Now, even as threads of renewed energy wrapped around her, she couldn't shake the uneasy feeling of knowing Maeve was keeping something from her, and that Chase was privy to it. Ashley was right. She was foolish to think Chase had warmed up to her. He was manipulating her, and now she wondered if Maeve was, too. She inhaled deeply, choking on months of deceit.

She wiped dripping streaks of dirt mixed with tears from her face, and spied Chase in the distance, watching her from the parsonage grounds. She continued weeding, pretending not to see him wave, but soon lifted her gaze, unable to resist the curiosity. She expected to find him still staring at her, but he was gone. It was just as well. She hoped he knew she hadn't waved back on purpose. Then she heard footsteps come up behind her.

"I hope you don't mind that I ordered this from Watson's Café for you, and took it upon myself to deliver it."

Ravenna whipped around to find Chase holding a large pizza box.

"I was thinking about the time I saw you with pizza that ended up in the sand, and figured buying you some more was the least I could do," Chase said.

"Why? Did you have something to do with the slice slapped from my hand that day?"

"Maybe indirectly. Will you accept it as a peace offering?" Chase held the box out for Ravenna.

Ravenna thought he looked sincere, and her intuition confirmed he was, but he'd fooled her before, and she refused to let it happen again. She wanted to accept it, to invite him in to share it, but she couldn't. "How about instead of pizza, you tell me why my grandmother and Jim were in your office the other day? If you want to make a peace offering, that's how to do it," she said.

"I didn't know—"

"What? That I was in the church that day? I was, and I saw them both enter and leave your office." Ravenna's eyes narrowed, watching Chase, waiting for a sign that her words struck a nerve, but his expression remained the same.

"It's true we had a meeting, but you know I'm sworn to secrecy and can't share what's said in my office."

"But you usually leave the door open. Anyone could walk by and listen in."

Chase shifted the pizza box. "It's an unfortunate circumstance of ministering to the opposite sex that for the sake of propriety, the door should remain open. I'm sure you noticed I closed the door during that meeting, for their privacy."

"Yes. I noticed it was closed when Faith walked in afterward, too."

"You must not have stuck around for very long then, because I opened it only a moment after she entered. Why are you so concerned about Faith, anyway?"

Ravenna ignored Chase's pointed question, but felt her cheeks flush. "You're not Maeve's or Jim's minister, so why do you need to keep what they said a secret?"

"I have to assume that someday I could be anyone's minister."

"Why do I feel like this is just about everyone keeping secrets from me?"

Chase's eyes softened, and he spoke with sincerity in his voice. "Lady Ravenna, sometimes people make mistakes. They make wrong assumptions, but can change their minds. Other times, people can be stubborn and keep believing the lies they tell themselves, even when they know the truth."

"Who's moved on and who's stuck, Chase?"

"The answer to that question sits inside a pizza box." Chase winked, placed the box on a bench in the yard, and left.

32

"HEY, IT'S BEEN A long day. I can't believe we sold so much of your jewelry today. How about we grab some dinner tonight? Better yet, let's go out to dinner," Klay said. "Why don't I call my dad and invite him, too?"

"I think it's time we had a little chat," Ravenna said. She grabbed a metal chair, positioned it across from her, then pointed to it. "Have a seat, my business partner."

Klay sat across from Ravenna and rubbed the back of his neck. "We sold twenty-six pieces today, so I'll need you to make an additional fifteen to replenish the inventory, but let's not worry about business right now. Let's have a nice dinner and talk about this over the weekend. Ashley's place? She always finds room for us, even on a busy Friday night."

Klay was the last person Ravenna wanted to have dinner with. It was bad enough that she had to work with him every day, but socialize with him? She didn't even know if she considered him a friend anymore. Friends don't bail when you face the most challenging time of your life. They hold your hand and mean it when they ask if there's anything they can do for you to make it easier. And Klay was the one person she thought always meant it, until Moon died. "No, I don't want to have dinner with you. It would be easy to lie and say I'm too tired, but I won't lie, and you know that. So here's the truth. I find it hard to care about someone who doesn't care about me."

"I care about you, Ravenna! I care enough that when I see you making crazy choices, like moving your apothecary to a Christian church, I come with you, even though I think it's the worst decision any witch could ever make. So here I am, monitoring jerkface because he's got something up his sleeve and we all know it, because I care about you. I think you should focus more on finding a new familiar so you can grant wishes again, and stop worrying about who killed Moon, because you can't bring her back. I'm sorry, Ravenna, but it's true. She isn't coming back. It's been five months, and it's time to move on."

"I know she's not coming back, and I don't want to find her killer because I think it'll bring her back to me. I don't even know what I'd say to the person who did it, except maybe that they suck, but I need to know. Did they kill poor Moon because I'm a witch? Does it have something to do with . . ." Ravenna pointed her thumb toward Chase's office and whispered, "Was it someone in this congregation? I need to know."

Ravenna started packing her things, and Klay followed her lead, locking the display cases. "Did you notice I fixed the bottom of this one?"

"So you're just going to ignore what I said?"

"I'm not ignoring you. I'm thinking."

"Well, stop thinking, and say something or do something."

Klay walked out into the hallway, and Ravenna joined him. She was locking the door when Faith walked by without saying a word, heading straight for Chase's office. She knocked on his door, and Ravenna faced Klay with her finger to her lips. "Shh." She strained to listen while pretending to have trouble with the doorknob.

Chase's voice was faint from this distance, but Ravenna heard him. "Open the door wide, will you?"

"What's going on with you?" Klay said.

"Nothing. I wondered if his door thing was because I'm a woman or a witch."

"If what was because—"

"Never mind. Let's talk outside."

They stepped out of the building into the crisp autumn air. All year Ravenna longed for fall days, and how they felt bearable because of the chilly winds that blew through her hair and whistled around her ankles. She noticed leaves in shades of red, orange, and yellow and listened to the sound of distant waves mixed with laughter and chatter coming from the beach and Ashley's restaurant. Ravenna thought fall was the season for making memories that would last a lifetime. But this year, everything was different.

Ravenna and Klay followed the sidewalk leading to her house.

"The apothecary is almost ready," she said.

"Every morning when I wake up, I ask myself how I'm going to get through one more day in this uptight hellhole. I can't believe I've lasted this long." Klay pointed to a white Cape Cod-style home on the side of the church. "Hey, whose house is that?"

"I'm pretty sure it's the parsonage where Chase lives."

Klay stopped and peered through the picket fence. "Kind of nice for a minister, don't you think?"

"That's Plymbury for you. You haven't even seen his office."

"Thank the Goddess, or maybe he should thank the Goddess. No telling what might happen if I were alone with him."

Ravenna shook her head and rolled her eyes. "His office is simple but elegant. A large window overlooks the gardens, and you can see all the way to the apothecary. I saw her from there once. She was running across my yard chasing a raven."

"Saw who?"

"Moon. She hops on her window seat in my bedroom sometimes, too. I think she's worried about me."

"Then talk to her when you meditate and tell her you're fine. It's time for her to move on."

"But I'm not fine, and she knows it. I need to know who killed her, Klay. I want her to know I cared enough about her to find out."

"Come on, you can't share headspace with someone for so long and not know that. She knows how much you loved her."

Ravenna stopped at the walkway to her house and grabbed Klay's arm. "Why won't you help me? I haven't said anything to you, hoping you'd come and tell me you'd changed your mind, but you didn't. You know how much this means to me."

Klay turned his back to her and leaned against the arbor at the entrance of Ravenna's walkway, his arms crossed, facing the ocean.

It was 5:15 p.m., and the smell of freshly fried seafood from Ashley's café mixed with seaweed filled the air, carried by the hum of conversation that ebbed and flowed with the rhythm of the ocean's waves.

"If she were human, the police would still investigate until they found her killer and justice was served. I owe that to her, because I loved her as much as any human I've ever known."

Klay ran his fingers through his hair and faced Ravenna. "I never really thought about it like that." He brushed a tear from his eye and pulled Ravenna into his chest. "I'm so sorry," he said, and wrapped his arms around her.

"I'm okay, Klay, but I need to know who killed her. Please help me get the closure I need."

Klay sighed and climbed into his car. "Come to dinner tonight, and you'll get all the answers you need. I'll meet you there in an hour."

"Wait! What do you mean I'll get my answers? Do you know something you're not telling me? What answers? Don't leave!" Ravenna said as his car rolled out of the driveway and up the street.

Ravenna's shoulders sank, and her head hung low as she shuffled down the walkway. She'd been away from the apothecary so long that she didn't even notice how run down the place had gotten, and made a note to weed between the cobblestones. Ravenna looked up, wondering if the flower garden was just as bad. That's when she saw her, sitting like a queen on her throne on top of a rock in the middle of it.

"Moon?"

The cat didn't move, and Ravenna made her way through the flowers toward her. "Moon, is that you?" Ravenna approached the rock and reached out to see if she could touch her, but the cat moved just out of arm's reach. Every time Ravenna inched closer, the cat moved further away.

"I'm going to find out who killed you tonight, so you can stop worrying about me. I'll be fine. You won't need to watch over me anymore."

Moon looked up at the weeping willow that overhung the driveway. Ravenna observed its branches drooping to the ground like a curtain of sorrow, revealing a deep hole in the middle. She was inching toward it when the raven flew out from behind it, startling her. It perched on the rock next to Moon.

Ravenna gasped. "Are you two friends?"

The raven lifted off the rock with its wings stretched across the sky, and Moon followed, darting across the flowerbeds, chasing the bird's shadow.

33

SKYE LOUNGED ON THE living room couch, still wearing her combat boots. Ravenna had a rule that no one wore their shoes indoors. Not because the floors were pine and could easily dent or because they could get dirty, but because she kept a Pagan home and believed that stepping on the floor with shoes was disrespectful to the Goddess. Also, when her bare feet touched the wood, it grounded her, and she wanted everyone to have that same experience in her home, especially Skye.

They hadn't spoken more than a few words in weeks.

"Why are you home? I thought you were working at Ashley's tonight."

"I saw a reservation for you, so I told Ashley I was sick and left."

"You left work because I was going to be there? How could you do that to Ashley on a busy Friday night?"

Skye reached for the TV remote on the coffee table and clicked the screen to life.

Ravenna spoke in a loud voice. "Are you going to—"

Skye turned up the volume.

"I don't like that you lied to Ashley, and if she asks me how you're feeling, I'm going to tell her the truth."

Skye stared at the TV, clicking through the channels.

"Can you please turn the TV off and talk to me?"

Skye's cell phone rang, and she jumped off the couch, holding it to her ear. "Yes, pick me up. I'd love to go," she said and ran upstairs.

"Take your shoes off in my house!"

Skye flew down the stairs as quickly as she'd run up them, still wearing her combat boots, but now with a pentacle t-shirt and a black lace miniskirt with fishnet stockings. She held a black leather jacket in her arms.

"So you're going out? What if Ashley sees you get in someone's car?"

"What does it matter? You told me you wouldn't lie, so tell her I went to a friend's house." Skye strutted into the kitchen.

"Whose house? When will you be home?"

The kitchen door slammed shut.

Ravenna had to do something. She scanned her witchy paraphernalia in the living room, full of ancient secrets and magic. She smelled a hint of the lingering fragrance of herbs, and reached for a spell book sitting on the table. She flipped through its worn yellowing pages, settling on the perfect one, and lit a tightly wrapped bundle of white sage resting in a quahog shell. Ravenna waited for the trail of smoke to fill the room, then lit a black candle to begin the magic that would snap Skye out of this recent funk.

But then she remembered her promise.

No magic, or she'd get kicked out of Chase's church. Ravenna struggled between her agreement with Chase and wanting desperately to repair her ragged relationship with Skye. Chase would never know, she thought, and she'd be out of his church in a few weeks anyway. But then her stomach flipped upside down, and the thought of breaking her word nauseated her. She snuffed the candle, and pushed and pressed the sage against the shell to extinguish it. She breathed a deep sigh and stood before the witch ball suspended before the massive window that stretched the room's length. The ball's glassy exterior absorbed green from the lush outdoor grasses and blue from the ocean beyond, mixing in a kaleidoscope of colors that twisted and turned with swirled hues of pinks and purples. And yet, even with all this color reflected on the witch ball's surface, the inside remained as hollow as she felt.

SHE WAS LATE. IT was 6:40 in the evening, and with a stomach full of upset and anxiety, Ravenna wasn't in the mood for eating or socializing. But that wasn't why she was there. She wanted answers about what had happened to Moon.

It was a crisp fall night, and Ravenna felt the sting from droplets of salty air striking her face while she waited for the hostess. The sun was setting, casting orange hues across the sky, and music played quietly in the background, making it seem like time stood still and Ravenna was intruding. The hostess arrived, and Ravenna followed her through the crowded mix of locals and tourists, chatting and laughing, sipping glasses of wine. Klay stood to greet her and asked the hostess to bring her a glass of Chardonnay. Ravenna's eyes darted between Klay and Rich, trying to see through tension as thick as the fog growing in the distance, pooling above the ocean waves. She studied Rich, a husky man in his late sixties, with weathered skin creased around his gentle gray eyes that spoke to a lifetime of hurt and pain. Rich, the only man Ravenna had really known as a child, always treated her like family.

"I didn't think you were going to meet us tonight," Klay said. "But now that you're here, why don't we eat?"

"I'm not hungry," Ravenna said.

"Well, I'm starving, so let's eat," Rich said.

Klay shot him a sideways glance.

"Where's Skye? I thought she worked on Friday nights?" Klay said.

"She went out with a friend."

"Ashley didn't need her? Hard to believe. Look how crowded it is."

"I didn't come here to talk about Skye. I came to talk about Moon. So why don't we do that? Good idea?"

Rich grabbed his glass of wine and drank it down, then waved to the waitress for another.

"Look, it's the witch in the newspaper!" a man with a red face, wearing a Hawaiian shirt, yelled from three tables away. He tried to stand, and the woman beside him grabbed his arm and pulled him down.

He fell back into his seat, then stood again. "I'm not afraid. I want to see her up close." He ripped his arm away from his wife and wove in and out of tables, slamming into chairs on his way toward Ravenna.

Klay stood between the man and their table and grabbed him around his shoulders. The woman chased after him, trying to pull him away from Klay's grasp. "Let's go," she said.

Rich coaxed Ravenna out of her seat and stood in front of her behind the table. The music inside stopped, and a crowd gathered.

The man wrestled with Klay. "I want to see a real witch up close."

"Joe, I'm going home if you don't stop this nonsense right now," the woman said. She pulled him out of Klay's arms and turned him to face his table, looking back at Ravenna. "I'd say I'm sorry, but I'm not. People like you are the devil incarnate."

"Then I guess we'll see you both again. In hell!" Klay hissed so intensely that spit shot toward the woman.

A man pointed at the woman. "All of you witches will burn in hell, but not these good Christians."

Ravenna felt a hand on her shoulder, causing her to jump. Rich swung around with his fist in the air.

Ashley raised her hands in surrender. "I'm sorry. I should have told you I was behind you. Stay right here." Ashley pushed through the crowd. "If you don't get back to your tables and stop yelling, I'm calling the police to clear everyone out. I mean it. My restaurant won't be a place for barroom brawls. Got it?"

Groans filled the air as the crowd dispersed, and everyone returned to their tables, whispering.

Ravenna hid her face in her hands.

"Here's your Chardonnay, Lady Ravenna. I'll be back with your drink in a few minutes, sir," the waitress said to Rich as though nothing had happened.

Ravenna didn't look at the waitress or thank her. She just wanted to keep hiding. She would have run home, but she'd have to cross the entire restaurant to leave. She was stuck, and felt the reality of it squeezing in on her.

"No one will bother you now," Klay said when Ravenna looked up.

"Good job. You did what any fine man does for a woman in distress." Rich smacked Klay on the shoulder. "I raised you right."

"Is that what you think I am, a weak, distressed woman?"

"We all need a little help every once in a while. I didn't mean you're always in distress."

"Maybe I'm not in distress. Why can't I stress just like you, and not be weak?"

"I didn't mean—"

The waitress returned to the table with Rich's wine and trays full of food. "Compliments of the owner." She placed the dishes on the table and pointed to the hostess stand. "Oh, and the gentleman over there, waiting for takeout, said to tell you that no one will bother you again. I heard him talking with that man, telling him to leave you alone and how unchristian his behavior was."

Ravenna looked over and saw Chase paying for his food.

"What's jerkface doing here?" Klay said. "I ought to go over there and—"

"It's too late," Rich said. "He just left."

The tantalizing aroma of grilled vegetable lasagna and portobello stuffed with spinach and feta wafted from the plates, filling Ravenna's nose with the comfort of home. But it soon dissipated when she inhaled the smell of piping hot, sizzling steak, leaving an acrid reminder of how much better her life could be.

"Crazy how well Ashley knows us," Klay said. He moved the steak in front of Rich. "I'll eat either of the other two. So what will it be, Ravenna, mushrooms or lasagna? What are you in the mood for tonight?"

"Answers to what happened to Moon."

Rich choked on the bite of steak he had just put in his mouth and drank down his second glass of wine.

"Is something bothering you, Rich?" Ravenna said.

"No, no, um . . . I have a hard time talking about loss. I have ever since Naomi walked out on us to shack up with her other family, but that was years ago. Sorry, Klay, I didn't mean to talk about your mother like that in front of you."

"Sure. I haven't seen her since I was four, though, so it doesn't bother me."

"Fair enough, but she's still your mother. Unfortunately."

"I think it's more unfortunate for you than me, Dad."

"Stop! What's going on here? This is not about your wife or his mother, so what's all this nonsense really about?" Ravenna said through clenched teeth.

Klay and Rich stared at Ravenna. Neither said a word.

"I'm not leaving here without my answers."

"Just tell her, Dad, because if you don't, I will. I can't do this to her anymore."

"I thought we agreed that—"

"Tell her!"

Rich's shoulders fell, and he looked down at the steak he'd cut into bloody pieces. He let out a sigh and looked at Ravenna. "I'm the one who hit and killed Moon."

Ravenna sat in stunned silence as a fiery pain erupted in her heart, reverberating throughout her body. The ocean seemed to mock her disorientation, echoing in her ears, so that she struggled to process what she'd just heard. Her breaths came in short bursts, each one shooting a sharp jab through her chest as she tried to get hold of herself, but her entire world shook from its foundations, and betrayal washed over her like an icy wave.

"I'm so sorry, Ravenna. I didn't mean to, and would never have deliberately hurt her. It was an accident. I swear."

"You know he didn't do it on purpose, right?" Klay said.

Anger coursed through Ravenna's body. All at once, incoherent thoughts flooded her head, and she spoke as if talking to herself. "You killed Moon. All this time, Klay was protecting you. You wouldn't help me. I trusted you. Rich killed Moon." Unable to focus on anything, Ravenna stared into space until she heard Klay calling her name.

"Ravenna? Ravenna?"

"How could you? How could you lie to me? I trusted you. You had no intention of telling me, because you wanted to protect him."

Rich talked fast. "I made a mistake and drove after drinking too much. I was heading back from Jake's bar in the center of town and didn't realize I had hit her until I got home and saw my tire. Klay told me that night it was Moon, and how could I tell you? I was drunk." Rich's eyes grew red and wet.

"You both lied to me all this time!" Dazed, Ravenna rose and staggered across the restaurant, trying to navigate her faltering steps around the dizzying blur of tables.

Klay caught up and grabbed Ravenna's arm to help steady her walking.

"Let go of me now!" Ravenna pulled her arm from Klay's grasp and stumbled over her feet. "If I never see either of you again, it will be too soon."

34

Beds are as much for passing out drunk as for sleeping in, and that's what Ravenna did when she returned from the restaurant to an empty house. She sat in her bed with a bottle of wine, watching the blades of her bedroom ceiling fan whir in a blur of chaos, like the world around her she wanted to forget. She hadn't slept soundly for weeks, and the wine slid down her throat with ease. It didn't take long on an empty stomach for her head to haze, forcing her heavy eyelids shut.

Ravenna awoke to the kitchen door slamming open. The vibration shook her body, reverberating for what seemed like an eternity before fading away, leaving a banging pulse inside her head. She heard voices coming from the kitchen.

"I asked you to take me home, not deliver me like a package to the doorstep," Skye said.

"I thought you might throw up and never make it that far," Klay said. "How much did you drink, anyway?"

"It's none of your business."

Ravenna heard a chair slam into the kitchen table.

"It is when you call me for a ride home."

"Would you rather me not call?"

"No. You did the right thing."

"Then get off my ass and go home now."

"Don't you dare talk to me like that, or—"

"Or what? You're not my father."

Ravenna picked up her phone. Three o'clock in the morning, and no missed calls or texts. She was grateful Skye was home safely but had no intention of facing Klay, so she stayed in bed, listening.

"I may not be your father, but I've always loved and cared for you as if I was. So what gives, Skye? This isn't like you at all."

Ravenna heard a screech from chair legs being pulled across the floor.

"Hold on there. Let me help you into the seat," Klay said. "Now, don't move. I'll make you some coffee, and then I want to know what's going on."

Ravenna wanted to burst into the kitchen and tell Klay to leave. Skye wasn't his kid. She needed her mother, but a pounding headache prevented her from doing little more than listening.

"Here, sip this water. I added some mint to help clear your mind and prevent you from getting sick. Have you ever gone drinking before?"

"No. This is the first time, and I never want to drink again."

"That's what they all say. So what made you drink tonight?"

"Why not? My best friend Charlotte wants nothing to do with me anymore, and it's not every day you find a friend who accepts you're a witch. You know what I mean?" Skye said.

"What happened with Charlotte?"

"It was after we got kicked out of the UU Church. She said everyone was talking about it, and people in town don't like that we're witches anymore."

"Here's some coffee for you. What else did she say?"

"Her parents were afraid that if she hung out with me, they'd get kicked out of the church, too."

"I'm so sorry, Skye, but just give her some time. She'll come around."

Ravenna heard Skye sob and Klay offering her a tissue.

"I didn't realize this was so hard for you," Klay said. "Why didn't you tell me sooner? I thought we were close, and that you knew you could trust me?"

"Because you went to the church with Mom. Great Maeve always said to stay away from Christians, and they're bad news. So how could Mom go? Why did you go with her, and why didn't anyone ask me to go, too?"

"Please believe me, Skye, that I only went to keep your mother safe. I can't wait to get out of that dungeon, and you'd hate it, too. But try to have a little understanding for your mom. She's hurting right now and needs you."

"Well, I am, too, and no one's bothered to ask me what I need. She pawned me off at Ashley's café so she wouldn't have to deal with me."

Ravenna somehow found herself leaning against the kitchen doorframe, her eyes barely open, wincing from the fan's light shining on her face. "I didn't pawn you off anywhere, Skye. I didn't want to mix you up in this mess."

Klay jumped up from his seat and looked Ravenna up and down. "Why are you still dressed in what you wore to dinner last night?"

Skye stood, wobbled, and fell into the table. "I'm going to sleep now."

Klay caught her. "Come on. I'll help you upstairs."

"No, you won't! Skye, I know you've been drinking, and it's four hours past your curfew."

"No, I just tripped on my foot." She attempted to walk, and Klay held her arm to steady her. "Um, yeah . . . I lost track of time. I tried to call and text you, but you didn't answer." Skye glanced sideways at Klay.

"That's right, she tried to call you, but when you didn't answer, she called me."

"Haven't you done enough damage? It wasn't enough that you lied to me about Moon, but now you're helping my daughter lie to me, too? For the record, my phone has no missed calls or texts."

"Haven't you ever heard 'call for a ride and no questions asked'?" Klay walked Skye past Ravenna, staring at her with furrowed eyebrows.

Ravenna shot back, "Haven't you ever heard that lies are a poison that kills trust?"

The pounding in her head grew louder, making her regret she'd gotten out of bed. She kept her eyes semi-shut and felt around the butcher block countertop up to the cabinet, searching for a coffee mug.

"Thanks, I'd love some coffee," Klay said when he returned to the kitchen and saw Ravenna scrambling for a cup.

Ravenna poured a mug for herself and drew in the earthy scent, hoping it would spring her to life, but deep inside, she knew nothing could. She faced Klay, peered over the rim, and lowered her voice to a growl. "Get out of my house."

"I just saved your kid's life, and that's all you have to say? Not even, 'thank you, now get out of my house'?"

Ravenna shook, inhaling deep breaths of steam from her coffee. She took a sip, and the hot, bitter liquid mixed with Klay's presence turned her stomach sour. "Did I mention you're fired?"

"What? You can't fire me. I'm your business partner!"

"I'll get another one."

"No, you won't. I'm not leaving." Klay grabbed a mug from the cabinet. "Move over so I can pour myself some coffee."

Ravenna ignored him and fixed her gaze on the whirling ceiling fan sucking up his words in a dizzying circle of indifference. Klay's presence lingered as only the ghost of a man she once knew.

"I need to talk to you," Klay said.

"It's a little too late."

"Please, Ravenna. I can explain."

"I asked you to get out of my house, and I'm not asking again."

"I'm not leaving until you hear me out." Klay took his empty mug and sat at the kitchen table, his face unyielding, his caramel eyes full of stubborn determination.

Ravenna considered calling the police but didn't want to give the neighbors one more thing to talk about. How was she supposed to convince people she was no different from anyone else if the police showed up and escorted her business partner out? It would be the next headline in *The Boston Globe*. "Fine. Make it fast."

"Will you sit?"

Ravenna rolled her eyes, topped off her coffee, and grabbed a piece of rosemary bread from the breadbox for protection. She sat at the head of the table.

"You're my best friend, and I'd never do anything to hurt you on purpose," Klay said.

Ravenna wrapped her hands around the bread. "So, what, lying isn't deliberately trying to hurt me?"

"No. Please, let me explain."

Ravenna tore off a piece of bread and soaked it in the hot brown liquid. The curious blend tingled in her mouth, instantly relieving her headache. "You have five minutes, and then I want you out of my house."

Klay stood with his empty mug and walked to the coffeemaker.

"I don't recall saying you could have coffee. You won't be here long enough to drink it."

"Come on, Ravenna. Do you think I'd want to hurt you? I've always stood by you, even when you married Tristan. I thought it was a mistake to lie about him, but I never said a word to anyone. I never told Maeve or Skye the truth. You live that lie to protect you, Maeve, and Skye—your family lineage. Yet you act pretentious, claiming that you'd never lie and only tell the truth? You think it's okay to lie to protect the people you love, even if it means hurting someone else you love. That's okay in your world, right? I did what you would have done, Ravenna. Did you ever think of that? Knowing that my dad killed Moon wouldn't bring her back, and yes, I wanted to protect my father." Klay sat back down and took a sip of his coffee. "And it's cold. Damn fan."

"You wanted to protect your father from me?"

"No. Not from you or because of the fire. I wasn't at all worried you'd hurt him. You know that, right?"

"Then what were you worried about?"

"My dad told you last night he was drunk. A DUI could have cost him up to two and a half years in prison, a hefty fine, or his license. All he could think about was his kennel, so he didn't want anyone to know. Since my mother took off, breeding those Doberman Pinschers has been the only reason he wakes up in the morning."

"That doesn't explain why you didn't tell me. I would never have ever said anything about him being drunk."

"Really? If someone asked if you knew who killed Moon, you would have lied? I thought you said after the lie about Tristan that you'd never tell another lie again. All I ever hear from you is, 'I won't lie. I won't lie.' Give it a rest, Ravenna. Sometimes lies give us dignity that telling the truth would strip away. They let us make choices without the judgment of others."

"Get out of my house."

35

Ravenna took Ashley to Boston for an appointment with her neurologist at Massachusetts General Hospital because it was getting harder for her to drive, but it wasn't the only reason. Ravenna was her healthcare proxy, and Ashley was getting more concerned about her disease progressing. After taking an intravenous steroid that was supposed to stop her last relapse, it ended up not helping as much as she'd hoped, and Dr. Chen had ordered an MRI.

"Wow. I can't believe Klay lied to you," Ashley said in the waiting room. "I guess it makes sense he was worried about his father, but I thought you meant more to him than that. You've always been the first person he confides in when there's a problem."

"I thought so, too, but obviously, I was wrong," Ravenna said.

"What's going on with Klay these days? I get he didn't want to hurt you more than you already hurt, but that's not like him."

"I know. I think he's still mad about the shop going to Chase's church or something." Ravenna checked the app she'd installed on her cell phone after Skye's drinking incident to be sure she was heading to the café.

"But he went with you anyway. Call me crazy, but I've always thought he wanted more than friendship with you, and what could be better than sharing a business with the person you love?"

"Ash, he and I have been best friends since first grade. Neither of us has ever wanted anything more. I know, because he had his chance and never said anything when I told him about my engagement to Tristan."

Ravenna shared with Ashley what Klay said that day on the beach eighteen years ago.

"HEY, KLAY, I'VE BEEN looking all over for you. I suppose I should have known you'd be here fishing," Ravenna had said. "Any chance you can take a walk on the beach with me? I have something to tell you."

"It can't wait until later at the shop?"

"Maybe, but I want you to hear it from me, not someone else."

Klay reeled in his line and placed the pole next to his tackle box, and they strolled along the shore in silence. Ravenna was deep in thought, trying to figure out how to break the news to him, wondering if it would make him jealous.

"Come on," Klay said. "What are you waiting for? We've walked for at least a mile now, and you haven't told me anything. Is this some kind of joke to get me to stop fishing? I know how much you hate me for killing fish, even if I need to eat them to survive."

"Seriously? You don't need to eat fish to survive. And no, it's not a joke." Ravenna wiggled the fingers of her left hand in Klay's face so he could see the diamond engagement ring Tristan had given her the night before.

"Whoa! Oh, wait. Are you engaged?"

Ravenna bobbed up and down on her toes. "Yes! I'm so excited. I had to come and tell my best friend first."

"But what are you going to tell Maeve?"

"I thought you'd be excited for me. Don't I get congratulations, a hug, or something?"

"Sure, congratulations, I guess, but what will you tell Maeve? If she knew he—"

"Why are you so worried about her? I want to live my own life." Ravenna's eyes narrowed, glaring at him. "She can't control who I marry and doesn't need to know anything other than what a fantastic guy Tristan is. Besides, Tristan's out of town more than he's here, so Maeve never has to know, and I'll never tell her. And you won't either, right? You wouldn't want to be the reason my family gets torn apart, would you?"

"No, Ravenna. I want to be the reason it stays together." Klay glanced down and kicked his foot in the sand.

"Oh, thank you, Klay. I knew you'd be there for me, just like always." Ravenna smiled and wrapped her arms around his neck.

"SEE WHAT I MEAN, Ash? He's always supported me, but never said anything about wanting more than a friendship. And now even that's destroyed. I don't know if I can ever forgive him for this." Ravenna checked her cell phone again to confirm Skye had arrived at Ashley's, and noticed six attempted calls from Klay.

"I think you should try. I'd forgive you if you hurt me to protect Skye, and wouldn't you forgive me if I were protecting one of my kids?"

Ravenna's jaw tightened, and she shifted in her seat. "Of course, our kids always come first, and we'd do anything for them, but Rich isn't Klay's child. So what's the connection you're trying to make here?"

"You know Klay's cared for Rich since his mother walked out. That man's a mess, and he can't get over it. Klay might as well be Rich's father. Cut him some slack, because he loves you and Skye more than anything. I know he does, and you don't find that kind of loyalty every day. Please don't make him choose between you and his father."

When she didn't answer his calls, Klay started texting, and Ravenna's phone wouldn't stop vibrating. She read them and shoved her phone in her pocket. "Oh, I won't, because I don't want to talk to him or his father. Decision made."

"I'm sure Rich is suffering for what he did, too, and maybe knowing how much he hurt you will finally get him to stop drinking. Wouldn't that be something positive that could come out of all this upset?"

A woman opened the waiting room door, holding a clipboard. "Ashley Watson."

Ravenna followed the nurse and Ashley to an examining room.

"The doctor will be right in," she said and closed the door on her way out.

Ashley sat on the examining table, and Ravenna listened to the paper sheet crinkle with every move Ashley made. The wall behind Ashley displayed a neurological poster detailing the spinal cord, reminding Ravenna of the seriousness of the situation that had brought them there. It already seemed the disease had stripped everything away from Ashley, leaving a harsh, cold reality as intimidating and relentless as the examining room.

Dr. Chen gently tapped on the door and stepped into the room. She called up Ashley's chart on the computer screen. "The MRI shows active lesions and swelling on your spinal cord and brain. Between this and the lack of response with the steroid treatment, I'm concerned that your MS might be more active and progressing."

Ravenna reached out to hold Ashley's hand, and saw her eyes tearing and her lips pinch together, quivering, holding back a sob.

Dr. Chen looked her in the eye and spoke gently. "I'm sorry, Ashley. The disease is progressing, and your disability is starting to accumulate."

Ravenna felt her body shudder, taking in what the doctor said.

"We can try another steroid, but you'll experience the same side effects as the ones you already experienced."

Ashley shook her head and whispered in a cracked voice. "No. I can't do another steroid. Please? It was brutal."

"I understand. Let's monitor you, then, and see if you can go into remission on your own. You'll need to get plenty of rest, and be sure you're eating healthy and avoiding stress."

Ashley nodded, and Dr. Chen handed her a slip for a follow-up appointment and a tissue. "Feel better," she said and left the room.

"I'm so sorry, Ash. Is there anything I can do for you?" Ravenna regretted saying it as soon as the words left her mouth.

"I'll let you know when I'm ready."

36

RAVENNA ALWAYS FELT RELAXED after yoga, but today, when she arrived home and spotted Klay's car parked in her driveway and him sitting on her front porch, her muscles tensed. He had left messages and sent texts for days, but she had ignored them, so it didn't surprise her to see him there. But that didn't stop her head from hurting when she ascended the porch stairs, swallowing a lump of pain. "What are you doing here? I thought I told you I didn't want to see you again."

Klay looked at her through a veil of sadness, running his hands through his thick wheat-colored hair. Ravenna felt herself waver.

"I need to get back to work. Okay, wait. That's not what I meant," Klay said.

Ravenna was silent, steeling herself with her hands on her hips.

"Did you listen to my voice messages or read my texts?"

"No. Note to self: remove Klay from my contacts."

"Oh, come on. Look, I'm sorry. I didn't choose my dad over you, and I had him tell you himself. If he hadn't, I promise, I would have told you."

"Really? When? Because you knew that same night! You let me go on a wild goose chase for weeks, trying to find Moon's killer. You told me to search alone because you wouldn't help me anymore, saying it was time to let it go, but you knew your father killed her, and you never told me." Ravenna heard angry waves beginning to crest in the ocean and a fiery sunset sky casting an orange glow on the globes of the hydrangeas lining the porch. She covered her face with her hands as tears slipped through her fingers, falling on the blue clusters below, browning and killing them. Her voice cracked as she spoke. "I don't think I can ever trust you again."

"If you think I made a choice between you and my father and I intentionally tried to hurt you, then I don't know what else to say. I'll start looking for another job." Klay descended the steps and walked toward his car.

Ravenna stood frozen, watching him walk away. In that moment, an overwhelming sense of loss penetrated her hard shell. She witnessed flashes of her life without Klay—lonely days in the apothecary, a gnawing emptiness that threatened to consume her—and she realized that she was about to lose the one person who had stood by her through everything. She swallowed her pride, and called out, "Klay, don't go. Since losing Moon, I haven't been myself. I'm not sure why I needed to know who killed her, but at least I can sleep now. Thanks for arranging the dinner."

Klay ran back up to the porch and embraced her. "I'm so sorry, and I promise you can still trust me. My dad's on his way here and has something for you. He wants to apologize, and I'm sure it will cheer you up."

"I don't want to see him. I can't look at him again. He killed Moon, and I just can't."

"Ravenna, please? It was an accident, and he feels awful about it. He hasn't been able to sleep, either. So let him do this, because he has something for you and hopes it might help heal your heart just a little."

"Nothing can heal my heart." Ravenna wiped the tears from her face and caught sight of Rich's car driving down the street.

"He's excited, so give him a break? Please?"

She didn't want to give anyone a break, and her jaw dropped when Rich parked his car on the street and walked toward her, holding a Doberman puppy. He wore a wide grin under his blue baseball cap, his eyes fixed on Ravenna. "I'm sorry for any pain I've caused you, but please forgive me, because I think I have your new familiar right here. He's a special little guy, and I hope you'll accept him as a gift from me."

Ravenna knew Rich's dogs were prize champions, the best of the breed, with a two-year waitlist. He'd lose a lot of money giving her this puppy. But a Doberman? What would people think? She held her hands up with her palms facing Rich, who was now halfway across the flower garden. "Don't come any closer. I can't. I won't. And look, he has clipped ears, and his tail's cropped, too. That's animal cruelty. Besides, he's a dog, and I need a cat. No, no, no."

"I think he'd be perfect for you. He'd be great protection, too, and look how adorable he is. Don't hurt his feelings. At least hold him and see if you like his personality. He's the best of the whole litter, for sure," Rich said.

"And loves belly rubs. Honestly, he's a sweetie pie," Klay said.

"A sweetie pie? I haven't heard that about a Doberman before. You two are joking, right?" Ravenna said.

"It's no joke. This guy has it all. His temperament is as precious as any Lab I know, and he's the best from any litter I've ever had. He's an unmistakable champion, and I want you to have him." Rich moved his head to prevent the puppy from licking inside his mouth. "He loves his kisses, too, this little one."

"Stop. Both of you, stop. Sure, the puppy's cute, but do you forget I'm a witch? I can't accept a mutilated dog. It goes against everything I stand for."

Rich moved toward her, holding out the puppy.

"I said, stop! Don't come any closer to me. I want a familiar that can communicate with me, not a guard dog, and I don't want to scare people even more. Thanks, but no thanks."

"But he's perfect for you, Ravenna. Just give the pup a chance, three months, and if you aren't happy, we'll find him a new home, no questions asked," Klay said.

"Klay's right. I won't have any problem finding him a new home. He's perfect." Rich scrunched his face and pushed the pup's face away from his. "Well, except for all the licking."

"I can't. Take the puppy and leave. I'm sure you'll find him a wonderful home, but it won't be mine. Thank you, but no thank you."

"You won't just give him a little belly rub?" Klay said.

"No. Take the puppy and go home!" Ravenna turned on her heel, entered the house, and slammed the door behind her.

37

A week later, Ava inspected newly stocked pieces of sea glass in the shop. "Will you join me for the service today?" she said.

Ravenna was running out of excuses, and didn't want Ava to think she was trying to avoid her rather than Chase. "I'm tied up with clients until after the service, but do you want to grab lunch when it's over?"

"Oh, yes! We'd love for you to join us for lunch," Ava said.

"Us?"

"Oh, you didn't know? After the services, some women go to Watson's Café for lunch."

"I didn't, but don't let me intrude. We can plan another day, just us." Ravenna cleared her throat, trying to get Klay's attention to help her bail.

"Don't worry, Faith won't be there. She's a realtor, and I was happy to hear Barbara say she was showing mansions down by the waterfront this afternoon." Ava laughed. "So come with us. Please?"

Ravenna didn't think it could hurt to have lunch with some women from the church, and maybe it would be an opportunity to get to know each other better. She also knew Ava would tell everyone she didn't want to join them if she didn't go. "What time?"

"Noon. You can come too, Klay," Ava said.

"I thought it was just women. Are men invited, too?" Ravenna said.

"It is mostly just women, but sometimes a guy or two joins us."

"Thanks, but somebody has to stay here, and that's me," Klay said. He leaned back in his chair, smiling.

"See you later," Ava said and headed to the service.

"I thought you'd take any excuse to leave this church," Ravenna said.

"Hmm . . . let me think. Alone in a room here, aside from customers, of course, or socializing with a bunch of Christian women. Yeah, alone works for me," Klay said. "Have fun."

"I fired you once, and now I think I should fire you again."

RAVENNA ARRIVED AT ASHLEY'S fifteen minutes early to sneak in some time with her before Ava and the women arrived.

"I can't believe you're having lunch with those people. If I felt better, I'd serve your table myself. On second thought, maybe I wouldn't. If I heard something noninclusive, I'd serve food that would make them all sick." Ashley waved her hands across the table like she was doing a spell.

Ravenna observed Ashley, trying to discern if she knew what she was doing.

"I'm probably projecting the anger I'm feeling about Jason. He's back in town and filed another custody suit against me, claiming I'm an unfit mother because of my declining health."

"Oh, Ash, I'm so sorry. How does he even know?"

"I don't know. He probably hired a private detective, or maybe one of the younger kids said something to him. What does it matter? This is just one more stress my body can't handle right now. I can't even imagine a life without caring for my kids."

Ravenna thought Ashley looked like she was holding back a sob, trying to distract herself by scanning the surrounding tables. "Let me know if you want to talk at my place. I'm always here for you."

"They haven't set the court date yet, but if I'm not in remission by then . . . I can't take a chance of losing my kids. You wouldn't let that happen, so you'll help me, right?"

"I love you, Ashley, but I . . . Let's see when the date is, okay?"

Ravenna spotted Ava, approaching the table with two women.

"Hey, Ravenna, did you invite someone else to join us?" Ava said.

Ashley stood to relinquish her seat. "I'm the restaurant owner and a good friend of Ravenna's."

"You never told me you knew the owner."

"I didn't realize Ashley was such a celebrity," Ravenna said.

"I'm not the celebrity. You are, and I'm fine keeping it that way," Ashley said. "Let me know if you need anything, and I'll send some drinks over. How many of you are there?"

"Just us, plus the pastor," Ava said.

Ravenna saw Ashley's eyes bug out and felt like she was looking into a mirror, because hers did, too. If she'd known he was coming, she never would have agreed to meet for lunch. "I didn't know Chase was having lunch with us."

"Is everything all right? I mean, is there a problem with him joining us?" Ava said. "I told him everyone who'd be here, and it thrilled him to join us. And he's a pleasant sight to look at while you eat, don't you think?"

The two other women laughed and whispered like high schoolers to one another.

"If you'll excuse me, I need to use the ladies' room." Ravenna stood and followed Ashley.

"I thought I told you he was bad news? Why are you having lunch with him?" Ashley said.

"You were right. Chase met with Maeve and Jim, the guy downtown who wouldn't rent me his space, and I called him on it. He wouldn't tell me what they talked about. Why did you give him pizza for me?"

"What pizza?"

"The other day, he came here, ordered a pizza, and delivered it to my house."

"I didn't know the pizza was for you. He just ordered it." Ashley poured drinks from behind the bar.

"He gave me some cryptic message about people moving on and people being stuck and answers being in a pizza box, and I've been trying to avoid him since. I didn't know he was coming for lunch. How can I bail?"

"I don't think you can. Just ignore him. Talk with the women as much as possible, and leave. I'll pop over and check in on you."

Ravenna and Ashley carried the drinks and a basket of bread to the table.

"I didn't know you were a server, Ravenna," Ava said.

"She's not, but she is a loving friend who'd give you the shirt off her back." Ashley glanced at Ravenna with a mischievous twinkle in her eye. "I mean, if she had something under it."

The women gasped, and Ashley laughed, disappearing into a sea of customers. Ravenna thought if Ashley planned to help by saying things to shock these women, then this lunch wouldn't go very well, even if it was funny.

"So why have you stopped coming to services?" Joan said. Ravenna studied the straight brown pixie cut framing her face and her perfect posture. Deep lines were etched around her mouth and between her eyebrows, making her appear as if she were constantly frowning.

"I've just been so busy with my shop, and it's hard to break away," Ravenna said.

"And about that," Joan said, then glanced at Michelle.

"We think it's time for you to leave the church. Enough is enough," Michelle said. "We don't want to be influenced by evil."

"What happened to Christians helping those in need? Is this why you agreed to come today, to give Ravenna a hard time?" Ava said. "Because I won't stand for it."

"Hello, ladies. I'm sorry I'm late. What did I miss?"

The women flashed their whitest smiles at Chase, and Ravenna could have sworn they were batting their eyelashes, too.

"Oh, you didn't miss anything, Reverend Wilkinson. We're just getting to know each other," Joan said.

Ravenna eyed Ava, hoping she would tell Chase the truth, but she just sipped her drink, looking down at the table.

"Why don't we order?" Ravenna gestured for the waitress, hoping to get lunch over with.

"Are you in a rush, Lady Ravenna? I just got here," Chase said.

"Not at all. Why don't I grab Ashley and have her bring you a drink? What would you like?"

"I'm sure the waitress can take my order when she's ready."

"I was just asking Ravenna how much longer she might be in our church," Michelle said with a plastic smile.

"As long as it takes to fix her shop," Ava said through gritted teeth.

"It shouldn't be much longer," Ravenna said.

"That's too bad. We love having you in the church with us, and it will be sad to see you go," Michelle said.

"Yes, very sad," Joan said.

Ravenna shifted her eyes between the two women at the table. She wanted to call them liars and throw their drinks in their faces, but it was more important that Chase saw her getting along with everyone. He had the most influence over his parishioners and this town, and she needed him to help change people's negative opinions of her.

The waitress appeared, and everyone ordered food and additional drinks.

"So what do Wiccans believe about hell?" Joan said.

"Maybe we should talk about something else," Ava said.

"Actually, I'd be interested to know the answer, too," Chase said.

Ravenna scanned the room, hoping Ashley might be nearby. No luck. "We believe in hell, but Wiccans don't believe it's a physical place. It's a state. Anyone at any point in their life can live in hell or heaven—even you. So now I have a question. Why would a Christian want to go to heaven if their kids might not go with them? That makes heaven hell, too, doesn't it?"

"I agree. Jesus's arms are wide, and he has enough love for all of his children so that none shall perish," Ava said. "Don't you agree, Reverend Wilkinson?"

"I agree that heaven would not be a place I'd enjoy for eternity if my children weren't with me," Chase said.

Joan gasped. "You don't even have children," she said. "It's not up to us to decide. Christ Jesus makes that choice, and I would go with or without my children."

"Reverend Wilkinson, I think you've been spending too much time with witches," Michelle said. "I'll be sure the congregation knows you need prayer."

Chase half smiled.

Joan fished for her cell phone inside her pocketbook, and Ravenna spied her looking at a blank screen. "Something just came up, and Michelle and I need to leave."

"Sorry we can't stay, but maybe next time," Michelle said.

Joan dropped a fifty-dollar bill on the table, and Ravenna didn't know if she was relieved that they were leaving, or more stressed now that she was alone with Ava and Chase.

"Leaving so soon?" Ashley said as she arrived. "I hope the holdup on the food isn't the problem. Sometimes we're so busy it gets backed up in the kitchen, but most people don't mind the wait."

Joan and Michelle scurried past Ashley without even acknowledging she had spoken to them.

"Your food should be out soon," Ashley said. "Did you want me to bring out their dishes, too?"

"Why don't you wrap their meals to go," Chase said. He was relaxed, sipping his glass of wine.

Ava fished in her bag and pulled out a twenty-dollar bill. "Could I please also have mine to go?" she said.

Ravenna felt paralyzed. Her thoughts jumbled together into a chaotic mess, and silence hung in the air with the weight of Chase's gaze on her.

"I can pack everyone's meals to take home if it's easier," Ashley said.

"That would be great. I wouldn't want Chase to think he has to sit here with me, and I don't mind eating at home," Ravenna said. She stood up and hugged Ava.

Ava whispered in Ravenna's ear, "If it were me, I don't think I'd be so quick to give up a chance to be with Chase alone." She grabbed her takeout box and waved on her way out.

"I don't feel obligated to have lunch with you, Lady Ravenna, so if you'd rather not sit with me, I understand," Chase said.

"No. Please don't misunderstand, because it's not that at all." Ravenna's body started to overheat, and her palms began to sweat. "It's fine. Let's stay and have lunch."

Ashley returned with two more takeout boxes and set them on the table with the check.

"Ash, if it isn't too much trouble, we've decided to stay. Could you bring us two plates?"

"Sorry, Ravenna, but I need the table," Ashley said.

Ravenna knew Ashley was trying to help her get out of having lunch with Chase.

"Oh, okay. I'm sorry, Chase, but we'll have to leave after all," Ravenna said.

"Sure, no problem. I'll walk you home."

"Across the street?"

"Sure, why not?" Chase settled the bill and scooped up the takeout boxes.

Ravenna reached into her pocket and pulled out a twenty-dollar bill for him.

"Forget it. I already took care of it." Chase flashed Ravenna a smile that made her lose her breath.

"Why don't you take the extra meals?" Chase said when they neared Ravenna's kitchen door. "I'll put them in the fridge for you."

"I'm vegetarian," Ravenna said.

"What about your daughter? Is she vegetarian, too?"

"Not strictly. Why do you want to come inside my house so badly? Are you looking for something in particular? Because I can promise it looks just like anyone else's house."

"Prove it," Chase said with a twinkle in his eye.

Ravenna enjoyed seeing a playful side of him. But she still didn't trust him, and couldn't decide if letting him in was a good idea. So she threw Chase's words from months ago back at him. "Well, to think a real live Christian minister wants to enter a witch's house. I suppose it doesn't matter that it's not raining outside because even if it were, you wouldn't melt, would you?"

"I suppose I wouldn't, but I know now neither would you."

Maybe she was too hard on him. Chase hadn't tried to hide his meeting with Maeve and Jim; he just hadn't shared the details. And he had helped with the drunk guy at Ashley's the night she had dinner with Klay and Rich. Ravenna smirked, and opened the door to let him in. "If you enter, you'll be alone with me, and I always close my kitchen door." Ravenna noticed the ceiling fan spring to life in response to her heartbeat speeding up a notch. Chase's eyes roamed the room the way each consecutive ocean wave took in more of the shoreline.

"I should have expected it to look rustic, but it almost feels like there's no difference between the outside and the inside. You have so many herbs and flowers. They're amazing." He pointed to the drying racks. "They're even on the ceiling. Do you sell them?"

"No. I use them in homemade drinks, teas, and sachets." She took the takeout boxes from him, put two in the fridge, and the other two on the table. "I'd invite you to stay for lunch, but I think your curiosity is settled now, right?"

"I could use a glass of water if you don't mind, but would you turn off the fan? It's chilly in here."

"Er . . . well, um . . . I can't. It's . . . a faulty wire. Klay will fix it at some point. How about some sparkling water with fresh mint?" Ravenna handed him a glass. She felt drawn to him, how his eyes crinkled slightly when he smiled and how his fingers brushed against hers, sending a shudder through her body. She knew he sensed it, too, by the way his voice grew softer, and his hand lingered just a second too long against hers on the glass when she handed it to him.

"How old is this table?" Chase sat and ran his hand across the surface.

"It's been in my family for generations. The table is the one thing that every Greene agrees on. If you want the house, you take the table with it."

"There's no table like this in my family. They prefer modern, but this feels more personal. So your mother lived in this house and ate at this table, too?"

"Yes, and Maeve and her mother before that, and so on. Do you feel the energy? My mother's energy, in the wood?"

"What was she like?" Chase said.

Ravenna wondered why Chase was asking questions about her mother and not her, but wanted to answer him without sounding annoyed.

"I don't know. After falling, she died giving birth to me at the bottom of the living room stairs."

Chase choked on his water.

"Is the mint too strong? Let me make you another one." Ravenna got up from her seat.

"No, no, please sit. I swallowed the wrong way. You say your mother died falling down the stairs?"

"That's right. I kind of just blurted that out, didn't I? Some people wouldn't want to live in the same house their mother died in, but I was born here, and

I'm a witch. So I'm not afraid of spirits, especially not my mother's." Ravenna forced herself to focus on the conversation. But every time his gaze met hers, she felt a surge of adrenaline threatening to unravel her composure.

"I see." Chase stared at the mint floating in his water, looking lost in his thoughts.

"Well, you wanted to come inside. You certainly don't have to stay if you're uncomfortable. Listen, I realize we disagree on what happens to our spirits after we die, but I accept that you believe something different from me. Can't we give each other the freedom to follow our own paths?"

"Lady Ravenna, I don't believe Christians hold the copyright to Jesus, but I do believe every path leads to him. Jesus is God, even if you don't know it yet."

Ravenna shifted in her seat, folded her arms across her chest, and wanted to say how offensive that comment was. Instead, she said, "Does being right trump compassion? If I think something different, is it more important that you're right than it is to give me peace, to let me hold on to my beliefs and you to yours? You know, compassion for each other."

"This isn't about being right. It's about spreading the word of Christ Jesus so that all will find salvation in him. Christians are called to do that work."

"What if I don't want to be saved? Does that make you think I'm evil? Do all my questions make you think I have a rebellious spirit?"

"I find you refreshing, Lady Ravenna, but still pray you'll accept God's grace." Chase got up from his seat with his takeout box and opened the door. "Next time, you'll have to show me the rest of the house if you expect me to believe you're not hiding something," he said and descended the breezeway steps.

38

RAVENNA HEARD THE FAMILIAR sound of Faith's heels storming into the church. When she blew past the church office, Ravenna assumed she was going to Chase's, but she walked into the shop seconds later. Her eyes blazed with anger, and she pointed her finger in Ravenna's face. "How dare you entice him into your home and seduce him like that!"

Klay turned away from the customer he was helping. "Invite who into her home?"

"Reverend Wilkinson. Who else? She's been waiting to bewitch him since day one, and now she's gone and put a spell on him, luring him into her home. Did you think I wouldn't find out? Oh, I saw it, when I was leaving a showing next door to your disgusting hovel."

The woman Klay was helping slinked out past Barbara, now standing in the doorway.

"You invited him into your house?" Klay said.

"I don't know what she's talking about." Ravenna caught a whiff of Faith's seductive floral and spicy perfume.

Faith shot back, her voice sharp with anger, "Don't play dumb with me. I saw him entering your house."

"Right, he came into my house, and I gave him a glass of water."

"What was in it? What did you give him?" Faith said. "Tell me now."

Barbara gazed up at the ceiling. "Lord, have mercy, for he knows not what he did."

"Did something happen I should know about?" Klay said.

"Goddess, no. I don't know what they're talking about," Ravenna said.

"No Christian minister would enter a woman's home alone unless a witch seduced him, and he didn't have the strength to resist. Lord have mercy on him," Barbara said again.

Ravenna thought she sounded like she was worshipping in a church service.

Tears burst from Faith's eyes and poured down her face. She choked on her sobs, and her body trembled as if she had witnessed something unspeakable that destroyed her. Her cries echoed in a heart-wrenching symphony of pain and despair.

"I must have missed something. Why's she crying?" Klay said.

"Faith, if the good Lord can forgive him for the evil thrust upon him, so can you. Now collect yourself, wipe those tears, and visit the man. I'm sure the spell will break once he looks at you," Barbara said. "Go on." She shooed Faith out of the room, and Ravenna heard Faith's heels clicking down the hallway. Barbara turned back.

"You may have fooled some people in this church, but not me. What you've done is despicable and pure evil, the devil's work. I pray that if a devil child is growing inside of you, it dies along with you, and that my daughter will mother him the purest of angels," she said.

"Wait a minute. What's she saying? Are you pregnant?" Klay said.

"There is nothing inside me that isn't of the Goddess herself. And no, I'm not pregnant!" Ravenna said, and ran out of the church.

Ravenna barreled down the street, breath shallow and ragged, leaving the church far behind her. She approached the beach, and frigid fall air sliced through her clothes. She wrapped her arms around her body, and stared at the dull gray sky meeting the ocean at the horizon and the waves slamming against the shore. Seagull cries echoed across the empty beach, and the smell of salt suspended in the air filled her nose. Ravenna sank into the sand, letting herself sob and hugging herself tighter for warmth, feeling like she'd just met winter's harsh arrival. She needed to leave the church quickly, and stay far away from Chase. It would ruin her reputation again if rumors started spreading that she'd seduced him, only this time they'd be worse. She needed to speed up the apothecary renovations, and convince Faith that she was wrong and she could have Chase all to herself.

In the distance, Ravenna heard a man's voice calling her name. It was like Klay to close the shop and come after her. He knew she'd need a friend who understood her, and he'd want to help her feel better. She stood and turned to call back to him, but instead of seeing Klay in the distance, her eyes found Chase. Unsure what to do, she bolted away down the shore, but it didn't take long for Chase to catch up.

"Please don't run. Let's talk," Chase said.

"I don't want to be seen with you. I refuse to be accused of doing something I didn't do."

Chase looked around the desolate beach and pointed to the dunes. "No one is here to see us. Look, even the patio of Watson's is empty in this colder weather."

"Why are you here?" Ravenna's mouth was numb, barely able to form words.

"You're shivering. Let me walk you home, and we can talk."

"No!"

"At least take my jacket. Here." Chase took his coat off and approached her, holding it out in both hands.

She wanted to say no, but the bitter cold was distorting her senses, so she succumbed. Chase wrapped the jacket around her, and she was instantly warmed from the inside out, the warmth passing between them melting the numbness away like snow under the sun. Chase let go, leaving the jacket on her shoulders, and the scent of salty air was replaced with his musky cologne.

He moved back to leave some distance between them. She ached for him to move closer again.

"I'm sorry that coming to your house caused all that distress, but I assure you it won't happen again."

"Faith will be happy to know that."

"How about I take you to dinner? No one can misinterpret anything if we're in public, can they?"

Ravenna wasn't sure why he wanted to take her to dinner, but she looked into his eyes and saw a sincerity that made her heart pound against her chest. There was something about Chase that drew her, a sense of curiosity and excitement she found hard to resist. "I . . . don't know." She felt the stress-cued hives crawl across her cheeks. "I appreciate the offer, but I'm not sure it's a good idea."

Chase grinned, and his eyes crinkled at the corners. "It's just dinner, Lady Ravenna. Nothing more, nothing less. And I found a vegetarian place you'll love."

Ravenna bit her lip. She wanted to accept, but part of her was afraid of getting hurt again, fearful of being misunderstood.

"And let's meet there. It's outside of Plymbury," Chase said.

Ravenna nodded.

"Friday night at seven o'clock? The Lantern in Marshfield. You can return my coat then."

Ravenna didn't know what had possessed her to agree and was trying to think of a way to renege before he reached the footbridge off the beach. Chase was halfway across the sand when he turned around. "Oh, and just for the record, I have zero interest in Faith," he said. And winked.

39

M aeve joined R avenna and Skye for dinner for the first time in weeks. Ravenna knew Maeve had been avoiding her, trying to teach her some cryptic lesson about family and loyalty, and had only showed up to discuss the apothecary reopening and Skye's approaching birthday. Turning eighteen meant Skye would be old enough to learn sea glass magic and assist Ravenna doing wishes in the shop, and Maeve would want to be involved in training her. Ravenna pushed down the turmoil that always threatened to bubble over when she thought about it.

"How soon will the new apothecary open? You know, you need to train Skye if you want her to help at the Annual Wish Festival next May," Maeve said.

Skye paused her forkful of vegetable lasagne mid-air, gazing between Ravenna and Maeve with wide eyes. Her face glowed with a radiance that reminded Ravenna of Tristan. He used to look at her the same way, hopeful that one day she would tell him he could stay home and no longer have to travel for months at a time. But she never had. Instead, Ravenna had continued living a lie, and he loved her so deeply that he lived it with her.

"I want to teach you, Skye, I do. But it will need to wait a while longer." It saddened Ravenna to disappoint her, but lately, no matter what she said, Skye just found a different reason to hate her.

"I heard you slept with Reverend Wilkinson," Skye said, as though it was a fact.

Maeve choked and spat out her mouthful of food. "No. Tell me it's not true. Right now, Ravenna, tell me. How could you?"

"You believe that? Don't you know the people in this town will say anything to turn everyone against me? Now even my family believes them?"

"You managed that yourself when you agreed to sell your jewelry in his church, and to stop doing wish magic," Maeve said.

"Give me a break. What choice did I have? Were you going to support us, Maeve? No, I didn't think so. What about you, Skye? Were you planning to quit school and work full time? Did you also want me to take a waitressing job at Ashley's?"

"Waitress shmaitress. Anything would have been infinitely better than what you did, and it only would have been for a few months. I don't know what possessed you to go to that church. Well, I guess I do now. You gave yourself away to the man who wants to destroy our lineage. Why aren't I surprised?"

"Wow! You actually do believe I slept with him."

The room grew silent aside from the buzzing whir from the ceiling fan, whose blades cut deep with a numbing chill.

It was Skye who finally broke the heavy silence. "My life would be so different if Dad were still alive. He would never have allowed you to go to that Christian church. Great Maeve's right. Christians suck the life out of you."

"You were six months old when your father died. How would you know what he would or wouldn't do?"

"I told her, Ravenna, that Tristan was such a sweet man with a heart of gold. He loved you with a genuine affection that most women only dream about having even once in their lifetime. He was gentle, kind, giving, and nature-loving. Honestly, there aren't enough words to describe how perfect he was. I wish you'd known him, Skye." Maeve rested her hand on top of Skye's, giving it a gentle squeeze.

"I can guarantee that Tristan would have supported my decision to move the shop to Chase's church. He wouldn't have given it a second thought."

"Never," Maeve said. "No witch would ever allow such a thing. And he was one of the finest witches I've ever known."

"Damn it! I've had enough. You want to know the truth? I'll tell you the truth." Ravenna slammed her fist on the table. "Tristan wasn't a witch at all. He was a Christian!"

Skye's mouth dropped open. Her head shook slightly from side to side, as she tried to comprehend the shocking blow.

"That's right, Skye. Your father was a Christian; you could have been born with two brown eyes. That's the risk I took, because I loved him that much. As for you?" Ravenna pointed her finger at Maeve. "You will never again tell me what I can and cannot do! I wanted you to love me, so I lied. Leave, if that's what you want to do. And Skye, I never would have lied to you if I hadn't felt it absolutely necessary. Your Great Maeve over there would have taken you away from me without a second thought if she knew your father was a Christian."

"Great Maeve, is that true? Would you have taken me away from my mother?" Tears shone on Skye's face.

Maeve dropped her fork on the plate and stared at the salad. A tear fell from her green eye, wilting the lettuce, turning it brown. "I can't believe you've kept this from me all these years. So that's why Tristan traveled so much, and always worked on Wiccan holidays," she said, as if to herself.

"Yes," Ravenna said. "You would have known he wasn't Wiccan if he worshipped with us."

"Skye's half Christian," Maeve said to her plate, then looked up. "Yes, Skye, I suppose I would have taken you away. But I would have had good reason to keep you away from Christians."

"But Great Maeve, you didn't hate my father."

"I thought he was a witch, and I loved him. I never would have given him a chance if I'd known he was a Christian." Maeve wiped Skye's tears with her napkin and cupped her hands around Skye's face. "To think, all these years, my great-granddaughter has had Christian blood running through her veins."

"Great Maeve, do you still love me?"

"Yes, of course, I still love you."

Skye wrapped her arms around Maeve's neck and kissed her face. "I love you, too."

Ravenna watched the tender exchange between Skye and Maeve, her chest tightening with a mixture of relief and anguish. The truth she had guarded for so long now hung in the air, raw and exposed. Her hands trembled slightly as she gripped the edge of the table.

"Just great," Ravenna said, her voice barely above a whisper, laced with bitterness. "I've carried this secret all these years, and now you two console each other as if I'm not even here. Do you have any idea what it's been like, living in constant fear you'd take my daughter from me? Or what it was like loving a man I could never fully share with my family? And now, after all these years of me protecting you both, you embrace each other!"

"Mom, I—"

"No." Ravenna cut Skye off, holding up a hand. "You don't get to comfort me now. Not when you so easily accept Maeve's love despite knowing she would have taken you away from me." She turned to Maeve, her green eye throbbing. "And you. You claim to love Skye unconditionally, but you just admitted you would have stolen her from me if you'd known the truth. How is that love?"

Maeve's face hardened. "I was trying to protect our bloodline, our family legacy, Ravenna."

"Our legacy? The only family legacy here is your prejudice and all the prejudice before you. Tristan was an amazing man, even though he wasn't a witch. I loved him with all my heart, and he loved me. And Skye is perfect because of it, regardless of her father having been a Christian."

Ravenna's outburst left a heavy silence in its wake. She looked between Skye and Maeve, seeing the hurt and confusion in their eyes. For a moment, she regretted what she'd said, but resolve quickly replaced her remorse.

"I've spent my entire life trying to bridge two worlds to protect the people I love. And in doing that, I've lost myself. I've lost the trust of my daughter and the respect of my grandmother, the woman who raised me." Ravenna's eyes narrowed, and she pointed her finger at Maeve again. "But I won't apologize for loving him." She took a deep breath. "Now, I'll say this: I won't be making any sacrifices for anyone anymore."

Ravenna stood up from the table and made her way across the kitchen to leave, but turned to face Maeve and Skye. "And I have one more thing to say. The rumors are rumors. I didn't sleep with Chase. But I am going to dinner with him on Friday night."

WINTER

40

RAVENNA LIT A CANDLE on the altar in her meditation room and sat cross-legged in front of it. The wish wall still hadn't returned, and the silence enveloped her like a warm embrace on this cold winter night. She peered out the attic window, watching snowflakes dance, shimmering with an otherworldly light. Despite the cold outside, the silence's warmth seemed to radiate, creating an aura of healing encompassing the entire room.

A gentle tap came before the door opened a sliver. "Can I come in?" Skye said.

Ravenna nodded and glanced down to see if Skye had removed her boots.

"I took them off. Can we talk for a minute?"

Skye's voice was gentle, just like her father's had always been. This was the side of her daughter that Ravenna cherished, and had missed with an ache that pained her beyond any hurt imaginable.

"Why didn't you ever tell me Dad was a Christian?" She sat cross-legged next to Ravenna. "Didn't you trust me not to tell Great Maeve?"

"Oh, Skye, of course I trusted you, but I didn't know how you'd react with all the hatred Maeve's been feeding you all your life. And I knew at some point you'd think about it, and want to ask me what you're here to ask." Ravenna stared out the window, unable to look at Skye.

"But I have one green and one brown eye, so doesn't that mean I can do wish magic? Oh, Mom, it's all I've ever wanted to do with my life. Please tell me I'll be able to."

Ravenna pushed a teardrop away. "I don't know, Skye. I regret not telling you sooner and preparing you for the possibility that you might not be able to draw on the wish magic. Maeve has always been so fixated on the family lineage that I knew it would shatter her, and in sparing her, I've now hurt you. I'm so sorry."

"I think it would have hurt you more, Mom, to lose Maeve."

Ravenna's eyes widened. "What makes you say that?"

Skye's downcast, mismatched eyes followed her finger as she traced the ankle pentacle tattoo that Klay had taken her to get, stopping only to wipe away her own tears. "I've seen the way you look at Great Maeve, Mom. It's like . . . like you're always seeking her approval. And I know you don't have anyone else. No parents, no siblings. Just us and Great Maeve." Silence hung between them for a moment before Skye continued, her voice barely above a whisper. "Sometimes I wonder if . . . if I'm enough for you."

Ravenna's breath caught in her throat. She reached out, gently lifting Skye's chin to meet her gaze. "Oh, Skye," she said, her voice thick with sorrow. "You are more than enough. You're everything to me."

Tears welled up in Ravenna's eyes as the weight of her choice crashed down on her. "I didn't just regret not telling you sooner," she said, her voice cracking. "I've been tormented by it. Every day, watching you grow, seeing your excitement about wish magic . . . it tore me apart inside. But you're right. I was terrified of losing Maeve, of us being alone. I'm so sorry I failed you, Skye."

"I understand, Mom. You were scared."

Ravenna shook her head. "Understanding doesn't make it right, Skye. I chose to protect myself and Maeve's feelings over preparing you for the truth. I convinced myself I was protecting you." Ravenna's shoulders sagged as she continued, "I've spent so long trying to be the perfect witch, the perfect granddaughter, that I forgot the most important thing—being the mother you deserve. I put Maeve's approval above your needs, and that's not okay."

"If you tried to teach me, would we know then?" Skye lifted her head, her eyes pools of sorrow, pleading for comfort from a mother who'd let her down.

"Yes, Skye. I'd know right away."

Ravenna couldn't bear seeing Skye so heartbroken, and her thoughts drifted to thinking about dinner with Chase later in the week and her agreement with him not to do magic. She couldn't teach Skye.

"If I can't do magic, would you still choose me over Great Maeve?" Skye said.

Ravenna nodded. Holding back a sob, she whispered, "I should have made that choice a long time ago. You're my daughter, Skye. Nothing—not Maeve, not my fear of being alone, not even wish magic—is more important than you."

Skye threw her arms around her mother. And as Ravenna held her daughter, cherishing the closeness she'd been deprived of for months, she silently vowed to herself that no matter what came next, Skye would forever be with her.

41

"How do you expect me to protect you when you make the stupidest decisions of anyone I've ever known? You're like a ticking time bomb waiting to detonate, and you'll blow me up with you." Klay slammed the kitchen door behind them and dropped the buckets of sea glass on the table.

"People don't get blown up when they know a bomb is going to explode unless they want to," Ravenna said. "And be careful with those. I didn't just freeze my ass off so you could break them all."

Klay rolled his eyes and ran his hand through his hair. "That doesn't even make sense. Nothing you say or do anymore makes sense."

"I didn't tell you so that you could freak out and give me a lecture. Chase and I will be in a public restaurant, and I didn't want you to hear it from someone else."

Klay ripped his coat off and threw it over the back of a chair. "Yeah, like when you told me you were engaged to Tristan? That announcement came too late, didn't it?"

"What do you mean? Did someone else tell you before I did?"

"Never mind."

Ravenna hung her coat on the rack. "Klay Mitchell, if you have something to say, say it now."

Klay eyed the coat hooks. "Wait. Whose jacket is that? I haven't seen a man's coat in this house since Tristan lived here." His face changed from confusion back to anger. "Oh, man. I actually believed you when you said Faith lied!"

"I told you the truth."

Klay grabbed his coat from the chair. "Don't expect me to pick up the pieces of this relationship fiasco. I was there for you when Tristan died, but I won't be hanging around a second time."

"What relationship? It's just dinner. He loaned me his coat because I was cold on the beach." Ravenna shifted, trying to avoid Klay's angry gaze.

Klay opened the door to walk out. "And since when does a guy ask a woman out to dinner, and it isn't a date?"

"Um, let me think. Oh, that's right, you have. And we've eaten with your father, too."

Klay stared outside into the distance as he put his coat on.

"You know I didn't sleep with him, so what's this all about? Are you upset because you want to have dinner with me?"

"I thought you didn't want me as your friend anymore because I didn't tell you the truth about Moon."

"Close the door, Klay. Please sit down, and I'll make us some hot tea."

Ravenna set out two mugs filled with hot water, and added fresh lemon balm and mint from the magical garden. "Listen, I told Maeve and Skye the truth about Tristan. I see how much pain my lie has caused my family, when I did it all to protect them. I would have been much better off dealing with the consequences of telling the truth from the beginning. So I guess I'm saying you were right, that I thought it was okay for me to lie, but not for you. But I still wish you had told me the truth about Moon from the beginning."

"I said I was sorry, and I still am. I can't believe you told them about Tristan. I assume Maeve didn't take it well?"

Ravenna handed him one of the mugs. "Not at all, but I'm sick and tired of her hatred toward Christians. It's bad enough that she didn't realize she was talking about my late husband like that, but he was Skye's father. She needed to know Skye's half-Christian."

"And Skye?"

"She's shaken up, especially knowing she might not be able to do wish magic."

"Okay, but we always said that if she couldn't, we'd use my wish to enable her to do wish magic. Nothing's changed, has it?"

"I didn't tell Skye you'd offered because I can't do any magic right now, and that includes your wish if she needs it. No magic for her or Ashley." Ravenna plopped into the chair across from Klay.

"Ravenna, in two weeks we'll move back to the Sea Glass Apothecary, and jerkface wouldn't even hear about it until we're long gone."

"Don't you think he'd make my life hell again if he found out? He knows where I live, and I can't. Not now."

"Maeve's right. You have gone mad. What could prevent you from helping the people you love? Just tell jerkface thanks for dinner, you're all set, and the deal is over."

"Klay, come on. Things are getting better, and you want me to throw all these past months away? I won't do anything stupid, but I need to go to this dinner with him." Ravenna stared into her tea, stirring it, watching the swirl of herbs whisked against their will, uncertain of their destination. She refused to be like them anymore.

She was looking forward to dinner with Chase, but had no intention of telling Klay that.

42

"Hey Ash, I know you're busy," Ravenna said into her cell phone. "But if I were going out with a guy, and he said it was just dinner, nothing more and nothing less, what should I wear? Should I wear my regular skinny jeans and peasant shirt, or something nicer? He asked me to dinner when I was wearing them and hasn't ever seen me in anything else, really. And what about my hair? Straight like I always wear it, or should I curl it, or do an updo? Ugh! Why don't you ever answer your phone? I hate leaving messages, and I don't have much time to figure this out." Ravenna ended the call and scanned the contents of her closet.

Skye was standing at the threshold of Ravenna's bedroom. "I think you should be yourself, Mom. You always look beautiful. But what does it matter? It's not like this is a date with Reverend Wilkinson, because ministers can't date. Besides, he's not just a simple Christian like Dad was. He's like the king-Christian." Skye rolled her eyes.

"Priests can't date, but ministers can. And I don't know if this is a date, but I'm going to find out."

"Are you serious? I haven't even met this guy and don't want to. Ever. Plus, you've never dated since Dad died, so why do you need to start now? Why him? Can't we just go back to how our lives were before he came to town? He's ruined everything."

Ravenna sensed desperation in Skye's voice, laced with a struggle to understand. In a way, she was mourning the loss of the life she once knew, now facing uncertainty. "Skye, if I had it to do all over again, I wouldn't have lied to you about your father, and you would have known all along you might not be able to do wish magic. But whether or not I have dinner with Chase tonight, that won't change. We can't go back. All we can do now is move forward together."

Skye picked up Ravenna's pentacle belt buckle from her dresser and ran her hand across it. "I've always wanted one like this, and I still do. If I can't do magic, I'd rather have a father who's a witch that can't do magic either. We'd be able to celebrate the holidays together, light candles and incense, and do spells from our family's Book of Shadows, like we do now with Klay."

Ravenna knew Skye thought of Klay as a father. When Tristan had died, Klay hadn't hesitated to step up and take on the role that Skye needed filled. "All children need a mother and a father," he'd said. No matter what happened in their lives, Ravenna knew Klay and Skye's relationship would always be the same. "This is just one dinner, Skye. Nothing's changing."

"It already has."

"No, it hasn't. Klay will always be like a father to you, Skye, and if you want to live your life as a witch, then I need to go to this dinner, whether or not it's a date. Chase needs to be convinced we aren't bringing evil into this town. Please trust me?" Ravenna wrapped her arms around Skye. A wave of nostalgia swept over her. "Chase and I have been discussing our faiths, and he's trying to be open minded. I need to take every opportunity to keep building this bridge. You understand, right?"

"No, I don't. You can ignore him, and you don't have to date him to make things better for us. Give me a break."

"No, Skye. I don't, but I want to, and I'll accept whoever you choose to date, too."

Ravenna's cell phone buzzed in her back pocket.

"Go ahead, answer your phone, Mom, because I have nothing else to say. I thought I could talk to you, but obviously I can't." Skye pulled out of Ravenna's arms and left.

Ravenna hesitated, unsure what to do, and missed Ashley's call. She listened to the message.

"I hope I'm not too late. Dress like you always do, hair too. And you better tell me who this guy is that's got you all in a frenzy trying to impress him."

Ravenna groaned and threw the phone on her bed.

43

THE PARKING LOT WAS almost full. Ravenna found a spot at the far end and turned off the car. She cracked her window and breathed the crisp air that carried the scent of winter despite the unseasonably warm temperature. Ravenna took a deep breath and exhaled slowly, struggling against her pounding heart and racing thoughts. She closed her eyes, trying to calm her frazzled nerves as a whirlwind of anxiety swirled around her. A gentle tap on the window made her jump and clutch her chest. Chase stood smiling outside the car door, gesturing for her to exit. She stepped out, and their eyes met. A shiver went through her body.

"I'm sorry I scared you. I thought we could walk in together," Chase said.

"It's okay. I'm fine. I wasn't expecting you to knock on my window. I thought maybe you were already inside." Ravenna tried to ignore her warm cheeks, and handed him his coat. Chase winked, making her cheeks hotter.

They entered the restaurant nestled off the path from Marshfield Beach. Ravenna couldn't help but admire the charming, cozy atmosphere with its blend of contemporary farmhouse and rustic styles, the tables lit by flickering lanterns. The hostess led them to their table and presented menus with dishes featuring local ingredients. Ravenna noticed a separate vegetarian menu.

"I reserved this table because I thought you'd appreciate the view," Chase said.

Ravenna looked out the window and saw a winding brook surrounded by trees. The fading sun cast a warm glow, making it appear like the trees dripped honey.

"Do you come here often?" Ravenna said.

"No, but I've heard great things about the place, so I came to see it earlier in the week and reserved this table."

"Do you like the view, too?"

"Of course. I appreciate the natural world just like you, only I don't worship it."

"I don't know if I'd say that I worship nature, but more that the Goddess lives in and through all things. She's energy that's everywhere."

"Even in this table?"

"Yes, and in this rose." Ravenna picked up the bud vase from the table and placed it down quickly to hide the nervous tremor in her hand.

Chase studied the flower, then lifted his gaze to Ravenna, causing her heart to leap into her throat. She didn't think she could sit across from him for five more minutes, never mind an entire meal. The waitress took their orders, returning with a beer for Chase and white wine for Ravenna.

"So why did you ask me to join you here?"

Chase lifted the jacket from the seat next to him. "Because you had to return my jacket, right?"

"Sure, because I couldn't have returned it to you at the church."

Chase shifted between her brown and green eyes as if unsure which to settle on, exposing the slightest hint of insecurity that made her smile into her wine glass.

"You were so upset when I found you at the beach, and I wanted you to know I'm aware of the rumor Faith's been spreading."

Ravenna felt her face and neck burn with embarrassment. "I never would have let you in my home if I knew—"

"Knew what, that Faith would do anything to scare you away from me? I hope she won't stop you from inviting me in again, because I only saw the kitchen. I still have the rest of the house to see. I need to settle my curiosity." Chase flashed a smile powerful enough to light up the candlelit restaurant, radiating a gentle kindness.

Ravenna couldn't help but bask in its warmth until the waitress served their dishes. They had piled her plate high with rice noodles, grilled vegetables, and a cashew cream sauce. She inhaled, and the combination of the food and Chase's musky cologne smelled tantalizing. Only then did she realize Chase had also ordered a vegetarian meal, a thick black bean and sweet potato burger with a side salad. "There were so many choices on the menu. You didn't have to order vegetarian."

"I wouldn't want to offend you, Lady Ravenna. And I'm thrilled with my choice."

Ravenna reached for her fork, and a strange tingling pulsed through her fingers. The room shifted and blurred, and she struggled to breathe through a combination of nervousness and attraction. She looked up and caught him watching her with an intensity that made her stomach twist, but she forced herself to continue the conversation. "You told me you have no interest in Faith. Why?"

"Why did I tell you, or why do I have no interest in her?"

Ravenna felt another flush of heat on her face. She wasn't sure she wanted the answer to either question, but chose the latter. "Why no interest in Faith? She's going through an awful lot to get your attention. She's a Christian and wants, how should I say it . . . to make you happy? Wouldn't any guy want that?"

"Maybe any guy who doesn't also want the heart of a woman," Chase said. His eyes followed the movement of Ravenna's hand, and she realized she'd started stroking the length of her hair in an attempt to calm herself.

"Is that why you're not married? Because no woman has given you her heart?"

"I'm not married because I've been so focused on fixing a past wrong-doing that I couldn't accept a woman's love."

"But you can now?"

"More than you know, Lady Ravenna." Chase half smiled and took a bite of his burger. "So tell me, why have you stopped coming to services?"

"Because I'll be leaving your church soon."

"Oh?"

"I meant to tell you. My shop will be ready in two weeks, so I'll be doing magic again soon. And don't worry, I'll take my cell phone and the waves with me." Ravenna wondered if Chase had ever believed her about the noise of the wish wall. It didn't matter. She just hoped it would leave with her.

"I see. Just when I'd gotten used to having you around. But that doesn't explain why you've already stopped coming to services. I'd hoped you'd still consider joining us on Sundays after you return to your apothecary. In fact, I quite expect it. And I also expect you to continue not doing any magic." Chase's sharp gaze pierced through the air, landing with unwavering confidence.

"What did you just say? Are you telling me I can't do magic in my shop?"

"That's right."

Ravenna's anger grew like waves crashing against her mind, threatening to drown her. She'd kept good on her bargain, and now Chase demanded more. She wondered how she could have ever trusted him, and wanted to lash out, to scream at him. But she knew she couldn't, not if she wanted to help Skye and Ashley.

"How much longer?" she demanded. "How long will you pull your strings to control me and prevent me from living my life?"

"As long as it takes for my congregation and the community to believe you're a Christian."

"What? Why do they need to believe that?"

"So I can continue dating you."

Ravenna's anger subsided abruptly, replaced by disbelief. She didn't know whether to believe him. What if all this was a hoax to manipulate her out of doing magic? Ravenna's hand shook, and her wine glass wobbled and fell. It broke on the table, creating a small waterfall cascading onto her lap, soaking her jeans. She jumped out of her seat, and Chase motioned for a waitress who appeared within seconds to help clean the mess.

"I'm sorry. I don't know how that happened." Ravenna attempted to pick up a piece of broken glass.

Chase grabbed her hand and squeezed it gently. "It's only a spill," he said, and stared into her eyes. She paused, her stomach fluttering, feeling light-headed. His words might as well have been "It's only a spell," because his energy was tugging at her, pulling her toward him, away from all rational thought. And in that moment, she believed it wasn't about the magic at all, but about a Christian minister who wanted a witch.

Ravenna snapped out of it when her cell phone rang. It was Skye, and she always answered when Skye called. "It's my daughter, and I have to answer it," Ravenna said, pulling herself together. She walked quickly toward the restaurant's entrance for better cell service and privacy.

"It's Ashley. Skye told me where you were and gave me her phone because she knew you'd answer it."

"Is Skye okay? Is something wrong?"

"Yes, something's wrong, but it's not Skye. It's you. Are you freaking serious? Get the hell out of that restaurant and away from Chase, now. I love you, Ravenna, but the man is out to get you, and I'll prove it. Meet me tomorrow at his church an hour before it opens."

"But Ash, that's low tide and—"

"I don't care what you say to him, but get out of that restaurant now, and meet me tomorrow morning. Got it?"

"Yes. I'll meet you to prove you're wrong, and get you all off my ass."

Ravenna ended the call and returned to the table. "I'm so sorry. I know we're at an awkward moment, but I need to leave because there's an emergency with my daughter. Another time, okay?"

"Of course, your daughter comes first. Let me know if I can do anything."

Ravenna reached into her bag and pulled out some cash.

"Please, I'll take care of it, so long as you promise we can finish a meal together sometime," Chase said and winked.

Ravenna wanted to finish this meal, but she had to prove to Ashley that Chase wasn't trying to hurt her, that he genuinely wanted to have a relationship. Or maybe she just needed to prove it to herself.

44

AT FIVE O'CLOCK THE following morning, Ravenna and Ashley entered the church's unlit hallway.

"This place is eerier than I thought, especially in the dark," Ashley said.

Ravenna turned on a light.

"Are you crazy? Shut that light off. Can Chase see inside the church from his parsonage?" Ashley slammed down the light switch.

"How would I know? Maybe through that window." Ravenna pointed to a window down the hall. "What are you worried about, though? He knows Klay and I come to work early sometimes."

"It's better he doesn't suspect you could have been in his office today, just in case we don't leave things the way they were."

"What? You didn't tell me you wanted to snoop around Chase's office!"

Ashley held a finger to her lips. "Shh. Keep your voice down. And not me. We."

"Look around, Ash. There's no one here, and I'm not going to invade his personal space. Come on, this is crazy."

"It's not personal space, or we'd be in the parsonage, rummaging through his t-shirts and underwear. But I'm telling you right now, if nothing turns up here, that's next. I'll prove to you he's got it out for you."

"Ash, I think you're being paranoid." Ravenna walked into her apothecary. Ashley followed, holding Ravenna's arm for balance.

"Yeah, you're damn right I'm paranoid. Have you already forgotten about the crowd who came after you at the Annual Wish Festival, and every other awful thing that's happened since Chase came to town? You're a witch, Ravenna, and you realize Christians hanged, drowned, and burned millions of you at the stake, right?"

"Of course I know that, but this is the twenty-first century. People don't kill witches anymore."

"Maybe not, but Christians aren't accepting of them either, and Chase has plenty of influence to make your life hell. But I don't need to tell you that, do I? We don't have much time, so where's his office?"

The waves on the wish wall in the apothecary room roared to life. Ravenna knew they heard Ashley's voice and were ready for Ravenna's healing magic. With each passing second, they grew louder.

"Come on, Ravenna, we need to get out of here before the waves give us away."

"Even if I told you where his office is, how will we get inside?"

Ashley pulled a hairpin from her pocket and held it close to Ravenna's eyes, grinning. "Do you know how often I've forgotten my key and locked myself out of my café? MS affects your memory, too, so I'm always prepared." Ashley dimmed her cell phone's flashlight and wobbled down the hallway. "Now, where's his office? Tell me, or I'll find it myself."

"Fine!" Ravenna grabbed Ashley's arm and helped steady her while walking to Chase's office, thinking there was no way Ashley could unlock the door. Then she'd give up on this nonsense for a while, at least until she concocted another foolish idea. But within seconds of standing at Chase's office door, Ashley had it unlocked and opened.

"Okay, that's enough. Close the door, and let's get out of here." Ravenna bounced on her toes. "I'm not comfortable doing this."

"Get out of here? No way. I'm proving this guy wants you hanged so that you'll get over him fast. I'm searching with or without you, Ravenna. So, are you with me?" Ashley's lips pursed, and she folded her arms across her body, waiting for an answer. "Decide already. We don't have all day."

"You're wrong, Ashley. So, yeah, I'll do this to prove it to you."

"Awesome. Get in. Close the door and lock it. Keep your flashlight as low as possible. You look through the desk drawers, and I'll look through the filing cabinet."

"What are we looking for?"

"I don't know, but something will prove Chase is on a witch hunt."

Ravenna didn't believe it. She pretended to rummage through Chase's desk drawers while Ashley opened a filing cabinet. His cologne permeated the room, clinging to every handle, drawer, and paper. She opened folders without looking at the words inside and sank her face into the centers, inhaling the intoxicating scent. She wished Chase was there with her, alone in his office, so they could drink in each other's scent until the moonlight receded, giving way to the early morning sun.

"Damn it . . . nothing here," Ashley said after thumbing through the last filing cabinet drawer.

Ravenna smiled. "And nothing here either. Can we go now?"

Ashley eyed the framed photos strewn across the far table and moved in to get a closer look. "Wait a minute. Who are these people in the photos, and who's this?" She shined her flashlight on the photo of a young boy, a woman, and a man wearing a suit, his face riddled with scars. She picked it up from the table to show Ravenna.

"I've seen it before. What about it?"

Ashley turned the frame and examined the back. "Nothing's written here. I wonder who it is. The man's much older than the woman."

"Come on, Ash, who cares? Put it down."

"Wait. I want to—"

Ravenna grabbed the photo to put it back on the table, but Ashley wouldn't let go. They tugged it back and forth until Ashley lost her balance. Ravenna grabbed her arm to prevent her from falling, dropping the picture to the floor where the glass broke. "Oh, shit! Let's clean it up. Put the photo back on the table, Ash. Hopefully, Chase won't notice it's broken for a long time."

"Wait. Look. What's that?" Ashley pointed to a small piece of folded paper on the floor next to the photo. "It must have come out of the frame."

Ravenna picked it up, shook off the broken glass, and opened it. As she read the words on the page, her heart pounded with such force it hurt her chest, making it difficult to breathe. Her body trembled, and short, shallow breaths made her dizzy. She collapsed backward against the table, sending more photos crashing to the floor. Ravenna leaned against the table's edge, staring at the paper, shaking her head.

"Ravenna? What does it say?"

She handed it to Ashley.

To Whom It May Concern,

Look to the Greenes of Plymbury if another Christian or I meet an extraordinary fate involving fire. There you will find your answer. And as the Good Lord has instructed by his holy word, do not let the witch live.

Praise be to our Lord, Christ Jesus. Amen!
Reverend Chase Wilkinson

Photo: Reverend Andrew Boyle (my grandfather), Francine Boyle-Wilkinson (my mother), and me, Chase Wilkinson (four years old).
Date of Note: March of the year I became minister at Living Waters Church in Plymbury, Massachusetts.

"That date's two months before the fire at the Annual Wish Festival. I knew he was out to get you . . . but kill you? What's this all about? Ravenna?" Ashley flashed the dim cell phone light in Ravenna's face, waking her from her trance. "I know this is shocking, but you've got to snap out of this. The church opens in five minutes, and we need to get out of here."

Ashley took a photo of the letter and dropped it on the floor with the rest of the mess. "Be careful. There's glass everywhere."

Ravenna stomped on the glass hard with her boot's heels, crushing it with vengeful anger as water welled in her eyes and flowed down her face. With each smash, the sound of shattering glass grew louder. Ravenna relished crushing it, taking out her frustrations, and punishing the glass for her foolish, naïve heart. She stomped harder and harder until Ashley grabbed her arm.

"Stop! Shh! You're too loud. Listen."

Ravenna focused, listening while trying to control her sobs. Faith's heels clicked down the hallway with an additional pair of footsteps.

Barbara's voice in the hallway was clear inside the office. "Here's the key, sweetheart. He'll be so happy to see you."

Ashley pointed to a door next to a bookcase. It was their only chance of not being discovered. Ravenna struggled to regain her composure through labored breathing. They tiptoed quickly across the glass-littered floor. The sound of their feet seemed to echo through the room. A key inserted into the office doorknob signaled that they were running out of time. Ravenna glanced behind her shoulder while turning the knob next to the bookcase. It opened. She and Ashley slipped inside the closet and shut the door. Ravenna held her breath and listened through the door over the beating of her racing heart.

"Mom. Mom, get in here now. Mom. Now!"

"Oh, my," Barbara said.

"Who would do this and how? Don't you have the only other key to Chase's office?"

"Yes, and when I came in this morning, it was right where I'd left it in my office. I'd better let the pastor know."

"Okay, I'll stay here and clean up."

Ravenna heard glass being pushed around and things being placed on the table. They needed to get out of the closet. She glanced at her cell phone to be sure it was on silent, then texted Klay: YOU CANNOT TEXT ME BACK! Ashley and I are hiding in a closet in Chase's office. Faith is here, cleaning a mess on the floor. We need help getting out. I'll explain later. HELP!

Ravenna heard someone walk into the office and hoped it was Klay.

"What are you doing in my office, Faith? And what happened to my pictures?" Chase said.

"I don't know, but I thought I'd help clean up."

"Please move away from those pictures and leave my office."

"Oh, I don't mind. I'm happy to help."

Ravenna heard someone else walk in.

"Whoa, what happened in here, and who was the guy bolting out of the building?" Klay said.

"What guy?" Chase said.

"I don't know. It was a guy I'd never seen before. He just ran out of the building and into the parking lot. If you hurry, maybe you can catch him. You too, Faith. You never know. Maybe you're enough to stop him."

"Yes, of course," Faith said.

Ravenna heard Faith's shoes speeding down the hallway.

Klay opened the closet door. "They're gone, but not for long. Hurry and head to the ladies' room. I'll text when the coast is clear, but you have a lot of explaining to do." Klay headed toward the apothecary.

Ravenna and Ashley went in the opposite direction to the ladies' room.

RAVENNA GRABBED TISSUES FROM a stall and wiped her leaking eyes.

"That was close. Smart thinking to send Klay a message to help us," Ashley said.

"I can't believe I fell for him. I thought he cared about me." Ravenna stared at a small hole in the wall. "He lied to me all along and planned to destroy my family. How could I be so stupid?"

"If you're stupid, I hate to think about what I am. No guy is worse than Jason, and I married the asshole. Maybe I should have searched Chase's office alone. I'm sorry," Ashley said.

"I need to pack and get out of here, now." Ravenna splashed cold water on her face and tapped it dry with a paper towel. She finger-combed her hair and took a deep breath. "Let's go."

"We can't leave this bathroom until Klay texts, and you're not moving the apothecary for two more weeks. Got it? The last thing you want is Chase to suspect you."

"Ugh!" Ravenna clenched her fists. She didn't know if she could stay in Chase's church for two more weeks, not after seeing that note. She wanted to confront him and get answers to the questions burning inside her, but Ashley was right. For two weeks, she needed to stay and avoid Chase.

Ashley held Ravenna's shoulders and looked deep into her eyes. "You can do this. Ravenna. You've been here for months, so two more weeks won't change anything except that he won't suspect it was you snooping around his office."

"Then what? What happens in two weeks? So I move out and into my apothecary, but I still need to keep my family safe."

Ashley took a deep breath and sighed. "Promise you won't do anything until we discuss this, please?"

Ravenna's phone vibrated with a message from Klay: Hurry! You only have about three minutes.

"Let's go. Send me the picture you took of the note," Ravenna said.

Ashley hugged Ravenna. "I will."

"Hey, Ash? Thanks for preventing me from making the biggest mistake of my life, even if it hurts like hell."

Ravenna opened the door, and they stepped into the empty hallway.

45

THE CHURCH HAD A quiet melancholy aura, like someone had died, and people whispered in the hallway about what had happened earlier in Chase's office. They said the pastor had run after a man, but he'd disappeared into the marshes long before Chase laid eyes on him, and Chase had locked himself in his office ever since.

Ravenna was leaving her ninth voicemail for Maeve. "I get it. You're mad at me. I lied to you, and you've been avoiding me, but I need to talk to you. Please, Maeve, call me or come to the church or something."

Ravenna texted Skye. *Can you text Great Maeve and tell her I need to talk with her? It's important, and she'll answer you.*

A return text appeared from Ashley with a picture of the note from Chase's office. *Skye asked me to text you. Maeve's out of town. Something about a witch convention, and she won't be available until she returns.*

Ravenna felt her stomach clench. *When will she be back?*

She wouldn't say.

Who wouldn't say? Maeve, or Skye?

Maeve.

Ravenna handed her cell phone to Klay. "This is just great. I'm a sitting duck, afraid for my life, and Maeve is off flying on her broomstick with a bunch of witches. Here's the note that was behind the picture."

"What were the two of you thinking going into jerkface's office alone?" Klay said in a loud whisper.

"It was Ashley's idea, and I didn't think we'd find anything, but now I regret not properly looking at any of the folders inside his desk."

Klay studied the phone, pinch-zooming the words and scanning the handwritten text. He scrolled back up, rereading as if he couldn't believe what he'd seen, then lowered the phone and frowned. "I don't think you need anything more than this."

"What should I do?"

"I knew that asshole was up to something, and it's really serious. How could he have known the fire in the apothecary would happen, and how did his grandfather get burned? It couldn't have been the day in your shop, because this photo was taken a long time ago."

"I know. I need to talk to Maeve. I remember Moon telling me she was keeping something from me when my shop burned down, and I have to ask her what it was. It might be connected. She might know something."

"Wait a minute, now something else makes sense—"

"Shh! Someone's in the hallway, and I don't want them listening to us." Ravenna moved closer to the doorway and heard Ava and Barbara talking.

"I'm not here to see Reverend Wilkinson. I'm here to see Ravenna," Ava said.

Ravenna glanced at Klay, and he shrugged his shoulders.

"Fine, but if I see you going further down that hallway, I'm coming after you. The first person in the minister's office today will be Faith," Barbara said. "After all, she is a sight for sore eyes."

Ava moved closer to Ravenna's room. "Sure thing. I'm sure Faith's all he's thinking about right now," she called back to Barbara, who was standing guard in the hallway.

Ravenna wasn't in the mood for company, but pulled herself together for Ava's visit.

"I'm sure Chase would rather see anyone but Faith right now," Ava said more to herself and laughed. "Can you believe what happened to Chase's office this morning? Why would anyone go to the trouble of breaking in to destroy family portraits?"

"Religion's separated families for centuries, and I'm sure ministers make plenty of enemies." Klay stood behind Ravenna and nudged her back. "Don't you agree?"

"Yes. It's unfortunate. So what can I do for you, Ava?"

Ava grabbed Ravenna's arm and closed the door. "I have to tell you something important."

"What if a customer comes?"

"Listen, some women from the prayer group met today to pray for Chase and what happened this morning, so I joined them. They said you've brought the devil into this church, and what happened to Chase is only the beginning. They were praying against you, Lady Ravenna."

"It's all in their heads. I don't even believe in the devil."

"I know. You don't have to tell me that. But I had my blue sea glass with me, and you were right because it gave me the strength to say what I had to. I led the next prayer against the evil of rumors, foolish accusations, and people who would rather harm their neighbor instead of love them. Then I lifted you in prayer for protection from people who can't see the evil that lives inside them. That broke the prayer group up pretty fast."

"Wow, you did that for me?"

"Yes, because I know your heart, and I'd hate to see it wrapped in a hard shell because people couldn't see the truth."

"Thank the Goddess," Klay said. " If I were a Christian, I'd drop an amen right now, but I'm not."

Ravenna shed a tear from her green eye and hugged Ava. "Thank you, and especially for being a genuine friend."

"I should have spoken up sooner, but I'm glad I finally did. I just wanted you to know."

Klay opened the door and ushered Ava out. "Thanks, Ava, but I'll have to ask you to go now, because we have a business to run." He waited for the outside door to close. "I thought she'd never leave."

"That was abrupt, considering she stood up for me against a bunch of nasty women."

"You have bigger things to worry about than those women, and I wanted to tell you this before we got interrupted."

"Tell me what?"

"Okay, it's another lie I kept from you." Klay blocked the doorway. "But before you get all mad at me and run, please hear me out."

Ravenna folded her arms across her chest. "I don't think I can take much more today, so please don't crush me any more than I already have been."

"I'll do my best. Maeve came to my house months ago."

"Why would she go to your house?"

"She said she had a dream we'd had a new litter of puppies and wanted to see them. We always have puppies, so it didn't seem so strange. Okay, her being at our house was, but the dream wasn't. You know what I mean."

"What happened?"

"Nina, the mom, is very protective of her babies, so we said she'd have to wait until they weaned, but she refused and marched right through the house to their pen. Nina growled at her, but Maeve looked into her eyes, and that dog mellowed like I'd never seen. Then she picked up a pup and told Dad and me he was your new familiar, and to make sure you take him because she wanted you protected."

"Was that the pup you brought me that day?"

"Yes."

Ravenna walked to the window on the far side of the room and gazed out at the bare weeping willow. Its snow-covered, heavy and overburdened branches drooped to the ground, twisted, like her tangled emotions.

"Do you still have him?"

"We were waiting for a good time to ask you again to adopt him, but I'm not asking. I don't know what Maeve knows, but she's right. You need protection."

"Bring him to my house after dinner tonight."

46

RAVENNA LEFT ANOTHER VOICE message for Maeve. "Okay, you win. Klay is coming here with the dog, and I've already named him Jet. So why a dog, and what's so special about this one? I'm sure any dog would have protected me."

She paced, wondering if her house was big enough for a large dog like a Doberman, and if Jet would be happy. Ravenna gazed out the living room window; the yard was big enough, and the beach was only a few hundred feet away. But inside was small and cluttered with herbs, sea glass, and other witchy trinkets. Ravenna contemplated the best places for his bowls, bed, toys, and leash. She settled on hammering a nail on the left side of the kitchen door frame, draped the leash over it, and placed the food and water bowls beneath it. She was sure Jet would take over the house, but still hadn't decided if she'd let him sleep in her bed or confine him to the living room.

"Mom, you look nervous," Skye said.

Ravenna realized she was biting her fingernails. "I'm fine. I've never had a dog before, and I'm not sure I know how to take care of one."

"Did you ever have a kid before me?" Skye put her hands on her hips. "No, and you figured it out. Right?"

"The most challenging part about raising you was during the months you didn't talk and couldn't tell me what was wrong. They still are, except now it's your choice."

"Maybe I am telling you what's wrong, but you're choosing not to listen, and Jet can speak in his own dog way. If you listen, you might understand."

"You're not making this any easier for me."

"I didn't know I was supposed to. I can't wait to see him when I get home from work tonight."

When Skye left, Ravenna entered the kitchen and caught a whiff of the dog food she'd set out. She thought about how different it smelled from cat food, how much she still missed Moon, and what it would be like living with a dog she couldn't talk to mind to mind.

Fifteen minutes later, she heard the crunch of tires on the clam shells of the driveway and took a deep breath.

Klay held the puppy at the kitchen door, whimpering and wriggling. "He's trying to get to you, Ravenna."

She lifted her hand to Jet's face and placed two fingers on his head. "I'm afraid to pat him, because I don't want to hurt his taped ears."

Jet pushed his wet nose into Ravenna's hand.

"Don't worry. His ears healed weeks ago. They're only taped now to teach them to point up instead of drooping down, and I'll retape them every couple of weeks until they learn to stay up."

Ravenna moved her face close to Jet and looked into his amber eyes. "But doesn't his ears being taped bother him? Who cares if they flop?"

They don't bother me, Jet said and licked Ravenna's face.

Ravenna pulled back, thinking she imagined hearing Jet talk to her. "Did you hear that?"

Klay shrugged his shoulders. "Hear what?"

I want them taped because when they stand up, I'll look fierce like my dad. Jet let out a growl.

"Jet, no. Don't growl," Klay said. "I'm sorry, but we can train him not to growl at you."

"Leave him alone. He told me what he'll be like when he's more like his dad."

"Good one, Ravenna. You can't let him growl at you like that. He needs to be trained to know what's acceptable and unacceptable behavior."

"Klay, I didn't make that up. He's talking to me."

"That's not possible. He's a dog. One of my dogs, and trust me, they don't talk."

Ravenna scooped Jet from Klay's arms and sat in a chair. She petted his back and kissed his face while Jet licked hers.

I knew you'd love me as much as I loved you the day I first saw you, Jet said. He rested his head on Ravenna's shoulder. *I was sad when you said you didn't want me, but every night I dreamed you'd come back for me.*

As Jet spoke, Ravenna felt their bond strengthen, like vines intertwining, wrapping themselves around her heart and mind. As their connection grew, Ravenna's head filled with pure white light, easing the ache of losing Moon, and her magic surged to life, crackling and sparking around them like lightning. Tears streamed down Ravenna's face, falling onto Jet's glossy black fur, shining with a mystical blue glow. It lifted from his fur like wisps of smoke, enveloping them in a shimmering cocoon. Ravenna knew she and Jet were bound as one, their souls interwoven into an unbreakable tapestry of love and magic.

Oh, Jet. How could I not have known? Ravenna hugged and kissed Jet. She didn't want to let him go. *I love you, Jet.*

"Was that smoke what I think it was?" Klay said.

"Yes, Klay. You and your father bred my familiar. Maeve knew it all along, but she didn't tell me because I wouldn't have listened then."

"Whoa! I can't believe it." Klay laughed and petted Jet. "Hey, little guy, you have a lot of responsibility, but for now, let's get you fierce, just like your dad."

Jet let out a low growl and licked Ravenna's face.

47

Ravenna squatted in front of Jet, making eye contact so he would pay attention. *When we go inside the church, walk close to the office wall and under the windows because I don't want the secretary to see you, okay?*

Ravenna had managed to avoid Chase for the past two weeks and she didn't want to have a run-in with him today. That was all she needed, to have Barbara cause a scene that would bring Chase running.

Why? Jet said.

Let's just say that technically, you're not supposed to be here, but we'll be leaving soon.

Why?

My shop is being fixed, so I work here for now.

Why?

Because I didn't have anywhere else to go.

Why?

Ravenna laughed and stroked the side of Jet's face. *You're a typical toddler full of endless questions. A man works here, and I think he wants to hurt me. I was hoping you could pick up on his scent and tell me more.*

Jet raised his head and pushed out his chest, commanding attention and respect. He focused and readied himself until he caught sight of Klay in the parking lot and ran toward him, jumping with excitement.

"Hey, Jet. Sit. Good boy." Klay petted Jet, showing him the same enthusiasm. "I know you've never had a dog, Ravenna, but you're supposed to hold the leash."

Ravenna took the leash from Klay. "Well, I wasn't expecting him to just take off."

"It looks like I need to train you both."

They walked inside, and Jet followed his instructions. Ravenna caught Barbara looking into the hallway, then standing with a raised eyebrow, eyeing below the windows. Klay waved, but Barbara flew out of the office before he put his hand down.

"I knew I saw you holding a leash. Oh!" Barbara pushed herself flat against the wall and froze. "Is that . . . a . . . a Doberman?"

"He's only a pup. Couldn't hurt a fly at this age," Klay said.

Yes, I could. Jet let out a growl toward Barbara.

"Help," Barbara said in a low cry and gulped. "Somebody . . . please . . . help . . . me."

Jet, don't growl at her. Remember, I didn't want her to see you, and now you've scared her, Ravenna said.

But—

No excuses. Be nice to her.

Jet whimpered.

"See, Barbara, he's just a pup. He didn't mean to scare you," Klay said and petted Jet's head.

Barbara crept toward her office with her back against the wall, her eyes fixed on Jet. "Get him out of the building." She slipped into the office and slammed the door. Ravenna heard the lock turn. Barbara pointed at Jet through the windows and then to the church door. Then she scrambled to her desk and picked up her cell phone.

"Should I take him home?" Ravenna said.

"Just ignore her. What's she going to do, call the police? I can hear it now. Hello, Plymbury Police? I have a dog in my church, and I need him arrested for growling at me. Oh, he's just a puppy, and there aren't any signs anywhere that say no dogs allowed, but I don't want him here. Oh. Yes, sir. I understand you're not an animal control officer," Klay said and laughed.

"How do you know? Maybe that's who she's calling."

"If he shows up, I'll talk to him."

Ravenna jumped when the door to the church opened, and Ava walked in.

"Oh, look how cute that puppy is with his ears all taped up," Ava said. "Is he friendly?" She didn't wait for an answer, but knelt to pet his head.

Barbara cracked open the office door and pinched her lips into the opening. "Stay away from that dog. He's vicious and just growled at me. He would have torn my arm off if I didn't make it into my office in time!"

Jet licked Ava's face. *She's nice. I like her.*

"He doesn't seem so vicious to me. You're a sweet boy, aren't you? Is he yours, Ravenna? Since when do witches have dogs? I thought they only had cats."

"Don't believe everything the media tells you," Klay said.

The church door opened again, and Faith walked in. "Why is that ferocious beast still here? He almost killed my mother. Get out of my way. I need to get to the office and see if she's okay."

"Be careful, Faith. He's a killer," Barbara said.

Ravenna led Jet toward the apothecary, watching Faith hustle into the office as fast as she could on five-inch heels.

Why are they lying about me?

Sometimes people don't want to know the truth because it frightens them, and a lie is like a false flicker of light they think will ward off the scary shadows.

I'm not afraid of the dark. Jet stood tall.

I'm not either, Jet. Not anymore.

"Let's get into the apothecary and start packing," Klay said. "Thanks for offering to help, Ava."

"Why not? One of my steady volunteer gigs wanted to hire new people, so now I have much more time during the day."

"Will you look for another volunteer job?" Ravenna said.

"Sure, but I'd like to help you over the next week or two until you get settled in your new . . . well, old place, if you'll let me."

"Sure. That would be . . ."

Everyone stopped talking when Chase walked past. He went into the office to speak with Barbara and Faith.

"I know you didn't want to be disturbed, pastor, but there's a vicious dog in here," Barbara said.

"He almost killed my mother," Faith said.

"Well, you look fine to me, Barbara."

"Yes, I got away within an inch of my life, because it was growling and baring its teeth, ready to tear me apart. You'll have it removed from the building, right?"

"Now, why would I do that? All seems quiet now, and if you stay in your office where you're supposed to be, there won't be any more problems."

"You're going to leave a witch with a vicious dog in our church? I think you should turn around and go tell her to remove that beast, and not bring it here again," Barbara said.

"Mom, it looks like the pastor is burdened with something much more pressing. Reverend Wilkinson, could you ask her to take him home?"

"I think you should both leave Lady Ravenna alone. She'll be moving out soon enough."

"Praise Jesus," Barbara said.

"Now, if you'll excuse me, I need to get back to work," Chase said.

Ravenna eyed Faith marching down the hallway, following Chase to his office. Barbara slammed the office door.

Could you smell his scent, Jet?

Yes. I got it.

Ravenna petted Jet's head.

"That's odd. Jerkface would have looked for any excuse to make your life difficult. Why not this time?" Klay said.

"Maybe he's afraid of dogs," Ava said and giggled.

"Wish I knew. I would have brought one here weeks ago," Klay said. He picked up cardboard boxes with bubble wrap inside and handed them to Ava and Ravenna.

Ravenna packed away her jewelry repair tools, but Chase's odd behavior lingered in her mind. He'd deliberately tried to distance himself from her, which made her yearn to see him even more. She knew she needed to stay far away from him, but even after two weeks of avoiding him she couldn't help pining for the mystery of his presence and the excitement of his allure.

48

Ravenna scanned the church shop, where she'd sold a piece of sea glass jewelry to the worship leader's wife just yesterday. It wasn't until now, when she was packed and ready to leave the church, that Ravenna realized how many allies she'd made. Sure, some still turned their noses up and treated her like the devil incarnate, but most had accepted her and had expressed how much they'd wished she could stay. They offered their help and well wishes, promising to visit her at the Sea Glass Apothecary.

Except Chase.

Ravenna hadn't spoken to Chase since their dinner at The Lantern, and wondered if he could know she was the one who had broken into his office. She thought he would have confronted her about it if he knew, but he hadn't.

Klay and Ava returned from the car, talking and laughing.

"We've packed everything. Well, except for that." Klay pointed to the material in front of the wish wall that still hadn't vacated the room.

"Oh, I'll take care of that for you," Ava said and reached for the cloth.

Klay grabbed her hand just before she pulled it down. "Let's bring everything from the room behind the sanctuary back here first, because Ravenna promised she would."

"There isn't much in there. We sold most of it during the church's summer fair, and new donations will start rolling in soon. They'll store those in this room now that you're leaving."

"Ava, could I have a minute alone with Klay?" Ravenna said.

"Secret business talk, huh? I'll be waiting outside." Ava stepped out.

"What should we do about the wall? We can't leave the cloth, but if we take it down, anyone who comes in will see it," Ravenna said.

"Let's think about this. Oh, I know. How about we don't give two shits if they see it? We're out of here, and the wall will leave when it's ready."

"Klay, I've worked too hard to have these people turn on me now." Ravenna peeked behind the cloth, confirming that the wish wall was still there. "I'm excited to return to my shop, but I can't do anything that will cause Chase to turn people against me again."

"Does that include not doing magic anymore?"

"Chase asked me not to do magic when I returned to my shop, so I don't want to change anything about the plan until I talk with him."

"You're going to continue to let this asshole run your life?"

Ravenna felt herself burning from the inside out and knew Klay could see the hives beginning to crawl across her face and chest. She took a deep breath to calm herself, thinking about what he'd said. No one was controlling her. She had her own life, and for the first time, she was living it. Ravenna fixed her gaze on Klay, and spoke with a steady, unwavering voice. "Let me make perfectly clear that Chase is not controlling my life. I'm choosing not to do the magic, and to have Christian friends."

"You're compromising who you are to have friends who only accept you if you're more like them?"

"Klay, I've let others tell me who I am my whole life. Now I'm giving myself the freedom to figure it out myself."

"How is not doing magic figuring it out?" Klay clenched his fists.

"I have no pressure. No one expects anything from me, and I don't have to wear the weight of everyone else's problems on my shoulders every day."

"So you're saying you'd rather be selfish than help people?"

"I'm saying I'd rather not be who everyone else wants me to be. Including you."

"You can never change, Ravenna, no matter how hard you try. Witchcraft runs in your blood, and your insides will always ache to do magic."

Ravenna stilled herself, listening to the whispers of her inner being, feeling the familiar surge of energy within her. She couldn't deny the truth of her heritage. No matter how hard she tried to ignore it, magic did pulse through her with an insistent beat. Yet, for the first time, she wasn't yearning to awaken it. She preferred the stillness, the quietness, and with Jet by her side, she knew a sense of peace again. Her head was no longer empty, and her body felt whole again. It was enough.

"Klay, you've given me all I need in Jet. He fills the emptiness and balances the restlessness of my magic, and no one else ever has to know he's magical. Let me try this my way."

49

Ravenna and Jet strolled along the seashore on an unseasonably warm December day. The snow had melted, and the ocean water shimmered like liquid crystals under the sun. Jet caught sight of a seagull swooping to snag the contents of a washed-up clam and bolted toward it, barking and tugging his leash.

No, Jet!

He looked back and returned to heel at Ravenna's side, making her appreciate all the time Klay had spent training him. After three miles, they approached the crossover to leave, and Ravenna spotted Faith in the distance, wearing a tie-dye scarf twisted into a sleek dress crisscrossed at her neck around a wide, flat gold necklace under an unzipped Canada Goose parka. Faith's elegance shone like a quahog glistening in the sun. But Ravenna knew that beneath her striking appearance lay a hollow emptiness, like the aftermath of birds picking away at a clam, leaving nothing but an empty shell.

Faith leaned against a post with a grin wider than the ocean. "They accepted the offer," she said into her cell phone. "I'm tied up right now, but I'll come by later this afternoon with the paperwork for the purchase and sale agreement."

Faith glanced over her shoulder as Chase approached her from behind.

Ravenna moved to the far left side of the crosswalk with Jet, hoping they wouldn't notice her.

"All set? I reserved a table for us," Chase said.

"More than all set."

If Ravenna could have seen Faith's eyelashes, she knew they'd be batting at Chase.

A man stopped twenty feet in front of Ravenna on his way to the beach. "Wow, a Doberman. You don't see those every day. Clipped ears, too, and with an evil witch." He spoke in a loud bass voice, and circled as wide as he could around them. Ravenna just wanted the man to pass without calling more attention to her.

"You better hold that leash tight, because I'm suing you if he bites." He pointed a scornful finger at Jet. "It looks like you used a potent spell on him, though, because no good woman can control a beast like that. You're both vicious. Vicious dogs."

A wave of nausea rose from Ravenna's stomach when she caught Chase running toward the man, abandoning Faith. Chase wrapped his arm around the man's shoulders and led him toward the beach. "Hey, Ron. There's no need to worry about the dog. He has a very responsible owner."

Chase didn't make eye contact with Ravenna, but Faith's eyes locked onto hers. Faith's upper lip lifted in disgust and she gave a dismissive tilt of her head as she headed toward Ashley's café. The snub stung, not because it came from Faith, but because she was meeting Chase for lunch.

The man that just ran by smells like the scent in the church, but he helped us, Jet said.

Remember when I told you that the waves of the ocean can look gentle and safe, but underneath could be an invisible riptide that can drag you under and swallow you up? Well, people can be just like the ocean's unpredictable tide, and it's challenging to know when you can trust them.

Jet turned around, baring his teeth before Ravenna realized Chase was behind her.

"Whoa, boy! It's okay," Chase said and extended his hand for Jet to smell it. "You left the church, Ravenna, and never even said goodbye."

"You'd avoided me for weeks, and from the looks of things, it seems you've moved on. Your date stormed off and is waiting for you inside the restaurant. Okay, no, she isn't. Now she's on her way over here."

Faith stomped toward them, sending mini sandstorms in the air. "Are you joining me for lunch, or are you hobnobbing with that wicked witch and her despicable dog?"

Jet let out a growl, and Ravenna tugged his collar in warning.

Faith backed up, keeping her eyes focused on the dog. "That brute should be at home, locked up where he can't hurt anyone, right, pastor? I just saw him almost attack you."

"Faith, come now. He didn't almost attack me. I came up behind Ravenna, and he was warning me not to get too close without her knowing. It's good for her to have that kind of protection, because some people in this town want to harm her. Don't they, Faith?"

"Harm? I . . . um . . . er . . ."

Jet let out another growl.

Faith backed up in slow, small steps. "Why's he growling?"

"He knows when someone doesn't like him," Ravenna said. She didn't like Faith either, and she was fed up with the snide remarks and tasteless attempts to win Chase over. But it didn't matter anymore. Chase had never cared for her. He only wanted her to trust him so that he could harm her. Ravenna had to keep reminding herself of that, because her heart told her something entirely different, making it impossible to completely let him go.

"Faith, why don't you grab our reserved table, and I'll join you in a minute," Chase said.

Faith huffed, and set off. Halfway down the crosswalk, she turned around. "Don't be long, because that witch isn't worth a minute of your time."

"Lady Ravenna, I think you left something at my church, and I wanted to return it." Chase reached into his shirt pocket and handed Ravenna Ashley's anklet. "I found it in my office closet. You know, the day someone ransacked it."

Ravenna's hand shook as she reached out to take it from him. Chase knew who'd broken in, and he knew Ashley had been with her. That was why he'd been avoiding her. Maybe he had been waiting, hoping she'd confess. "I can explain. I—"

Chase held up his hand. "You still have to show me the rest of your house, and I never saw your apothecary, either. I'll come by when it's ready."

Chase left to meet Faith, and Ravenna's heart crumbled like sandcastles broken down by careless waves.

50

A LAMPPOST AT THE end of the cobblestone walkway cast shadows across the frosted early morning ground. Ravenna stared at her Sea Glass Apothecary's freshly painted seafoam green door, then looked up at the dark, velvety sky. She'd waited months for this day.

The apothecary was ready.

Ravenna raised the key to the knob and inserted it. The door clicked open with ease, and the icy ocean breeze grabbed hold of it, pushing it open. A bell above the door chimed softly, its vibration wrapping around her like a warm embrace. Ravenna stepped over the threshold. Inside, the scent of fresh paint and polished wood mixed with the faint, salty tang of the sea. The shop had transformed. The charred remnants of the fire had been replaced by gleaming wooden display cases lining the walls, ready to be filled. The wide pine floorboards led to a new sales counter at the back of the shop, and large bay windows ran across the right side of the store, framing a view of the sleeping winter flower gardens.

Ravenna swallowed as emotion welled inside her, knowing this was the same space she had poured her heart and soul into. It felt different, reborn from the ashes, with a sense of resilience that pulsed through the silent room. She ran to the door of the wish room and studied the original silver star etched with her name, now with two points stained black from the heat of the fire, affixed to a new oak door. Ravenna pushed the door open with excitement and anticipation.

Her hopes fell when she scanned the room, and her eyes fell upon the bare walls. She held back the pressure of tears behind her eyes, hoping the wish wall would return when it was ready.

RAVENNA BOUNCED UP AND down in Skye's bedroom doorway. "Skye. Skye. Wake up."

"It's Saturday. Why can't I sleep?"

"It's the Sea Glass Apothecary. It's ready, and I wanted you to be the first to see it."

Skye's eyelids lifted, and she raised her hand to block the rising sun creeping in through the sheer window curtains. "Seriously? What time is it? You couldn't wait until I woke up?"

"Aren't you excited? Don't you want to come back to work with me?"

Skye pulled the covers over her head, wrapping them tightly around her. "Go away. I want more sleep."

Ravenna studied the contours of Skye's body, curled up into a ball beneath the blanket, and heard the rise and fall of a soft whimper turn into a mournful sob. "What's wrong, Skye? This should be a time of celebration, not sorrow."

Skye's cries grew louder.

"Please take the blanket off." Ravenna tugged at it, but Skye pulled it tighter.

"Okay, then I'm going to sit at the edge of this bed until you talk to me."

Skye groaned and ripped the blanket off her head. "What do you want?"

Skye's swollen red eyes and matted hair made it looked like she'd been crying for days. Ravenna remembered Tristan, too, used to hold everything inside, but eventually, the pressure squeezed so much out of him that he had to let it all out to reset himself and be able to breathe again. Ravenna knew enough to wait, because it would only be a matter of time before Skye would tell her what was tearing her up inside. The next ten minutes seemed like hours, and Ravenna struggled to stay calm. She wanted to hug Skye, give her a tissue, and open the curtains, but she knew any movement would make her hide again.

"Why would I want to come back to the apothecary? You won't teach me how to do wish magic, and even if you did, I probably can't do it," Skye finally said.

"It's not all about wish magic. This apothecary will still be yours one day, and I can easily teach you how to make sea glass jewelry and run a business. But honestly, I miss you, and want us to spend more time together."

Water leaked from Skye's eyes. "So that's all you have to say. You won't teach me wish magic, and that's your final answer?"

"Why is it all about the wish magic for you, Skye? It's an immense burden and responsibility to hold the decision of a person's fate in your hands. And once you start, there's no way out. The weight of that obligation grows heavier every day, and life should be easier than that. I want so much more for you, and you have such a bright future full of possibilities."

"What about what I want? Does that matter to you? Can't I find out whether I can even do the magic?"

"I know wish magic sounds romantic to you, but you'll be living for everyone else and not for yourself. Besides, you're too young to know what you want. Let me teach you how to make sea glass jewelry and manage your own business."

"Ashley already offered to help me learn how to run a business, and helped me with my college application. I applied to the University of Nevada in Las Vegas for the Restaurant Management program, and if I'm accepted, I'll start next September."

The words hung between them, as sharp as broken glass. Ravenna's heartbeat quickened, pounding like the sound of betrayal in her ears. She attempted to steady the hurricane of emotion swirling around in her head, blinking once, twice, trying to wipe away the hurtful words. She spoke past a lump of pain. "I guess restaurant management it is, then. I know you'll be wonderful at it. Good luck getting accepted."

"That's it? That's all you have to say?"

"What else is there to say, Skye? You've made up your mind." Ravenna stood to leave.

"Because you didn't give me a choice."

"That's not true, Skye. You don't know how lucky you are. I gave you the freedom to choose, which was never given to me."

Ravenna left the room, thinking how she'd fought for every scrap of independence in her life, constantly feeling the weight of family expectations pressing down on her shoulders. And now, she had no choice but to give Skye the same freedom she'd always pined for—to choose her own path. Still, it stung, and she couldn't help but believe Skye was making the wrong choice.

51

"This place looks incredible," Klay said, inspecting the new wish room.

"I wish Maeve was here to see it. I still haven't heard one word from her." Ravenna checked her cell phone.

"She probably needs more time to cool off. I can't imagine accepting the truth about Tristan is easy for her. Knowing Maeve the way I do, she'll show up as soon as the doors open for business," Klay said, and chuckled.

"Well, she'd better come home soon, then, because it won't be long now."

"This shop is yours, Ravenna, not Maeve's. You don't need her approval on your changes. They're spectacular. I just finished arranging all the sea glass jewelry in the display cases, so we're all set for reopening. Except . . . there's still one thing missing." Klay pointed to the bare wall where ocean waves had roared and stars had twinkled with hope.

"I wonder why it won't come home. Maybe it's waiting for Maeve, too," Ravenna said.

"I don't know, but it's beyond me why anyone would want to stay in that church." Klay pulled out a crystal bowl filled with sea glass stars from a box on a chair. He was about to set it down when Ravenna grabbed it, and shoved the bowl into a filing cabinet.

"Oh, I get it now. I wouldn't want to come back either if I served no purpose." Klay stared at the closed drawer. "I hope you never change your mind about me."

"Look, I've been going over the apothecary's finances. I realized I don't need to do wish magic to support Skye and myself, because I make plenty of money selling my jewelry. And since I won't be doing magic, I'll have much more time to make additional pieces."

"What about him?" Klay pointed to Jet sitting by Ravenna's side. "Isn't he supposed to help you do magic?"

Yeah, I want to help do magic. Jet pushed his head into Ravenna's hand, making her pet him.

Let's not worry about that right now. Your cones aren't even off your ears yet.

Last time Klay taped them, he said they'll stand on their own, and I won't need posts anymore.

"Did you tell Jet he may not need more tape?" Ravenna said.

"You're changing the subject, but yes. He's six months old, and I've been testing his ears untaped for long stretches. They seem pretty perky. I almost didn't even do them this time, but I figured once more, just to be sure. You don't want a Doberman with floppy ears."

It's okay. I can wait because my ears need to be tall and scary, like my dad's.

Ravenna smiled. "Could you take the tape off now so I can see them? Please, Klay?"

"Sure. We can take it off and see how they do."

Klay sat on the floor, and Jet approached him with his nose pointed downward for easy access to the top of his head. Ravenna watched Klay's fingers search for the tape's edge, then peel it away from Jet's ears. His movements were careful and serious, unlike his typical laid-back demeanor. She observed his quiet strength, the whispered soothing words to Jet, and thought there was something magical about it. Klay pulled off the last of the tape, and Jet's erect ears stood tall and proud.

"I knew they were ready." Klay smiled and clapped his hands.

Ravenna reveled in the satisfaction in Klay's eyes, and her heart swelled. It was a simple moment, but one she'd never forget.

Jet shook his head, then lifted his eyes toward Ravenna. *How do they look?*

Wow! You look like such a big boy. Ravenna ran her hands along Jet's silky fur and the smooth inside of his ears. Her fingers stuck to a glob of adhesive on the edge, and she carefully picked it off. Then she kissed him on the top of his head between his ears. *You're so handsome. I love you, Jet.*

Jet licked Ravenna's face.

"I think this guy's done being taped, but if you see even the slightest droop, you need to let me know so I can tape them again, okay?"

Jet began jumping around the room, shaking his head and growling. *I'm all grown up. I'm all grown up.*

Ravenna grabbed Jet's leash and hooked it onto his collar. "Can you watch things while I'm gone? I want to take him for a walk. The cold won't hurt his ears because they're not used to it, will it?"

Klay grinned. "No, but watch them."

"I will." Ravenna led Jet outdoors and followed the sidewalk up the street.

Why are we going this way? The beach is the other way, and I want to go there. We will. I have some unfinished business I need to take care of first.

52

Ravenna's boots pressed against the icy steps of the church. The biting winter air swept across her face, the pain of it carrying a sharp reminder of the photograph and letter she'd found in Chase's office. And even though Chase had come to her rescue several times since then, she still didn't trust him, and hoped not to see him today.

Jet stood by her side as they entered the church. His sleek, black coat shone like a polished gemstone over his muscular body. Ravenna looked down at his discerning, intelligent eyes and erect ears, appreciating his regal air of authority. Jet was devoted to her despite his intimidating appearance. He yearned for her love and companionship, offering unwavering loyalty and protection. She was grateful for it, especially after seeing that letter. But she knew nothing could protect her from the uncontrollable excitement that overtook her whenever she saw Chase.

Just like last time, Jet. Stay close to the wall, and under the office windows.

Ravenna strode next to Jet, dropping her hand so Barbara wouldn't see the leash. She glanced through the windows but didn't see anyone.

It isn't like Barbara not to be in her office. She makes as good a watchdog as you. But she can't growl like I can. Jet let out a low rumble.

Yup, and that makes you extra special.

On the way to her old apothecary room, Ravenna didn't see anyone in the hallway, either. She placed her hand on the cold brass doorknob and attempted to turn it, but it wouldn't open. She began shaking it left and right with more force, but it didn't budge.

Damn. They locked the door. Now what? I have to get in there.

You don't have a key?

No. I mailed it back because I didn't want anyone to think I had bad intentions. Wait a minute. Barbara must have gotten it, so it has to be in the office somewhere. Okay, Jet, I have to look in there, so I need you to stand guard and warn me if someone's coming.

Ravenna led Jet to the office door and opened it. *Stay here.*

But if they see me, they'll know you're inside.

Listen to me: no growling or barking. Just talk to me, and if you see someone coming, find a place to hide down the hallway and let me know where you are. Okay?

Okay. Jet sat watching the hallway with his chest pushed out and his head held high.

Ravenna slipped inside and rummaged through Barbara's desk. She opened and closed drawers slowly to prevent the metal from squeaking and calling attention to herself. Inside, she found chocolate bars, half-eaten bags of potato chips, and a bookmarked diary that Ravenna's curiosity forced her to open and read the most recent entry.

> *Dear Christ Jesus, my Lord,*
> *I write to pray that our pastor finds his way back to you, as he has gone astray. If it's not bad enough that he willfully invited that witch demon into this house of worship, she has fooled and enchanted him. And even now, in her absence from the church, he cannot let her go. I pray he confesses his sexual sin to Faith so they can find peace in matrimony together, because you and I both know that Faith is his only destiny. Amen!*

Your faithful servant,
Barbara

Ravenna flattened the journal on the desk, grabbed a red marker, and wrote over the text:

The pastor has not sinned, but you have. Do not cast judgment on any of my children, or I will turn my back on you.

Ravenna closed the journal and put it and the marker back where she had found them. She turned her focus on the walls. Next to the copy machine, she spied a small rack of hooks with dangling keys and crept over to it. There were so many, and she needed to hurry. She scanned them all, and as much as she wanted to grab the keys to Chase's office and the parsonage to ensure Barbara wouldn't give them to Faith, she refrained.

I'm in front of the guy's office whose scent you wanted me to smell. Hurry!

Ravenna tucked the key labeled "Fair Storage" into her pocket and ran out of the office to meet Jet. On her way down the hall, she spied Jet, cornering Faith against Chase's closed office door. Chase opened the door, and Faith pushed herself into his arms and buried her head into his chest. "Oh, pastor, protect me."

"What's going on out here?" Chase said.

Ravenna felt her fingers burn with jealousy. "I'm so sorry. His leash slipped from my hand, but he won't hurt her."

Good boy, Jet. You can back away from them now.

"What are you doing here, Lady Ravenna?" Chase said.

"And why is that beast here with you?" Faith wrapped her arm around Chase's waist and put her hand on his chest.

Chase tried to pry Faith from him. "You can let go now. Ravenna has the leash, and the dog won't hurt you."

"No, I can't. She can't hold him back if he decides to eat us for lunch." Faith pushed deeper into Chase's chest, wrapping both arms around his waist.

Chase reached his hand out to Jet. "Come here. What did you say his name was?"

"It's Jet," Ravenna said. *Let him pet you, Jet, and be extra nice.*

I don't want to. This is the guy you said wants to hurt you.

He won't hurt me right now if you're nice.

Jet pushed his head into Chase's hand.

"See, Faith. There's nothing to worry about. Why don't I keep Jet busy, and you can scoot down into the basement to help your mother retrieve the files I need? I'm sure by the time you come back, Jet will be long gone."

"If it's all the same, I'd rather stay with you, because I'm scared. I think people would understand if I joined you in your office, with the door closed." Faith shot Ravenna a sideways glance.

Ravenna stared at Faith as she groped at Chase's chest. Her gaze lingered on Faith's fingers and the intimacy of the gesture, stirring a yearning so profound inside of her that it left her breathless.

"I don't think that's necessary, and you'll be plenty safe with your mother." Chase peeled off Faith's hands and pushed her by the small of her back toward the hallway.

"Fine." Faith's stomps echoed on her way to the basement door.

"Did you come to see me, Lady Ravenna? Because I'm afraid I need to leave for a pastoral visit."

"Oh, yeah, um . . . I probably should have called first. No problem, because it's not important, and I wanted to stretch Jet's legs. I'll catch up with you another time." Ravenna forced herself to turn away from Chase, but felt that familiar tug that refused to let her go.

Chase gently grabbed her arm to turn her around. It felt like a spark igniting between them.

Jet growled.

No, boy. Shh.

Their eyes met, and the world and its religious boundaries disappeared for a moment. Sounds became muted, and colors more vibrant. The charged air hummed with an intensity that made her skin tingle. She felt it stronger than ever, pulling them together as if she were standing on the edge of a cliff, the wind whipping around, tempting her to leap. Yet she resisted, pulling her arm from his grasp. "You should get going to your appointment." She cast him a smile that did little to hide the tremor in her voice.

"Come on, Jet," she said. "Chase has someplace he needs to be, *and so do we.*"

Chase winked with a twinkle in his eye, and moved off down the hallway.

BARBARA AND FAITH WOULD return from the basement soon, and Ravenna had no time to waste. She unlocked the door of her old apothecary with the key she'd stolen from Barbara's office, and she and Jet slipped inside. Ravenna closed the door behind them and switched on the light.

You need to be quiet, Jet. I don't want anyone to know we're in here. She bent down and kissed Jet's head. *I love you. You're such a good boy.*

Jet licked her face.

Stay by the door and tell me if you hear anything.

Ravenna moved to the center of the room and inhaled the familiar scent of musty books and polished wood. She examined the newly donated furniture, delicate china, and jewelry, tracing their surfaces with her fingers, and saw visions of the stories each one carried. It occurred to her that these once-gleaming surfaces, dulled by time and jammed together for space, were a housed hodge-podge of forgotten memories. Each item in the room was more than just a donation. It was a piece of someone's life, a fragment of their story, forgotten and surrendered. But Ravenna wouldn't abandon hers. She was here to reclaim it.

Ravenna squeezed through the maze, trying not to disturb the Jenga of donations, but knocked a teacup from a topsy-turvy stack. It fell to the floor with a loud crash, and she froze, holding her breath, listening for anyone who may have heard it.

Do you hear anyone on the other side of the door, Jet?

Yes. Someone's coming.

Shh.

Ravenna heard Faith's heels speeding toward the room.

"Where are you going in such a hurry, Faith?" a woman said in the hallway. "I've been looking all over for you, because my niece is selling her house and needs a realtor."

The sound of Faith's shoes faded away, and soon the sound of their voices was gone. After a few more minutes of careful silence, Ravenna stepped over the shards of china and continued to the fabric she'd left hanging on the far wall.

Ravenna curled her fingers around the edge of the sheet. In one swift tug, she tore it away, unveiling the wall underneath. There was the wish wall, a once vibrant and spectacular living display, now reduced to a silent, faded mural on the cold sheetrock. The moon had transformed into a flat, two-dimensional disc without radiance. The waves, now frozen crests, didn't roar in their customary dance with the shore. The stars, stripped of their brilliance, were lifeless, distant echoes of forgotten dreams. It was as if the wall, once brimming with magic and filled with wishes, had surrendered to a wretched fate, evaporating into a mere painting. Each brush stroke held a dreary gray haze that seemed to hang in the very air above the surface. Once alive and overflowing with the dreams and desires of countless hearts, the wish wall was now a somber memorial of lost hope.

Ravenna's soul ached at the mournful sight, and her green eye stung with pain as sharp as a wound inflicted by shards of broken glass. The wish wall was her family's beacon, their lighthouse in the stormy sea of life. But now, its light had dimmed, and its magic was extinguished. She traced her fingers over the frozen waves, lifeless stars, and dull moon, each detail a painful reminder of what she'd destroyed. Ravenna fell to her knees, tears streaming from her eyes. The room filled with an echoing silence as if time held its breath, mourning the loss of the wish wall's magic.

I hear someone in the hallway, Jet said.

"Shit." Ravenna wiped her eyes and wove her way through the clutter to Jet. She held her breath, trying to quiet her speeding heartbeat so she could think of a way out unnoticed, or at least a reason she'd be in there.

They're coming in, Jet said.

Ravenna eyed the knob as it turned, and the door swung open. Jet's body tensed. He let out a menacing growl, and Ava stood petrified in the doorframe, clutching a stack of books.

No, Jet! Ravenna grabbed Ava's arm and pulled her into the room, slamming the door shut behind her. "Is anyone out there? Did anyone see you?"

"Wow. You two scared me half to death. What's going on?" Ava petted Jet.

"Did anyone see you?"

"No. Barbara was in her office when I walked by, and ignored me. Is everything okay? You look upset."

"I broke in to get something I thought I left behind, but I don't know why I bothered. I should have known it wasn't here. Can you help us out of here?"

"Why did you care if anyone saw you? You could have asked if it was here."

"You know how Barbara feels about me. She never would have let me in."

"Yeah, but I also know how Chase feels about you." Ava raised her eyebrows, placed the books on a nearby table, and elbowed Ravenna. "Why didn't you just ask him?"

"How about we talk about that later? For now, would you mind helping us get out?"

"Sure, I'll keep Barbara busy so you can sneak out."

"Oh, and somehow return this, too, without her knowing where you got it." Ravenna handed Ava the key. "And one more thing?"

"Sure, what is it?"

"Come by the apothecary soon. I have something important to ask you."

53

RAVENNA WAS MEDITATING IN the apothecary's wish room when she heard the bells above the entrance clang piercingly, turning the regular charming jingle into an alarm that tensed her body. Jet ran toward it, growling.

"Please help! Lady Ravenna, it's my mom. She needs help."

Ravenna flew out of the wish room to find Jet with Gina in the middle of the shop. Ashely's daughter was tear-streaked and red-faced.

"What's wrong, honey?"

"It's . . . my dad." Gina struggled to catch her breath from crying. "He's . . . moved back . . . to town."

Ravenna handed Gina a water bottle from the counter and led her to a seat in the wish room. "Slow down, Gina. Take a drink and catch your breath."

Gina concentrated on composing herself, and Jet placed his head in her lap. She stroked his head and half smiled when she pressed his ears down, and they shot back up.

"He has pretty cool ears, doesn't he?" Ravenna said. "Now, can you tell me what's wrong?"

"My dad moved out of Boston and bought a mansion on the beach next to the café. We didn't know who bought it until he just showed up. He told my mom he needed to watch her, because she couldn't take care of us right. Then he said he was taking us away from her, and he was taking the café, too." Gina's eyes welled again, and Jet shoved his head under her hand.

"He's living in Plymbury?"

"Yeah, but not just anywhere. Right next door to the café."

"Where is your dad now?"

"He's at the café. I ran over here because they got into a huge fight. He was yelling and said he was going to take us to his house. Mom left my brother and sisters at home with the sitter this morning, but I ran over here. I don't want to live with him. Please don't make me go. I can't leave my mom. She's feeling worse than ever and needs me. Please, can you help?"

Ravenna glanced at her watch. "Doesn't the café open soon?"

"Yes, Mom drops me off at school and comes back to open, but my dad's there. We have to help her." Gina shot up from her seat and pulled Ravenna's hand.

"One second, Gina. I think someone else can help." Ravenna grabbed Jet's leash from the wall and clipped it to his collar. "Why don't we see how your dad feels about Jet?"

Okay, Jet, now's your chance to be big and bad like your father, Ravenna said, leading him and Gina across the street.

Jet let out a growl. *I can do it.*

I know you can.

Jason's voice from inside the café jarred Ravenna like a roar of thunder in a clear sky, shattering the calm morning. The sound of glass breaking drowned the yelling with a sharp, violent pitch that echoed through the desolate street.

Ravenna handed Gina her cell phone. "Go back to my shop and call the police. Don't leave there for any reason until someone comes looking for you, okay?"

"But I want to go with you. My mom needs me."

"If you want me to help, you need to listen to me. Make the phone call and wait at my shop. Hurry."

Gina ran back to the apothecary with the phone.

Jet, I'm taking you to the back entrance so Jason won't see you. Wait until I enter the front door, then sneak up behind him.

When they reached the back door, Ravenna unclipped Jet's leash and kissed his head. She led Jet into the back room and pointed beyond the doorway to Jason standing behind the bar. *There he is, and you can see the front door just beyond the bar. Wait for me to come inside.*

Ravenna exited and ran to the front of the café, where she spotted Faith standing at the entrance. Ravenna turned around to avoid her, deciding to meet Jet in the back again.

"Lady Ravenna? Where did you come from, and what's all the yelling in there?" Faith chased after her.

"I don't know what you're talking about, Faith. Why don't you go home?" Ravenna waved a dismissive hand behind her and continued walking.

"Why don't you go back to your evildoings across the street? I came to meet my client. I sold him the house next door, and now he's buying the café, too. Ashley must have told you."

Ravenna stopped and spun to face Faith. "He told you that? He said he was buying the café?"

"Yes, and isn't it so coincidental that his last name is Watson? That's why he wants this place."

"It's coincidental, all right."

Ravenna didn't want to waste one more second talking to Faith. Ashley needed her. She marched toward the front door, with Faith following close behind. Ravenna opened the door but hesitated, listening to an eerie silence. Jason wasn't standing behind the bar.

Faith pushed her way past Ravenna. "Move out of my way."

Then Faith screamed, and Ravenna dashed in after her.

"I knew that dog was vicious. Get him away from my client. He's going to kill him!" Faith scooted behind Ravenna for protection.

Ravenna spotted Jason pressing against the dining room's far wall with Jet growling and baring his teeth in front of him.

Jason was pushing himself into the wall, covering his face with his arms. "Help! Help!"

Ashley lay on the floor next to Jason. Ravenna ran to her, grabbed her arm, and lifted her into a seat. *Good boy, Jet. You keep him right there until the police come.*

Jet let out a growl.

"Are you okay, Ash? What happened?" Ravenna said.

Ashley's breaths were a fragile whisper, laced with the raw aftermath of her ordeal. Her eyes had a haunting mix of fear and disbelief as if trying to comprehend the reality of what had just happened. Her hands shook, and Ravenna clasped them. The color had drained from Ashley's face, leaving her ashen with sorrow etched into every line. Her voice trembled as she spoke. "Jason came at me with a glass, threatening to hit me. His eyes were so full of rage, and I froze. He grabbed me from behind and wrapped his arm around my neck. He was choking me." Ashley lifted her hand to her neck and then to the side of her head. "I felt the cold glass on my face, and all I could think was that it was all over. Jason was going to kill me." Ashley stared at Jet keeping Jason cornered. "Just when I thought there was no way out, your dog launched himself at Jason. He bit down on his leg, sending us both to the floor. Jason got up, and your dog backed him into the wall. He saved my life, Ravenna."

Ravenna looked at Jet. *I'm so proud of you.*

Jet let out an extra fierce growl.

The police barreled into the café with Faith latched onto the arm of the head officer. She pointed at Jet. "There he is, officer. Take out your gun, because you can see I was telling the truth. That dog is vicious. He needs to be put down."

Jet, you can get off him now and come sit beside me. "Mind your own business, Faith. Officer, Jet didn't hurt anyone. He was protecting Ashley. Jason attacked her."

The officer handcuffed Jason.

"They're lying! The dog attacked me out of nowhere," Jason said.

"Come on. We can sort it out at the station," the police officer said.

Faith was following Jason and the officer out of the café. "Wait. You can't arrest my client. He did nothing wrong."

"You haven't heard the end of this, Ashley," Jason said on their way out.

"Wait, you know her? I thought you were buying the . . ."

Gina ran into the café with another officer trailing behind her, and hugged her mother. "I'm not going with Dad, Mom. Please don't make me go."

"You, your brother, and sisters won't be living with him. Not if I have anything to say about it." Ashley attempted to stand but fell back into her seat, the stress from the attack compounding the weakness of her MS.

Ravenna's thoughts lingered on Ashley and her children. She shuddered, thinking about what could have happened if Jet wasn't there, and what might happen if Ashley's health continued to decline. Ravenna loved Ashley and knew it was a burden she could remove if only she'd perform the wish magic. But the thought of Chase crashed into her mind, and she knew with an unwavering reality that performing magic again would leave her without a lifeboat on a sinking ship.

Let's go now, Jet. We've done all we can.

54

RAVENNA RETURNED TO THE apothecary with Jet, and found Chase and Ava waiting for her. She caught Chase examining a sea glass bracelet from the spirituality-themed display case, holding it before his eyes and turning it in his hand.

"Oh, hey. I hope you don't mind that we let ourselves in," Ava said. "The door was open."

"Hello, Lady Ravenna," Chase said and held up the bracelet he'd been inspecting. "Just how does someone gain spirituality from this sea glass?"

Jet growled.

No growling unless I tell you to.

I didn't need your help with that guy across the street.

You're right, and I'm so proud of you, but this is different.

Ravenna shook her head. "I'm sorry. Why are you two here?"

"You told me to come by because you had something to discuss. Reverend Wilkinson saw me open the door, so he came in, too. We didn't expect to find the place empty." She petted Jet on the head. "He looks so handsome without his ears coned."

Jet licked Ava's hand.

Chase put the bracelet back into its case. "Do you always leave the door unlocked when you leave?"

"No, but it was an emergency."

"I see. I hope the fire's extinguished now."

Ravenna interpreted Chase's words as a veiled threat, and her mind filled with the haunting image of another mob storming her shop. She didn't trust him, and her rational mind was skeptical about his intentions, questioning his every move and word. Yet she couldn't control her aching heart, yearning to be kissed by his lips and held in his arms, dreaming of a sanctuary of peace and harmony.

"So, why are you here?" Ravenna said.

"Why don't you have your discussion with Ava, and I'll pick up some coffee at Ashley's. How do you ladies like your coffee?"

"Oh, I was just there. I wanted some coffee this morning . . . but . . . um . . . the coffee machine is broken. Ashley said they'll fix it in an hour . . . but the café's opening late. Maybe you should return to the church and come back later."

"Are you trying to get rid of me, Lady Ravenna?"

"She would never do that, Reverend Wilkinson. I think Ravenna needs a few minutes alone with me, but you can't go to Ashley's because she needs time to fix her coffee machine. It's as simple as that."

"Why don't I leave you two alone, then?" Chase walked toward the door.

Ravenna felt the tension in her neck and shoulders release, and ignored her heart's cry for him to stay.

"I'll take a walk on the beach and come back before I freeze. See you soon," Chase said, and left.

Jet growled a low rumble.

Stop it, Jet.

"Even I can feel the sexual tension between the two of you. How long will you deny it?" Ava said. "How cool? A Christian minister and a Wiccan. You don't see that every day."

"It's not something you see any day, so get the thought out of your mind. I don't think Chase wants anything but to make my life miserable."

"And you? What do you want, Ravenna?"

"To change the subject."

Ava giggled. "Okay, fine, for now."

"Good, because I asked you here for a reason. I'm sure you've noticed Ashley hasn't been feeling well, so Skye's working more at the café than here, and I need help. Since you're looking for another volunteer job to fill your time, I thought maybe you could work for me instead. But only if you let me pay you."

"Wow! Work with you here? I can't believe it. This is crazy and exciting." Ava's eyes shimmered like rising sunlight on the ocean, and every curve of her face shone as if sun-kissed. It thrilled Ravenna that this brought her so much happiness, and she knew Ava was the perfect person for the job. But then, something in Ava shifted. It was subtle, like a cloud passing in front of the sun, and the smile on her face wilted.

"What's wrong?"

"Are you sure you want a Christian working in your apothecary? You remember that I'm a Christian, right? I don't have any plans to convert."

Ravenna laughed and pulled Ava in for a hug. "Yes, I know you're a Christian, and no conversion is necessary, only friendship. Wiccans don't proselytize, but I do need to teach you all the metaphysical properties of each piece. It's a lot to learn. Are you up for it?"

"I can't wait. When do I start?"

"How about today? Klay will be here soon, and he's the perfect person to teach you. And I'll need you to help watch the shop when Chase returns, because I'm sure he's up to something."

"Oh, Ravenna. Can't you see it? You're so perceptive about seeing things hidden beneath the surface of everyone else, but it's like you refuse to see underneath your own skin. What's under there, Ravenna? Don't you have a piece of sea glass jewelry that would reveal it? Or maybe you just need a mirror." Ava grabbed one from the countertop and held it facing Ravenna. "Tell me you don't see what I see in your green eye."

"What do you see, Ava?"

"I see a woman who's afraid. She's afraid not only of confessing her love, but of what it might mean if she doesn't."

Ravenna peered at Ava over the top of the mirror. "Eyes reveal what the observer believes is true, and the observer can change their mind when such absurd claims are denied."

"You can deny it all you want, but I'm sure of what I see, Lady Ravenna. And so are you."

Ravenna raised an eyebrow and grinned. "I knew you'd be perfect for the job."

55

KLAY ENTERED THE APOTHECARY thirty minutes later with Chase at his heels, and saw Ava. "Oh, just perfect, one Christian behind me and another in front of me. It's like a Christian sandwich, and I'm the dead meat in the middle."

"Don't be so dramatic. Ava works for me now, doing Skye's shifts, and I need you to train her," Ravenna said.

Klay pointed his thumb over his shoulder. "Next, you'll tell me he left the church and works here, too. I'm putting my foot down. No Christian ministers in a New Age apothecary."

"Hilarious, Klay with a K. I assure you, I won't be working here. However, I will admit, it's quite a charming space, and look at those magnificent garden views." Chase swept his hand across the expanse of the windows.

"That's nothing. Almost every room in the house has a breathtaking view, but I think you already know that," Klay said.

Ravenna glanced at Klay sideways with widened eyes.

"No. I'm afraid I don't, but I look forward to finding out."

"Oh, I would love to see your home," Ava said.

"I believe I've booked a private tour," Chase said.

"What? You're going to take him for a tour of your house?" Klay said. "Are you nuts? Didn't you learn your lesson the last time?"

"That's a great idea. You two go ahead, and I can wait for the next one," Ava said.

"Since there's a purpose to this tour, I'd like to see what's behind there." Chase pointed to the wish room door. "It's a private space, yes?"

"That's right." Klay moved between the door and Chase. "It's private. Invitation only, and I don't recall you being invited."

Jet joined Klay, growling at Chase.

"Good boy," Klay said.

That's enough, Jet. If I need you, I'll let you know.

Chase put out his hand to let Jet smell it.

Be nice. You can watch him, but no growling.

Okay.

Chase petted the top of Jet's head. "See, he remembers me. Now, about that room."

"Does that mean you're satisfied with the apothecary?" Ravenna said.

"Satisfied? What?" Klay grabbed Chase by the arm. "Let's go. You've been here long enough."

"Let go of him, Klay. You and Ava have some inventory to stock, so why don't you do that and stop interfering in my life?"

"Fine." Klay let go of Chase.

Ravenna opened the door to let Chase and Jet inside the wish room. She watched Chase stepping over the threshold. His tall silhouette darkened the doorway before he entered, and his presence commanded her attention. Something about the way he moved, with a certain refinement and confidence, sent her heart aflutter.

The room was a sanctuary, a haven, a place where dreams took form and desires became reality. The walls whispered silent prayers, and the veil between the physical and spiritual world thinned. Here, Ravenna could hear the universe. White sage lingered in the air, a sweet, smoky perfume that hinted at ancient rituals and hidden secrets. Chase scanned the room, his eyes wide with awe and apprehension. He moved as though realizing he had stepped into a sacred space. His gaze lingered on the empty wall where shadows flickered, cast by the flame of a black candle. His fingers brushed lightly over a sea glass necklace on the table, its seafoam green hue glowing under his touch. Ravenna debated explaining that touching a witch's magical tools was impolite, but saw a flicker of something in his eyes. A spark of understanding, an unexpected connection. Chase looked up. His eyes met hers, and she felt something connecting their worlds, forged through mutual respect and shared curiosity.

"I use this space to meditate and escape it all."

"Is that all you use it for?"

"It's where I perform wish magic." Ravenna held her breath, waiting for his reply.

"How many wishes?"

"None in this new room."

Chase stared at the empty wall. She waited for him to say something, anything, or to move closer to her.

"Maybe it's time to see the rest of the house," Chase said.

RAVENNA LEFT JET WITH Klay, and she and Chase entered her home in the other side of the building. Somehow, her living room appeared more interesting to Chase than the wish room. He inspected every inch of the space and settled his gaze on the coffee table, where a cluster of ritual tools hummed with Ravenna's power. He moved closer to her family's Book of Shadows.

"Please ask before you touch anything," she said.

Chase gave her a curious look, and she knew this request was unusual for him.

Chase pointed to the thick, leather-bound book. "Why do I have to ask? It's sitting on the coffee table for anyone to see."

Ravenna appreciated his desire to understand something foreign to him but wanted to respect the boundaries of her family lineage. "This Book of Shadows holds my family's spirit, our energy. It has belonged to the Greene family for generations, and is attuned to me. You could say it's sacred and inappropriate, or even rude, to touch it without asking. It's my family, our beliefs, our identities." Ravenna steadied her eyes on Chase, hoping he'd understand and respect the sanctity of her space.

"Lady Ravenna, are you saying there's something wrong with me—my energy, as you call it? And what does that mean?"

"Oh, no. Please don't take it personally, because it's not just you. It's anyone. You must own something you treasure so much that if anyone touched it, you'd feel it violated your very being?"

"Come to think of it, I do. I think you've seen the photograph of my grandfather, my mother, and me. You've even touched it."

Ravenna felt like he had punched her in the gut and knocked the wind out of her. "Chase, please let me—"

"No need to explain, Lady Ravenna, but let's make this fair. Shall we?" He sat on the couch and lifted the heavy book from the table onto his lap. "So, I can look inside?"

Chase was right. She had violated his sacred space, and if looking in her family's Book of Shadows would help him forgive her, then so be it. She had nothing to hide. Ravenna nodded and eyed Chase studying the pages, running his fingers across them, stopping on words like *spell*, *magick*, and *chant*.

"This concoction of mud and herbs is supposed to soothe and heal the eyes. Am I right?" Chase said.

"Yes."

"Hmm. Jesus, too, concocted a mud mixture to restore sight to those who were blind."

Ravenna stood in silence.

"Lady Ravenna, I don't mean to upset you. You've touched my most treasured possession, and I wanted to experience yours."

"It was an accident."

"It was an accident that you and your friend Ashley broke into my office and destroyed my most treasured possession? So is it safe to say that if I broke into your home, I could say it was an accident that I leafed through this book?"

"Okay, I've had enough. I'm not playing any more games."

"I assure you, Lady Ravenna, I'm not playing games, either."

Ravenna sat next to Chase and looked into his eyes. "What do you want from me? I know you're trying to kill me, so why don't you just get it over with?"

Chase laughed and reached out, attempting to wipe the tears from Ravenna's eye. She grabbed his wrist before he could touch her.

"Lady Ravenna, I'm not trying to hurt you, but I am trying to understand and learn why I've fallen for you. Do you deny you've fallen for me, too?" His eyes, shining with anticipation, met hers.

Ravenna's breath hitched. A tempest of silent whispers and unspoken desires swirled around them. It was more than just a physical attraction. It was a supernatural connection, a spellbinding web of love and passion, floating them in a magical sea of emotion. Ravenna let go of his wrist and shot up from the couch, breaking the enchantment.

"I can't. Since we're asking questions, how did your grandfather get burned, and why did the letter behind the photo say you wanted to kill me?"

"You honestly don't know, do you?"

"Know what? Tell me. What don't I know?"

Chase returned the book to the coffee table and rose, brushing past Ravenna on his way to the windows. He peered out to the ocean, then looked up. "Isn't that a witch ball?" He pointed to the colorful glass sphere hanging over his head. "Why do you have one? I thought they were to keep witches away."

"Do you trust every Christian you meet?"

"No, and I suppose you're having trouble trusting me, too." Chase shifted his eyes to Ravenna. "Please believe that I have your best interests at heart when I say that I can't be the one to tell you this. You'll have to ask Maeve." He took

Ravenna's hand and pressed her fingers to his lips, sending a chill through her body that made her ache for more.

"Please, Chase? I need to know."

"Come to the church if you still want to see me after you talk to Maeve." Chase released her hand and gave her a solemn wink.

Ravenna tried to say she couldn't ask Maeve, that she didn't know where Maeve was, but Chase was out the door before she could utter a single word.

56

SEVERAL DAYS HAD GONE by, and there had still been no sign of Maeve. Ravenna worried that something might have happened to her, and then had a fleeting thought that life would be easier if she didn't return. But Ravenna wanted her to come home. She loved Maeve and wondered if, now that Maeve knew Tristan was a Christian, she could talk to her about Chase.

Ravenna hadn't felt this way about anyone in years. She had forgotten what it was like to be distracted by surges of excitement whenever she thought about a man. She couldn't help but relive Chase's gentle kiss on her hand, and his serious wink when he'd left. She longed for more of him, and wished she'd pulled him close and kissed his lips. Chase had had his chance to harm her but hadn't, and she believed he sincerely didn't want to. But she still couldn't walk down the street and confess her love for him. First, she needed to know about the photograph and letter, and it seemed Maeve was the only one who could tell her.

Skye was dusting display cases in the apothecary with Jet beside her.

"I'm so happy you've found an hour to work with me before school. Are you glad to be back?" Ravenna said.

"I need to get to Ashley's. When is Ava going to be here?"

"She's not working today, but Klay is on his way. Have you heard anything from Great Maeve? I'm so eager for her to see the new shop."

"No," Skye said.

278

"Is that the truth, or just a way to avoid telling me?"

"I have a deal for you, Mom. You teach me wish magic, and I'll tell you where she is."

"Skye, you know I can't."

"Right, because Reverend Wilkinson is making your life hell, even when you're all giddy welcoming him into our house. Ashley and I watched you from the restaurant. It didn't look like you were so afraid of him."

Ravenna's jaw dropped, and the bells above the door chimed. Klay strolled in, Jet running to greet him.

"Are you talking about what happened with jerkface in your house? I'd like to know, too," Klay said.

"Why does everyone need to know everything I do?" Ravenna said.

"Sometimes I think you forget you're a famous witch. I'm surprised the local paparazzi aren't stalking you and taking pictures whenever you're with him," Klay said.

"Maybe if it's a secret, then you should be more secretive. Just sayin','" Skye said.

"It's not a secret."

"What's not a secret?" Klay said.

"That Mom's all head over heels for Reverend Wilkinson. I guess it's not enough that she ruined my life by marrying my dad, who was Christian. Now she wants to ruin it all over again."

"That's enough, Skye. I won't put up with any prejudice coming from you. You're half-Christian, too, and you wouldn't be here if I hadn't been with your father."

"Don't remind me."

"Maybe it's time to see if Skye can do magic," Klay said.

Skye looked at Ravenna with wide, expectant eyes.

"We'll talk about it when Maeve gets home. I need to talk to her first. When you speak with her next, Skye, tell her I'm not the only one waiting for her to come home. You are, too."

"Thanks for trying, Klay." Skye grabbed her backpack behind the sales counter and headed for the door. "See you later, Jet."

Klay began counting the float in the cash drawer.

"How about you don't interfere in my relationship with Skye?" Ravenna said when Skye had left.

"Really, since when? I've never heard you say that before. At least, not until you decided you'd rather have jerkface in your life." Klay slammed the drawer shut. His words reverberated through the apothecary, and Ravenna felt their sting seep into her skin.

"Klay, please. Take a walk on the beach while I smudge the room, and don't come back until you're free from negativity."

"Sure. I'll walk, and why don't you take a cold shower?"

Ravenna locked the door. "Okay, you want to fight, then let's do it. Get it all out, because I want this place smudged and peaceful after."

"Peaceful? That's a joke. Nothing is peaceful, Ravenna. Our lives have been turned upside down by jerkface. Is there no end to it? Why do you insist on letting him rule us? Oh, I know. It's as plain as the bare wall in the wish room. You love that asshole, but he doesn't deserve you."

"Then who does, Klay?"

"Someone who appreciates you for who you are, and doesn't make you someone you're not."

"Or maybe someone who doesn't care about my magical abilities, and loves me without them."

"Ravenna, wake up. He only loves Jesus. You threaten everything he knows and believes about God. He can't figure out how someone ordinary like you can perform miracles like Jesus did. I suppose it never occurred to him that maybe Jesus was a witch, too. What am I saying? Of course it didn't, because he thinks

Jesus is God, and has never even considered that every single one of us is a part of a higher consciousness, that we're all God. Do you want a guy who doesn't even acknowledge the Goddess in you? Go for it, Ravenna. Let me know how that works out for you." Klay snagged his jacket from the wall hook, and Jet grabbed it in his mouth, trying to stop him.

"If Tristan accepted me for who I am, so can Chase."

"Who the hell are you, Ravenna? Because none of us know anymore. No, boy! Let go of my jacket."

"I'm the sa—"

"Don't answer that. I don't want to hear it. But tell me, will jerkface even allow you to smudge your apothecary? Just think about everything you're giving up, Ravenna." Klay pried the jacket from Jet's mouth and stormed out.

Ravenna collapsed over the sales counter, trying to calm herself by taking slow, deep breaths. The hurt and anger in Klay's voice slammed against her heart like a tidal wave, threatening to drown her.

57

"I GOT THE COURT date. It's April first, and I'm sure it was deliberate. His attorney wants to make me look like a fool." Ashley leaned on a purpleheart wood cane in the apothecary. "Please tell me you won't let him?"

"I'm sorry, Ash, but you can fight this again and win."

"Not if I enter the courtroom like this." Ashley balanced against a display case and lifted her cane for Ravenna to see.

"When did you get the new stick?"

"A couple of weeks ago. Skye didn't tell you?"

"Skye doesn't tell me anything these days. She wouldn't even tell me you helped her apply for college until she threw it in my face."

A heavy silence hung in the air.

"Ravenna, I didn't . . . she said you asked for my help."

Ravenna sipped a hot coffee from Dunkin' and lifted her eyes over the lid. "Ash, I know your oldest is only eleven, but when she's a teenager, don't trust everything she tells you."

"I should have asked you, but I just assumed—"

Ravenna held up her hand. "Forget it. I'll deal with it when I find out whether she's accepted."

"Then I suppose this isn't a good time to ask for a favor?"

Ravenna braced herself, trying to think of any excuse for a way out of telling Ashley she wouldn't do wish magic.

"I didn't want to tell you because I hoped it would reappear." Ashley glanced at her feet. "I lost the anklet you made me, and I know you're going to tell me that losing healing pieces means you no longer need them, but my health has gotten much worse since I lost it. So I was hoping maybe you could do the wish magic for me?"

"It's not a good time, Ash. Klay and Jet will be back any minute, and we need to review the financials before we open. But I forgot to tell you—I knew you lost your anklet because I found it . . . um . . . at the café. It must have slipped my mind."

"Slipped your mind? I need that anklet, Ravenna. My health depends on it. How could you keep it from me?"

"I hope you know I'd never hurt you. Is that what you think? That I didn't want to return it to you?" Ravenna pointed to her workbench. "It's sitting over there, waiting to be fixed."

"And you said nothing about it until now?"

Ravenna felt a swirl of sorrow behind her eyes. She had watched for years as Ashley struggled with her health. A surge of guilt washed over her as she realized her selfishness. She'd allowed her tangled feelings for Chase to overshadow her concern for one of her closest friends. Sure, Chase had discovered the anklet, but Ravenna couldn't let Ashley know. She feared the conversation that would follow, the inevitable lecture about Chase's attempts to destroy her life, and couldn't bear to listen. Her heart longed for Chase, whispering about fairy tales and happy endings. But, for now, it seemed easier—kinder, even—to let Ashley believe Ravenna had left her feelings for him back at the church. "I wanted to surprise you by making a new one and incorporating pieces from this one, too, because it has your energy all over it. I'm sure your health will improve between this new piece and the necklace I already gave you."

"Oh, Ravenna, that means so much to me. I didn't mean to accuse you of anything. I'm just not myself these days. The added stress of the police letting Jason go—"

"What? The police let Jason go? Did you at least file a restraining order against him?"

"I tried, but it was his word against mine, and since he didn't hit me with the glass—"

"Are you joking? You had to prove he'd hit you before they'd do anything about it? What if he comes after you again?"

"I can't worry about that right now. All I want is to heal so I can keep my kids. It's all I care about and can think about these days. Please, Ravenna, can you do the wish magic for me?" The bells on the door chimed as it opened. Ashley started and almost fell when she whipped around to see Klay step in with Jet.

"It looks like maybe you're more concerned about Jason than you say you are," Ravenna said.

Ashley eyed Ravenna, and Jet ran to greet her.

"So long as I have this brave guy, everything will be fine. You're my hero, Jet." Ashley petted his head with her free hand.

"He's something special, all right," Klay said.

Jet stood tall and proud. *I love my family.*

"Did I miss something?" Klay said.

"No, but you and I need to finish those financials before the shop opens for business."

"What fin—"

Ravenna looked at Klay with wide eyes and tilted her head toward Ashley.

"Oh, right, those financials."

"I'd better get back to my café, too, but let's make those plans soon. I really can't wait much longer." Ashley hobbled out of the apothecary.

Ravenna moved behind her workbench and held up Ashley's anklet, rubbing the sea glass in her hand, feeling its energy. It was alive, pulsating with a vibrant, fiery force that Ashley's multiple sclerosis had dimmed. She could feel the toll the disease had taken on her friend, the pain and fatigue that clung to her. Ravenna wanted to help, to use the magic that flowed through her veins like a wild river . . . but there was something else in the anklet. A presence that wasn't Ashley's.

It was Chase's.

A hint of his energy, like a silent whisper in the wind. A subtle reminder of why she couldn't help Ashley. She held the anklet, feeling the cold glass against her skin, soaking in her friend's energy, promising to be there, to love and support her, without doing magic.

"What was that all about?" Klay said.

"She wants me to do wish magic to heal her MS."

"And you used me as an excuse because you're not going to, are you?"

"No."

Klay headed for the door.

"Where are you going? We're opening in ten minutes."

"Don't ever ask me to lie for you again." Klay walked out and closed the door behind him.

58

THE MAGICAL HERB GARDEN was unchanged, as green as it had been before she had buried Moon there ten months ago. A small rock with an impression of her paw print sat as a marker of her gravesite. Ravenna pulled weeds nearby and heaped them into a pile, allowing the catnip space to grow unobstructed in the spring. *I miss you so much, Moon. My heart still aches,* Ravenna said. She reached to pass her hand across the cold, hard stone, then felt a tap on her shoulder and jumped to her feet. It was Maeve, finally back from who knows where.

"Where have you been? Why didn't you answer any of my calls or texts?" Ravenna saw Maeve watching the catnip sway in the chilly breeze over Moon's grave, then look beyond to the ocean, where the icy blue waves capped with white foam and rumbled to the shore.

"Do you know why I picked Moon for you, instead of another kitten in the litter?" Maeve said.

"Because you knew she had the gift of telepathy?"

"Telepathy shmelepathy. They all did, but Moon read my heart and told me she'd keep you grounded and safe forever."

"Safe from what?"

"I didn't know then, but I do now. Chase." Maeve moved down from Ravenna to help weed the magical garden. "Do you have a spade in the shed? These weeds are harder to pull."

Ravenna retrieved the spade and a small rake. She dropped them beside Maeve. "I think Moon wanted to protect me because she knew you were keeping something from me. So what is it?"

"Why would I hide anything from you?"

Ravenna had no intention of telling Maeve what Chase had said. She wanted the truth with no coaxing. "So you can look at me and tell me you've always been honest?" Ravenna studied Maeve's contorted face and thought the truth must have rotted her insides all these years. But Maeve's demeanor shifted to a broad smile when Skye hurtled toward them, with Jet on his leash pulling to break free.

"He's too strong, Mom. I tried to take him for a walk, but he wants you," Skye said.

Jet stopped in front of Ravenna, staring at her without moving. Skye dropped the leash and huffed with her hands on her hips.

I told you to let Skye take you for a walk, and I'd be back inside soon. Why don't you want to walk with Skye?

I wanted to see you first, Jet said.

Is something bothering you?

No. Jet rubbed his head into Ravenna's hand.

"Am I taking him for a walk or not? I don't have all day," Skye said.

You need to go for a walk with Skye and behave. I'll be in soon to give you lots of belly rubs. Ravenna kissed Jet, and he licked her face all over, making her giggle. She grabbed his leash and handed it to Skye. "Thanks, honey."

"Why don't you and Jet stay for a while? I could use some help with weeding," Maeve said.

Ravenna knew Maeve was trying to avoid the inevitable conversation about to happen.

"Love you, Great Maeve, and I'm glad you're home. No offense, but I'd rather walk Jet." Skye and Jet trotted toward the beach.

"What's going on with her? She seems so distant from you lately," Maeve said.

"You have to ask? She doesn't like Chase any more than you do, Maeve."

"Smart girl."

"Or manipulative great-grandmother."

Maeve pointed the spade at Ravenna's face and hissed, "You think I'm the reason she doesn't like him? No, Chase caused that all by himself. Did you ever stop to think about the heartache he's causing her? Because of him, she's lost her bond with her mother, and now she can't follow her dreams because you're still refusing to do magic. She can't trust you, Ravenna. You're not the same person anymore."

"Then we're even, because I don't trust you either, and I know you're hiding something from me." Ravenna's anger subsided when she saw Maeve's face drop like she had punched her in the gut. "Maeve, I told you the truth about Tristan, and now I want you to tell me the truth. I deserve to know whatever it is, and I think you've kept it from me long enough." Ravenna's eyes narrowed, and her jaw tightened.

"I don't know what this is about, but I'm done talking." Maeve walked toward the far garden beds, and Ravenna followed her. She knew Maeve was lying and trying to avoid the subject, but she wouldn't give up without getting answers.

Maeve stopped in the rose garden full of multicolored buds that bloomed magically all year long, even in winter when the snow covered them like a thick layer of blown-in insulation, keeping them warm and protecting them from harsh winds. But nothing could protect Maeve. Ravenna wanted answers and wouldn't stop pressuring her until she got them. "I saw a picture of a man, and I think you know him."

"I've known a lot of men in my lifetime."

"You wouldn't recognize him, because scars from third-degree burns covered his face."

Maeve froze.

"So you do know him."

Maeve lowered herself to sit on the ground, scratching herself on rose thorns. She stared at the blood trickling from her legs, paying no attention to the dirt from her hands rubbing into the cuts through her torn pants.

Ravenna squatted. "Please, Grandma. Tell me what happened."

"Where did you see the picture? What did you hear?" Maeve said.

"It wasn't just a picture. There was a note in the frame that said if something happened to Chase's family, our family did it. The disfigured man was Chase's grandfather."

Maeve shook. She rose from the ground, trembling, and took Ravenna's hand. She led Ravenna along a pathway to a stone bench in the middle of the rose garden. Ravenna waited, watching as Maeve took deep breaths, swallowing back words she wanted to set free.

"Please, Grandma? What's going on?"

"Oh, Ravenna." Maeve let out a heart-wrenching sob. "I think I killed your mother."

Ravenna stood in stunned silence for a moment.

"What? How is that possible? She fell down a flight of stairs and hit her head at the bottom. Did you push her down the stairs?"

"No. It happened when your mother was nine months pregnant with you. She was due any day, and we'd taken a trip downtown to buy you an outfit to wear home from the hospital after you were born. Windy was so excited."

"THIS DRESS IS PERFECT, Windy. Don't you think?" Maeve had said.

"This is the one, Mr. Dalton. Could you wrap it with a pink bow? I know I'm having a girl," Windy had said, smiling and cradling her belly.

"Of course, but please, call me Jim. I've been dating Maeve long enough that the formalities aren't necessary."

"I'll tell you what," Windy said. "When you close your shop just for one day and come visit my baby, I'll consider you like family. Deal?"

"Deal." He wrapped the dress and handed it to Maeve with a kiss when a customer walked into his shop.

"I'll be right with you," he said.

"I think you'll help me now," a tall man wearing a clerical collar said. He stood behind Windy.

"Sure. Of course, Reverend Boyle. What can I help you with today?"

"I have what I need right here. Come with me!" He grabbed Windy by the back of her collar and dragged her out of the store, across the street to Beach Plum Park.

"Stop. Let go of her!" Maeve said.

She and Jim ran after them. Boyle slammed Windy's back against an enormous oak, shoving his red face into hers, saying something undecipherable through gritted teeth. She struggled but couldn't get free. She tried to push him away, but he didn't budge. He grabbed her stomach and squeezed it so hard his knuckles turned white. Maeve wanted to help her, but Jim held her back. Windy kicked Boyle and was raising her hands to push him away when Jim let go of Maeve and leapt forward himself, grabbing Boyle from behind and holding him with his arm around his neck. It was too late, though. Instinctive, defensive fire had already shot from Windy's fingertips, and flames engulfed Boyle's body. Horrified, Maeve watched both men fall to the ground. Jim rolled to extinguish the fire on his arm and hand.

Windy's skirt had caught fire, too. She ran toward the fountain, but tripped on her torn dress, hitting her head on the fountain's edge as she went down. Maeve ran to her. A small crowd that had gathered extinguished the remaining fires using water from the fountain, as an ambulance approached.

Later that evening, in intensive care, the doctors weren't sure Windy would survive, so they took the baby by C-section. After the surgery, Maeve entered Windy's hospital room and sat by her bed, holding her hand. Windy was weak and barely conscious, but Maeve had to ask. "What about the family legacy if this gets out? What will happen to the baby? No one can know what happened, Windy. It would put us all in danger. Do you have enough strength to grant me a wish? I'd do it myself, but a witch can't grant their own wish."

Maeve pulled a white sea glass star from her pocket and placed it on the hospital tray in front of Windy. "I wish everyone who witnessed what happened today could not speak about it. Can you do that for me, Windy?"

"Yes. I'll do it for my daughter," Windy managed to say. She lifted her head, groaning and wincing in pain, then fixed her green eye on the star.

"Light that once hung in the sky, you turned to glass and fell from high, into the ocean and tumbled free. Now grant this wish. So mote it be!"

Windy's right eye turned from grass green to a bright, iridescent emerald hue that illuminated the star. The light inside the sea glass flickered, dislodged from the star, and floated above her.

Windy gurgled. She gasped for breath as the monitors began to shriek in alarm. The light from the sea glass above them fizzled into darkness as the vital signs on the monitor flatlined.

"Windy. Windy! Nooo!"

"THE MAGIC KILLED HER, Ravenna. I killed my daughter. She couldn't handle the magic in her state, and I asked her to do it. How could I have been so selfish? Why was the family lineage so important to me that I killed my daughter? After all these years, I still can't forgive myself," Maeve moaned through her guttural sobs. "I'm so sorry I never told you the truth, Ravenna, but losing the family lineage would mean your mother died in vain."

Ravenna squeezed Maeve's arms. "My mother shot fire from her hands? Who else in our lineage shoots fire? Do you? Who else? Tell me now!"

"I never have, and no one else I know of except you. Ow! You're hurting me."

"My whole life, I've been living a lie. A lie that you told me." Ravenna let go of Maeve, studying her face, noticing its crooked dishonesty for the first time. She stared at the worry lines around Maeve's green and brown eyes, wrinkles that Ravenna remembered growing deeper each passing year, never knowing they protected a deeply hidden family secret. Maeve—the woman who had loved and nurtured her, taught her how to use magic and warned her only to use it when it helped others—had used magic selfishly, and it had killed her mother. "You killed my mother, and for what? And why were you and Jim in Chase's office? What does that have to do with this?"

"I wasn't with my witch friends all this time. Jim and I figured out Chase was Boyle's grandson after he threatened Jim."

"Threatened him?"

"Chase didn't want Jim to let you rent his available space, because he was trying to destroy our family. So we finally scheduled a meeting with Chase in his office to warn him to back off. Afterward, I visited a nursing home in Alabama to pay Reverend Boyle a visit."

"How could you?" Ravenna clenched her fists.

"Ravenna, please listen to me. I went to find out if Boyle had sent Chase to destroy our family, but he hadn't. Chase made that decision alone. Please, I'm begging you. Have the good sense to stay away from him."

"Really, Grandma? Maybe it's you I should stay away from." Ravenna stormed into the apothecary and locked the door.

THE NEXT MORNING, RAVENNA sat at the bottom of her living room stairs where the supposed accident had occurred, and where forty-one years of Maeve's lies unraveled, pulled apart thread by thread. The agony of Maeve's betrayal tormented her, and the cold, haunting echo of her grandmother's lies wrapped her in a blanket of shattered trust.

She remembered Maeve weaving tales of enchantment and goodness about magic, painting it as a beacon of hope in a world full of darkness, but the terrifying truth of her power cast a long, ominous shadow. She was a fire-shooting witch, just like her mother, and there seemed to be no way to control it.

The soft, wet brush of Jet's tongue against her cheek stirred Ravenna from her thoughts and the nausea in her stomach calmed.

Are you okay? Jet said.

I love you, Jet. Thanks for the kisses.

It's time for breakfast. Jet retrieved his food bowl from the kitchen and dropped it at Ravenna's feet.

Just let me make a quick phone call, she said, pressing speed dial. "Hey, Ava. I need to run an errand this morning. Can you and Klay take care of the shop and Jet until I get back?"

"Sure. Is everything okay?"

"No. Yes. Thanks." Ravenna ended the call with a single tap of her thumb.

59

THIRTY MINUTES LATER, RAVENNA entered the church. Barbara stood guard in the hallway.

"What are you doing here? I hope you're not planning to break into the pastor's office again. Haven't you done enough damage?" Barbara said.

"That's a tough job, Barbara, protecting the building. Maybe it would be easier if you installed security cameras."

Barbara flicked her hands at Ravenna to shoo her away. "Just go back to that evil witch shop of yours."

Ravenna heard Chase's voice booming down the hallway.

"If I've told you once, I'll tell you one hundred times, Lady Ravenna had nothing to do with what happened in my office. It's all too easy to blame a scapegoat. Until we know who did it, maybe we should remember what happened to Jesus."

Ravenna was relieved to hear that Chase hadn't told Barbara that she'd been involved in the break-in. Then she realized he'd just lied.

"Lady Ravenna, I've been waiting for you," Chase said.

"Reverend Wilkinson, it's not a good idea to let someone like her into this church again. Let us not forget what the devil is capable of." Barbara eyed Ravenna up and down with a scowl.

"Please, join me in my office, Lady Ravenna. Barbara, if you've nothing better to do than lay false accusations, I have plenty more work to give you."

"That won't be necessary," she said, huffing and stomping her feet back to her office.

CHASE GAZED OUT HIS office window, speaking as if to himself. "It looks so different in the winter. Nothing's growing here, but if you peek to the right, you can see plenty growing in your yard." Chase nodded toward Ravenna's house, then faced her.

"That's strange. I mean . . . I must have . . . different flowers than you?" Ravenna said.

"Lady Ravenna, you don't need to make excuses. Your gardens are spectacular, and you wouldn't be here if you didn't know by now that I know what you're capable of. Close the door and have a seat."

"Close the door? What about Barbara?" Ravenna said.

"I don't believe I invited her. Did you?" Chase winked.

Ravenna chuckled and felt her cheeks flush. Chase had wavered from his steadfast belief in leaving the door open when he was with a woman. Her lips parted, ready to question him, but nothing came out, so she closed the door.

"Please." Chase motioned for her to sit across from him at his desk.

Ravenna fidgeted in her seat, only realizing that she was twirling her thigh-length hair when she observed Chase's eyes following her hands.

"I assume you spoke with Maeve," he said.

"Were you ever going to tell me?"

"Tell you what, Lady Ravenna?"

"About my mother and what happened to your grandfather. What if Maeve hadn't told me? You know my mother was only trying to protect me, right? He attacked her, and he's the reason she . . ." Ravenna stopped herself, realizing it was unfair to blame Chase's grandfather for her mother's death when Maeve more likely directly caused it. "You knew my mother didn't die in my house. You knew the truth all along, and you didn't tell me."

"It took me a while to realize you didn't know about all this. And yet, you shot fire from your fingers. How did you suppose that happened?"

"I didn't know I could until Maeve told me my mother did, too. People can lift cars when a loved one's crushed under them, so I . . . wait a minute." Ravenna stood up, thoughts swirling in her head, and stumbled to the window. Skye had been in the apothecary that day, and Ravenna remembered that all she could think about was protecting her. It wasn't black magic. It was a loving, saving act by a mother for her child. But Ravenna's mother had taken protecting her even a step further when she agreed to perform the wish magic for Maeve, even though it cost her life.

Ravenna noticed something out of the corner of her eye and looked up, spotting the raven flying in circles, so close that its wingtip brushed against the window with each pass. She looked down at the grass below, and spied Moon following the raven's shadow. "Do you see them often?"

"See who?" Chase said.

"The bird and the cat." Ravenna pointed to them.

"I don't know what you see, but it doesn't matter. None of it does anymore."

Ravenna turned around, surprised at how close Chase was. They almost touched. She felt their heartbeats in sync, each throb echoing the other's rhythm. Her gaze locked onto his, drawn into the depths of his soft, azure eyes. It was a mystical connection that surpassed words, creating an invisible thread that pulled them even closer. She knew he felt it, too, and yearned to touch him, to end this dance on the fine line between desire and restraint, but she needed more answers. "You came to Plymbury to kill me," she said.

"I did." Chase looked down, breaking their shared gaze. He reached over and lifted the photograph she and Ashley had broken. It was in a new frame. Chase ran his fingers over the glass, almost making Ravenna feel sorry for him.

"Ever since I was a small child, my grandfather would point to the scars on his face. 'Never again, Chase,' he said. 'Don't let this happen ever again. Not to anyone in our family, and not to any Christian.' When I was older, I asked how it happened. He tried to tell me, but only one word would come out: 'Witch.'"

"Oh, Chase. It must have been awful as a child to associate us with something so horrific." Ravenna took Chase's hand in hers, fighting the desire to wrap her arms around him.

He dropped her hand. "Please, Lady Ravenna, let me finish before you decide to have sympathy for me."

Ravenna lifted her hand and cradled the side of his face, watching his eyes light up. She gently pulled him toward her, focusing on his lips, but he moved her hand away and continued speaking.

"In time, we discovered that Windy had hexed my grandfather. He couldn't speak about what had happened, but we learned he could write it down on paper. After reading the words he wrote, I felt a calling, Lady Ravenna. God help me, but I believed I needed to become a minister to destroy you and your family. I made it my life's mission. So when Reverend Todd left Living Waters, I knew I had to get the job." Chase's eyes welled with tears.

A shiver of dread crept up Ravenna's spine as Chase's words laid out the horrifying truth that he had devoted his entire existence to her demise. It wasn't a simple difference in faith and belief between a Christian and a witch. Hatred and malice continued from one generation to the next ones, made worse by a physical attack and a mother's instinct to protect her unborn child. Chase hadn't been just a vague threat lurking in her periphery all this time. He had been a predator waiting to strike.

The gravity of his hatred finally seeped into Ravenna's heart, and an overwhelming wave of vertigo washed over her. The room whirled, spinning in a wash of terror. Her vision blurred, and the edges of her world closed in. Then, as if someone had flipped a switch, she plunged into darkness.

60

CONSCIOUSNESS WASHED OVER RAVENNA like a mystical tide, gently floating her back to the shores of reality. Her eyes fluttered, revealing a hazy swirl of smoke beyond her lids, and she recognized the familiar aroma of sage burning as if in some distant dream.

"Ravenna? Ravenna?"

She opened her eyes to find Klay standing over her with flushed cheeks, his breathing labored.

Klay squeezed her hand. "You know who I am, right?"

Ravenna nodded, smiling.

"What happened? Jerkface won't tell me, and the paramedics want to take you to the hospital," Klay said.

Ravenna felt a hand stroking her face and shifted her eyes away from Klay, catching sight of Chase kneeling behind her. "Praise God you're okay," Chase said.

Barbara pushed her way past the paramedics. "Praise God? Reverend Wilkinson, she's possessed you, and you're not of sound mind. Lord Jesus, please help us." Barbara raised her hands and gazed at the ceiling. "The pastor's influenced by the devil right in this very office. Please, Lord, remove the evil darkness so the pastor might see the light. Jesus, our glorious savior, help him find his way back to you."

"Barbara. I assure you, I'm of sound mind, and the prayers aren't necessary."

Ravenna heard Faith's heels clattering down the hallway and attempted to sit up.

Klay eased her shoulder down. "Don't get up."

"Klay, what are you doing here?" Ravenna said.

"Faith came to the apothecary to tell me you were here. I came to get you away from him, but then I saw the ambulance pull in and ran to see if you were all right. I was hoping to find jerkface on the floor, not you. I'm so glad I got here when I did."

"Where's Jet?" Ravenna said.

"Back at the shop with Ava."

Faith ran into the room and knelt next to Chase. "Oh, pastor. What did this evil witch do to you?" She caressed his arm and face.

Chase shot up to his feet to evade her touch.

"Move away, folks," a paramedic said. He pushed a blood pressure cuff onto Ravenna's arm. "Can you tell us what happened, ma'am?"

"I don't know. I was talking, and woke up on the floor," Ravenna said. "I have no interest in going to the hospital."

"I think you should get checked out. I'll go with you," Klay said.

"Is this your significant other, ma'am?"

Faith answered, latching on to Chase's arm. "Yes. Yes, sir. They're a couple, and he should go with her."

"Yes, of course," Barbara said. "Everyone knows they're a couple. And rightfully matched, if I say so, just like my Faith and the reverend. Just look at the happy couple."

Chase removed Faith's hand from his arm and moved closer to Klay as the paramedics lifted Ravenna onto a gurney. "Let me take care of Lady Ravenna while you go back to the apothecary. I assure you, I'll keep her safe," Chase said.

"Yeah, sure. You also have a bridge to sell me, right? I'm not going anywhere."

"You heard the paramedic, Reverend Wilkinson. Let Klay accompany the witch, and Faith's presence can heal you," Barbara said.

"Sounds like a good idea to me," Klay said.

"Please, Klay? Ava can't handle things without you at the apothecary," Ravenna said.

"Then I'll close the shop for the rest of the day, because I'm not leaving you with him again." Klay gave Chase a sideways glare and scowl. "I won't let you hurt her."

Ravenna rubbed her eyes. "Okay, Klay, that's enough. I asked you to watch the shop, so I'd appreciate it if you could please return to work."

"I'm not leaving."

Chase peeled Faith off him again. "I think you heard Lady Ravenna. She wants you to go," he said.

"Yes, Klay, please. I appreciate your concern, but I'm fine with Chase."

"Okay. I see how it is." Klay lifted his hand and swung a fist through the air, planting it on Chase's face.

Faith screamed and buried her head into Barbara's shoulder.

Ravenna gasped, wincing as if she could feel the raw force behind the blow. "Klay, stop!"

Chase staggered back a few steps, eyes wide in surprise. His hand reached up to cradle his cheek.

"Plenty more where that came from, asshole," Klay hissed as the paramedics held him back.

Shock was etched on Chase's face. He took a deep breath, visibly swallowing his initial urge to retaliate, and lowered his hand from his face, revealing a red mark already turning into a bruise.

"Oh, Goddess. Chase." Ravenna slid off the gurney and ran to him. His eyes met hers, and he gave her a small, sad smile.

61

RAVENNA PLACED AN ICEPACK on Chase's cheek. "How bad does it hurt?"

"Not too bad. Faith and Barbara are much more painful," he said, and grinned. "I didn't think they'd ever let me leave the church."

"I'll get you some arnica ointment and mix in some cayenne pepper for the inflammation," Ravenna said.

Chase's hand shot out, gripping her arm. "Please?" His eyes locked onto hers. "Don't go."

Ravenna quivered, hearing in his words the unspoken love they both tried so hard to ignore. Her heart pounded in her chest, aware of the raw intensity Chase's words carried and the way his fingers held onto her arm, warming her skin. His hand moved from her arm up to cradle the side of her face with a feather-light touch, sending that familiar jolt circling and sparking around them.

"I'm sorry my story was so painful to hear, Lady Ravenna, but I wanted to be honest with you. No secrets. I know who you are, and I wanted you to know who I was. But you must know by now I don't feel that way anymore."

Ravenna heard the sincerity in Chase's voice and saw the honesty in his gaze. His words were a soothing lullaby that calmed her stormy thoughts.

"I have something to show you." Chase reached into his pocket and pulled out a ring.

It wasn't grand or ornate, but had an elegant simplicity that captivated Ravenna. A single diamond nestled between six prongs, surrounded by a warm gold band softened by the passing of time.

"This belonged to my grandmother. She was a woman of incredible strength and grace, living with a harsh, prejudiced man, yet she showed nothing but kindness and acceptance for everyone she met. She would have loved you." He paused, looking at the ring as if seeing it for the first time. "I used to think she was weak and bent too easily under the weight of my grandfather's wrath, but I was wrong. My grandmother was the strongest person I've ever known, a true Christian, living by the principles of love and forgiveness, even when it was the hardest thing for her to do."

"She sounds incredible," Ravenna said.

Chase looked up at Ravenna, his eyes mirroring the sincerity of his words. "She gave me this ring the day before she passed away, and told me to give it to the woman I would spend the rest of my life with. I thought it was trivial. Just another piece of jewelry. But now . . . now I realize how meaningful it is."

He held the ring out to Ravenna, his gaze never leaving hers. "Lady Ravenna, there is no one else I would rather give this ring to. No one else embodies the love, the strength, the acceptance my grandmother did. You are the woman I want to spend the rest of my life with. Will you marry me?"

Ravenna's eyes gazed into his as her breath caught in her throat, and the room seemed to shrink into insignificance around them. There was only Chase and the pure love that hung between them like an invisible thread weaving them together, binding their destinies. She was aware of every breath he took, every beat of his heart against her own. Time seemed to slow. Each second stretched into eternity as their faces drew closer until their lips finally met in a passionate kiss. Her hands tangled in his hair as she tried to pull him closer to erase any distance between them. Their kiss held the promise of a thousand unspoken words, a silent vow that whispered a love that transcended the barriers of religion.

"Yes," Ravenna whispered with a ragged gasp, lost in the whirlwind of emotions threatening to consume her. She ached, yearning for more of him, for the closeness their kiss had promised.

Chase slipped the ring onto her finger and covered her face with delicate kisses, each one a soft echo of the passion ignited between them. Ravenna's fingers moved to the top button of her shirt, but Chase gently pulled her hands away before she could undo it.

"Lady Ravenna." His voice was steady despite the emotions Ravenna knew raged within him. "I respect your faith more than you can ever know, and I know you respect mine." She felt his lips curve in a rueful smile. "We have to wait until we're married."

62

AVA DROPPED A SEA glass necklace on the display case, squealing and throwing her arms around Ravenna, squeezing her too tight. "Oh, I just knew it. You're meant for each other, and this is such wonderful news. Have you set a date yet?"

"We only just got engaged." Ravenna laughed and pulled away from Ava's grip.

"At least I know he won't ask me to be his best man," Klay said, and chuckled.

"You might have a better time getting along with people if you don't punch them without good reason," Ravenna said.

"Who said I want to get along with him? And I had a good reason. You're just oblivious."

"You punched Reverend Wilkinson?" Ava said.

"Yup, and unfortunately, only once. Don't bother sending me an invitation to the wedding, Ravenna, because I'm not going," Klay said.

"You seriously won't come? You're my best friend."

What about me? Jet said.

Don't worry, Jet. You're my familiar. It's better than a best friend. Ravenna petted Jet's head.

"Klay, you just have to go," Ava said.

Ravenna approached Klay and placed her hand on his, distracting him from taking inventory.

Klay eyed the diamond on Ravenna's finger. "You know you deserve something much bigger than that, right?"

Ravenna pulled her hand away. "Look, Klay, you know I'm not happy about what you did to Chase; he was only trying to help me."

"He was trying to keep you away from me, but it doesn't matter anymore. I've meant to tell you for a while now. I'm giving you my two weeks' notice."

"What?"

"Come on, Ravenna, you had to see this coming."

"Klay, you're my business partner. We signed a contract, partners forever. You can't just leave like that. Please take some time to think about this. The shop needs you. Skye needs you. I need you."

Klay laughed.

"What's so funny?"

"You can hire anyone as qualified as me to run the shop. As for Skye, I plan to visit with her. But you, Ravenna, that's laughable. You made it clear yesterday that Chase is the one you want. If it makes you feel any better, I won't want to be around you anyway once you're baptized."

"Yesterday? Chase and I were having a conversation, and I passed out. I just wanted us to finish what we were talking about."

"Oh, you finished it all right. The ring says everything, doesn't it?"

"Klay, you've misunderstood. And who said anything about me becoming a Christian? Chase said he respected my faith."

"It's just a matter of time, Ravenna. We all see it coming."

"No, Klay. You're wrong."

"Am I? Are you doing magic? Will you ever do magic again? I'm sure not doing magic was a condition of the marriage, right?"

"We didn't even discuss it."

"So let me get this straight. You agreed to marry jerkface without talking about your magic. Now I've heard it all."

"I haven't even thought about it, Klay."

"You have a daughter who desperately wants to do magic and a close friend who's losing her kids, and you haven't thought about it? I have one question for you, Ravenna. Is it worth it? What's jerkface sacrificing for you? Who is he hurting by marrying you?"

"It won't be easy for him to tell everyone he's marrying a witch."

"A witch that's becoming a Christian. How hard could that be? They'll be partying in the streets."

"What's wrong with being a Christian?" Ava said.

"What's wrong with being a witch?" Klay said.

"Nothing, but why can't Ravenna be a Christian?" Ava said.

"Loving relationships go two ways. Give and take. It's not all take just because one person thinks their faith is more important than the other's. So, tell me, Ravenna. What did he give up for you? Oh, I know. He gave up wanting to kill you."

"Kill you? What are you talking about?" Ava said.

"That's not fair, Klay. He isn't the same person he was all those months ago."

"He wanted to kill you?" Ava said.

"Right. Jerkface wants to marry you because he decided he wants to get into your pants instead."

Ava gasped. "Christian men aren't like that, Klay."

"Ava, all men are like that. Christian men just don't tell you."

"Come on, Klay. Don't be so callous. You've said nothing like that to me before," Ravenna said.

"All men? Then who are you aching to sleep with, Klay? You're Pagan, so tell us," Ava said and giggled.

"Yeah, who?" Ravenna glanced at Ava with a smile.

Klay grabbed Ravenna and turned her to face him. He held her face in his hands gently, and gave her a loving kiss on the lips. "You, Ravenna. But only once you love me like I've loved you for the past eighteen years. And forget the two weeks' notice, because I'm out of here now."

"She's engaged! I'll pretend I didn't see that!" Ava said. "I'm sorry I asked."

Ravenna froze as Klay released her and turned away. Her world plummeted. Klay wanted more? More than friendship? She shook her head in disbelief. All these years, their bond had been unbreakable. Klay, her rock, her confidante, had never even breathed a word of this before. He had been her safe harbor when she couldn't think about being with another man after Tristan's death. And through it all—her engagement to Tristan, his death, and until now—Klay had been there without a trace of dissent, without even a hint of how he truly felt.

She watched Klay grab his things and walk out, speechless, wondering how she'd been so blind. Or maybe he had been too good at hiding his feelings. Either way, Ravenna couldn't bear the thought of life without him, even if she'd never thought about loving him the way he had just confessed to loving her.

SPRING

63

RAVENNA STIRRED VEGETABLE BROTH and tomato sauce together, the robust aroma of chili powder and cumin mingling with them. She added an eighth of a cup of maple syrup from a client's farm in Vermont, giving the chili an unexpected but welcome twist Ravenna hoped would help Chase savor the beans without missing the meat. Now, in the last few minutes of cooking, she added frozen corn for a pop of color.

The door opened, and Ravenna glanced at the clock. It was Maeve, ten minutes early. Ravenna hadn't told her Chase would be joining them for dinner.

"Why did you invite me tonight?" Maeve said. "I thought you'd never speak to me again after I told you about your mother."

"Maeve, sit down. Let's talk for a minute before my dinner guest arrives."

"Dinner guest? Who's joining us?" Maeve sat at the old rustic table and ran her finger in circles over a knot. "Sometimes I think about all the Greenes and their friends and family who once sat at this table."

"I bet Jim sat here with you, too," Ravenna said.

"He did, but I broke it off with him when your mother died. How could I think about loving a man when I couldn't even love myself after what happened to Windy?"

"But he tried to save her life, and helped save mine."

"I'll always be indebted to him for that, but I could never give him the love he deserves." Maeve changed the subject. "Did I ever tell you how much Windy loved this table? She said if the house ever burned down, she'd save it."

"If the house burned down, she would have been the one who'd started the fire."

"How could you say that?"

"Because it's true, Maeve. Look, I'm going to tell you what's on my mind because I don't want any more secrets between us, and you're just going to have to learn that I'm my own person and can make choices in my life that you may not like or agree with. It doesn't mean I don't love or want you in my life, and I hope you feel the same way about me." Ravenna reached out to place her hand over Maeve's, and felt a cool breeze start from the ceiling fan. She was taking a deep breath, ready to tell Maeve about Chase, when Maeve looked down and gasped.

Maeve grabbed Ravenna's hand and held her ring finger close to her eyes. "Is that a diamond? Is that an engagement ring?"

"Yes," Ravenna said. "It was his grandmother's."

"I'm so excited, Ravenna! I can't believe you're getting married. I want to congratulate you both together. Do you have any champagne?"

Ravenna laughed, thrilled at Maeve's excitement and acceptance. "I don't have any, but we don't need it." Ravenna rummaged through the refrigerator. "I have grape juice."

"Juice shmoose. I'll run over to Ashley's real fast and get a bottle of champagne before Klay gets here."

Ravenna's smile dropped. There was a knock at the door.

Maeve threw the door open, and her face turned sour. "What are you doing here? We're celebrating tonight, and I don't believe we invited you."

"Yes, Maeve. I did invite my fiancé."

Maeve's face drained of color. Every tense muscle in her face seemed to scream in disbelief, and she blinked her eyes as though trying to wake from a nightmare.

"Something smells fantastic. I can't believe a vegetarian meal can smell so good," Chase said. He entered the kitchen and hugged Ravenna, kissing her head. "Maeve, is something wrong?"

"Yes. You're wrong. You can't marry Ravenna, damn it. I won't allow it!"

"You waited until now to tell her?" Chase looked up at the ceiling fan. "I thought Klay was going to fix that fan? It's freezing in here."

"Fix the fan?" Maeve rolled her eyes. "She can't fix the fan because it has a mind of its own, and no one has control over it. Ravenna, you can't marry a man who isn't a witch. I thought you learned your lesson with Tristan."

"Maeve," Ravenna said through gritted teeth.

Chase laughed. "I'm pretty handy. Tell me where the fusebox is, and I'll fix it."

"No, Chase. It's okay. Klay will get to it soon. Skye, dinner's ready!" Ravenna called upstairs, her voice echoing through the house. There was no response, but Ravenna hadn't expected one. Skye wasn't thrilled about meeting Chase.

Chase turned his attention to Jet, crouching down and extending a hand for him to sniff. Jet was wagging his tiny tail.

"Dinner will be ready soon," Ravenna said. She returned to the chili and added more pepper. She had planned to make tea with the lavender she had gathered from the herb garden, but threw it into the pot instead, thinking everyone could use some calming. "Skye! Dinner!"

Chase reached for the dishes on the counter. "I'll set the table," he said.

Maeve pointed at Chase on her way to the door. "I've had enough. Don't invite me to dinner with him again."

"Great Maeve, where are you going? I just got here," Skye said as she entered the kitchen.

"Skye, go get your coat. You're coming with me because I'm not eating here, and neither are you."

"What did I miss?" Skye said.

"The whole point of this dinner is for Skye to get to know Chase. She's staying here."

"I want to go with Great Maeve."

"You go ahead, Skye. We can catch up another time." Chase said.

Skye grabbed her coat from the hooks.

"Reverend Wilkinson, let me make one thing clear. You may have Ravenna convinced you're all innocent and in love, but not me. Christians don't marry witches, especially not Christian ministers. They only marry Christians, and I know you won't set a date until Ravenna becomes one of you."

"We haven't even talked about a date. And what if I want to become a Christian?" Ravenna said.

"How dare you." Maeve's face was purple with anger. "What about your daughter? That man will go nowhere near Skye. Do you hear me?" Maeve pointed at Chase. "I don't know how you got that bruise on your face, but I hope it hurts like hell because I know you deserved it. Let's go, Skye."

The door closed behind them, and Chase pulled Ravenna close, embracing her.

"Please don't listen to her. It will take her some time to get used to us," Ravenna said.

Chase lifted her chin and gazed into her eyes. "What the Good Lord has intertwined, no individual can pull apart."

Ravenna leaned into his chest, ignoring the pang of his disregard for the Goddess.

64

RAVENNA PULLED THE CORD through the last piece of sea glass, tied the sliding knot, and cupped the anklet in her hands over the burning sage, allowing the smoke to infuse it with healing energy. She thought this piece was much more potent than the one she had given Ashley before, and with the court date tomorrow, Ravenna couldn't wait to give it to her. She slipped the anklet into a black velvet drawstring pouch and put it into her pocket.

Come on, Jet. Let's go for a walk on the beach.

Jet jumped in circles. *Yay! We're going to the beach.*

"Ava, I'm taking Jet for a walk. Would you mind watching the shop while I'm out?"

I'll be out, too, Jet said.

"While we're out."

"Sure, and enjoy the weather out there."

Ravenna led Jet outside to a warm spring breeze carrying the tangy scent of the sea. They set off across the street, and Ravenna noticed a flyer in the window of Ashley's café advertising the upcoming Annual Wish Festival. It read: *Only a few weeks to decide your magical wish. Make it good because you only get one in your lifetime!*

Ravenna spotted Ashley inside the café and waved to get her attention, then pointed to the flyer, making a tear-it-up gesture with her hands. Ashley raised her hand to ask her to wait, and hobbled with her cane to the bar.

Let's go inside and give her the anklet you made.

Dogs can't go inside restaurants unless they're service dogs, but Ashley will come out in a few minutes.

I'm a service dog. I help do magic.

Let's talk about that later, okay?

As she waited, Ravenna saw three women coming toward her. The first woman, silver hair cropped in a crisp bob without a strand out of place, said, "Aren't you Ravenna Greene, soon to be Ravenna Wilkinson?"

"I'm sorry. Do I know you?" Ravenna said.

"No. But everyone knows you're engaged to Reverend Wilkinson. Welcome home," she said. The woman eyed Jet and took a step backward.

"Welcome home?"

"You know, into Jesus's loving arms. Welcome. We're so excited to have you on our team."

"Amen," the other two women said.

Ravenna half smiled. "Team?"

"You know what I mean—the Christian side of things. And you won't need that anymore." She pointed at Jet. "The good Lord will give you all the protection you need once you're baptized."

You don't want me anymore? Jet dropped to the ground.

I love you, Jet. Don't listen to her.

She said you don't need me.

Don't listen. "Who said I was getting baptized?"

The woman laughed and flashed a fake smile. "It's the talk of the town. Everyone wants to attend, and the pastor agreed that when it happens, it will be right on Plymbury Beach for everyone to witness. After all, it's not every day that a famous witch like you becomes a Christian, and the whole town's so excited to welcome you. Aren't they, ladies?"

The second woman's chestnut hair was swept into a French twist so tight that it pulled her lips into a flat line. "Oh, yes. We can't wait," she said.

"Would you like to join us for lunch? It's a perfect excuse to ditch that devil of a dog. He's evil, you know. Well, of course, you do because you're one of us now," the third woman said. Her loose, gray wavy hair framed piercing eyes full of Christian zeal.

Why are they saying mean things about me? Make them stop.

I can't, Jet. People think crazy things when they're afraid, and nothing I say can change it.

But they're not being mean to you.

Yeah, I know.

The second woman walked a wide berth around Jet, her eyes riveted on his every move. She held the café door open for Ashley, who was trying to make her way outside. "We were just telling Ravenna how thrilled we are that she'll marry Chase. It's the talk of the town, and you must be equally excited," she said.

Ashley pointed inside the bustling café. "I'm sure you'll find plenty of folks inside who would be happy to talk about it."

"May the Lord bless you with healing," the woman said. "Are you ready, ladies? Let's have some lunch."

Ashley's face lost its plastic smile when the door closed behind them. "Please tell me you won't marry him and that this is all some kind of joke," Ashley said. "I'm going through champagne faster than I can order it. People are toasting the end of the Greene legacy. As soon as you change your name to Wilkinson, it's all over for your family and this town."

"I . . . haven't even thought about . . . changing my name. I didn't take Tristan's last name."

"Ravenna, Chase isn't just any Christian. He's a Christian minister. Everyone expects you will because Christian women don't usually keep their maiden names, and everyone knows what that will mean for your family."

"But I'm not Christian, and Chase knows that."

"He also knows the name Greene isn't just any last name. Your last name might as well be Witch. I'm sure he'll expect you to change it."

Ravenna folded her arms in front of her. "He respects me and my faith, and I don't think it's an issue."

"You didn't think he was out to get you, either, until I proved it to you. You remember the photo and the letter, don't you? I can't just stand by and watch this happen to you and your family, Ravenna."

"So you're going to walk out on me, too?"

"Who walked out on you?"

"Let's start with Klay."

"Oh, no. Klay." Ashley raised a hand to her mouth. "He must be devastated."

"He quit working for me two days ago, and said he's never coming back. Do you think he means it? I can't help but think he just needs time to cool off."

"Ravenna, you need to wake up. Your whole life is drastically changing, and you can't just expect the people who love you to be happy about this. When someone's life changes so significantly, it changes the lives of everyone who loves them."

Ravenna glanced up at the trees surrounding the café while waiting for Ashley to finish her lecture, and caught sight of the raven soaring in the sky. It was as if it was trying to get Ravenna's attention.

"Look at me, Ravenna. Damn it. Look at me! My health is getting worse by the day, and you don't even care that I'm going to lose my kids and the café. All you can think about is marrying a man who ruined all our lives. Did you at least bring the anklet for me?"

"Ash, it's not like that. I love you, and want to help you heal."

"Right, so long as it doesn't mean doing magic for me."

Stung, Ravenna pulled the pouch out of her pocket and handed it to Ashley. "Good luck in court tomorrow."

As Ashley hobbled back to the café, the truth hit Ravenna like an early spring frost, blanketing her in icy realization. Amidst her whirlwind obsession with Chase, she'd allowed one of her closest friends to continue to suffer. A wave of remorse swept over her, and the revelation stung, burning her conscience.

65

RAVENNA SAT AT HER workbench, trying to focus on drilling holes in the sea glass she'd collected earlier that morning, but her mind wandered to Ashley and her court appearance. She prayed to the Goddess that the anklet would be enough to prevent Ashley from needing her cane, and that maybe the judge would see she could manage her kids despite her illness.

Ravenna got up to stretch, and spied Maeve in the yard. Jet grabbed and tossed every weed Maeve pulled, entertaining himself while she tended the garden. Ravenna laughed at his antics, but her attention was drawn by a commotion from Ashley's café that pierced the air. She darted out the front door of the apothecary to see what it was. Maeve and Jet joined her in the driveway.

"What's going on?" Maeve said.

"Shh. It looks like Jason," Ravenna said.

"That can't be good. Where are all those people coming from?"

A crowd had swarmed around a sleek black SUV parked outside the café. Jason yelled at the kids, "Get inside the car. Now!"

Ashley clutched his arm with desperate pleas and tears streaming down her face. Ravenna strained to listen, but Ashley's words got lost in the chaos.

Jason ripped his arm free of Ashley's grip. He pushed Ashley away. Unable to maintain her balance, she fell backward onto the pavement. The crowd gasped, and Ravenna felt a burning sensation in her fingers. *Let's go, Jet.*

Ravenna pushed into the crowd, but couldn't squeeze through the mass of people. Two men lifted Ashley to her feet. Jason gunned the car's engine and drove toward the dispersing crowd. People scattered, creating a path for his escape. As the SUV sped away, Ravenna caught sight of Ashley's youngest daughter, her small hand reaching out of the tinted window, crying for her mother.

Ravenna's breath hitched. She bent over, clutching her chest, panting short, shallow breaths, devastated that the anklet hadn't worked. Jet leaned against Ravenna's leg to comfort her. Ravenna straightened and watched the two men escort a shaken Ashley back into her café.

"This is horrific. He must have gotten custody of the kids today," Maeve said. "How could this have happened?"

Ravenna shook her head. "I can't believe it."

"You won't do the wish magic for her, will you?"

"I'm engaged to Chase, Grandma. I can't."

"Engaged schmengaged." Maeve flicked her wrist toward Ravenna. "Can't, or won't? There's a difference."

"Maybe both. But I don't even have the wish wall."

"Windy did magic without it, and I bet you could, too. If you really wanted to."

Ravenna couldn't listen to Maeve trying to manipulate her. She turned and made her way up the drive toward the apothecary, contemplating how to help Ashley. And then it came to her.

In a burst of excitement, Ravenna dashed into her bedroom and yanked a box from beneath her bed. She opened the lid and ran her fingers over the green shard of sea glass cradled by a platinum ocean wave. It pulsated with an ethereal glow, and Ravenna couldn't suppress her grin. Her heart fluttered with excitement and anticipation.

Tomorrow, she'd bring Ashley the persuasion necklace.

66

THAT NIGHT, RAVENNA WOKE to pounding on the door, and Jet barking and growling.

"Wake up and let me in. Let me in, Ravenna. I'm not leaving!" a voice said outside.

Ravenna threw on her robe and checked her phone. It was 3:00 a.m, and there were seven missed calls and more texts than she could count. All from Ashley.

Skye flew down the stairs, meeting Ravenna in the living room. "Who is it, Mom?"

"I think it's Ashley."

"Why would she come in the middle of the night?"

"I don't know." Ravenna opened the kitchen door, letting in a tear-filled, unstable Ashley.

"I can't . . ." Ashley struggled to catch her breath. "I can't sleep . . . without my kids home in their beds. Do you think . . . he's abusing them?"

"No, Ash, I'm sure they're fine. It's temporary. You'll take him back to court and fight."

"I almost went to his house, but changed my plans when I saw Faith's car in the driveway." Ashley swiped away her tears and took a deep breath. "She better not be sleeping with him while my kids are in that house. I'll tear her throat out."

"Come in. What are you saying about Faith?"

"She was with him in court today to talk about the café, but there wasn't enough time, so they postponed it."

"All this stress can't be helping your health, Ash. Take some deep breaths and calm down." Even using the cane, Ashley needed Ravenna's help to a chair at the kitchen table.

"Nothing's helping my health, and the anklet you gave me is useless." Ashley reached down and tore it off her ankle, sending sea glass flying through the kitchen. "And I don't need deep breaths. I need to heal and get my kids back home with me."

Jet leaned into Ashley to comfort her, but she ignored him, folding over the table and sobbing into her arms. "I need my kids. I can't live without them. Oh, please, God. Someone help me."

"Skye, go grab the box under my bed. Hurry."

Skye returned and handed the box to Ravenna.

"I know what you need, and I regret not giving it to you sooner."

Ashley lifted her head, her face lit with hope. "Really?"

Ravenna handed her the box, and Ashley ripped off the cover. The sight of the persuasion necklace seemed to freeze her in place. Her face fell, and her bright eyes lost their new shine as if a shadow had taken away her joy. Her expression was of unmistakable disappointment. She lifted it from the box with trembling hands, her grip tight and accusing. "You think this is what I need?"

"Yes, it worked for you last time, remember? I should have given it to you yesterday. It can change everything."

Ashley stared at the necklace as though looking past it, lost in thought. She held the chain between her hands, raising it as if to drape it around her neck, but she abruptly yanked her hands apart, breaking the chain and sending the pendant flying.

Skye ran to retrieve it. "Mom, the glass shattered."

"Ashley, why? How could you do that? It was your only hope."

"It wasn't my only hope, Ravenna! You were. This wouldn't have happened if I had wished for magic last year. I hate myself for not asking then, and I hate you now for caring more about Chase than me. I thought you loved me. I trusted you." Ashley began to sob again.

"Mom, why won't you do the magic for her? Why? You can help her, and you won't. You're not the mother I know and love. I would do it for you, Ashley, if I could. I swear I would."

Ashley's sobs intensified, her body trembling. She stood, clutching the table for support, then tried to walk but couldn't. Ravenna leapt to her, pushing the cane under her hand, and scooped under Ashley's arm to help her. Ashley pushed her away, losing her balance as she did, and plummeted to the floor, smashing her head against the leg of the table.

"Ashley? Ash? Skye, call an ambulance!"

67

Ravenna sat beside an unconscious Ashley while a nurse connected her to wires, monitors beeping and buzzing.

Fifteen minutes later, a doctor walked in. "You must be Miss Greene, Ashley's healthcare proxy?"

"That's right," Ravenna said.

"My name is Dr. Driscoll, and I'd like to update you on Ashley's condition. A fall like Ashley's usually results in no problem. However, hitting a head hard enough can cause a buildup of fluid in the brain, and the resulting pressure keeps a patient unconscious."

"She'll be okay, though. Right?"

"We've done several tests and I'm waiting for the results, but sometimes patients never wake up from comas. Also, in patients like Ashley with MS, if they survive, it can make the progression of the disease worse, depending on how severe the resulting damage is. I'll keep you updated," he said and left.

The doctor's words hung in the sterile hospital air. She stared at Ashley lying there, still and ghostly pale against the white sheets. Ravenna couldn't tear her gaze away from Ashley's unconscious body, tracing the slow rise and fall of her chest, trying to etch every detail into her mind, terrified it might be her last memory of her. The possibility of death, or making it through with her MS even worse, was a shock that made Ravenna's mind race, thoughts tumbling over each other in a tumultuous wave of fear. Tears welled in her eyes, blurring her vision.

Ravenna grabbed her cell phone from her bag and texted Klay.

EMERGENCY! It's Ashley. I'm with her in the hospital. She may not make it. Hurry! Bring a star!

68

RAVENNA HEARD FAMILIAR FOOTSTEPS echoing down the hospital corridor, stopping at the nurse's station. She met Klay in the hallway, closing Ashley's door behind her.

"What happened?" he said, staring at her.

Ravenna's restrained facade crumbled when she heard Klay's voice. Her hands trembled, and her composure shattered like glass under pressure, spilling its contents. She spoke through heart-wrenching sobs, words punctuated by gasps for breath. "She fell and hit . . . her head. She might not make it. It's all . . . my fault. She was stressed about losing . . . her kids . . . and fell."

Klay reached out to pull Ravenna in close, and wrapped his arms around her. "Oh, Ravenna. Why do bad things have to happen to the people we love before we realize how much they mean to us?"

"Klay, I need you, I can't live without you, even if I can't—"

"Shh. Let's not worry about that right now. You need to take care of Ashley." Klay reached into his pocket and handed Ravenna the sea glass star. "I knew you wouldn't let her down."

"Help me, Klay. I feel like I'm drowning."

"What's wrong?"

She swallowed hard, her throat tight with guilt. "Ashley asked me so many times to heal her of MS." The memories of Ashley's different pleas echoed in her mind, each one a haunting reminder of what she had refused to do. "But she can't ask me to heal her head from this fall." Ravenna's voice broke on the last word, her sorrow spilling into the space between them. "If I do the magic for the MS, like she asked . . . there's still a good chance she might not make it." Ravenna cried tears full of fear, regret, and desperation as she finally allowed the magnitude of Ashley's situation to wash over her. She tried to steady herself, but the sorrow was a tidal wave, relentless and all consuming. "And if I heal her for the fall instead, she'll still have MS, and no wish left."

"Ravenna, she made you her healthcare proxy because she trusts you to make these types of decisions on her behalf. Think about what you'd choose if you were her."

"I don't want the responsibility of that decision."

Klay dropped his arms. "So you'd rather do nothing?"

"I want to do this for her, Klay, and I'm so grateful you're here. I just want to do the right thing. And there's another problem."

"What is it? Chase?"

"No. Please don't make me think about him right now." Ravenna took a deep breath. "I don't know if the magic will work without the wish wall."

"Oh."

"I destroyed it by not using it, and if the magic doesn't work without it . . . then I've lost the ability to grant wishes."

"Goddess, Ravenna. Why didn't you think about all this before you went and fell in love with jerkface? Wait a minute. Didn't you tell me your mother performed magic in the hospital without the wish wall?"

"Yes, but the wish wall was still in the apothecary and alive. I'm sure that star joined the wall somehow, because every time I walked into that wish room, there was one star that shone brighter for me than all the rest. I think it was my mother's wish."

"Well, you won't know unless you try, and there's no more time to waste, Ravenna."

"I know. Will you watch the door for me, and make sure no one comes in?"

Klay hugged Ravenna before opening the door to Ashley's room for her. "I'll keep watch out here. You can do this, Ravenna. I believe in you and in the Goddess. This is why you have this gift—to change people's lives for the better."

"I've never been so scared to perform magic before."

"Because this time, the magic matters to you personally."

Ravenna entered Ashley's room, leaving Klay behind. Every step she took was weighed down by the gravity of her remorse and the burden of her guilt. She slid into the chair beside the bed, reached for Ashley's cool hand, and squeezed it with a silent promise in the warmth of her fingers.

"Ash?" Her voice disturbed the stale silence of the room. "I can't bear seeing you in so much pain. I'm sorry it had to come to this for me to open my eyes. I just pray it's not too late." The words choked her, pressing down on her with the weight of how much she loved Ashley and her fear of losing her. She held the star in her trembling hand over Ashley's still body and struggled to recite the rules for wishing.

"A person can have only one wish . . . in their lifetime. The wish . . . cannot provide financial gain."

Ravenna stopped to compose herself. After a deep breath, she continued.

"The wisher cannot . . . travel in time. The wisher cannot . . . bring someone back from the dead." Ravenna's voice faltered as the stark truth of those words struck her to the core. A chilling thought crept into her mind—if Ashley died, she couldn't reverse it. *Please, Goddess,* Ravenna thought, *don't let her die.* She swallowed and continued in a hushed murmur. "And the wish can harm none."

Then Ravenna choked out the wish itself, praying she'd made the right choice. "Goddess, Ashley wishes to be cured of MS."

Ravenna only then realized that she had been gripping the star with such intensity that her knuckles had turned white. She uncurled her fingers, wiped the tears from her cheeks, and focused on the star.

Her right eye turned from grass green to a bright, iridescent emerald hue that reflected in the star. It illuminated in her hand, and she recited the wish chant:

"Light that once hung in the sky, you turned to glass and fell from high, into the ocean and tumbled free. Now grant this wish. So mote it be! Please, Goddess."

The light inside the sea glass flickered, dislodged from the star, and floated above Ashley's body. Ashley let out a gurgle. The light fizzled into darkness, and the patient monitor flatlined. "Ash. Ashley? Nooo!"

RAVENNA RAN INTO THE hallway. "Help! Ashley needs help!"

Over the hospital loudspeaker, she heard alarms interrupted by an announcement: *Code blue. Code blue in ICU. Code blue. ICU.*

Emergency personnel surged past Ravenna, making a beeline for Ashley's room. Ravenna latched onto the arm of a man in a white jacket.

"I'm afraid there's no time for conversation. You need to stay here, ma'am." He removed her grip and continued his hurried stride.

Ravenna spotted Klay darting down the hallway.

"The magic, Klay. It didn't work. It killed her, just like my mother. I made the wrong choice."

A nurse appeared before them, her voice soft yet firm. "Let me bring you to a private waiting area. I'll inform the doctor you'll be there."

Klay gathered Ravenna next to him with an arm around her shoulders as they trailed behind the nurse. She ushered them into a room, and a chill ran through Ravenna at the thought of Ashley no longer being with them. She moved to stand at the room's solitary window looking out over the courtyard, but the view offered Ravenna no solace. Instead, it felt like a cruel reminder of the life that continued outside.

Klay placed his hand on Ravenna's shoulder, bringing her back to the present moment. She had no idea how long she'd been standing there, but her body was stiff and achy.

"I made the wrong choice, Klay. I'll never forgive myself. How can I tell her kids they have no mother, and that it's all my fault? I lost one of my closest friends, Klay, and I killed her. How can I live with myself?"

She felt Klay's hand squeeze her shoulder. "Ravenna, this wasn't your fault. You did what Ashley had asked you to do. You did your best, and I'm sure Ashley knows that. You're not alone. We'll get through this together." He wrapped his arms around her. "And when the time is right, we'll figure out how to tell Ashley's kids, and make sure they know how much their mother loved them."

"I'll fight for them. They can't stay with Jas—"

A knock on the door interrupted Ravenna. The nurse entered. "Does this belong to you or Miss Watson? It was on the floor of her room." The nurse placed the star in Ravenna's hand.

"I must have dropped it when I ran out."

"You can see Miss Watson now. The doctor will join you soon to discuss the next steps," the nurse said.

Klay squeezed Ravenna's hands. "I'll meet you at the nurse's station."

Ravenna plodded down the hospital corridor, a tight knot of anxiety coiling in her stomach, nauseating her. She didn't want to see Ashley like this. She wanted to remember her alive and full of life.

When Ravenna reached the door, she hesitated and considered turning back, running away. But she took a deep breath and pushed the door open.

"What took you so long? I thought you'd never come back," Ashley said.

Ravenna gasped at Ashley sitting up in her hospital bed, alive and well, and lifted her hands to cover her gaping mouth. She shook her head. "Ashley?"

"The doctor says I'm healed, and it's a miracle. He didn't believe it, so he sent me for an MRI, and all my lesions were gone, too. I feel incredible, and I'll get my kids back, Ravenna. You healed me!"

Ravenna struggled to understand Ashley's words, and her vision blurred as tears welled up in her eyes. She blinked them away and Ashley was still there, watching her and laughing. It wasn't an illusion.

"You're alive. You're actually alive."

"I'm more than just alive, Ravenna. I'm healed from MS." Ashley's sparkling eyes held Ravenna's gaze. "How can I ever thank you? You didn't just help me, Ravenna. You gave me my life back."

Ravenna eyed the star in her hand and squeezed it, thinking she'd just gotten her own life back, too.

69

RAVENNA GAZED OUT THE window while waiting for Skye to return from school. After spending over eleven grueling hours in the hospital with Ashley, exhaustion made her eyelids heavy. But she couldn't close them, because the world seemed livelier and brighter, and she didn't want to miss a moment of it. Every leaf, every blade of grass, danced in the sunlight as if the universe reflected a clear light that seemed to emanate from Ravenna herself.

Jet poked his nose into Ravenna's thigh to get her attention.

What is it, Jet?

Does this mean I can help you do magic?

Yes, Jet, and I'll need you to help Skye, too. She doesn't have a familiar.

She's coming, Jet said.

Ravenna spied Skye in the distance, about a tenth of a mile away, and she and Jet ran out to greet her.

Skye bent down to pet Jet's head. "Hey, Jet. Mom, what are you doing out here? You haven't met me coming home from school since I was ten. Is Ashley okay? Oh, no. Please tell me she didn't die?"

"No, Skye, she's fine. But I have some news, and couldn't wait to tell you."

Skye's eyes narrowed as if trying to read the story in her mother's facial expression.

"Ashley's cured of MS. She's healed."

"The doctors cured her MS? How is that possible, and why did it take so long?"

Ravenna laughed.

Skye walked toward the house along the cobblestone walkway with her. "I don't see what's so funny."

"Wait, Skye. You didn't let me finish. And don't go in the house. I need you in the apothecary."

"I have homework to do before working at Ashley's. Tell me what happened!"

"I did Ashley's wish magic, and she's healed. And the magic didn't just remove the MS. It removed the fluid in her brain caused by the fall, too. She's perfectly healthy. Well, as perfectly healthy as a woman in her forties can be."

"You did wish magic? You really did it?"

"Yes, now come with me." Ravenna grabbed Skye's hand and marched her toward the apothecary. Jet followed close behind.

"What's this all about?" Skye said.

The shop bells chimed, and Ava greeted them at the doorway. "How is everything with Ashley? Is there anything else I can do to help, other than watching the store for you?"

"Ashley's fine. She'll be back in the café soon, I'm sure."

"Praise God!"

Ravenna had never heard Ava say that before and didn't know why it surprised her so much. It made her think of Chase, but right now, she needed to do what she'd intended. She would talk to Chase later. "Ava, I'll be in the wish room with Skye. Can you take care of the shop a bit longer, and Jet, too?"

"Sure."

"Mom, what's this all about?"

Ravenna grabbed Skye's arm again, leading her to the wish room.

"I'm not a child. I can walk by myself, you know."

"Are you ready?"

Skye pried Ravenna's hand from her wrist. "Ready for what?"

Ravenna heard a roar behind the door and flung it open. She gasped in joyous disbelief. "Oh, my Goddess."

"Mom, the wall. It's back," Skye said.

Ravenna stared at the once empty wall, now midnight blue with thousands of twinkling stars fading in and out. The waves climbed higher and higher, crashing into the most explosive roars Ravenna had ever heard. In the middle of the room, there was a light floating in the air. "Look, Skye," she said, pointing at it. "That must be Ashley's star, joining the others."

Skye threw her arms around Ravenna's neck and squeezed her tight. "Oh, Mom. This is the happiest day of my life. Thank you for healing her."

Ravenna sat Skye at the table. She lit a white candle and pulled the dish of sea glass stars out of the filing cabinet.

"What's this all about?" Skye said.

"Do you want to do magic?"

"Wait, what?"

"Do you?"

"More than anything, Mom!"

"Then let's find out if you can."

Skye wrung her hands. "I wasn't expecting this today. I . . . don't think I'm ready for this. What if I can't?"

"What if you can?"

"I'm serious, Mom. What if I can't?"

"Let's find out, Skye."

"What do I have to do?"

Ravenna stroked Skye's hair. "The most important thing is to relax, because the Goddess can't guide you if you're a bundle of nerves. Focus on the flame of the candle and your breaths."

While Skye composed herself, breathing deeply with her eyes on the candle, Ravenna texted Klay. *Can you please come to the apothecary? I think Skye might need you.*

Ravenna watched for Skye's face to soften and her shoulders to relax. "Okay, I think you're ready."

Skye shifted her vision from the flame and stared into Ravenna's eyes. "Now what?"

Ravenna took two stars from the bowl and handed one to Skye. "When I focus my green eye on the star, a tiny spark of light flickers inside it, and my eye changes from grass green to emerald green. Watch."

Ravenna held the star in her palm and focused on it. In an instant, the light flickered deep inside the star. "Did you see my eye turn color?"

"Yes."

"Okay, now I want you to do the same thing with your star."

"I'll try." Skye held the sea glass in her palm. Ravenna studied Skye, focusing on the star the same way she had. Nothing. She looked at Skye's green eye. Nothing.

"Nothing's happening. Am I doing it wrong? Am I not a witch?"

"Don't you worry, Skye. Magic or no magic, you're a witch. Try again."

Skye tried three more times. Nothing.

Tears rolled down Skye's face. "I want this more than anyone has ever wanted it, and I can't do it." She put her elbows on the table, cradled her face in her hands, and cried. "Please, Goddess. Please?"

Ravenna rubbed Skye's back to comfort her. "Oh, honey, I know—"

Klay's voice called out from behind the door. "Can I come in?"

Ravenna let him in. "Thanks for coming, Klay. I've been asking too much of you today."

"Anything for Skye." Klay saw the wish wall. "Oh, wait. How did that get here?"

"Why did you ask Klay to come?" Skye said.

"Because he can help you, if he's still willing. And, Klay, I don't know how it happened, but the wall's ready if you are."

Klay sat down next to Skye and wiped a tear from her eye. "Listen to me, Skye. As much as we hoped it wouldn't come down to this, we all knew you might not be able to do magic. You didn't know this, but I've had my wish saved up for you. If you want this as much as I believe you do, then let me wish it for you. You're like a daughter to me, and nothing would make me happier."

"Oh, Klay, I love you so much, but how can I let you give me your wish? What if you ever need it? I can't take that from you."

Klay took Skye's hands into his. "Wishes are prayers that the Goddess answers for people who've lost hope. If I give you mine, then not only do I give you hope, but hundreds, if not thousands, more people will have hope, too. Skye, take my wish because that is my wish—for you to give more people hope. Please?"

Skye kissed Klay's cheek and wrapped her arms around his neck.

"Is it all right if Skye stays?" Ravenna said.

"I wouldn't want it any other way," Klay said.

Ravenna opened the door. *I need you, Jet.*

Jet trotted in and settled beside Ravenna, his gaze steady and alert.

Ravenna handed Klay the bowl of sea glass over the white candle that had burned down to half its original height. The waves on the wish wall rumbled with anticipation. "Pick your star, Klay Mitchell."

Klay cradled a star in his palm over the table. He cast a fond look at Skye, his face beaming with the most heartwarming smile Ravenna had ever seen from him. Skye's eyes met his, and she returned the smile.

"Are you ready?" Ravenna said.

Klay shifted his gaze to Ravenna. "Yes."

Jet, are you ready to help me?

Yes. Yes. Yes.

"I need to go over the rules for wishing.

"A person can have only one wish in their lifetime. The wish cannot provide financial gain. The wisher cannot travel in time. The wisher cannot bring someone back from the dead. And the wish can harm none.

"Klay, please state your wish."

"I wish for Skye and her bloodline to continue the magical lineage of her ancestors. So mote it be."

Ravenna focused on the star in Klay's hand and recited the wish chant.

"Light that once hung in the sky, you turned to glass and fell from high, into the ocean and tumbled free. Now grant this wish. So mote it be!"

Wow! Jet said.

Ravenna's right eye turned from grass green to a bright, iridescent emerald hue that illuminated the star. The stars on the wall blinked faster, and the waves became louder. The light inside the sea glass turned white and flickered, dislodging from the star, floating up in the air, attaching itself to the wall. Other stars surrounded the new one, dancing around it in a circle while the ocean waves swelled and crashed like a triumphant symphony.

We did it. I did my first wish, Jet said.

Ravenna giggled and reached over to pet Jet's head. *That's right, Jet, and you were so helpful.*

Klay picked out another star from the bowl. "Here, Skye, let's see that eye of yours light up."

Skye took the star from Klay and breathed a deep breath, focusing on the star. "Okay, I'll try."

Ravenna held her own breath, her eyes riveted on the sea glass.

Nothing.

She glanced at Klay, feeling her heart race with panic. His eyes darted from hers to the star. Ravenna followed his gaze and squealed when she saw the glass shimmering with white light, and Skye's eye transform from grass green to a vibrant emerald hue.

70

For two days, Ravenna had avoided answering Chase's phone calls. She carried the burden of having to tell him she'd done magic, and she knew the conversation needed to be in person. She approached the church and was ascending the stairs when Barbara flung open the door.

"You're no longer welcome here. Houses of worship are for Christians, not witches. By the way, thanks for the tip about security cameras." Barbara pointed to a camera above the entrance. "As you can see, it works."

Barbara wouldn't let Ravenna pass when she stepped onto the landing.

"Of course I'm welcome. I'm engaged to the minister," Ravenna said.

"Don't remind me. How a Christian pastor could believe a witch would ever become a Christian is beyond me. We all know once a witch, always a witch."

"Please move so I can go see my fiancé."

Barbara moved just enough to let Ravenna squeeze by. "Fine. I'm sure the pastor will also say you're no longer welcome here. Everyone knows ministers don't fall in love with witches unless they put some spell on them." Barbara mocked Ravenna, placing her hands over her heart and batting her eyelashes. "Oh, I'll stop doing magic for you, Chase, and I'm sure one day I'll welcome Christ into my heart and become a Christian, too."

"Chase told you I wanted to become a Christian?"

"He didn't have to. You're manipulating him, and he believes it. It doesn't matter, though. Faith has her sights on a much better catch these days."

"Jason?"

"News travels fast in Plymbury, doesn't it?"

"Barbara, I am not obligated to explain myself to you, but here's some advice. Keep Faith away from Jason. The man's abusive."

"It seems it's not enough that Faith's let go of Chase in favor of a man with, let's say, a more secure financial status. You seem intent on destroying any chance she might have at happiness, just because he's your friend Ashley's ex-husband."

"No, Barbara. That's not it at all. It's because he's an asshole."

Barbara gasped. "Such language in a house of worship."

Ravenna chuckled and knocked on Chase's office door.

CHASE OPENED THE DOOR and pulled Ravenna in tight for a hug. "I went by your house twice, and no one was home. You didn't answer my phone calls—"

"I'm sorry. I didn't mean to alarm you, but I was in the hospital with Ashley. She's fine now."

"Come in." Chase closed the door behind Ravenna. The furrowed lines on his forehead smoothed, and his narrowed eyes opened, a radiant sparkle lighting up his face.

"I have something important I need to talk with you about," Ravenna said. "Why don't we go walk on the beach?"

"This sounds serious."

"It is."

Chase grabbed his jacket and followed Ravenna to the corridor.

Barbara shot out of her office. "I told you he'd kick you out. Only he's doing one better. He's escorting you out."

Ravenna ignored Barbara, but Chase didn't. "Lady Ravenna is always and forever welcome in this church so long as I'm here, and it would be wise for you to accept that fact. I assume you enjoy working here, no?"

Barbara headed back to her office, throwing a "Humph!" over her shoulder.

Ravenna and Chase stepped outside, greeted by the sun casting a warming pastel glow. The air smelled of the sea mixed with the aroma of blooming spring flowers.

"I have a better idea," Chase said. "Let's talk in your yard. The view is breathtaking from my office window, and I'd love to finally see the tulips up close."

Ravenna grinned and led Chase home to a secluded corner of the garden, where a rustic wooden bench worn smooth by time and weather sat nestled under the shade of cherry tree branches, heavy with delicate pink blossoms. Fallen petals carpeted the surrounding ground, and the air carried a sweet scent mingled with the earthy aroma of fertile soil.

Chase studied the gardens. "It looks like the tulips are a blanket of flowers all the way to the church from here. It's almost as beautiful as you are."

Ravenna sighed. She felt the unwelcome heat of hives as they blossomed on her chest and began their crawl to her cheeks.

"Lady Ravenna, what's weighing on you?"

Ravenna loved how even once they had become engaged, Chase still called her Lady Ravenna. She wanted to hold on to this moment for as long as she could. She reached out to hold Chase's hand, lifting it to her lips and kissing his fingers. "Will you kiss me?" she said.

Chase framed her face with the soft touch of his hands and leaned in. His lips met hers, filled with passion and longing, a kiss that seemed to ignite a dazzling display of sparks around them in a celestial dance. Ravenna couldn't help but wonder if this feeling would ever stop.

Chase pulled away, leaving Ravenna longing for more. "I've been thinking about the wedding. The sooner, the better. I assume you don't want to elope, but I don't want my family or parishioners to ruin our day. Would you consider it?"

"First, I need to talk to you about something else."

"What could be more important than our wedding day?"

Ravenna blurted it out. "I did magic . . . for Ashley. She's cured of MS."

Chase lowered his gaze to the ground. "I see."

"She's one of my closest friends, and I couldn't just let her lie in a coma when I could help, and—"

"Shh." Chase looked into Ravenna's eyes and placed his hand on her thigh. "I understand, Lady Ravenna. Sometimes, we feel that prayer is insufficient, particularly when we realize the Lord has different intentions for those we care about the most. I understand it's a temptation for you. One that I imagine will take time to overcome, but confessions like this help us move in the right direction."

Ravenna thought about the word he'd used. A confession, an admission of guilt. Chase was trying to comfort her for making a mistake. But this wasn't a confession. Nor had it been a mistake. It was a statement of truth that came with elation, whether or not he liked it.

"I also did magic for Skye. You don't need to know the details, but it was important to her. We'll both be granting wishes at the Annual Wish Festival in three weeks."

"I thought we made an agreement, Lady Ravenna."

"We did while I was using a space in your church."

"I also asked the same of you when we met at The Lantern, that you refrain from using magic even after you were back in your apothecary."

"Chase, I have no intention of keeping this agreement throughout my marriage, and I don't feel guilty or ashamed about it. I was born into a family of witches, which makes me a witch. I'm proud of it."

Chase's gaze was distant, locked on the horizon where sea and sky merged into a blurry line. The rhythm of the waves seemed to captivate him, reaching frothy crests and retreating to the sea.

Ravenna broke the silence. "Did you think I'd become a Christian?"

Chase chuckled. "I'm not sure I ever thought you'd call yourself a Christian, but I believed you'd let Christ into your heart, and that's good enough for me."

"What are you saying? You expected me to live a Christian life?"

"I thought you yearned for it."

Ravenna rose, letting her footsteps guide her down a path toward the magical garden, passing a parade of vibrant tulips. She entered the archway formed by interweaving branches of ancient trees that marked the entrance to this enchanted sanctuary, humming with the whispers of her ancestry. Chase trailed behind.

"Do you hear them?" Ravenna said.

"Hear who?"

"My ancestors. Their spirits live here, and I visit whenever I need strength or guidance. It's like how you pray to God."

"Spirits don't stay on earth. If they're Christian, they go to heaven. Otherwise, they go—" Chase cut himself off.

"To hell?"

Chase whispered, "Yes."

"Shh. Close your eyes, Chase. Listen."

"I don't hear anything," Chase said.

"Only a Greene can hear them. They're my family, my spirit guides. They're not in hell, but right here, and have been for all of my ancestors before me. I'll join them one day to help guide Skye and her children."

"It's romantic, Ravenna, but if you accept Christ into your heart, you'll know what it means for a parent to truly love his child."

"I do know what it means, Chase. My mother saved my life, and I just saved Skye's after you and your grandfather tried to destroy us. It's true that I wanted to run away from the prejudice I've had to endure throughout my life, but I don't want to give up my heritage, and I don't want to change my name to Wilkinson. I'm proud to be a Greene. I'm proud to be a witch."

"You're playing God with your magic."

"No, I'm not, Chase. The Goddess uses me to help people, just like God uses you. We have unique gifts."

Ravenna watched Chase's eyes roam over the mystical garden, drinking in the magic. It was as if he was trying to tune his senses to the subtle symphony of nature around him, yearning to catch the elusive whispers that danced in the breeze. She could almost see him straining to hear the ancient call of her ancestors, reaching out to him from across the veil of time, longing for a bridge between their worlds.

"Lady Ravenna, I may not see things from your perspective, but I accept you. When I discovered the ocean wall in the room you used in my church, I realized . . ." He paused, swallowing hard before continuing. "I've overlooked so many things, turned a blind eye, and I could for an eternity. Just run away with me. Let's get married."

Ravenna felt a surge of emotion threatening to overwhelm her. She loved this man with every fiber of her being, yet she knew what she had to do. Her voice was steady, her resolve unwavering. "Chase, I love you. My heart has intertwined with yours, and I don't think it will ever untangle." She slipped the ring off her finger, a tear dropping from her green eye onto the stone, and placed it in his palm, surrendering a piece of her soul. "But I can't marry you."

Her eyes held his, brave and resolute, even as they glistened with tears. It was the most difficult stand she had ever taken, but she knew she had to, for both their sakes.

"I can't bear the thought of losing you, but I'll do anything to bring you happiness," Chase said.

"If you mean that, then let me and my family live in peace—as witches."

"I will," he said. He winked, as he shed a tear.

71

Ravenna and Maeve entered Ashley's café for an early breakfast. The scent of freshly brewed coffee and warm pastries floated in the air, mixing with the hum of conversations and the whirring of the espresso machine.

Maeve elbowed Ravenna. "Look over there."

Ravenna caught Ashley darting from table to table with a tray full of steaming cups and plates piled high with mouthwatering food. Her face was flushed from exertion, but her eyes sparkled, and she wore a constant smile. Ravenna couldn't remember seeing Ashley so healthy. Her movements were fluid, effortlessly managing the demands of the busy café, and Ravenna heard whispers of surprise filling the room.

"Ashley looks fantastic!" one woman said.

"Whatever she's doing, she should stick with it," a man said to the woman sitting beside him.

"I wonder if Ashley got her wish early this year," another said.

Ravenna found a corner table and raised a hand to catch Ashley's attention before she and Maeve settled themselves.

Ashley darted over to their table.

"Ash, look at you. You're like a teenager running around this place helping customers." Ravenna looked down at Ashley's leg. "And I don't see a stick by your side."

Ashley laughed and sat in an empty seat. "I heard you and Chase broke up a few weeks ago. I can't say I'm sorry, but I hope it wasn't because you helped me."

"It was my choice," Ravenna said.

"Yeah, she finally came to her senses," Maeve said.

Ravenna glanced sideways at Maeve.

"Where's Jason?" Ravenna said.

"The judge saw how healthy I was at our second court appearance yesterday and dismissed the case for the café. It's still mine."

"Crazy what a little magic can do," Maeve said.

Ravenna handed Maeve the menu. "Why don't you just decide what you want to eat."

"Same as I always get."

"Ash, I'm so happy for you. What about your kids?"

"That won't be as easy. Jason and Faith tied the knot at the Plymbury Town Hall yesterday. I imagine he's trying to prove he's a stable family man, and we all know she only married him for his money. But I filed an appeal for custody, and they'll set a new court date."

"Is there anything else I can do?"

Ashley hugged Ravenna. "You've given me all I need, and I love you for it. I'll get my kids back. Sorry I can't stay and chat more, but I've got to get back to work. I'll see you tomorrow."

72

Skye pointed out the window of the Sea Glass Apothecary. "Mom, look. I can't believe it. There are twice as many people in line for the Annual Wish Festival as last year."

"It's a good thing you can help me. Are you sure you're ready? By the end of the day, you'll be exhausted."

Skye pushed up onto the balls of her combat boots, her body rising with grace despite the rugged footwear. She spun, arms outstretched in a wide arc, and her black lace miniskirt billowed out, transforming her into a whirling dervish of anticipation and excitement. "I'm more than ready," she said, her voice filled with joy. "I've waited my whole life for this."

Jet ran around Skye, following her turns. *Me, too. I can't wait. I waited my whole life, too.*

Ravenna laughed.

Skye stopped turning and waited for her balance to return. "When are Klay and Great Maeve coming?"

"I just heard from them. They're working their way through the crowd," Ava said.

Ravenna gazed out the window and watched the sun over the maypole, its ribbons flapping in the breeze. She heard people in line outside chatting, anticipating having their wishes fulfilled by two witches with one green and one brown eye. A mother and her daughter.

"Why do you suppose the crowds are so huge this year?" Ravenna said to anyone who was listening.

"Breakup or no breakup, Chase loves you, Ravenna. He's been talking up this festival all over town and in church," Ava said.

I guess he wasn't so bad after all, huh? Jet said.

Ravenna petted his head. *No, Jet. Not bad at all, but it's okay. Sometimes, people can show they love each other more by giving them freedom. When you care about someone so much that you don't want to mold them into what you desire, that's when love's the truest.*

Jet growled at someone banging on the door.

"It's probably reporters. They'll have their chance when we open for the day," Ravenna said.

"Mom, it's Ashley. I'll let her squeeze in."

Ashley rushed inside with her children clinging to her, but as soon as they caught sight of Ravenna, they ran to hug her.

A lump formed in Ravenna's throat. "Please tell me you and Jason worked out visitation rights, and you didn't just steal your kids."

"I don't have to work out a visitation schedule or go to court. Jason and Faith brought the kids to the café last night. They said they bought a town-home in Brookline, and there's no space for the kids there. I think he knew he'd lose if we went to court again, so he asked me to have my attorney draw up papers, giving me full custody. Poor Faith. She would have been better off with Chase."

Ravenna ignored the Faith comment and hugged her friend over the kids still latched onto her legs. "Wow! Ashley. That's incredible. We need to celebrate."

"Let's go, kids. We'll see Ravenna later."

Ashley opened the door to leave, allowing Klay and Maeve to squeeze inside.

"Maeve, I thought I asked you not to wear that Romani outfit again this year," Ravenna said.

"It's fine," Klay said. "I almost lost her three times in that enormous crowd, and the only way I could find her was by listening for the clanking of all those gold bracelets."

"Outfit shmoutfit. I'll wear what I like, and you'll wear what you like." Maeve looked over her shoulder and batted her eyelashes. "Besides, I wanted to look extra special for my date with Jim tonight."

"I thought you ended that years ago?" Ravenna said.

"We were just keeping our distance because of your mother's wish magic that bound people from talking. But the cat's out of the bag, so why not pick up where we left off?"

Ravenna raised her eyebrow and grinned.

Klay took Skye's hand and led her toward the back of the shop. "Before we open, I have something to show you. Everyone, come with me."

Behind the sales counter, Klay pulled out a gift bag and handed it to Skye.

"What is it?" Skye said.

"Open it up and find out."

Skye gently pulled out something flat that was wrapped in layers of tissue paper. She rested it on the counter and unpeeled each layer until she spotted a silver corner. "Oh!" She ripped the rest of the paper off in haste, gasping when she saw a shiny silver star with the name *Skye* etched in the middle.

"Klay, it's spectacular, and so thoughtful," Ravenna said.

"Now you have matching stars," Ava said.

Klay retrieved a hammer and small nails from underneath the sales counter and affixed the star right next to Ravenna's on the oak door of the wish room.

Skye wrapped her arms around Klay's neck. "I love you so much, Klay. You're not just my dad. You're the witch that gave me magic."

Klay kissed Skye on the cheek and motioned for Ava to open the shop door. "If everyone's ready, let this magical day begin."

The shop filled with wall-to-wall people and reporters in seconds. Skye greeted the first person in line for a wish. She motioned for the woman to follow her into the wish room while reporters snapped photographs from above the crowd. Ravenna and Jet followed, closing the door behind them.

Ravenna studied the woman, who was only in her mid-twenties. She carried an air of weariness, burdening her with an invisible load that forced her shoulders to slump and her head to bow.

Ravenna pulled out a chair for her to sit at the wish table. "What's your name, and how can Skye help you today?"

"I'm Shannon." She waited for Ravenna and Skye to sit down. "I've suffered from depression my whole life. I hate myself. I hate the way I feel, and want it to stop. All I want is to be happy."

"Skye can certainly help you with that," Ravenna said.

Jet pushed his head under Shannon's hands to help calm her.

Skye lit the white candle and handed Shannon the bowl sitting in the middle of the table. "Please pick a star."

"Am I supposed to pick a certain one?" Shannon said.

"Nope. Just whichever one you feel is calling you," Skye said.

Shannon picked one and inspected it, then clutched it to her chest.

"I'll need to go over the rules for wishing with you, so please listen carefully," Skye said.

"A person can have only one wish in their lifetime. The wish cannot provide financial gain. The wisher cannot travel in time. The wisher cannot bring someone back from the dead. And the wish can harm none. Sound good?"

"Yes," Shannon said.

"Okay then, here we go," Skye said. "Hold the star in your hand over the table so I can see it."

Shannon's hand shook, and Jet rested his head on her lap.

The stars on the wall blinked fast, and the waves roared with purpose. Shannon's eyes darted between Skye and Ravenna.

Ravenna reached her hands across the table and cupped underneath Shannon's. "It's okay. You can relax. You're in excellent hands with Skye."

Skye focused on the star in Shannon's hand. Her right eye turned from grass green to a bright, iridescent emerald hue that illuminated the star.

Ravenna's gaze locked on Skye, taking in the utter concentration on her face. The surrounding air seemed to pulsate with Skye's energy.

Skye recited the wish chant:

"Light that once hung in the sky, you turned to glass and fell from high, into the ocean and tumbled free. Now grant this wish. So mote it be!"

Shannon stared at the light inside the sea glass that turned white, flickered, and dislodged from the star. She followed it as it floated in the air and attached itself to the wall. The other stars surrounded the new one, dancing, and the ocean below rumbled with joy.

Ravenna felt the magic taking effect in a ripple of energy that swept across the room.

Tears of overwhelming pride welled in her eyes, knowing her daughter had just used her magical abilities to help someone in need.

73

AFTER A LONG DAY of fulfilling wishes, everyone gathered at the beach. Ravenna approached Ashley's food hut to order some of her favorite pizza, and ran into Reverend Jennifer.

"Hello, Lady Ravenna. I've been meaning to contact you," Jennifer said. "It seems there was some kind of mistake last year. We'd love to have you and Skye return to the UU church."

"I need to get food for my family, but maybe we can discuss this another time," Ravenna said.

Jennifer continued talking as she walked away. "There's nothing to discuss. You and Skye can return anytime, because you're always welcome. I hope to see you soon," she said, and waved.

Ravenna watched Jennifer jog toward the coast to meet up with some people, and spotted Maeve and Jim holding hands, walking Jet along the shore. Ravenna smiled, thinking Maeve looked happier than she'd ever seen her. She was continuing toward Ashley's food hut when Chase appeared in front of her, as though he'd just materialized outside of the crowd.

"I don't think I appreciated how big this festival was in your honor last year, Lady Ravenna," Chase said.

"Ava told me what you did for Skye and me. Thank you."

"I always keep my promises."

"Will it ever get easier?" Ravenna said.

"Will what get easier? Do you mean seeing each other without wanting to run away together and never return? Not for me, but maybe for you."

Ravenna followed Chase's eyes, gazing at Klay sitting in the sand with his arm around Skye.

"I never understood why you chose me over him," Chase said quietly. "I may not like him, but it's clear how much he loves you, Lady Ravenna."

"I know."

Ravenna turned back to face Chase, but beachgoers were wedging between them on their way toward the water. Chase stepped back to let them through, and winked at her before surrendering himself to the crowd.

Acknowledgements

To all my esteemed MFA in Creative Writing professors and my academic advisor at Southern New Hampshire University, how can I thank you? Your profound knowledge and guidance have been instrumental in helping me shape this thesis novel. I am deeply grateful for all I learned. Thank you!

To Professor Weston Ochse, you were one of the most memorable professors I had the pleasure of knowing. The world has truly lost an incredible writer and human being. May you rest in peace.

To Professor Holley Cornetto, you were a lifesaver, guiding me through the complicated twists and turns of subplots. Start placing your bets because this is only the beginning.

To Professor Jan Watson, you are a kind and gentle guiding spirit. In addition to offering me the most encouraging and helpful feedback on my novel, your unwavering belief in me and my story throughout my three thesis terms was invaluable.

To my phenomenal copy editor, Arin Murphy-Hiscock, your timely return to my life was a blessing, and I sincerely appreciate your help and support when I needed it most.

To my beloved husband, Tim, your unwavering support and selfless sacrifices have been the foundation of my journey. Your passionate desire to see me live my dreams has been a driving force. I am forever grateful for your love and presence in my life. I love you more than words can express.

To my friend and colleague, Pastor David Woods, your teachings and support have left a lasting impression on me. I am grateful for the impactful lessons I've learned from you and the Journey Community of Faith congregation.

To the First Church of Wicca, being your high priestess was the most incredible honor of my life. I hope this story helps you to be seen.

And to my parents, Francine and Richard, I wish you were here to see this.

I did it. I finally did it!

About the Author

© Alec Hovey Photography

KENDRA VAUGHAN writes wicked awesome Magical. Mystical. Meaningful. fiction from the suburbs of Boston and has an MFA in Creative Writing from Southern New Hampshire University. *The Plymbury Witch* is her first novel. Visit her at www.KendraVaughan.com.

Connect Online
Facebook: @KendraVaughanAuthor
Newsletter: www.KendraVaughan.com/Newsletter
Blog: www.KendraVaughan.com/Blog

Author's Note

Thank you for reading! I hope *The Plymbury Witch* resonated with you in a meaningful way.

Your thoughts and opinions mean a lot to me, and I'd greatly appreciate it if you could spare a moment to share a review. Reviews play a crucial role in helping other readers find my work and encourage me to continue writing. If you could leave an honest review on Amazon, Goodreads, or your preferred book discovery platform, it would be wonderful. Thank you for being so supportive!

With magic,

Kendra

Printed in the USA
CPSIA information can be obtained
at www.ICGtesting.com
CBHW021844190924
14678CB00010B/373

9 781961 103016